GENA SHOWALTER

THE
PHANTOM

CANARY STREET PRESS

CANARY
STREET
PRESS™

Recycling programs
for this product may
not exist in your area.

ISBN-13: 978-1-335-00928-9

The Phantom

First published in 2023. This edition published in 2024.

For questions and comments about the quality of this book,
please contact us at CustomerService@Harlequin.com.

Canary Street Press
22 Adelaide St. West, 41st Floor
Toronto, Ontario M5H 4E3, Canada
CanaryStPress.com

Printed in U.S.A.

To the incredible Jill Monroe. A divine connection,
best friend, business partner and absolute blessing.
Thank you for the emergency read and invaluable feedback!

To reader and contest winner Shaquitta Morton.
I am humbled by your support! Thank you for helping me
spread the word about my books.

And to superwoman Naomi Lane, Queen of Creativity,
Lady of a Thousand Talents and
Grand Duchess of Generosity. You are a treasure!

PROLOGUE

Excerpted from *The Book of Stars*
Author unknown
Warning: Living text subject to change

They are ancient warriors, evil to the core and loyal only to one another. Known as the Astra Planeta, Wandering Stars, Warlords of the Skies—the beginning of the end—they travel from world to world, wiping out enemy armies. Drawn to war, they turn even the smallest skirmish into a bloodbath.

Glimpse these warlords, and you're soon to greet your death.

Having no moral compass, they kill without mercy, steal without qualm, and destroy without guilt. Their aim is simple, their goal fixed. Revive a mystical blessing to experience victory for five hundred years, whatever the cost. A necessary requirement in their endless battle with Erebus the Deathless, the Dark One, Master of the Depths. Without this blessing, the Astra automatically acquire a curse. Five hundred years of utter defeat.—Page 1

The time has come to renew the blessing or lose it. One after the other, each of the nine Astra will be charged with an impossible task. Two have already proven successful. Let the third now demonstrate his worth. His name is Roux Pyroesis, Son of Mars, the Torture Master—the Crazed One. A violent past has left him unable to experience the touch of another without experiencing terrible pain.

Using a trinite blade, Roux must cut out the heart of the most powerful female in existence: the Ation queen. For a ruthless killer and expert in agony, there should be no easier task. End another life? With pleasure. For this battle-hardened warrior, a victim is a victim. But how will he react when he discovers his newest target is a beauty he can touch without experiencing pain—a fierce harphantom gifted to him by Fate?—Page 10,521

THE INVASION

Harpina, the harpy realm
Two months ago

"I would do bad things for a maple-glazed donut," Blythe the Undoing said to the warrior with his back to her. She smiled when he slowly pivoted. A window display of at-home guillotines loomed behind him. *The* must-have this summer season.

They stood in the middle of the town square, surrounded by overcrowded shops and harpies in a hurry to get somewhere. How could Blythe not notice the grade A man-beef amid the chaos? He was six feet three of sculpted muscle, golden skin, and rugged appeal, with a wild dirty blond mane.

Just her type.

"Any interest in acquiring a maple-glazed donut?" Blythe inquired, twirling a lock of hair around her finger.

"Perhaps." He gave her a languid once-over. "Tell me more about these bad things."

He stood beneath an awning, at home in the shadows. He'd obviously tried to blend in with the other males in the realm, wearing a well-fitted white cable-knit sweater, worn jeans, and scuffed combat boots. Standard nice guy attire. Not really her thing. But thick leather wrist cuffs and multiple spiked rings hinted at the rough alpha within.

"I don't know if you can handle the heat," she said, flirting.

Leering at her, he asked, "Are you sure a sweet thing like you can handle *my* heat?"

Blythe inwardly fanned her cheeks. Well, well, well. No more hints about the alpha within. He'd decided to show off. "Me? Sweet?" She batted her lashes at him. "I come with a warning, handsome. Small dynamite, big boom."

After all, she was the centuries-old daughter of the legendary Tamera the Widow-maker and two ancient evil gods.

Yes, Blythe had three parents. No, she didn't want to consider how.

Anyway. With such a stellar bloodline, she wielded abilities even the oldest of immortals struggled to comprehend. Granted, she hadn't used those abilities in eight years, and her skills were embarrassingly rusty. But. Once upon a time, she'd been a highly skilled and merciless assassin.

Although, yes, she might be considered sweetness itself when compared to a manticore. A being able to morph into a wonderfully grotesque combination of a lion and a scorpion. And that's exactly what this guy was. The mane always gave them away.

Manticores topped the short list of the fiercest, slyest shifter species in existence. Her favorite flavor of jam. Didn't hurt that this particular manticore practically burned her corneas. Hot, hot, hot!

Voice throaty, he said, "Then I'd better acquire a maple-glazed donut."

"Yes, you'd better." Slits in her top allowed the small wings on her back to flutter freely as she stepped into the shade, pressing against him. "But first, I should make a down payment."

Laban, her consort of eight years and the father of her only child, Isla, wrapped strong arms around her waist and grinned. "You are too sexy for your own good."

"I know," she deadpanned.

He snorted with amusement. "I'm glad you're mine, little love." Pinching her chin, he forced her full attention on him. His dark eyes glittered with her ultimate favorite: possessiveness. "Say I'm yours."

She slid her palms up his chest, over his shoulders and through his soft hair, rasping, "You're mine."

"Never forget it." He swooped down, and she rose to her tiptoes to meet him. Their lips met in the middle.

Harpies catcalled and offered lewd suggestions. Who cared about a crowd of witnesses when you had two hundred and fifty pounds of man-candy ready to be unwrapped and devoured? Besides, Blythe had been desperate to kiss him ever since he'd suggested they spend the day shopping for anything and everything her heart desired.

Frenzied for her, he pushed her up against the window display. How she loved this male. From the very beginning, he had addicted her. She *required* him. Like any harpy consort, he calmed the worst of her tempers, healed her deepest wounds with his blood, and roused her most insatiable lusts. But their connection went far deeper than that. Any time apart proved painful, body and soul.

"Momma! Daddy!"

The familiar voice rang out, and Blythe and Laban ended the kiss in an instant. They both panted as they shared a wry grin. She eased from her mate just in time to catch Hurricane Isla in her arms.

"Hey, baby." She kissed the tip of her daughter's nose. "Aren't you supposed to be school shopping with your classmates, learning how to distract shopkeepers and steal from stores as a unit?"

"Yep."

When the little darling offered nothing more, Blythe cut off a laugh. Oh, how she adored this precious bundle of energy and optimism. A miniature version of herself. Same sleek black hair. Same skin tone. Same light blue eyes. Well, one light blue iris for Isla; the other was a rich brown identical to Laban's.

The girl toyed with the neckline of Blythe's favorite T-shirt, twisting the material between her fingers. "Want to see what I stole all by myself?"

Do not smile. "I do." Her darling had always excelled at thievery. She was almost as good at it as drawing. Well, the drawing of locks and keys, anyway, and only locks and keys. Isla's obsession. Each month, she auctioned off the artwork to family members, forcing them to pay up or destroy her feelings. It was a constant source of amusement for Blythe.

Brimming with excitement, the seven-year-old

whipped a small, bejeweled dagger from the waist of her pants. A dramatic, adorable *ta-da!* moment.

Pride puffed Blythe's chest. Everyone agreed: if you didn't guard your goods, you didn't deserve to keep them.

Well, everyone but Laban agreed. He frowned. "We talked about this, mini B." The nickname he used when Isla skirted trouble. He swiped the blade from the wee one's grip. "You are to avoid battles of every kind. That means you have no need of weapons."

A stinging retort brewed on the back of Blythe's tongue, and she barely managed to tame it. This. This was her main point of contention with her beloved consort. His unnatural fear that mother and child were destined to be harmed irreparably.

Blythe understood the reason. He hailed from a patriarchal society where males were warriors and females were fragile. Laban expected his girls to eschew danger, not seek it. A frustrating viewpoint to overcome for any combat-hungry harpy. Meaning, any harpy ever born. Blythe more so than most. Before meeting the love of her life, she'd lived for the challenge of battle and the high of victory.

On the other hand, Laban had given up his expectation of eternal pampering to be with her. Harpies just didn't play that way. And he'd come so far over the years. In the beginning, he could barely leave the house without engulfing both Blythe and Isla in some kind of bubble wrapping. Now, at least, he didn't flinch or even intervene if Blythe got mouthy with another harpy.

On the other, other hand, she'd given up just as much to be with him. After centuries of blood, sweat, and toil, she had surrendered her dream of becoming harpy

General. Harpina's version of queen. This, after earning nine of the ten stars required for the role.

Those stars still decorated her wrist. Permanent tattoos meant permanent reminders. From potential leader of the entire population to a partner and mother. A change she'd never regretted. But a little more understanding on his part would go a long way.

Isla's shoulders rolled in, and her bottom lip rolled out. "But, Daddy. Martha and Pepper already have a full arsenal. Lulu even got a flamethrower for her birthday."

"We'll discuss the dagger when you get home from school, honey." After Mommy made Daddy forget his irrational fear. And his own name.

Scowling, he crossed his arms over his chest. "I've already rendered my final verdict."

"Un-render it." Blythe blew him a kiss with her middle finger.

"Yeah, Daddy," Isla said, revitalized. "Un-render it."

He pursed his lips, saying nothing. But he also softened.

Blythe kissed her daughter's cheek, then set the darling tyke on her feet. "Return to class. Miss Eagleshield is probably worried about you and beating up innocent bystanders for information."

"Oh! I'll help. I'll demand they tell me where I am, and practice using my fists of fury when they answer. Okay, love you, bye!" Isla geared to rush off, but the ground shook hard, stopping her.

Suddenly, the whole world felt as if something vital had been kicked off its axis.

Blythe clutched the girl close as a huge sand cloud swept through town. Her vision blurred. Her nostrils stung, and she coughed. A strange current electrified the air. Intense. *Wrong.* Instincts spiking to high alert, she palmed a dagger of her own.

"What's happening?" Laban demanded at the same time Isla cried, "Momma?"

"I don't—" A horn blared, three long blasts. The Stop What You're Doing and Battle For Your Life horn. A sound Blythe hadn't heard since an invasion of vampires six hundred years ago. Aggression rippled through her wings.

Shouts and stomping footsteps told her fellow warriors were mobilizing. Preparing.

The sand cloud thinned, the world clearing up in seconds... Blythe inhaled hard, the scent of cedarwood and spiced oranges filling her head. A soft, rich fragrance utterly at odds with the massive black wall now blocking the end of the street. A giant of a male stood in front of it.

Enemy! Her wings rippled with more force. Old habits flared. Tensing to defend, she catalogued the invader's details as swiftly as possible. An enormous helmet made from the skull of some kind of mythical beast covered his face. He was shirtless. Muscular. Beyond muscular. Tattoos decorated every inch of his torso—*moving* tattoos. The plethora of images pranced over tanned skin. Leather pants hugged tree trunk–like thighs. Metal tipped his boots.

Something about him was familiar to her. But what? She knew she'd never met anyone so...big. One did not forget a male like him. What even was his species? Definitely nothing she'd fought before. A shock, considering she'd lived thousands of years and encountered hundreds of different immortals.

He stood in place, as still as a statue, with his chin

tipped back, his shoulders and spine straight, and his legs braced apart. His arms hung at his sides. He held no weapons, but then, it wasn't like he needed them. Long, sharp claws extended from his nail beds.

"If you wish to live," a rough voice boomed across the land, "you will stand down. If you wish to hurt, you will attack. The choice is yours. At the moment, I seek only a conversation with your General."

The voice didn't come from the direction of the giant. Meaning, there were more invaders.

Blythe's stomach flipped. How many others assembled nearby? And to what end?

"There's been some kind of mistake," another voice boomed, this one smug and recognizable. Nissa, the current harpy General. "I ordered strippers for *next* Tuesday."

Snickers and laughter rose, blending together.

"By the way," Nissa continued, "you're as good as dead. I'll be seeing to your demise myself."

Blythe heard only a slight clink of metal before a round of horrified gasps blended with cries of shock. She knew. The General had fought the speaker and lost. That quickly.

Trepidation pricked her nape. There'd be no stopping a war now.

"No mercy!" someone shouted.

Harpies hastened toward the giant. Finally, he moved. With inhuman speed matched by no one, he cut down anyone who neared him. Blood sprayed in arcs. Harpies collapsed. Severed hands and feet flew here and there, stacking up around him.

Blythe's jaw slackened. Such savagery.

"Run! Hide! Protect our daughter," Laban shouted

over a symphony of shrieks. "Please, love. I'll find you."
He sped toward the other male.

She almost teleported to his side, an ability few knew
she possessed. Her consort seriously expected her to run
and hide while intruders maimed her kinsmen? Never!

Blythe descended from a long line of warriors. Before she died over a decade ago, her mother had killed
more enemies than anyone in Harpina's history. Her fa-
thers were Erebus Phantom, creator of phantoms, and
Asclepius Serpentes, creator of snakeshifters and gorgons. Three dominant species flowed through Blythe's
veins. So, she would fight at her consort's side whether
he liked it or not. Together, they would ensure this brute
with moving tattoos experienced agonies too vast to
comprehend. She had only to—*Protect our daughter.*

The most important words Laban had spoken echoed
inside her head. Blythe cursed. *Run and hide Isla it is.*
Then she would return to the battlefield.

Tiny wings flapping, she swooped the trembling girl
into her arms and cast one last look at her consort as
he reached the giant. Blink. Laban collapsed like the
harpies—only his head went flying.

Shock pummeled Blythe, nearly drilling her to her
knees. What…how…*what?* No. No! She hadn't just seen
what she thought she'd seen. But as his severed head
hit the cobblestone and continued to roll, reality pummeled her.

"Laban!" she screamed. Her beloved, headless. Immortals like him could recover from many things, *most*
things, but not that.

He was dead.

Gone.

There'd be no bringing him back.

Isla must have witnessed the assassination, too. "Daddy," she cried, hurling herself from Blythe. The little girl ran as fast as her legs would carry her—straight toward the giant.

"Isla!" Panic shoved Blythe forward. She gave chase, cutting through the chaos. Harpies sprinted in every direction, quickly swallowing the child, blocking her small form from view.

An ear-piercing shriek ripped from her throat. Grief and rage boiled in the undertone. If the brute harmed such a defenseless child…

No! Can't lose my child, too. Blythe teleported. Suddenly, she stood directly behind Isla, who stood directly in front of him, clutching the bejeweled dagger, ready to strike.

Had she stolen the weapon before Laban rushed off or had she lifted it from his corpse? A sob clogged Blythe's throat.

Menacing red eyes glowed inside the shadows of the giant's helmet. Those wild orbs locked on her, and something buzzed along her spinal cord. A sense of knowing. As if they'd met before. No time to unravel the mystery.

What happened next happened both at lightning speed and in slow motion. The enemy swung both arms, a split second away from swiping those blood-tipped claws through her treasured offspring. She grabbed Isla by the shoulders, forced her to dematerialize, and yanked her inside Blythe's own body. Then she, too, dematerialized and dove into the perfect shield—the oversized frame of her consort's killer.

In essence, she possessed him. An ability wielded by all phantoms. Most couldn't hide their presence, but

Blythe could. Without the warrior's knowledge, she sank deep, deep, deep inside his conscious mind. A place to listen and learn while figuring out a safe time and place to exit.

A time and place she could slay her host in the worst possible way. After she toyed with him a bit.

Except, for the first time, Blythe lost track of the outside world. Even worse, thousands of voices screamed at her at once.

Echoes of his thoughts? Another first!

Sharp pains ripped through her mind. Could Isla hear this awful deluge? Feel this? But, but…too many layers! Too loud! Blythe couldn't think; she needed to…she…

With all her considerable might, she attempted to slip out of him. Argh! She failed.

Imprisoned? Had she doomed Isla, too? *Forever?*

2

THE SIGHTING

Roux Pyroesis gripped hanks of his hair and tugged. One moment he'd glimpsed a black-haired, blue-eyed beauty on the battlefield, the sight of her like taking a hammer to the gut. The next she'd vanished, momentarily forgotten as thousands upon thousands of screams erupted in his head.

His prisoners had escaped their mental cells again.

He tugged his hair harder, hating the full-time penitentiary erected inside his subconscious—a consequence of his best and worst ability.

Roux could drain an immortal and utilize their life force as fuel. But. Anytime he did it, their soul ended up trapped within his own. All he could do? Hold the captives inside a mental dungeon, out of sight and out of mind.

Every so often, inmates fought their way free from the massive, shadowy labyrinth of cells, each frothing with fury and determined to punish him for his misdeeds.

Except for one. That one remained in solitary confinement. Roux ground his teeth. Upon occasion, he visited the male.

As usual, his world faded to black as he focused on the deepest, darkest corridors of his mind. A terrible thing to do while engaged in a realm-wide takeover.

Thankfully, well-honed instincts fired up anytime he shut down, creating a shield of energy around him. Any harpies or consorts who attempted to stab, claw, or hack any part of him dropped, out for the count.

Amid the chorus of screams, Roux confined his captives once again. Victim by victim. Beings who'd withered into shells of their former selves. No longer could he tell who was who or what was what. He only knew what they'd once been. An assortment of vampires, banshees, sirens, gorgons, sorcerers, gods, Amazons, and shifters.

How much time passed before a hand slapped his shoulder, bypassing the shield, he wasn't sure. His eyelids popped open as the cacophony of noise faded into a dull whisper.

A fellow soldier stood at his side, patting his shoulder. Silver Stilbon, a son of Mercury and third in command of the Astra Planeta. A trusted brother-in-arms known as the Fiery One.

Details crystalized in an instant. Roux remained on the battlefield, exactly where he'd stood before. The conflict had ended, with sprays of crimson already drying on the trinite barrier he'd helped teleport into the world.

Around him, piles of dead consorts and sleeping harpies missing their hands and feet. The sleep came courtesy of the other Astra who must have forced the issue, changing the very atmosphere of the realm. On the horizon, the once glaring sun was in the process of setting. Hours had passed.

Was the black-haired female among the casualties, or had he imagined her? One second, she'd stood before him. The next, she hadn't.

Had she flashed, moving from one location to another with only a thought? Unlikely. Flashing wasn't an ability harpies usually possessed. More than that, Roux was able to clock the start and finish of any mode of teleportation, and she had stayed put. Like a phantom, but not like a phantom. There. But also not there, exuding a strange hum of power.

That's right. He'd felt the brush of it a split second before she'd vanished. Who was she? *What* was she?

He conjured her image, hoping to unearth answers. Instead he discovered unwanted fascination. *Not beautiful, but stunning.* She possessed a delicate bone structure, with eyes like wounds, hemorrhaging agony. Her red lips were parted, as if she couldn't quite catch her breath. She held on to a wee girl—a child who'd looked like her miniature.

Yes. Roux remembered the young one, too. Mother and daughter?

The moment he'd spotted the youth, he'd altered the trajectory of his swing. To win a war, he would commit atrocities. And had, often. But harm a wee one? Never. It was a line he refused to cross. The only line. What if he'd done it inadvertently during his blackout?

Chest clenching, he searched the sea of bodies in his

vicinity. When he found no sign of either female, relief sparked. Except, they hadn't escaped the realm, either. Not with the Astra on guard. So where were they?

Had the pair been a figment of Roux's broken mind? No, surely not. Unless they were. But they couldn't be. No way his passionless mind had the capacity to concoct a fantasy female as lovely as the mother.

A sliver of critical information seemed to hover on the periphery of his awareness. Perhaps the key to unlocking the mystery of her. He had only to reach it.

Why couldn't he reach it?

"She was there," he muttered, "then she wasn't." Same with the girl. "There, then not there." How? *How!* "There. Then not."

"Be at ease, my brother." The shirtless Silver offered the kindest smile he was capable of mustering: a swift baring of his teeth. His long black ponytail contained more blood than the walls. So did his bronzed, *alevala*-stained skin. On his chest and arms, those revolving tattoos displayed the faces of everyone he'd killed for the sake of his blessing tasks. Peer at one of the markings long enough, and you would relive the memory through Silver's eyes.

Roux, too, wore his own terrible deeds in his flesh. All Astra did. "I am well." His version of well, anyway. This was a time of celebration, not worry. "Why wouldn't I be? We won." As always.

"That we did."

"What of our comrades? Any casualties?"

"None." Eyes like mercury glowed with satisfaction, softening Silver's overly harsh features. "As usual, the Commander ordered each of us to select a female we think he might wish to wed. We were to bring our selection to the harpy throne room. You failed to appear, and I came looking."

The word *us* snagged Roux, as always. He and the other eight war gods first met countless centuries ago. They were rescued as children by Chaos, Ruler of the Abyss, then trained for war together. Roux never tired of being part of a unit.

Today, their unit embarked upon a new blessing task. The Commander—Roc—was to marry and sacrifice a virgin in thirty days.

Roux scanned the sleeping harpies once again. Who to pick? Roc had always preferred warrior women. But weren't all harpies supposedly warrior women? So, Roux would go with hair color. But which hair color did the Commander prefer? Roux had never paid attention to the bedmates of his brothers-in-arms. Had never *cared* to pay attention.

Due to the circumstances of his birth, he'd never experienced the slightest spark of sexual attraction. He saw those around him as friend or foe, nothing more, nothing less. Until the black-haired stunner.

Why did he continue to think of her? Why, why?

"Don't worry," Silver said, giving his shoulder a final pat and drawing away. The split second of contact was the most Roux could tolerate outside of combat. Another consequence of his birth. "Ian delivered two harpies. One for himself, and one for you. He informed us of your...predicament."

Relief eased a fraction of Roux's tension. Ian was the ninth ranked Astra and responsible for cataloguing the aftermath of every battle. Roux was sixth and had been for the past millennia; he'd been demoted from third after a few "bouts of madness."

"I will thank him," he said. This wasn't Roux's first blackout; only his first blackout involving a breathtaking harpy.

There. Not there. Where is she?

"Thank him later. Now that you're back in the game, we should head to the palace. The Commander has chosen his bride and completed the marriage ceremony. You are to report to the dungeon, where you'll guard the unchosen. I've already reinforced the cell, ensuring there will be no escapes."

The temperamental Silver did all metalwork for the Astra. There was no one better.

"Gird your loins, stab yourself in the ears, and thank yourself later," the warrior added. "These harpies aren't like any other species we've encountered."

Stab himself in the ears? Surely there'd be no need for such an extreme measure.

"I'll be fine." As Roux flashed to the dungeon to see to the prisoners, he did his best to scrub the black-haired female from his mind.

He failed. *There. Not there.*

Weeks later

I should have stabbed myself in the ears.

"Did you know tattoos are exactly like vodka?" A familiar feminine voice echoed from the dungeon walls. But then, a familiar feminine voice *always* echoed from the dungeon walls. "They make my clothes fall off. Wanna come to my place for a drink, gorgeous?"

Behind him, snickers abounded. Roux stood guard near a cell filled with ten harpies. A spot he rarely vacated. Hadn't taken him long to learn the prisoners never, ever, shut up. In a bid to disconcert him and escape, they constantly ridiculed and propositioned him, doing their best to harass him.

"Be honest," another said. "That's a Breathalyzer in your leathers."

"Excuse me, Officer Sexy," a third piped up, bending over to wiggle her backside in his direction. "I'm ready for my total body frisking."

Roux never deigned to respond. The object of his obsession preoccupied him, plaguing his thoughts day and night.

He saw her waking or sleeping, if he dared to close his eyes and sleep in this dreadful place. He sensed her presence at odd times, too, but so far he'd found no sign of her nearness. Once, he thought he heard her whisper into his ear, teasing him.

I don't know if you can handle the heat.

The statement taunted him. The heat of what? Her gaze? Her words? Her touch?

A moan nearly slipped past his lips. A part of him wanted her hands on him. A desire he shouldn't entertain! No one could touch him for more than a few seconds without inciting an internal cringe. At the very least! Thanks to his father, he was damaged goods in any way that mattered.

He knew this, accepted it, because he had a chosen family now. His brothers-by-circumstance loved him, as he loved them. They squabbled, yes, but none of them ever lost sight of a simple but profound truth: they would willingly die for each other.

Sometimes, though, he couldn't help but wonder if they should be doing more than killing and conquering, amassing a bigger army all to do more killing and conquering. But only sometimes. And in the near future, they could do more. They would. Once he and the other Astra successfully completed this newest round of blessing tasks, they would ascend and kill Erebus Phantom, their greatest enemy, along with his legions of soulsuckers. No greater outcome than that.

But of course, he also wondered what would come afterward for him. Would the Astra split?

What would Roux do with his free time? Other Astra employed a concubine. He kept a maid.

Did the beauty in his thoughts have a male?

How had she stood before Roux one moment and been gone the next without flashing? She hadn't ghosted inside him. His impenetrable inner shields had been engaged. More than that, he'd played host to many of the spectral species in his early years. Phantoms, ghosts, wraiths, and demons. This was not any of that.

The mystery rolled on, consuming his days. And his nights.

The timing for this couldn't have been worse. He should be focused on Roc's task. How the Commander seemed to be doing the unthinkable—falling in love with his latest bride.

If, at the appointed time, Roc failed to sacrifice her, the Astra would lose everything they held dear. A circumstance Roux could hardly fathom. To betray the males who had served you for eons, merely to save a specific female? Couldn't the Commander select another?

A sharp pang tore through Roux's temples, a slight puff of air leaving him. For days, these pangs had attacked him with greater frequency and intensity.

The next one nearly dropped him to his knees. As

something warm and wet leaked from his nose, Roc's wife, Taliyah, snaked around the far corner, approaching the cell.

Roux tensed, but weakness invaded his limbs. His vision blurred. The world spun. The next thing he knew, he was laying on the floor, looking up at the pale firebrand who'd waged war against the Commander's heart.

Taliyah loomed over his fallen form, patting his cheek. "There you are," she said.

With a roar, he launched to his feet. "Why did I black out?" He'd heard no screams. "What did you do to me?" The questions shot from his tongue like poison-laced daggers. She *must* have done something. Phantoms were liars and manipulators, all of them.

The current Astra queen with a stubborn streak a thousand miles long held up her hands, palms out. "Okay. Let's de-escalate a notch, soldier. I did nothing, m'kay, but I now recognize what's wrong with you. I even understand how to fix you…kind of."

She could fix him? He ground his teeth, rocked back on his heels, and inclined his head, saying, "My…apologies." However he felt about this woman, she did bear a higher rank. Not only was she Roc's wife, she was also the new harpy General. For the time being, he owed her respect. "You have answers?"

Despite the sharpness of his tone, his words placated her, and she nodded. "The woman you saw during the battle did, in fact, possess you. I can confirm that. She is a phantom like me."

In his veins, blood froze. No. No! His shields were not so feeble.

Phantoms were mystically created by Erebus, the god the Astra battled for the blessing. Usually. But Taliyah was Erebus's biological daughter and unlike any phantom they'd ever encountered.

Taliyah wasn't done, either. "Here's the thing. She probably possessed her daughter first. Meaning, yes, you're carrying both mom and child inside your body. Knowing Blythe, she hoped you'd whisk them both to safety, where they could exit without your knowledge."

Finally, his obsession had a name. Blythe. "The little girl. Yes. I saw her. Then she disappeared, and *she* appeared. The woman. But I stopped. I was swinging, but I stopped. I would never hurt a child. But by then, the two were already gone. Then the darkness came." His brow furrowed. "If they remain inside me, why do I not sense them?"

"They're buried too deep. At least, that's what my niece told me when she took over your body and spoke to me."

What! The child had overtaken him? He opened his mouth, a curse poised at the end of his tongue. Then the rest of her admission caught his attention. Niece. That meant Blythe was more than a phantom. She was Taliyah's sister, a harphantom, and a daughter of Erebus. Enemy!

"No big deal," Taliyah interjected with a breezy inflection. "Nope! Not another word from you. Just let your shields down, and I'll draw them out."

No big deal? Seething, he crossed his arms over his chest. "Lower my shields for a phantom?" Any phantom? Never. Surely he wasn't so foolish. This might be a trick, after all.

Her expression hardened. "Do it willingly, or I'll make you do it by force. One way or another, I'm getting my girls out. No, you know what? You don't get to think about this, and you don't get to fight it. Kneel."

He laughed without humor. "I will not."

"I wear your Commander's stardust. I'm his wife and his *gravita*. I'm also acting harpy General, as well as the granddaughter of Chaos. You will show me the honor owed to me. Kneel."

Again, he ground his teeth. That she'd echoed his earlier thoughts…

The stardust was a problem. Astra produced it for a fated mate and no other…and Taliyah indeed wore the glittery powder on every inch of visible skin. She was the first to do so, though Roc had wed twenty others before her. But problem or not…

Even as Roux worked his jaw, he slowly lowered to his knees.

"Good boy. Now, this might sting a bit." Chin up and shoulders back, Taliyah eased closer… He tensed, his muscles like rock. Her body ceased moving just before contact, yet her spirit kept coming, slipping into him.

Electric pulses raced along his synapses, sharper than the pangs, and he stiffened. Pressure built in his torso. Then, he heard Taliyah whisper inside his head. "Blythe. Isla. I'm here. Follow my light and reach for me. I'll do everything else. Isla, help your mother. Blythe, you'll both be safe, I swear it. I'm not sure what you've witnessed, but you have my word the Astra won't hurt any of us."

For the second time, black dots wove through Roux's vision. Moderating his inhalations, he held steady. Finally, the pressure eased and the dots dulled. Taliyah succeeded, extracting Blythe from the confines of his spirit and the young one from the confines of hers. At first, the General worked with invisible beings. Then the pair solidified, becoming visible to Roux as well.

His tension instantly mounted. The daughter sank into unconsciousness while the mother fought to awaken. The most incredible scent wafted from one or both, and he wondered how he'd missed the intoxicating mix of honeysuckle and roses the day of the invasion.

As he drank in the sight of his dark-haired beauty, various words streaked through his mind. *Exquisite. Phantom. Enemy. Want. Mine!*

Want? His? Roux didn't…he couldn't…no. Impossible. And yet, parts of him warmed, soon growing hot. Hotter.

Sizzling.

Suddenly, he was gnashing his molars, emitting a low growl, and huffing his breaths, as if he'd sprinted across three galaxies.

The beauty slit her lids and leveled pale blue irises on him. Wrong. Pale blue no longer. Black flooded their depths. Hatred all but iced her skin, and it—she—captivated him.

What if he burned hot enough to melt her?

"Enjoy your last days," she rasped for his ears alone. "I'm coming for you."

3

THE BEGINNING

Present day

Blythe stabbed her target in the gut. Twice. A one-two punch with her favorite daggers. Merciless, she spun and rammed her combat boot into the underside of his chin. Upon impact, a blade ejected from the boot's toe, slicing into his mouth.

The life-size dummy with steel rods for bones seemed to smirk at her. *That all you got?*

Not even close. With a grunt, she elbowed his jaw, bending the rod, then punted his groin. Once again, the blade in the toe of her boot ejected on impact, slicing through his nut sack. For fun, she concentrated on those dangly bits until nothing but shreds remained.

Sweat dampened her skin, and her breaths came fast. Shallow. She'd been at this for hours. Ever since she'd tucked Isla in to bed. Training and strengthening,

strengthening and training. Blythe's new obsession. She was still out of practice, but she improved by the day, thanks to the gym she'd installed in her bedroom at the harpy palace.

"Look at you," her sister, Taliyah, said from the doorway. The tall, slender goddess leaned against the frame, gorgeous in a skimpy red dress, with her pale hair falling around her shoulders. "Rumor says a switch flipped in you when you escaped the Astra. Bye-bye, Good Blythe, hello, Evil Blythe. Ice-cold yet brimming with fiery rage. Utterly unlikable. Detestable even. So of course there's now talk of erecting a monument in your honor."

The interruption didn't stop Blythe. She danced around the dummy, throwing punches. By some miracle, she'd contained her icy, burning rage while Taliyah and Roc had won the first blessing task, and Halo, the second-in-command, had won the next. Now the need to attack the Astra—to maim one in particular—bubbled inside her without cease, threatening to erupt.

"Don't be too jealous, General Hussy," she said. "I'm not angling for your position. Yet."

A snort met her words. "It's General Huffy, and you *know* that. Anyway. I kind of miss my only mildly homicidal sister."

"You have Kaia, Bianka, and Gwen." Taliyah's other half sisters, and Blythe's cousins. Yeah, their family was complicated.

"Are you kidding?" the General exclaimed. "Not one of them has even killed their first battalion yet. They are sweet as sugar."

"Then you are out of luck, because the old me died with her consort." She attacked the dummy with more fervor.

Taliyah heaved a sigh. "Have the hallucinations started?"

"Nope." Most widows were forced to see their slain mates everywhere they looked for the rest of their days, unable to touch. The reason so many of their species opted to waste away in bed or go out gloriously in battle, taking a myriad of enemies along with them.

Many of the harpies who'd lost a consort during the Astra invasion hadn't even awoken from their forced slumber. The others were busy hallucinating right and left. But not Blythe. She slammed a fist into the dummy's face. She had yet to see Laban even once, and it wasn't fair. But she knew who to blame.

"The Astra I inhabited," she grated. "He filled my head with terrible memories I never lived, and there's no room for anything else." Horrors that revolved around a sobbing little boy he'd tortured. A child who had begged for mercy...at first.

A shudder rocked her, vibrating in her wings. *Detest the Astra!* He'd shattered every bone in the child's body. Removed his organs, including an entire husk of skin! Hung him upside down and drained him of every drop of blood, laughing all the while.

"I'm due my psychosis," she continued. Punch. "Deserve my insanity." Punch, punch, punch.

"His name is—"

"I know. Roux." Pronounced "rue." With a hiss, she clawed the dummy's face to shreds. "The name fits him well, considering I'm going to make him rue the day of his birth." She'd meant what she'd said when she exited his body. For the rest of her existence, she would live only for his death. "Nothing will stop me. *You* know this, yes?"

Another sigh seeped from her sister. "I do. But he's our ally, not our enemy."

"No, sister. He's *your* ally. He will always and forever be my only enemy."

The majority of harpies—those without consorts—were like Taliyah. They'd already forgiven the Astra for their crimes. Beefcake had to beef, right? The bulk of the sisterhood considered the nine warlords and their legions of soldiers to be friends. But not Blythe. Never her.

The Astra shouldn't be allowed to live while Laban, her only addiction, was now ash in the breeze. His body had been torched with the rest of the dead while Blythe was stuck inside Roux.

The problem was, the Astra were deathless. Even if she removed their heads, they would revive. For gods like them, such injuries meant nothing. Not when an ordinary weapon was used, anyway. But. Similar to Blythe and trinite—the very substance now walling her great city—the Astra possessed a kryptonite. Everyone did.

She had only to find theirs. And she would. Soon.

"At least speak with Neeka before you act," Taliyah said. "She's the most powerful oracle in, like, ever. Seriously, the woman can see everyone's future but her own."

"Fine. Where is she?" Blythe wouldn't turn down trusted inside information.

"Wellll. That, I don't know. She up and disappeared again. But don't worry. I've got my best spies on the lookout. Though so far they've only uncovered rumors about an underworld king who might have abducted her to his Hell kingdom for reasons."

Wait for the harpy-oracle's return? Nah.

"No, Daddy. No!"

Isla! Blythe flashed into the bedroom connected to hers. The precious angel tossed and turned under a lacy pink quilt. "It's all right, sweetheart. Momma's here," she cooed, caressing the little girl's face.

An anguished whimper escaped her child, and she briefly squeezed her eyes shut.

Taliyah materialized at her side, took in the scene with a glance, and deflated. "I'm never going to convince you to see things my way, am I?"

No. "Roux should be your enemy, too," Blythe replied with a quiet tone. "Isla will have no peace until I achieve vengeance."

Maybe she wasn't yet ready to take on Roux, but she *could* power up on soul—sustenance for her phantom side—and cause him some damage. It would be a start, anyway.

"Blythe," Taliyah began, sensing the direction of her thoughts.

"No. No more conversation." Determined, Blythe kissed her daughter's brow, then slipped into the spirit realm, becoming undetectable to all, even a fellow phantom like Taliyah, and flashed to her new snack closet. The barracks containing the Astraian army, located inside the wall the warlords had teleported around the city the day of their invasion.

The massive three-story structure was divided into ten sections, one for each Astra. There were rooms for soldiers on the bottom, with different facilities and offices in the middle, and a covered, windowed walkway on top.

Blythe couldn't occupy the structure for long without

weakening. When she weakened, her ability to cloak herself deteriorated.

Today, she would eat and run, staying no more than five minutes. A huge improvement, considering she'd lasted sixty-six seconds her first visit.

Sticking to Roux's portion of the structure, she stalked the corridors. Day and night, his soldiers took turns doing patrols throughout the world, on the lookout for her father and his minions. Those who weren't on patrol were either resting, training, or playing.

Coming upon the sleepers stretched out on a multitude of bunk beds, she rubbed her hands together. "Let's see what's on the menu today," she muttered. An eclectic mix of vampires, Amazons, banshees, and shifters. Males and females Roux had conquered throughout the ages, no doubt.

Hatred grew unchecked in her heart, sprouting thorns that pricked her veneer of calm.

She got to work, ghosting over the nearest sleeper, pressing her lips deep into his throat, and sucking out a single gulp of his soul before moving on to the next course. Her version of a sampler platter. This served two purposes. One, she affected a cluster of soldiers rather than a lone combatant. And two, no one would associate the slight, unexpected weakness with a phantom feeding.

Blythe glutted herself without reservation or guilt, consuming more than ever before. Some beings tasted sugary, others spicy, but all provided her with a warm burst of energy. When she finished, unable to hold another drop, she wiped her mouth and prepared to flash away with thirty-two seconds to spare. The perfect time to hunt her foe.

Someone burst into the room, crying, "Bossman is fishing in the maze again!"

A buzz of excitement crackled in the air. Everyone but those she'd sampled exploded from their beds, dashing out the door. Her appeteazers lumbered a little.

Hmm. Bossman—Roux?

Just in case, she teleported to the center of the royal garden. The heart of the realm's only maze. Bloodred flowers bloomed all around, sweetening the air. Large ebony spears grew from plant limbs, interlocking to create a wide circle around a stone bench. A contingent of harpies and soldiers clustered about, gaping at the male in the middle of it all.

Roux indeed. Sunlight bathed him. He wore a short-sleeve white T-shirt beneath a blood-soaked apron, the *alevala* decorating his arms on display.

He wasn't handsome by any means; his features were far too harsh for such a classic description. But. She pursed her lips. As much as she loathed to admit this, some females might consider him sexy hot. Over six and a half feet of muscle and sinew, he possessed a body built for war. Wavy blond hair appeared softer than silk while golden scruff on a strong jaw looked deliciously rough. Long lashes framed the most unusual yellow irises with striations of magenta, gray, and russet. The red had vanished completely.

Why, why, why is this Astra familiar to me?

Seeming bored, he wiped his crimson-stained hands on a rag. Though everyone else muttered about the carnage he'd just wrought, he remained quiet.

A vampire lay upon the bench, sobbing and frantically scanning his open chest cavity in the process of regrowing every organ but a racing heart, which remained whole. The original vital organs were scattered over the ground. A multitude of lungs, intestines, kidneys, gallbladders, stomachs, and livers. A thick metal hook protruded from each.

Blythe prowled closer, gaze locked on her target. Midway, she exited the spirit realm, catching his attention. And his scent. Cedarwood and spiced oranges. A fragrance as lovely as it was horrifying, bringing back memories of death and pain.

His blank expression never wavered—but he did go still, as if arrested by the sight of her. She knew the feeling. Seeing him in the flesh after inhabiting his body...being face-to-face with the male who'd destroyed her family... Rage deluged her. Another dose of hatred. Frustration. Intrigue. Curiosity. Even more rage and hatred.

"Everyone else," he calmly stated without glancing away from her. He dropped the rag inside the vampire's gaping wound. "Go."

The spectators shot off in varying directions. Someone carried the vampire away.

Blythe arched a brow at Roux. "What'd the vampire do wrong? Dare to breathe your air?"

"He did nothing wrong. He asked me how many times an immortal can lose certain organs before they cease regrowing. As one of his instructors, I decided to show him with a hands-on demonstration." Roux flashed, appearing directly in front of her. "The answer isn't twenty-eight."

"Well, I'm interested in learning the answer myself. How about another hands-on demonstration?" Wings fluttering, bones humming with fresh strength, she struck. A swift swipe of her claws, and she held a kidney in her grip. She offered him a cold smile and tossed the organ into the pile, saying, "One."

A stream of scarlet wet his T-shirt before the wound healed. The corners of his mouth turned down. "Your eyes turned black, a sign of aggression, yet I sensed no hint of it. How did you hide it from—"

Swipe. Again, she held a kidney in her grip. The sweet baby he'd just regenerated. "Two," she stated, matter-of-fact before softballing the brand-new organ his way. "And Roux? Hot off the presses. I *am* aggression."

Smiling wider, she stepped into a spirit realm and flashed to Isla for a quick check. Sleeping soundly. Excellent.

Blythe appeared in her private bathroom next, planning to clean up and figure out her next move. As she fiddled with the knobs in the shower, a movement toward the right caught her notice. Spinning, she prepared to attack.

Her gaze lit on familiar features, and she gasped. "Laban?"

"Hello, little love." He occupied a corner of the spacious room, peering at her with a soft expression of total adoration. A black robe draped him.

Realization struck with the force of a spiked baseball bat, and Blythe half laughed, half groaned. Her first hallucination.

"What took you so long?" She marched over, reaching for him out of habit. Her gore-covered fingers ghosted through his beautiful image, and she swallowed a sob. "I expected to lose my mind long before this."

"You aren't losing your mind. I'm real. I promise you." He, too, reached out, only to drop his arm to his side before contact. "Listen to me, sweetness. All right? Stop allowing your hatred to be your coffin. Live your life. Find happiness."

Uh… "What do you think I'm trying to do?" As long as Roux breathed, happiness would forever dance from her clasp.

"Please, Blythe. You aren't listening." Disappointment radiated from him—and it was directed squarely at her, making her squirm. "I need you to let go of…"

The words tapered off, his image fading.

"Laban!" She attempted to clamp onto him, somehow, in some realm, but he was already gone.

Tears stung her eyes. "Bring him back right this instant," she commanded her brain, slamming her fists into her temples. But Laban never reappeared. Her rage flared anew.

Forget the shower. Forget planning her next move. She *knew* what to do. Until she acquired the means to slay him, she must make Roux utterly miserable.

For days, Blythe secretly studied, researched, and followed her enemy, the Astraian torture master. She learned his habits. Searched out every rumor that mentioned his name. Collected details about him as if every tidbit were priceless in value.

Roux never knew. Yes, Astra were far more advanced than any other species she'd faced, but they weren't all-powerful.

What she'd discovered so far: He was the son of the war god, Mars. If a job called for the swift extermination of an entire planet, the Commander summoned Roux. Like any Astra, he could change the very air around him with only a thought, filling the atmosphere with poison, sleeping gas, or many other substances. But he did it with a speed the others couldn't replicate. A second preternatural ability allowed him to absorb souls into his mind. Something no one understood.

No one understood the reason his *alevala* writhed when he fought but stilled when he stopped, either. For the other Astra, the exact opposite occurred.

Though Blythe had tried to activate one, concentrating on an image with all of her might, she'd never relived a piece of Roux's past.

But no matter. That was a mystery for another day. This morning, she planned to initiate contact again.

Blythe teleported to the chandelier in the hall outside his bedroom. A favorite spot to observe his comings and goings. As cold as ice, she waited. Several minutes passed. Roux didn't appear. Nor did Laban. In fact, no other hallucinations of her consort had come.

Surely the Astra's fault.

Feeling petty, she unscrewed a bulb from the light fixture and tossed it at Roux's door. Glass shattered, jagged shards exploding in every direction.

In a blink, the Astra opened the block and scanned the area. Left, right. He frowned.

"On your way to the gym, Astra?" she asked with a smooth tone. He wore a pair of workout shorts that hung low on his lean waist. No shirt or shoes. "Gotta keep those muscles bulging, huh?"

He glanced up. Though zero emotion emanated from him, he seemed to sigh. "I understand your fury with me." His patient tone pricked her nerves. "I took someone you valued and—"

"You took someone I cherished," she corrected.

"Laban was a father and a consort. You, like all Astra, are nothing but death walking."

Roux tossed up his arms, as if exasperated. Still his features remained impassive. "How was I to know the manticore was special and not to be decapitated? He wasn't wearing a sign."

A new bomb of hatred exploded inside Blythe. She materialized in front of him, met his gaze—and extracted another kidney.

"Three." Giving him a saccharine grin, she dropped the organ at his feet. "Gotta admit, I'm really looking forward to taking number four."

With a huff, he slammed the door in her face.

"The conversation is on pause, then?" she called.

Early the next morning, Roux flashed to the trinite wall he and the other Astra had transferred to Harpina on the day of their invasion. The empty upper room located within his section, to be exact.

He peered out a large paneless window overlooking his assigned section of the marketplace. The very spot he'd first materialized. A violent storm brewed in the dark, gloomy sky. Cold wind blew in, the perfect complement to his troubled mind and its never-ending spinning wheel of irritations.

Blythe wouldn't dare appear here at least. As a phantom, she weakened in the presence of trinite. As a harpy, she would never approach a foe in a weakened condition. Meaning, he could steal a few moments for himself and think. Perhaps even puzzle out an answer to a series of questions he couldn't shake.

Namely, why did he seek her forgiveness for killing

a male who'd chosen to challenge him? Why did he wish she...liked him?

Why did he care about her feelings at all? She— stepped from thin air, mere feet away, and rested a shoulder against the wall while munching on a candy bar, total nonchalance.

He ground his teeth.

Roux didn't attempt to protect his vital organs. No, he was too busy cataloguing her every detail. Hair brushed to a shine and curling at the ends. Eyes like blue ice. No. Wrong. Eyes like onyx again. Cheeks pink with health. Or fury. The official harpy uniform clung to her curves: a metal breastplate with two intriguing cups, and a short, pleated skirt. Arm and shin bands adorned her, strapping a wealth of daggers to her limbs.

"Whatcha doing?" she asked. "Is Roux busy ruing the day he was born yet?"

Why not tell her the truth? "I'm contemplating what to do about you."

Far from cowed by the threat, she took another bite of her treat. "Have you tried tattle-telling to the General? Or dying for good? Yeah. I'm pretty sure that's the winner."

"I can stop you on my own." But had he? Nooo. Some foolish part of him *liked* dealing with her. The very crux of his problem.

"Oookay. Sure you can," she said, making a lewd motion with her free hand. She finished off the chocolate, tossed the empty wrapper on the floor, and wiped her hands together. "I no longer enjoy my sweets, by the way. Another crime to lay at your door."

He leaned toward her. She just... She smelled so nice. And she moved with such grace. An unexpected coil of heat circulated through his veins, a sensation as wonderful as it was terrible. His bones burned, his muscles like slabs of steel molded in a forge.

I don't know if you can handle the heat.

"What do you think you can do to me?" Head back, menace clear, he invaded her personal space. "If you haven't noticed, I'm bigger, stronger, meaner, and far more powerful than you."

Far from intimidated, she lifted a hand and ghosted her fingers along his jaw, never actually touching him as she softly proclaimed, "Astra, I'm going to make you suffer in ways you never dreamed possible."

He'd taught himself not to flinch when someone reached for him. For the first time, however, he had to stop himself from seeking further contact. What did she feel like?

He pressed his tongue to the roof of his mouth. What did the feel of her matter?

At least he thought he knew why she affected him like this. Blythe reminded him of his father's favorite mistress. A deranged ballet dancer who'd giggled and twirled about as Mars inflicted unspeakable agonies upon him. The only part of Roux's childhood with a positive association. Anytime he'd focused on the gracefulness of the female's motions, he'd almost forgotten his pain.

In a world of pain and darkness, she'd been a vision of softness and light.

If the mistress had been a taste of grace, Blythe was an entire meal. The harphantom never looked as if she walked; she appeared to float.

"You can try," he told her, "but you will only waste your time. I've lived too long and survived too much."

"I'll see your denial and raise you two fingers." She lifted both hands and flipped him the bird.

He swallowed a sigh. "Is there anything I can do to appease your—"

"Nope," she interjected. Her firm tone offered no wiggle room. "I'll only hate you more if you try."

Frustration gripped him. He wasn't used to failure.

A muted scream suddenly filled every chamber of his mind. He stiffened. Someone had escaped his mental dungeon.

If Roux didn't act, other prisoners might follow suit. If he did perform a search and grab, however, he would have to retreat in his mind. A state many of the Astra referred to as "Roo Coo."

Cut short his time with Blythe? No. "Do you expect me to continue allowing your attacks?"

"Hey, that's a hundred percent on you. You're free to stop me anytime. If you can." The harphantom tilted her head, studying him. "Have you ever lost someone you loved?"

Inside, his breath hitched. *Blank mask secure.* Never reveal an emotion. A lesson he'd learned well as a child. Anything you felt could and would be used against you.

"I have, yes." He punctuated the words with a nod. "Your father killed my brethren and my old Commander." Erebus might not have taken the former leader's head, but he was still responsible for the male's death. "I miss them every day." The family he'd built was now forever incomplete...much like Blythe's.

He almost flinched.

Her mind must have traveled a similar path. Her irises turned black again. She swiped out her claws, intending to take another kidney.

Roux caught her wrist, stopping her at the last possible second. "Do yourself a favor and put your grievance with me on hold. The next blessing task nears. Erebus is soon to challenge a new warlord, and I won't tolerate interference from you."

"Give me a minute to etch that pearl in my memory bank. Roux won't tolerate interference. He suggests I forget my vendetta against him until he and his buddies successfully defeat my father and ascend, gaining more power and living their dream. Got it."

"I didn't utter a suggestion," he grated.

The corners of her soft pink mouth curled up, and his guts tightened. Uh-oh. He knew that look. Knew trouble came next.

"You know," she said, sounding contemplative, "if you hadn't murdered the male I loved, we probably would've been friends. But you did. And we're not. And for some reason, I've only gotten to see him once, so I'm cranky." Swipe.

She used her free hand to snag a kidney. "Four," she said, droplets of crimson falling from her hand. "In case you're wondering, it was just as satisfying as I'd anticipated."

The blip of pain should have heralded a brutal retaliation to prove he meant business. Instead, he growled and spun her into the wall, marveling over a spike of excitement.

Excitement. As if they were playing some sort of game.

Their gazes met, and he heated another twenty degrees.

"Do not push me, harpy."

The organ splattered on the floor. "Or what, Astra?"

Smirking up at him, she vanished. Not flashing but misting, as only her kind could do.

The urge to hunt her down choked Roux. To press her against another wall and…do something. With his hands. His mouth.

Once again, frustration rose to the forefront, overtaking him. He needed to get this female out of his head. Somehow. Soon.

4

THE GOODBYE

Blythe trailed Roux, slinking through a lavishly decorated corridor in the Harpinian palace. He turned a corner, heading for his bedroom, and three of her father's phantoms came into view. Their skin was pallid, their eyes milky white. As usual, Erebus had sent females he'd dressed in ragged widow's weeds.

The trio walked in a circle at the far end of the hall, directly in front of Roux's door. With monotone voices, they chanted, "Wait for Roux, tell Roux, laugh. Wait for Roux, tell Roux, laugh."

They spoke the order that had been issued by their maker, Blythe's father. And they would obey every action to the letter.

How Daddy Undearest loved to sneak his minions past Astra defenses. Not to inflict physical injury. No.

Such small groups of phantoms could do little damage to such powerful males. Erebus did it to wreak havoc in their minds. And it worked. Roux stiffened and withdrew a dagger.

That weapon! Trinite. Hissing, Blythe stumbled back a step.

As soon as the creatures sensed the Astra, they pivoted in unison, facing him, and tilted their heads to the side. They were nothing like Blythe. She had free will; they did not. They could do nothing unless commanded by Erebus. A terrible fate they had not deserved.

As Roux closed in, the women intoned, "Riddle me this. What fills your life and makes it empty at the same time? Regret. Ha ha ha. Ha ha ha. Ha ha—"

He killed them all with a slash of the dagger. The phantoms tumbled to the floor, where they quickly evaporated. Muttering under his breath, he stalked into his bedchamber.

Blythe followed him, ghosting through the door just in time to witness his beeline for the wet bar. He poured himself an ambrosia-laced whiskey with a trembling hand.

Oh, oh, oh. Trembling?

He poured himself a second glass, then a third, until the trembling tapered off. Only then did he plop onto the foot of a massive bed. Strain bunched his muscles as he propped his elbows on his knees and sank his face into his upraised palms. A picture of defeat.

Blythe thrilled. What had caused this delightful development?

"Get it together," he mumbled. "You have conquered worlds. Slain royals. Tortured answers out of the most formidable of challengers. There's nothing you cannot do."

And now he gave himself a pep talk? Grinning, she flicked the tip of her tongue against an incisor. He should look and sound like this more often. Made her feel less stabby. For a second or two, at least. Just long enough to inventory the sense of familiarity that had only strengthened. Something that made her feel *more* stabby.

Should she reveal herself or wait a bit longer?

"Hello, daughter." Her father's greeting ended the mental debate.

A beaming Erebus approached her side. And oh, how the Astra would have thundered if he'd known his most despised foe stood within murdering distance, tucked safely inside a hidden realm.

As usual, the god wore a long robe the color of pitch. The preferred apparel of the ancients, and exactly like the garment Laban had worn in her first and only hallucination. But she wasn't going to think about that. White corkscrew curls lay in total disarray around a face with heavily lashed black eyes and a large, hooked nose. Thick dark brows proved stark against Erebus's fair skin. A constant smirk ruined any hint of attractiveness.

"Unless you come with news, leave," she commanded. "You can torment the other Astra as much as you wish, but Roux is mine." Especially in here. His bedroom, her territory. A harpy did not cede territory.

"I do come with news."

Excitement glimmered to life. "Has the time come?"

He offered a slow nod, as if he savored the action. "It has."

Well, well. The next blessing task was now set in

stone, putting Roux up to bat. Soon, the Astra would journey to a prison world known as Ation to cut out the queen's heart. A task designed by Erebus and one Blythe approved.

How better to separate the golden giant from his brethren and Taliyah, with no one able to come to his rescue? "I'll be joining him."

"Of course you will. That was always the plan."

Once, female-centric species had shipped vile criminals incapable of rehabilitation to the prison realm. Easy to enter but impossible to escape, even if you possessed the ability to flash. Unless your father was a god, and you were a phantom. At least, Blythe expected one of her unique abilities to provide a way home. If she failed to return, well, it was a risk she must take. For Laban. For vengeance.

For Isla.

Finally, her daughter could begin to heal. Eventually, she would understand and even praise Blythe's efforts.

"When is he to leave?" she asked, a mental to-do list forming. Pack. Hug and kiss Isla goodbye. Warn her sister. Blythe adored Taliyah, despite the General's annoying defense of the Astra army, and she wanted the beloved woman prepared for the worst—the loss of the blessing and the beginning of the curse.

"Tomorrow," Erebus replied. "But *you* will go now, or you won't go at all." He delivered the threat without masking his giddiness.

"Wrong." Her fingers curled into fists. "I'll go in an hour."

Silent, he slinked about Roux's bedroom, examining the warrior's things, and Blythe followed, huffing with irritation. First her father looked over a stack of folded leathers resting atop the dresser next to a bowl of fruit. On the desk was a piece of parchment with the same three sentences scrawled over every inch of it. *She isn't mine. But she is. But she isn't.*

Interesting. She who? His concubine? And should Blythe kill the woman just for giggles?

"You *are* ready for this, are you not?" Erebus asked. "I haven't pinned my hopes on a mistake, have I?"

"I'm ready," she grated. He sought to manipulate her. But. She hadn't lied. She *was* ready. She'd fed on soul again this morning. She wore the harpy soldier uniform and had two short swords crisscrossed over her back. Daggers hung at her sides and waited inside her combat boots.

"Why delay, then?"

"Why move so quickly?" she countered. "You want me at my best, do you not?" Two could play the god's mind game. If Roux succeeded, completing his task, the entire Astra army would be one step closer to obtaining the blessing. If all triumphed, Erebus earned the curse. An eternal curse this time. No more getting another chance every five hundred years. The outcome of this war forever settled the issue.

"I know what will happen if you leave this room. You'll visit your brat. She'll say something disgustingly sweet, and you'll convince yourself to stay and strike at Roux another way. You'll lose."

Dang him. An argument she couldn't refute. Except for the brat part. Her father possessed the Blade of Destiny, an ancient weapon able to transport him far into the future while remaining entrenched in the present. At any given time, he viewed hundreds of fates at once.

"I've already ensured you'll have everything required for today's departure and total victory." He slid an odd-looking purple blade from a pocket of his robe, and a plain black pouch from another pocket. "This weapon is made of firstone. The only substance able to slay an Astra."

Blythe gaped. *Knew it!*

"When sheathed in this pouch," he added, anchoring the weapon inside the material, "Roux will not detect the blade. Better to surprise him..."

Gimme! She made grabby hands.

Her father held it just out of her reach. "Like Roc, Roux will have thirty days to win or lose his task. If you cannot kill him, you have only to keep him trapped in the Ation realm. When the thirty days ends, the curse will fall upon all Astra, and killing Roux will no longer be a problem for you."

With firstone in her possession, how could she fail? But. What her father proposed struck her as too easy. Too good. A trap?

Why set her up, though? What could be his end goal?

Granted, Erebus cared nothing for her or her safety. He never had, and he never would. And most days, she didn't care. He wasn't worth an emotion. Long ago, he'd attacked Harpina, murdering hundreds of innocent harpies, all to coerce her mother into spending the night with him to conceive Blythe. He was a bona fide monster.

After she ended Roux's life, she intended to target Erebus. The Astra were right to detest him. The Dark One had no redeeming qualities whatsoever. He was pure evil, loyal only to himself, and lacking any type of moral compass. But for now, she needed him. *The enemy of my enemy is my friend.*

"You were born to defeat the Astra from the inside out," he said. A mantra she'd heard before. "Do things my way, and you will succeed. Nothing will stop you."

Still her instincts pinged. Something more was going on here. "Why don't *you* venture into Ation?"

"And give the residents another male to covet?" He spread his arms, as if he were some kind of prize. "Believe me. You'll want them focused solely on Roux."

Her attention returned to the Astra. He jerked up his head, meeting her gaze, and she gasped. He could see her?

His lids slitted, and his lips compressed into a thin line. But. He didn't leap into a defense position. He scanned the chamber, crimson sparks burning brighter and brighter in his irises.

Hmm. Maybe he *couldn't* see her. She waited, curious to learn what he'd do next.

Moving as slow as molasses, he unfolded from the bed. The sheer breadth of him swallowed up the space, making the square footage seem to shrink. After cracking the bones in his neck, he rolled back his shoulders. Preparing for battle?

Erebus chortled with glee. "I don't know how, but one or both of us has been detected. How wonderful. How wonderful indeed."

Wonderful? Not really the word she'd pick.

"Best you go, my dear, before it's too late." Her father brandished a hand toward a wall, where a large red door with strange symbols carved into the wood appeared.

Roux ran his tongue over his teeth. "Show yourself. Come on. Don't be shy now."

"I grow tired of waiting, daughter." Erebus waved

the dagger in her direction. "Will you win, or will you lose?"

Blythe looked between the two males, wanting to face off with Roux here and now but also eager to oversee his vengeance. What if this was her only way into Ation?

"I'll go." Wings rippling, she swiped the firstone dagger and its sheath. A hum of power slipped up her arm, and she nodded with satisfaction. Right decision.

Growing more determined by the second, she strode over and twisted the red door's knob. An overwarm handle. No, not just overwarm but searing. She hissed as pain flared, but she didn't let go of her prize.

Determined, she pushed her way through the block...

Suddenly, she stood in the center of a damp, dark cave. Cold air roused goose bumps on her exposed flesh. But she couldn't complain. The air carried an intoxicating scent. Like nothing she'd ever encountered.

She looked here and there. Rocky walls speckled with crystal surrounded her. A steady *drip, drip* of water filled her ears. Hmm.

This was the infamous Ation? Yes, the smell rocked. But the sights left something to be desired.

She gazed over her shoulder, intending to snap questions at her father. Her jaw dropped. The door. It was gone. Had vanished as if it had never existed.

Deep breath in, out. If Erebus had sent her anywhere other than Ation... No, surely not. Why would he do so? He might not care about her well-being, but he despised the Astra as much as she did. She— Movement behind her!

Wings buzzing, Blythe whipped around, sliding the dagger from the pouch. A shadow traveled closer in a blink, swooping down and punching the top of her sternum. Impact sent her stumbling back amid a chorus of feminine laughter.

Thankfully, she recovered quickly. Wait. The being hadn't punched her sternum; no, the being had punched through the bone, meeting Blythe's spirit and adhering some kind of ruby to it. A ruby that manifested in her flesh only a blink later.

What was…why… A flood of weakness infiltrated her limbs. *So dizzy.* In seconds, she was tottering. Usually, such feebleness came when a harpy's wings were pinned. But hers remained free. Even still, only iron determination kept her upright with the dagger in her hand as her strength continued to drain.

The shadow slinked a wide circle around her. Then another. And another. The creature, whatever it was, drew closer each time.

Blythe attempted to flash but failed. She tried to mist. Another fail. *Too weak.*

The darkness receded as the shadow stopped directly in front of her. She jolted. A wraith. A species that fed on a specific emotion. None could assume a solid physical form, but all could change their appearance at will. This particular wraith had chosen a beautiful redhead with amber eyes and overlarge breasts squeezed into a skintight silver gown. Very evil queen chic.

"Hello, Blythe. My name is Penelope. Some call me Miss Murder. I answer to either."

She knows me? Blythe struggled to think as she attempted to swing the dagger, but again, she failed, her arm too heavy to lift. No, no, no. *Need to fight!*

The wraith chortled. "I'll take this, thank you very much." Penelope plucked the prized weapon and sheath from her grip. "By the way, it was your father who told me you'd be arriving tonight. He's paying me to oversee your...care. I hope you don't mind, but I've taken the liberty of forging a link between us." She grazed a red-tipped nail against the ruby. "From now on, I'll feast on your hatred anytime I open the link. Or anytime you decide to wallow in the emotion." A wicked grin bloomed. "Don't hate me—or do—but I'm not sure I've ever tasted anything sweeter. To be honest, I'm hoping to glut myself."

Betrayed! "Why?" Blythe eked out. Why would Erebus do this?

The other woman's grin widened. "Isn't it obvious, dear? You aren't the Astra's killer. You're the bait."

5

THE MYSTERY

Roux walked like a doomed man headed to his execution. He held a piece of crumpled paper in a tight grip. An invitation from Isla Skyhawk, Blythe's young daughter.

His lungs emptied anytime he glanced down at the paper. Hand-drawn locks and keys consumed every free space. The old iron ones with fancy swirls. In the center of the page, she'd written:

WHAT? A TEA PARTY.
WHEN? TWO MINUTES AGO. DON'T BE LATE.
WHY? YOU OWE ME.

No location was mentioned. Not that he required any kind of map to find her.

He should ignore the summons. He had duties to complete. By Roc's command, Roux must aid Ian and Silver as they fortified the palace against Erebus. Somehow, the god continued to bypass once impenetrable defenses, bringing his phantoms inside. But how could Roux turn down an "invitation" from a young girl who'd recently lost her father because Roux had brutally slain the male?

He bit the inside of his cheek, tasting blood. No doubt Isla wished to poison him. An act of revenge. Something most harpies revered. One thought kept him striding forward. He'd left her with a memory she would forever long to scrub from her mind; something too many others had done to him. If he could ease her inner agonies in any way, why not play along?

His dread magnified as he entered a small sitting room with yellow walls, gilt-framed portraits, crystal vases, and velvet sofas, all spotlighted by lavender beams of sunlight filtering through a stained glass wall. Delicate china was spread over a large oval coffee table.

Isla sat on a beaded pillow, concentrating with all her might as she poured steaming tea into a cup. She wore a pink leotard and a fluffy tutu, with her sleek black hair twisted into a bun.

Seeing her, he felt like someone shot him in the stomach. Would she shrink back with terror upon noticing him?

After placing the teapot on the table, she glanced up at him with mismatched irises. One blue, one brown. No, she didn't shrink back. She narrowed her eyes.

"Sit," she commanded, motioning to the pillow on the other side of the table.

Such bravery deserved a reward. "Yes, ma'am. I believe I will." Roux folded his enormous body onto a small pillow across from her and attempted to get comfortable. An impossibility. Never had he felt so awkward. "May I ask why you have no fear of me?"

Her brow furrowed, as if he'd asked an unanswerable question. "Why would I be afraid of you? I'm, like, a powerful goddess or whatever."

Yes, he supposed she was. "Does your mother know about this party for—"

"Nope," she interjected, so much like Blythe he figured he'd be losing another kidney before this ended.

Where *was* Blythe? What was she doing? Yesterday afternoon, mere days after Halo's triumph, she'd come to Roux's bedroom. He knew she had. He'd caught a waft of her delectable fragrance—mixed with her father's. But neither individual had appeared, or challenged him. Or approached him since. He thought he might, perhaps, miss the female.

Isla pushed a cup toward him, the action smooth. "I know your secret."

"Impossible. I have no secrets." He concealed nothing from the Astra, and they concealed nothing from him. Halo had even known about this tea party before Roux.

Apparently, this was his twentieth-something time to attend it. Not that he remembered any but this one. The others had taken place during Halo's blessing task. A challenge involving a repeating day, a mystical weapon in the form of a harpy-nymph, and twelve Herculean labors. Roux recalled only the final day of the challenge—when the tea party had not occurred.

He should have avoided it today, too. He didn't belong in a chamber like this. He didn't belong anywhere near a child. Any child. Especially the daughter of his victim. His past was too violent, his future expected to be much worse.

He sighed and met the girl's gaze. Her mismatched eyes lacked the mischievous sparkle so many other harpy children possessed. A somber air cloaked her. *My fault.*

He deflated. "Why don't we discuss your father?" Roux would issue an apology. Something! "There is much I—"

"No." The flat denial forbade further comment on the subject. Her irises flashed black, reminding him of her mother. Little pink nails sharpened into ebony claws.

Different parts of his torso constricted. Very well. "You were telling me about my secret?"

"Yep." She took a sip of her tea, then added a heaping spoonful of sugar. "It's pretty terrible—for you."

He drained his cup, simply to have something to do, surprised to detect no toxins in the liquid. "Enlighten me. Please," he added.

As she daintily added more sugar to the pot and poured him more of the already too-sweet liquid, she said, "You won't believe me."

No, probably not. He drained his second cup. "Tell me, anyway. That *is* why I'm here, is it not?"

"It is." She propped her elbows on the coffee table, rested her chin in her hands, and stared at him. "You're hiding a prisoner in your mind. Even from the other prisoners. Even from yourself!"

He double blinked. How did she know about his prisoners? Unless...

A roar nearly erupted from him. "You visited the dungeon in my mind while you and your mother inhabited my body?" Had seen the spirits trapped inside his head?

"Yep," she repeated, remaining as calm as could be. "By the way, you are super weird. Probably the weirdest person I've ever met. But I'm thinking of opening a mind dungeon of my own. Any tips?"

"Yes. Don't do it. And I hide no one, especially from myself." He remained keenly aware of every inmate. Didn't he? He might have forgotten who and what they were, might have failed to capture and reimprison the escapee, but he sensed their presence.

"You totally do," she said, and how confident she sounded. How gleeful.

"Who is it, then?"

"I'm not telling." Her focus returned to the tea. "I promised I'd keep his identity to myself, and I *never* break my promises unless I want to."

She'd offered a clue, at least. This supposed secret prisoner was male. And there was a single reason she'd want to guard his identity. She knew him.

If circumstances were different, Roux might believe he'd absorbed her father, the manticore. But circumstances weren't different and— Wait. "Did you *speak* with this prisoner?" The second the terseness of his tone registered, he inwardly cursed. *Fragile little girl. Do better.*

She added another dollop of sugar to the teapot, then poured more liquid into her cup and sampled the result. "Mmm. It's perfect now. Care for more, Mr. R?"

"No, thank you," he grated. "Why tell me about the prisoner without revealing his identity?"

Again, she flipped up her gaze. This time, she grinned, and in all the centuries of his life, no one had ever appeared more diabolical. An expression she'd inherited from her mother? "Now you'll search for him. Hopefully, you'll find him sooner rather than later. I'm eager for the two of you to chat."

He didn't know what to say. This must be a trick. Her version of revenge. A way to torment him with a supposition or distraction. She'd all but admitted it! So, no. He wouldn't visit the dungeon to locate this supposed prisoner and solve the alleged mystery.

He. Would. Not.

A hard rap sounded at the door, and he craned his neck to glance at the intruder. Spotting the Commander, Roux popped to his feet, standing at attention. Since Roc's marriage to Taliyah Skyhawk, Blythe's sister, the iron-willed warrior had displayed prolonged moments of uncharacteristic softness coupled with unexpected smiles. Today strain etched his every feature.

Roux wanted to spew out questions but held his silence. One did not speak before one's superior. He kept his gaze pinned over Roc's broad shoulder, exactly as a subordinate should. Not because the other god was stronger or more powerful; he wasn't. Roux did this to show his respect. Like all Astra, he valued title above sentiment. Emotion was always subject to change, but the authority in their designations forever remained the same.

"You can show yourself out," she announced, sparing Roc a single glance. "You weren't invited."

The Commander blinked with incredulity. To be spoken to with such irreverence, and by a child...

Roux cringed inside. Such disrespect was never tolerated from anyone. Ever. He gently explained, "A

Commander may attend any event that transpires in his territory, with or without an invitation."

To Roc, he spoke telepathically, using a mental link all Astra possessed.—*Any punishment due to her, I will take.*—From this moment on, he would protect the little girl and her mother from further hurt and harm. Because Isla was right; he owed them.

The Commander seemed to fight a smile.—*My next words may be punishment enough. The next blessing task is set, and you are the contender.*—

He frowned. Usually, they went in order of rank: Roc, Halo, then Silver, with Roux sixth. This guaranteed they worked the same task every five hundred years. This round, however, they battled for more than the blessing. They sought ascension. A rise in status and dominance, and a chance to obtain eternal freedom from the curse. Then, at long last, they would have the power to oversee the ultimate destruction of Erebus. For this reason, the Dark One, who pursued his own ascension, was allowed to change the order he faced his opponents as well as the tasks themselves.

"Come to the conference room the moment you tell her goodbye," Roc told him before flashing off.

"No need to say goodbye," the little girl said, offering Roux another of those calculating smiles. "I'll be seeing you real soon."

He noted the pain behind her expression this time, and he couldn't bring himself to leave. Not yet. "I know this means nothing to you but…" His jaw tensed. His throat tightened. Hands fisted, he sank to his knees, so that they were eye to eye. "I'm sorry I killed your father."

The smile vanished. Her lower lip wavered. Tears

welled, but she blinked them back. "You aren't sorry," she informed him with a firm tone. "But you will be. Now go. I'm done with you."

Sighing, he forced himself to teleport to the conference room. An open space with a long table and ten chairs. Roc already stood at the head of the table, a tower of might with cropped dark hair, bronze skin heavily marked by *alevala*, and eyes of gold with striations of gray.

"Any questions?" the Commander prompted.

Many. But he'd start with the most important. "What am I to do?"

"There is a supposedly inescapable prison world known as Ation. You will venture there, apprehend the queen within twenty-nine days, and return to Harpina. On the thirtieth day, you will present your prisoner to Chaos and remove her heart with a trinite blade."

Nothing out of the ordinary. All easily accomplished. So what was the catch? "What do you know of the queen?"

"Only that the current or former sovereign is a vampire, but the title can transfer to another at any time. Or has transferred. You may or may not meet the vampire but the one who rules after her. Or now." Roc pinched the bridge of his nose. "The time difference between worlds is confusing. Sometimes it's faster than ours, sometimes it's slower, but everything equals out in the end. I'm not sure how it works. Just look for the one who wears the crystal crown."

Halo Phaninon, their strategist, appeared, flashing into the room with Celestian "Ian" Eosphorus fast on his heels. The two flanked the Commander's sides, the three creating a wall of ferocity.

Though the two weren't related by blood, Halo resembled Roc in many ways. Similar brown hair, bronze skin, and odd golden eyes. And though Ian, who was black, looked nothing like the Commander, they shared the same parents.

The two males were just as different in temperament. Where Roc was all rough insistence and brute strength, his younger brother exuded unflappable confidence and smooth charm.

Both newcomers offered Roux a sympathetic wince. He kept quiet, waiting, as his mind whirled. Something had happened. What, what?

"Your suspicions were correct," Halo informed the Commander. Once, he'd been known as the Machine. An emotionless husk Roux considered one of his closest friends. During his most recent task, however, Halo had found his *gravita*. Now the warrior constantly exuded an enviable contentment Roux couldn't understand. "She's missing."

She who? Ophelia, Halo's mate? Taliyah?

"Erebus is overdue a spanking." Ian stretched his fingers, as if warming up for the job. "He sent another phantom with a message to my quarters, confirming her location."

Long ago, Chaos had chosen Ian to be the first leader of the Astra. A wise move. His abilities were awe-inspiring and vast. But he'd failed to sacrifice his bride during the original blessing task, welcoming the curse, and heralding the death of several Astra. After that, he'd lost his rank.

Just how many phantoms had Erebus snuck inside the palace? Why had no one informed Roux more had come?

All three males regarded him with something akin to worry.

"What?" he demanded, unable to tolerate the curiosity a moment longer. "If you doubt my ability to prove victorious, do not." It was the worst insult they could lob at him.

He might have his share of problems. The prisoners in his mind. Their screams. Bouts of blankness and madness. His utter hatred of physical contact. His unusual obsession with a black-haired, blue-eyed harphantom who rightfully despised him. But. Never had he failed these men; never would he. Roux had always—*would* always—cross any line to protect them.

"We have no doubt you will succeed," the Commander stated. "But there's a problem. Blythe found a path into Ation."

Hearing her name spoken aloud sent a jolt through him, making his spine go ramrod straight. This explained why she hadn't dropped by today's tea for kidneys at least.

"How?" he demanded.

"Erebus, I'm sure. I suspect she means to challenge you at every turn, impeding your victory however possible."

Enjoy your last days. I'm coming for you.

He worked his jaw. "Are you ordering me to kill your *gravita*'s beloved sister?" And if so, how was Roux to respond? He had never hesitated to follow a directive but he wasn't sure he could murder Isla's sole remaining parent in cold blood. Or hot blood. Never again scent that sweet mix of honeysuckle and rose?

Stiffness spread through him, making his body feel as hard as granite.

"I am not." Roc scrubbed a hand over his face. "I'm asking you to let her live, no matter what vile deeds she commits against you. When you return with the queen, I'd like a living, breathing Blythe to be with you. Taliyah won't forgive me if harm comes to her sibling."

Relief poured through him. "It shall be as you have requested."

"If she's injured along the way," the Commander added, "find a way to heal her. Because she lost her mate, she'll be unable to use blood as medicine. Bloodfruit doesn't help her. She can't keep it down."

A complication he hadn't considered. Mated harpies sickened when they drank from anyone but their consort, forcing widows to rely on a tree-grown blood substitute.

Perhaps Blythe required something stronger than fruit? She was a royal born of the gods who'd birthed phantoms and snakeshifters. "What of soul?" Did she vomit that, too?

"I don't know. Taliyah tells me as little as possible of her sisters."

No matter. "I will do whatever proves necessary." Words he meant with every fiber of his being. Now, on to business before he got lost in thoughts of the harphantom. "What do you know of Ation's terrain?"

"Ophelia shared the rumors she's heard throughout the years," Halo said. "Ation is supposedly like Earth, with mountains, plains, deserts, oceans, and forests. The seasons differ in different locations. Night replaces day and day replaces night. But beware of the monsters beneath the ground."

Monsters? No big deal. "When do I leave?"

"Today," Roc said, surprising him. "You'll need to

take any supplies with you. I'm told you'll be able to flash into the realm as well as throughout it, but you won't be able to leave. You'll be completely cut off from other worlds, unable to communicate with us." The Commander glanced at the clock behind Roux. "You have one hour to prepare."

"Just in a couple of minutes." Roux remained at the ready.

With only a thought, he summoned a backpack, weapons, all-terrain gear, gold, and anything else he might need, teleporting each item atop the conference table. Then, he strapped the sword, daggers, whip, bow, and quiver of arrows to his body and stuffed the rest inside the backpack.

A solo dagger possessed a trinite blade. There was no reason to cart in an entire arsenal comprised of the single substance able to kill the harphantom. At the same time, he must be prepared for the worst.

Lifting his chin, he met the Commander's gaze. "I'm ready."

6

THE CALM

Blythe stumbled across a sunlit expanse of soft grass and sharp stones, regretting her foolishness, and missing her daughter. She'd walked for hours with no end in sight. Earlier, Penelope had drained her so completely, she'd been unable to fight as the wraith stripped her out of her uniform and boots and forced her into a ridiculously sheer white nightgown. The plunging neckline displayed ample cleavage and really made her new wrist shackles pop.

Perfect "bait" attire. Never mind that bloody abrasions littered her bare feet and dirt smeared her calves.

The ruby remained embedded in the hollow of her throat, just above her sternum, allowing Miss Murder to drain her anytime, anywhere. Which she hadn't done for over an hour.

As soon as her strength returned, Blythe attempted to flash to another world. And bombed. She tried again, aiming for ten miles to the east within this very realm. Another bomb.

Unwilling to give up, she misted—nope. Slipped into a spirit realm? Not even a little.

Frustration razed her nerves. She'd been tagged with mystical shackles. They did more than limit her movements; they kept her helpless.

Penelope floated over the land, keeping pace beside a strange amalgamation of creatures. It was the size of a wolf with the hide of a stonefish and the horn of a rhinoceros, and it led Blythe forward using the nexus of chain that dangled from the center of her manacles. It kept the end firmly anchored in its mouth.

"Faster, girl," the spectral menace demanded as Blythe tripped over a rock. "I have places to be."

"What places? Why?" Knowledge equaled power, and right now she needed all the power she could get.

"Why is easy. I've sold you. The places are none of your beeswax. Is that the saying? Did I use it correctly?"

She worked her jaw. "Who bought me?"

"The queen of Ation. Who else? No other can afford my admittedly exorbitant rates."

Well, well. The queen herself. The very person Blythe sought. She picked up the pace as much as inhumanly possible. Which wasn't much.

"Don't hate me," the wraith continued. She flaunted a grin over her shoulder. "Or do. I do what I must to keep my people in peak condition for the coming of our Chosen One."

Chosen One? "Do tell."

"All I'll share is this. She's a being of exceptional ability who will free us from our suffering."

"Meanwhile you make others suffer?"

"And you are above such pursuits?"

She narrowed her eyes. Silence reigned as they exited a valley teeming with wildflowers, bypassed a crystalline lake surrounded by gorgeous red flowers, and paraded past an ancient village of women toiling to survive. Some were dyeing and weaving garments. Some skinned animals, while others stirred stews or carried large clay pots of sloshing water.

None approached, too afraid to even glance at the wraith. No one spoke, either. They simply went about their day, as if used to encountering prisoners who were being dragged to and fro. Maybe they were.

Blythe blamed Erebus for her predicament, yes, but also Roux. Mostly Roux. Had he kept his claws to himself, Laban would be alive, Isla would have two parents at her side, and Blythe would be blissfully happy again.

When Miss Murder moaned with pleasure, Blythe groaned. She knew what came next—another draining.

Sure enough, cold infiltrated her limbs. Tremors set in.

Any thought of the Astra delighted the wraith, shooting hatred along the link between them.

Deep breath in, out. As she attempted to blank her mind, an idea formed, both brilliant and risky. Blythe seized it. Desperate times, desperate measures. If she could glut the woman, the feedings would stop, and her strength would return full force. She could kill Penelope, ridding herself of the ruby.

Worth a shot.

Blythe returned her focus to Roux, to the memories

she'd stolen from him. The ones involving the torture of the boy. In her mind, she saw the Astra draped in a black robe, with the sleeves rolled up his forearms. He stood over the boy. A poor soul fettered to a bed of stone.

Expression gleeful, Roux pressed a multitude of branding irons into the child's flesh. Screams of agony echoed within her head, reminiscent of those she'd heard while inhabiting him. Hatred swamped her.

New moans left the wraith.

Another memory of torture made itself known, and more hatred flowed along the link, establishing a pattern. Concentrate, flow. And flow. And flow. Gah! The wraith might be a bottomless pit.

Blythe's knees buckled, and she toppled to the ground. Bad plan. Very bad.

The wolflike creature—she'd call it Amal—sustained its swift pace, dragging her behind it. Rocks sliced different parts of her. Amid an onslaught of aches and stings, she clambered to her feet.

The Astra will pay for every vile deed he's ever committed! Every wound I've received.

Every moment of my family's anguish.

A fresh tide of weakness crashed into her limbs. "I want my dagger back," she snapped, stumbling again.

"Dream on, girlie." Penelope chuckled with delight. "But whatever you're thinking, keep it up. Your hatred is delicious. The most potent I've ever sampled. Truly, my thanks for the top off."

Irritation flared. Blythe knew a bit about wraiths and how they operated. The only way to shed the ruby—without Penelope's aid or death—was to rid herself of whatever emotion empowered it. Sounded easy. It wasn't. She'd lived a long time and knew how emotions worked. They started out as seeds planted in the rich soil of your heart. Thoughts and words acted as water. Soon, trees sprouted and bore fruit, good or bad. More seeds, more trees. She couldn't even die and revive to remove the ruby. The roots remained ready to grow a whole new orchard.

To remove her new bling, Blythe must truly forgive Roux for his crimes against her family. But how could she forgive him, even temporarily?

He and his brethren deserved to suffer. No other outcome was acceptable. But, at the rate she was currently draining, she might die *without* reviving.

"Are we there yet?" she whined, and not just to be annoying.

"Unfortunately for you, we are." Penelope pointed ahead to an overcast area where a group of large rocks formed a wide circle. Reminded Blythe of Stonehenge in the mortal realm.

Twenty females congregated there, some perched atop the rocks, others standing guard outside the circle. She clocked two shifters, three vampires seemingly unbothered by the sunlight, six Amazons, one gorgon, five sirens, two harpies, and a manticore, who didn't look like some fragile thing in need of a man's protection, but a hardened warrior.

Blythe's gaze lingered on the manticore's golden mane. A lump clogged her throat. The ruby heated, and more of her strength whooshed away.

Each being wore a leather half top and short, slitted skirt, putting their weapons on display. A stunning, scarlet-haired vampire with green eyes bore a crown fashioned from black crystals. The Ation queen?

Harpies and vampires shared an ancestor. Thanks to a violent history, the two species rarely got along.

When Penelope and Amal halted before the guards, the suspected queen stepped from her rock, zipping to the ground and executing a graceful landing. As she approached the wraith, another vampire and an Amazon joined her, flanking her sides.

"*This* is our insurance policy?" The potential queen looked Blythe over and grimaced, clearly unimpressed. And who could blame her? There was nothing more humiliating than being caught in chains. "It's so...delicate." She shuddered.

It? Blythe's wings fluttered. "Careful, babe. This insurance policy comes with hidden fees." Blythe inwardly grimaced. Okay, so, as far as comebacks went, that one sucked. In her defense—no, she had no defense. She should be better at this, and it was her fault she'd gone soft the past eight years.

Snickers blended with murmurs of doubt. The doubt came from the harpies. Who should have rushed to vindicate Blythe. The sisterhood stuck together against all others, always, whether they knew each other or not. Or rather, they did in Harpina. But she wasn't in Harpina anymore, was she?

Teeth grinding, Blythe shifted her focus to the rocks. Hmm. Up close, she noticed blood-smeared carvings. Strange symbols she didn't recognize. Power wafted from each, prodding her curiosity.

"This chick isn't a prize," the fairest of the harpies said. "She's a participation ribbon."

Hold up. Insurance policy. Chick. Participation ribbon. Why did an ancient civilization of criminals sound so modern?

Penelope seemed to read her mind. Fluffing her hair, she said, "I acquired a collection of romance novels featuring the original heartbreakers and often read them to the masses. For a price. I suggest you put your name on the attendees' list ASAP. We fill up fast."

You've got to be kidding me.

The vampire with the crown held up a hand in a bid for silence—and she got it. Oh, yes. The queen. "Answer my question, wraith."

"I am one hundred percent certain she's the one you seek," Penelope said. "I've been assured the Astra will agree to your demands in order to save her life."

"Why?" the queen asked. "Is she his mate?"

"No," Blythe snarled, unable to hold her tongue. Let anyone think she belonged with Laban's killer? Never! "I'm his doom."

Once again, snickers sounded. Someone even mocked her. *"I'm his doom."*

"Ah, how cute is she?" The gorgon jumped up and down and clapped. "This phantom isn't as mindless as we heard."

So. They saw her as a phantom, not a harpy or even a combination of the two.

"Her sister is wed to the Astra's king," Penelope explained. "The warrior headed here is supposed to save her while completing his blessing task."

Well. Everyone had been fully briefed about the intricacies of the situation. And Roux, save her? Hardly. He'd be too busy dying.

Satisfaction played over the queen's elegant features. Everyone else attempted to mask their excitement but failed.

For some reason, this infuriated the vampire. "Do not forget," she snapped at the group. "He's mine."

"Wrong. He's mine." The Amazon at the queen's side moved as fast as lightning, swinging a sword, swiftly beheading the vampire. She swooped down to swipe the crystal crown from the grass. As she straightened, she settled the circlet atop her head.

The violence didn't disturb Blythe. She'd seen worse a thousand times over. She'd *done* worse. But wow. Just wow.

There was a beat of silence as everyone absorbed what had happened. Then a chorus of cheers erupted, but they sounded anything but cheerful. Blythe detected grumbles and bored tones.

"All hail Sheena," the women cried, "the new queen of Ation."

Sheena preened. She was a dark beauty, at least six feet tall, and marked with scars along each arm. "I'll be attending your next reading free of charge," she told Penelope.

"Of course," the wraith replied. "The queen usually does."

Extending her arms, the new ruler turned in a half circle to face her companions. "Any objections?"

The others darted their gazes, staying quiet. Not Blythe. "Do you plan to kill him?" she demanded.

Completing the spin, Sheena met her gaze and laughed. "Kill him? Are you kidding? He'll be the first male to enter this world. I plan to bed him again and again and again and again. When I'm pregnant and done with him, I'll gift him to the others. They can spend a night in his bed. For a price."

For a price. The theme of Ation. But. Allow Roux

to experience pleasure upon pleasure during his task? Although...

She'd followed him for weeks, yet she'd never seen him make use of his concubine in a sexual way. Nor had he shown favor to a harpy. Therefore, she had no idea about the kind of women who revved his engine. But come on. What hot-blooded, single warrior wouldn't relish time spent with sex-starved prisoners?

She balled her hands. As more weakness settled in her limbs, Penelope moaned with glee.

Amal's sudden roar tore Blythe's attention from the wraith. What? What had happened?

The other women squealed as they raced into formation, creating two lines of four and two lines of five, with Sheena two steps ahead of them all.

"Give her to me." The new queen stretched out her arm and waved her fingers in Blythe's direction. "Now."

"I don't know if I should," Penelope replied as Amal shifted its big body directly in front of her. "My deal was with Morgana. Only her mark decorates the Oath Stone."

Morgana, the former queen? Oath Stone? Wait. Blythe thought she remembered Oath Stones mentioned in history books. Used by the ancients to ensure beings kept their word.

"No, your deal was with the realm's leader. I am she, and she is me." Sheena waved her fingers again. "You'll have your payment by morning. Now give me my insurance."

"Very well. The deal stands." The wraith nodded to Amal, who dropped the end of Blythe's chain.

She pulled at her shackles. How she longed to lash out. To prove her superior strength. To punish. To excise the tension building inside her. But, as the ground shook, then shook again, gaining traction, she barely remained upright.

Sheena wasted no time, swiping the links and yanking. Blythe stumbled forward, unable to halt her momentum. The queen caught and spun her, putting them chest to back, then wrapped one arm around her waist. With her free hand, Sheena held a blade at Blythe's throat.

Blythe fumed. She, a former assassin with nine stars branded in her left wrist, had been rendered all but helpless.

Her gaze landed on the wraith and narrowed. "You'll pay for everything I endure."

"Sure. Okay." With a parting wink, the wraith faded until only a transparent outline lingered. And only for a moment. Both the outline and the beast vanished in a rolling white fog.

"This is really happening," someone behind her whispered. "In a matter of seconds, a man will enter Ation. A real, live man with a penis and everything!"

"Be quiet," Sheena snapped. "Be ready."

"I *am* ready," the whisperer replied.

The murk drew closer. Closer still. Would she find Roux inside it? Heart thumping, Blythe squinted into the miasma. Searching, searching…

Closer…

Blythe braced for impact. The vapor enveloped her, scented with cedarwood and spiced oranges, and air hitched in her lungs. Her eyesight hazed.

For several seconds, no one moved or spoke. No one dared to breathe. And it wasn't because of fear. Oh, no.

Anticipation crackled all around, hot enough to burn off the haze.

Suddenly, Roux towered before the troops. He stood roughly thirty feet away, his formidable body laden with enough weapons to equip an army of fifty.

He'd come prepared for war.

Blythe's wings shuddered, relief and hatred converging inside her. A confusing mix. Of course, her link to the wraith instantly reactivated, causing fresh weakness to pour through her limbs.

Deep breath in, out. She did her best to concentrate on the relief. The Astra was here, and he was killable. Her trip and subsequent suffering had been worth it. Forget her present state. It was temporary and subject to change. Vengeance could and would be had. Soon. And who knows? She might find a way home to Isla afterward.

A wave of homesickness nearly crushed her chest.

A god assured of his power, Roux examined the women around her without moving a muscle.

How she longed to snag another kidney. Perhaps his liver as well.

The softest breeze rustled locks of his pale hair over his brow. Per usual, he was shirtless. Finally, his *alevala* moved again, jumping to another location on his flesh. Unfortunately, now wasn't a good time to lose herself in his past.

Around her, the small army of nineteen whistled, catcalled, and offered lewd suggestions.

"The things I'm going to do to you, Torture Master," Sheena purred.

Silent, he slid his attention to Blythe. A blink-blink followed a languid perusing of her see-through nightgown. As if he couldn't believe what he'd seen, he did it again. Warmth suffused his irises. A lot of it. A telling reaction.

He liked the look of her. Good. *Knowledge to use against him.*

Finally the supposedly savvy warrior noticed the dagger poised at her neck, the ruby above her sternum, and the chains constraining her wrists. Flickers of red filled his golden irises.

Didn't want anyone else being responsible for her torment?

"Love those jumping tats…" With a dreamy sigh, a shifter glided from the formation, sashaying toward Roux. "Gonna get me a closer look." But she stopped and yelled in agony midway.

The others shouted commands to return.

Falling to her knees, grunting and moaning, the shifter clawed at her face. Blood streamed from her eyes, nose, and ears. Wasn't long before she toppled the rest of the way, going still and quiet. Dead?

The others quieted, too. Were they reeling with confusion like Blythe? What just happened?

"What did you do to her?" the other shifter snarled.

He ignored the female, his focus unwavering on Blythe. "You are unharmed?"

"I'm going to carve you open from nose to navel and pluck out your organs with my teeth," she purred at him. "I'll bypass your record for sure."

The zipper of his leathers pulled taut. "I'll take that as a yes."

Whoa, whoa, whoa. There was liking the look of her, and then there was getting turned on by her threats. One she could use to her advantage; the other she wouldn't tolerate. He shouldn't be allowed to enjoy a moment of his defeat.

A vampire noticed his reaction, too, and shouted, "I'm going to use you as a pincushion for my swords." Her shoulders rolled in after his zipper retracted. "That didn't do it for you?"

Okay. All right. His erection must have been a delayed reaction to the bounty of femininity before him, not some *War of the Roses* fetish.

Unfazed, he shifted his gaze to Sheena. "Release my harphantom." The words emerged calm, pleasant even, but there was no mistaking his note of command.

Uh, his harphantom? Blythe bared her teeth at him. "Not yours."

"I'll keep her, thanks. Here is what's gonna happen," Sheena announced. "You kill any more of my soldiers, and I will slice through her trachea. You attack us, and I will slice through her trachea. You drop to your knees and vow to do whatever I ask, or yes, I will slice through her trachea. Questions? Comments?"

"Go ahead and slice," he grated. "I've seen ordinary phantoms recover from far worse. She'll heal, I'll make sure of it, and you'll die."

Glaring at him, Blythe licked her teeth. "I don't need your help to heal."

"As if you'll be allowed to heal." The queen kissed her cheek before stroking the tip of the dagger over the ruby. "You see the jewel embedded in your female's skin? It came courtesy of a wraith. Her strength is being drained as we speak, her ability to recuperate supernaturally suspended. She will die a mortal's death, and not even a warrior like you can bring her back. But I have a way to revive her."

"I'm not his female," Blythe snarled. Harpies received one consort in a lifetime. No more, no less. She wouldn't claim Roux in any way, shape, or form.

"Perhaps I have the means to cure her, perhaps I don't. Yet," Roux said to Sheena, acting as if the bound harpy he strove to "protect" hadn't spoken. "Either way, your guards will die before you find out. You, I'll save to kill later."

With her free hand, the Amazon fanned her cheeks. "Anyone ever tell you a battlefield isn't the place for sexy talk?"

His lids slitted. "You make light because you do not understand with whom you deal. My name is Roux Pyroesis, and I am an Astra Planeta. Many refer to me as the Crazed One. Right now the harphantom is the only thing standing between you and the destruction of this entire realm. Harm her at your peril."

"Oh. I see what's going on here." Sheena tsk-tsked. "You make light because you believe we should fear you. You're so big, bad, and mad, after all. But soldier, we defeated the dragons who once ruled this world. You are nothing but a tasty meat stick."

He dropped a backpack at his feet and unsheathed two short swords, then motioned the females over with a nod of his chin. "Know this. If the harpy is injured, I will ensure your end becomes infinitely more humiliating than currently planned."

Being defended by the Astra was even worse than being restrained by the Amazon. Blythe's every nerve sang with resentment.

"You just made your next mistake." Sheena gave another tsk-tsk. "You consider my boast empty. Allow me to teach you a difficult truth, Astra. I say what I mean and mean what I say." She bent her head, kissed Blythe's cheek—and struck, slamming the blade through her windpipe, exactly as promised.

Sharp, piercing pain. Instant dizziness. Blood filled her mouth in a rush, spilled down her throat, and choked her.

Can't breathe. Spots of black grew over her vision. In the distance, she thought she heard Roux roar with unholy fury. Then her knees gave out, and she knew nothing more.

7

THE DECISION

Pure, unadulterated rage deluged Roux. The Amazon had *dared*.

He altered the unnaturally sweet-scented atmosphere, intending to put everyone to sleep. Again. For some reason, the lot remained alert and upright. Was his ability failing or were they immune to the gases? Something to ponder later. For now...

Threaten someone under his protection and suffer.

Roux ran at his foes, his plan clear. Incapacitate the Amazon with the crystal crown, the queen he'd come for. Dismember and slay everyone else. Afterward, he could feed Blythe his blood, or at least try. If she sickened, he would find another way.

Once she healed, and she would, he would return to Harpina with both the harpy and the Amazon. Then he would torture the Amazon for the allotted thirty days' wait, then present her heart to Chaos. Task complete, vengeance acquired.

Just before he breached the queen's perimeter, a manticore struck her from behind, cleaving her head from her body.

The Amazon toppled, the crown tumbling across the grass.

"No one touch that crown!" the manticore shouted.

Confused, Roux paused. His mind reeled. The new queen, gone. According to Roc, another being would be named ruler. The permanent one, or would she come next?

Perhaps he should kill every female but one? Warrior's choice became queen. Yes. He liked this plan.

The remaining immortals rushed to surround Blythe, forming a wall around her. A siren began to sing the harpy to...health? Death?

Can't risk it. Lurching into action, Roux lunged and swung his swords, intending to take out a shifter and the siren at once.

The group surprised him, banding together to block and defend each other, rendering his strike unfruitful. Hmm. They were willing to murder their queen but also loyal to others? Or only disloyal to she who bore the title of sovereign?

A macabre dance ensued. The gorgon utilized the snakes attached to her scalp, attempting to mesmerize him. The vampires bit to weaken not to kill. The manticore endeavored to sting and inject him with a paralyzing toxin. The sirens not singing to Blythe hummed a seductive melody meant to propel him into a sexual lather.

Despite their best efforts, he evaded every tactic and capability, taking down two sirens, a vampire, three Amazons, and the final shifter. But he didn't do it quickly. Minutes passed between each death, irritating him greatly. The females were more skilled than expected. Had they attempted to slay him rather than subdue him, they might have done major damage before losing.

And lose they would. Astra weren't like any other opponents. They'd lived too long, experienced too much, and labored too extensively, eradicating any disadvantages. But. No matter the losses or injuries the females incurred, they maintained a stalwart wall around the General's sister. As a unit, they proved more skilled, organized, and disciplined than ninety-nine percent of the armies he'd faced.

Must get to Blythe. If she couldn't tolerate his blood, maybe she would recover with his soul.

Can't fail her. Can't fail my Commander...

Growling, Roux delivered a series of painful blows to an Amazon, shredding different parts of her. Down she fell, now missing a throat, a heart, and her intestines. Before the other combatants could stop him, he stomped, the spikes on the bottom of his boot removing her head and finishing her off.

"We wish you no harm, Astra," the gorgon panted, doing her best to hold his gaze. Her species possessed the unique ability to look into another's eyes and turn flesh into stone. Fables claimed the metamorphosis transpired in a matter of seconds, but even the most talented of gorgons needed hours.

"Your wishes mean nothing to me." Swing.

She jumped back, his claws grazing her belly. Panting worse, she said, "Don't be so sure. Agree to bed each of us, and we'll let you have the phantom. Think of it. Your end goal is achieved, with hours of pleasure as a bonus."

He opened his mouth to refuse, but snapped his jaw shut before a single word escaped. To end the battle sooner rather than later and get Blythe in his possession? Perhaps he could bargain.

Needing a moment to consider his options, Roux halted his next blow midswing and moved out of the strike zone.

The females maintained their defensive positions around the harphantom, watching him with varying degrees of lust, hope, and satisfaction.

This bouquet of femininity hoped to use his body. He supposed he should be flattered? Ian would've been. Many other Astra as well. And ever since Roux had spotted Blythe in her transparent gown, sparking the heat, he'd ached for...something. Every cell in his body felt alive with purpose. For the first time in his life, he was curious about sexual matters.

How soft might a woman's curves feel against his palms? Would he react to the opposite sex as the other Astra did, always hungering for more? Would the heat flame out of control, remaking him? But to what end? Curious Roux might be, but tolerant he was not. Physical contact had never not bothered him.

So what would he offer these females instead of what they currently desired? Wait. What was he doing? He was a legendary warrior. A killer—a god. He fought until his challengers died, always, without exception.

"Do you agree?" the gorgon asked, hopeful.

"I'd rather rend each of you in half." He retracted his claws and withdrew the shiniest of his swords.

She held up her hands, palms out, and rushed to say, "Whoa. Hold up there, hot stuff. Do you refuse because you think your phantom is already dead? I assure you, she's alive and well."

The women parted, revealing Blythe at long last. Though the black-haired vixen lay on the ground, unconscious, her wound had closed, and her chest was rising and falling with her breaths. His breath came easier. Unfortunately, the ruby still glinted in the sunlight.

"We know you require an Ation queen to complete your blessing task. Well, you require her heart, anyway," a harpy said. A shapely beauty with rich brown hair, flawless skin a shade lighter, and big eyes a shade darker. "If you refuse our oh, so generous offer, the crown will go unclaimed until your clock runs out. And Astra? The crown means nothing unless it is willingly claimed. But, if you agree to our terms and sign the Oath Stones, we'll give you the phantom as a token of our goodwill. She'll be yours to do with as you please."

Oath Stones. His gaze slid to the circle of strategically placed boulders in the distance. He knew how they worked. Whoever chiseled their symbol in the stone, spoke a vow, and sealed it with their blood would be forced to keep their word. Zero exceptions. A practice once used by the oldest of the gods to circumvent betrayal. Not even an Astra could break its compulsion.

Roux needed someone to claim that crown. Thankfully, the females had just provided a way to force the issue. Far different than the females expected.

Halo might be the strategist, but Roux was an excellent problem solver. He had to be. Have other people trapped in your mind? Lock them up. Black out occasionally? Train yourself to instinctively shield yourself with electrifying power. Today's solution seemed obvious.

"Here is *my* offer," he said, sheathing his weapons. "You will place Blythe the Undoing into my care, as promised, but you will also hold a to-the-death tournament."

A tournament served multiple purposes. Rallied the competitive spirits of these alpha warriors, kept them occupied mentally and physically, and provided a queen for his task. If they took each other out in the process, leaving him with fewer bodies to cut down on his way out, even better.

He continued, "The winner will claim the crown, and I'll spend the night with her without killing her. I'll also escort her to Harpina." Where he would remove her heart, as ordered. If she revived afterward, as many immortals could, he might kill her again just for grins. He had no mercy to spare for the females of this world.

The group's lust, hope, and satisfaction morphed into excitement, suspicion, and cold calculation.

"My, aren't you a clever one, offering something we would kill anyone to acquire," the manticore said. The others chirped their agreement. "Give us a moment to discuss the particulars."

They rushed together, forming another circle around Blythe, once again shielding her from his view. He barely silenced a second roar. Nearly flashed closer to shove everyone aside. He wanted the widow in his sights.

Frantic whispers erupted from the group before they broke apart and faced him.

He almost smiled. He'd won. He knew it.

Once again, the harpy spokeswoman stepped forward. "We agree to your terms. With certain caveats, of course. We host the tournament and make the rules, not you. You can do nothing to affect who wins or loses. The games begin in ten days and last ten days. This gives us an opportunity to alert the masses. Gotta give everyone a fighting chance, you know? Also, while you're on Ation, you will live at the palace. The phantom can stay in your chamber, if you like, but you cannot stray far from royal grounds…unless you are on a date, then you must only remain near your date. Speaking of, you must spend at least six consecutive hours with each member of your welcome party, and you cannot commit murder during these times." She winked at him. "The order you choose to be with us is up to you. So is what happens."

Why let the masses participate, risking the crown? Or did these females have no wish to carry the title, despite its new perks? Perhaps they thought to use their wiles and lure him from his task, keeping him here.

Soon they would learn the error of their ways.

"Agreed," he stated. Ten dates and ten days of the tournament. One night with the queen. Nine days to find a way into Harpina with Blythe and the queen at his side. Perfectly doable.

A celebration erupted, an assortment of high fives, whistles, and victory shouts. One voice rose above all others.

"Sausage for everyone!"

He pressed his tongue to the roof of his mouth. "Let's get this done." With a thought, he teleported to the closest Oath Stone.

He had no need of a chisel. Not with his claws. Hand lifted, index finger poised over the rock face, claw extended, he announced, "As long as all females of this realm abide by our agreement—no harm comes to Blythe the Undoing, the harphantom in my care—I agree to the following. In ten days, a ten-day to-the-death tournament will commence, free of my interference. The winner will become queen. I will spend the night of her coronation with her. In return, I will remain near the palace unless I'm on a date, then I will remain near the date. As for the encounters themselves, I will spend six hours with each of the ten residents here, without committing murder. I will also escort the queen to Harpina."

That said, he scraped his personal symbol into the stone. A circle with two smaller circles inside it, the pair divided by a jagged line. The same symbol was branded into his nape, though it contained marks added by Chaos and the other Astra. Their symbols. This allowed them to telepathically communicate with each other. Usually.

Now on to part two of his oath. Roux sliced his finger with a claw and sealed the vow with a bead of his blood.

The compulsion took root inside him in an instant, and he nodded. "It is done."

His challengers celebrated with increased vigor, thinking they'd won some great prize. Think again. They should ask his maid about his idea of romance. He usually polished his weapons while she cleaned his room or mended and washed his clothes. Sometimes, when they were both feeling particularly social, she complained about the difficulty of removing bloodstains and dried viscera, and he grunted a response.

Ready for what came next, he summoned his discarded backpack. The straps appeared in his hand. Excellent. He might not be able to teleport things from other worlds, but he could still call for what he'd brought with him.

Hanging the weight of it from his shoulder, he strode over, picked up the crystal crown, and hooked it to the side of the pack. He returned to the women. Many reached out, intending to trace their fingers over his chest. A fierce glare and low growl stopped them.

"Move," he commanded, and they reluctantly backed up.

He crouched before the slumbering Blythe. The heat had never truly died and revived in seconds, reminding him of a low-grade fever. He swallowed a curse. No woman should be this lovely.

Scowling, he removed her shackles with a single tug, then tossed the metal aside. He had no need of such a restraint. Not when he had a better one in the pack.

As gently as possible, Roux gathered the beautiful harphantom in his arms and clutched her to his chest. Her slight weight barely registered, yet every inch of his body zeroed in on her. Her soft cheek pressed against his shoulder, her warm breath fanned his flesh, and her floral scent filled his nose.

The heat intensified until he felt engulfed by flames. Teeth gritted, he commanded, "Lead the way."

8

THE SHIFT

Hazy lights flipped on inside Blythe's head, illuminating a cluster of waiting memories she couldn't quite reach. Confused, she blinked open her eyes. *Where am I? Where's Isla? What happened?*

Too-bright sunlight seared her eyes, leaving her blinking rapidly. As heavy lids slid shut for good, other details made themselves known. Warmth and power enveloped her. Magnificent power. Fierce and strong. Incredible! The fact that her wings were pinned? Who cared?

Tension seeped from her. This felt oh, so right. Perfect, actually. This was everything she'd been missing.

Did her consort carry her to bed?

Her consort... There'd been a battle. An injury. A harpy only rested and recovered with a fated mate, death the only exception. Blythe was very much alive, rested and recovered. Right? Or did she not have a consort?

She had a child. That much she knew. A precious little girl she longed to enfold in her arms. But... *Why can't I remember anything else?*

Noises intruded upon her thoughts, coming from here, there, everywhere. Even in her head, where a haunting melody played without cease. A healing tune. That. That was what enveloped the cluster of memories. The vibration of sound created an impenetrable shield.

She wanted to work up a good mad about it...but mmm. The air smelled good. Really good. Really, really, *really* good. A shiver-inducing combination of cedarwood and spiced oranges.

Moaning, she burrowed into the source. How delightful. Both velvety soft and steel hard at once.

A hungry growl joined the outer clatter. A low-impact quake followed.

Threat? Her eyes sprang open, the act no longer a struggle. She took stock, cataloguing everything at once. Tattoos. Multiple silos, all windowed and as tall as skyscrapers. Dirt streets, not the cobblestone paths she was used to seeing. Groups of unfamiliar women of varying species wore primitive leather dresses and mingled about. Some stood near steaming pots and roasting game. Some trained with blades and spears. In a nearby pond, others washed clothes.

Whoever they were, whatever their task, they stopped to stare at her with expressions of awe. Hmm. What if they weren't focused on her, but the male who constrained her?

The male. Her maybe, maybe not consort. But he

must be. No way she was nestled against some strange man's chest. But…

Something's wrong. What wasn't she remembering? What, what? She poked and prodded at the song barrier, desperate for answers, but the melody endured, unbroken.

Determined, Blythe fought inside and out, twisting and contorting, seeking freedom from both the song and the male.

He held tight. When a handful of observers rushed over, he tensed. Did the women intend to help her? Hope crested—every female reached out—and crashed. They merely sought to caress him.

"Do not dare," a gravelly voice snapped. *His* voice. The male's.

Exclamations came, one after another. "Ahhh! He even sounds like sex!"

"Where did you find him, and how long can I rent him?"

"A real-life slice of man-candy!"

"We'll be making an announcement about him soon," someone called. "Now back off. We gotta get him settled in at the palace first. Oh, and no one touches the piece of glass in his arms."

Glass? Blythe?

"I will gut anyone who tries." His every word dripped with promise. "Understand?"

She went still. *He protects me?*

Amid rising murmurs, she poured what remained of her strength into eradicating the song. Finally, the notes split down the middle, memories surging forth. Laban. Invasion. Betrayal. Ation. Wraith. Roux.

Rage fueled her hatred, heating the ruby and bringing more of that dreaded weakness. But no matter. You didn't always need to be the strongest opponent to win a battle; you just had to be more determined. She erupted, hissing, cursing, and clawing.

"How are you so soft and so vicious at the same time?" he muttered.

She squirmed and fought and bucked. But the ruby continued to heat and weakness continued to flood in, allowing the song to repair itself. The next thing she knew, her memories vanished, and she was floating away in an ocean of nothingness.

"This is where you'll be staying."

Roux couldn't identify the speaker. The entire welcome party had crammed into a hallway at the top of the "palace." A silo set in the center of a circle of nineteen other silos.

With Blythe in his arms, he pushed past the group. Any blip of contact razed already-razed nerves. There. A door. He shouldered his way into a spacious bedroom.

"Feel free to drop off your baggage and join us on the third floor for a quick game of strip poker. Don't worry. We won't let you be late for your first da—"

He kicked the door shut, ending her invitation.

A quick scan revealed lavishly detailed furniture made from wood, stones, and metals. Candles flickered throughout, tinging the air with the fragrance of magnolia and melting wax. A set of open windows lured in golden sunlight and a cool breeze.

He teleported his backpack to a cushioned chair near the crackling hearth, then strode to the four-poster canopied bed. As gently as possible, he placed his sleeping bundle atop the mattress. He meant to walk away and find her clean clothes, but the sight of her arrested him.

Black locks spread over a white pillow, framing a face too lovely to be real. Long lashes fanned out, reminding him of a peacock's plumage. The most ridiculous thought he'd ever entertained. For once, her plump red lips weren't set in a grim line, turned down in a frown, or curved in a calculating grin. No, they were slightly parted, as if she prepared for his kiss.

His breath hitched. That. That was the most ridiculous thought he'd ever entertained. As if she would ever wish to kiss him.

Trying not to care, he reached out and traced a fingertip over the glistening ruby embedded in her throat. Warm. Because *she* burned?

A now familiar heat infiltrated his being, as wonderful as it was terrible. With a huff, he pivoted to begin his search for clothing at last. A chore requiring less than thirty seconds. The desired items hung in a wardrobe on the other side of the room. A plethora of leather tops, shirts, dresses, and sheer gowns. A pale blue one caught his notice. The perfect match for her eyes.

Not select it? Impossible.

The heat worsened as he returned to the bed, the swatch of material in hand. *Ignore it.* He traded her bloody garment for the clean one, never allowing himself to gaze anywhere but the pillow. A feat requiring every ounce of his strength. Still the heat increased.

The second he finished his chore, he exited the force field of her unnatural appeal and sank into the chair near the hearth. Only then did he let himself peer at her. And peer at her he did, unwavering, planning to

spring up at the first sign of wakefulness. Because...
just because.

He kept his gaze glued to her even as he dug into the
pack, removing a dagger and stone. After dropping the
bag at his feet, he sharpened the already sharp blade.
For hours. Watching. Waiting. Wondering who he was
soon to face. The snuggler who rubbed against him for
comfort or the she-beast who fought as if she would
happily die as long as she took her enemy with her.

She stretched atop the mattress. Roux froze rather
than spring up. He held his breath as she eased into a
sitting position. Baby blues glided over the room, slid
over him, then darted back and widened. He expected
a spill of black over her irises. The blue lingered.

Hope bloomed. Was he soon to interact with the
snuggler?

"Are you my consort? You must be. I slept in your
presence, and you're so familiar," she said with a soft
tone.

She had no memory? "I believe your kind makes an
exception for harpies near death."

"I neared death?" Moaning, she massaged her temples. "This song...what is it hiding?"

She didn't remember because of a song? But why
would the siren— The answer crystalized before the
question fully formed. Of course the siren had manip-
ulated Blythe's memory. To stop the wraith from uti-
lizing the ruby, draining the harphantom at a time she
needed to heal to survive, the siren had to take control
of her emotions.

"I am... Roux," he said, offering nothing more. How
should he handle this? Her?

"Roux," she echoed. She traced her gaze over him,

radiating curiosity and, dare he believe it, attraction? "Are your tattoos moving?"

He glanced down, and sure enough. The *alevala* moved, as if he waged war inside himself.

Reeling, he dropped the weapon and tool, dug a shirt from the pack, and yanked the material over his head. A type of armor for them both. He needed a barrier against the torment of her gaze, and she needed to not get trapped in his past.

"Well, that wasn't very nice, now, was it?" she chided. Half pouting, half smiling, she stood to steady legs. In a beam of light, the blue gown revealed more than it concealed. Her curves— He wiped his mouth.

Pure grace, she approached him, hips swaying, slits parting in the skirt, revealing hints of her thighs.

Sweat beaded on his brow. He couldn't…he shouldn't…

A scream exploded from the back of his mind. Jaw clenched, he gripped the arms of his chair. The mental interruption came from the escapee he'd noticed at the tea party with Isla. Someone he needed to capture and imprison at last. But miss this moment of comradery with Blythe to do so? No.

All sensual grace, the harphantom eased onto the ottoman in front of him. "Did something happen to me?"

He gave a slow, solo nod, afraid of startling her, reminding her of her hatred for him. "What's the last thing you recall?"

"I know I'm a harpy and a phantom, my name is Blythe the Undoing, I have a daughter named Isla, and I'm working to become General. Although, I can't become General with a child. So what am I missing?" Her brow furrowed. "I see flashes of you getting your smolder on but not much else."

No memories of the consort then, despite recalling her child. But what did she mean, Roux's smolder? "You're missing a lot. Though it would be easier to lie to you, I'll be honest. I am not your consort. You despise me."

"Are you sure? *Despise* is a strong word." A teasing smile blossomed as she slid her gaze over him. "Maybe I've been flirting with you."

The chair arms cracked. So badly he longed to reach out and shift a lock of her silken hair between his fingers. "I'm quite sure. On four separate occasions, you've extracted at least one of my organs."

Those ice-blue eyes glittered with mirth. A queen of delights, she waved a hand through the air, dismissing his words. "Foreplay, babe. That, I promise you. Judging solely by the book cover, I'm certain you are a story I've been eager to read, muscle to muscle."

The way her voice dipped... He gulped. Once he pried his fingers from the chair, he tugged at the collar of his shirt. She was a playful feast of carnality.

Oh, how Roux dreaded the return of her memory.

"You...find me handsome, then?" In that moment, he wanted this female to like him. A dream destined to go unfulfilled. "Or perhaps you meant you can't wait to crack my spine."

There was something in the core of his being that only Chaos and the other Astra could tolerate. A fact Roux had accepted long ago. He doubted Blythe would have favored him as a compatriot even if her consort still lived.

"Put it this way, Astra," she rasped, twirling a lock of hair around her finger. "You're a first edition, and I'm a highly motivated collector with cash to burn."

He had absolutely no idea how to respond to that. Thoughts left his head and gathered behind his zipper.

"Astra," she repeated with a frown. Her head tilted to the side, as if she were trying to work out a puzzle. She muttered, "Astra, Astra, Astra. Laban." Her frown deepened. "Invasion. Betrayal. Ation. Wraith. Roux." Her lids dropped, slitting.

Roux lunged in her direction, hoping to prevent what came next. Too late. She swiped and ducked, avoiding capture. He stumbled back with blood trickling down his side.

"Five," she snapped. Then she gasped, the organ falling from her clasp. She rubbed the ruby while wobbling on her feet. "I remember the rest now. Hatred. Weakening. Sleeping. I'm going to kill—" Eyelids sliding shut, she crumpled.

He caught her before she landed, clutching her to his chest. As he carried her to the bed, his inhalations came in quick succession. She was just so soft. So sweet. With such an incredible scent.

Reluctant, he placed her onto the bed and retreated to his seat by the fire, where he sharpened the already sharp dagger once again. And once again, his gaze remained glued to her.

Anticipation slithered through him. What would the she-beast do next?

Bright lights flipped on inside Blythe's head, bringing instant clarity. Laban. Invasion. Betrayal. Ation. Wraith. Roux. Flirting. Hatred. Weakening. Sleeping. Strengthening. Destroying the song once and for all. Waking. Committing murder—soon. Yep, all her memories were accounted for.

With a hiss, she popped open her eyelids and jolted upright, freeing her buzzing wings from confinement. She perched on an ultrasoft mattress, and she wore a clean, transparent nightgown. A spacious bedroom filled with amazingly detailed furniture surrounded her. The scent of cedarwood and spiced oranges saturated candlelit air. Night had come. Roux sat by a crackling hearth, a pile of weapons scattered about his feet. He was as still as a statue but wide-awake and staring at her, squeezing daggers in a white-knuckled grip. It would have been creepy if it hadn't been so sexy.

His intensity clashed with her rage—and gained ground. From wild inferno to dying spark she went. A cloud of smoke lifted from her mind, revealing a waiting revelation. *Night had come.* Hours had passed. Time she'd spent sleeping, vulnerable to attack while her greatest enemy hovered nearby. Oh, the horror!

Blythe ran her tongue over her teeth. Harpies only slept with their consorts, yes, but this didn't count. It couldn't. Like Roux had said, she'd been recovering from a near-death experience. Because of him. *Go ahead and slice.*

Reason abandoned her. She didn't care that Penelope had taken possession of her firstone dagger and nothing Blythe did today would cause permanent damage to the Astra. *Attack!*

Unleashing a war shriek, she hurled herself at the blond giant. Swipe. She clawed out his throat. Tit for trach. "One," she said, holding up her prize. New body part, fresh start.

He didn't tense or gasp. Healing in record time, barely even bleeding on his chair, he set his daggers aside with slow precision. His yellow irises spun with striations of magenta, gray, and russet. There was no hint of red, despite the violence of the moment.

Her rage roiled on and on and on. Except, now there was something else mixed with it. Something hot she couldn't identify.

He arched a brow. "Foreplay?"

Argh! "Absolutely not." She tossed the bloody mess in his face. Crimson splattered his skin. Somehow it looked good on him. "I'm a vicious killer." To prove it, she leaped onto his lap and attacked him with renewed force.

He let her do it. "For the record, vicious killers don't have to tell their victims they are vicious killers."

He was *teasing* her right now? "I will rain a thousand deaths upon your head!"

The beating continued.

"Are you done, she-beast?" he asked, almost sounding bored.

Oh, how she hated him! Hated, hated, hated. "I'm only beginning, wretch." Blythe whaled on him with every ounce of force at her disposal, put her all in the blow. When that failed to satisfy, she shredded his shirt. His flesh.

Rather than protect any part of himself, he petted her hair. What the— She failed to land her next blow and swiped only air.

"There, there," he said. Another stroke of his fingers through her tresses, and she failed to land her next *three* blows.

"What are you doing?" Trying to comfort her? Fool! And yet, the rage seeped from her. She sagged in place, almost as if—no! No, no, no. Only a consort could tempt a harpy from the worst of her tempers, and Roux wasn't her consort. He wasn't.

So he'd calmed her a little? So what? It didn't mean anything. An effect of the ruby probably. It must be.

With a huff of irritation, she hurled herself away from him.

"Did you harm yourself?" he asked, removing the remains of his shirt. "Do you require medicine or sustenance of any kind? I know you are unable to keep down blood, but what if you can process what comes from a stronger species? It might be worth a try."

"Stronger species? Like an Astra?" Pacing before him, she laughed without humor. "I don't need blood right now, and I can drink any soul, anytime." She'd never tasted her consort's soul, even by accident. He'd asked her not to, and she had respected his decision. He'd needed to preserve his strength to protect his girls.

Roux revealed no reaction, neither confirming nor denying her accusation. "How often do you need to feed on soul?"

"Whenever I wish or monthly." Whichever came first. Why was he being so solicitous with her, anyway? "Just so you know, I prefer death over ingesting any part of you." Best to hammer the point home until he *did* react.

"I don't recall offering," he quipped. "If you get hungry, go for the Phoenix. I spotted her on the walk to the palace. She might nourish you well. Blood or soul."

"Either way," she grated, "I don't need you to oversee my meals."

"Noted." He remained annoyingly casual. "Shall we talk, then, or would you prefer to use me as a scratching post again?"

"Scratching post. Obviously."

"Just be careful of my face." All but smirking now, he stroked his chin. "I know how much you enjoy looking at it."

Oh! The nerve! Blythe got serious and launched her next attack, once again diving into his lap. Punching. Clawing. Slapping. Elbowing. Kicking. He took the blows without complaint.

Though she didn't activate the link to the wraith, she began to weaken. Bones broke in her hands with every blow. Skin split, and blood trickled. It wasn't long before she merely swatted at him. But stop? No! *Must deliver pain. Must...feed.*

She slowed, her gaze dropping to his throat. Breath sawed in and out of her mouth. How good would he taste?

With the next swipe, the tips of her claws grazed his flesh. Not to harm but to caress. His eyes widened, and he sucked air between his teeth. Without thought, she kind of, sort of rested her palm on his chest. Maybe, possibly, she curled her nails into his skin, too, as if she intended to hold on forever.

Forever?

In a snap, she came to her senses and drew back. Appearing shell-shocked, he captured her wrist and flattened her palm against his bare chest. His racing heartbeat greeted her. She stood frozen—while burning up. He was an absolute furnace!

He moved her touch across his collarbone, forcing her to stroke him. Or maybe not forcing her so much as guiding her.

"What are you doing?" she demanded, far too breathless for her liking.

"There's no irritation with you," he said. Shock lit his features, smoothing his roughest edges.

"I don't care. Stop it!" Better?

He didn't stop it. He linked their fingers.

Too intimate! "Let me go," she commanded, tugging to no avail.

"There is no irritation with you," he repeated, drawing her touch to his well-defined abs. "I want more."

Oh, good gracious. Was he smuggling an eight pack of grenades in there? Her heart knocked against her ribs. Had she been standing, her knees would have wobbled.

Not just sexy. Needy. Sensual. Lethal to her common sense. Her toes threatened to curl with— No, no, no. But there was no denying it. A tendril of desire. As if she craved the touch of a man. This man.

Why, why, why would her body come alive now? With *him*?

The echo of the siren's song must be responsible for this, too. Or her brain was glitching, mistakenly assuming she stroked her consort. An understandable error, considering muscles felt like muscles.

Just before Blythe's fingers reached the Astra's golden happy trail, she rallied enough inner strength to wrench free of his grip and slap him across the face. Once, twice. Thrice.

Angry with them both, she snapped, "Don't do that again."

"Don't aid me, then." He wagged his jaw, as if she'd finally made an impact emotionally if not physically. Those multicolored striations spun around his pupils, faster and faster. Drawing her closer...

What are you doing? She wrenched away, furious

with herself. With him. "I'm going to examine my sur-roundings, and you are not going to complain."

"Can we discuss what happened the day of the Astra invasion?" he asked as she darted about. "I'd like a chance to explain."

Gnashing her teeth against a sudden onslaught of weakness, this one courtesy of Penelope, Blythe put down a crystal vase she'd lifted. "Why bother? Nothing you say can make things right." An apology wouldn't restore her consort. An explanation wouldn't reunite father and daughter, returning Isla's joy. "You did what you did, and I'll make you pay for it. End of conver-sation."

For now, while she dealt with the wraith, she should probably default to her original plan and do everything in her power to ruin Roux's mission.

"Very well." He resumed his dagger sharpening, as if he hadn't cared about her response. "Allow me to catch you up on our situation."

"Go for it. I'd love to hear your take." Opening a door, she discovered a closet brimming with leather dresses reminiscent of those she'd seen on others. The garments hung alongside scantier outfits like the one she wore. "Lucky for you, I've got my listening ears on today."

"We are in the queen's palace, though there is cur-rently no queen. In ten days, a ten-day tournament will begin. Winner becomes ruler. In the meantime, I will be dating the females who survived their introduction to me."

"I see." Irritation surged. And *only* irritation. Ab-solutely nothing else. Not in the slightest degree. But. If the Astra thought to satisfy a harem of eager lovers while waiting for the tournament to begin, he needed to think again.

"Tell me about the wraith who marked you," he said, changing the subject. "Tomorrow, I'll find her and have the jewel removed from your spirit."

Blythe yanked a leather dress free from the rack, cracking the wooden hanger. Though it galled and stung her pride, she considered accepting his offer. To kill him, she required full strength. The best way to get it? End Penelope. If he wished to take out her other enemies, who was she to stop him?

"What do you require in return?" With the garment in hand, she eased to the bay of windows and peered out. They were at least twenty stories up, higher than any silo around them. Bonfires and torches crackled here and there, illuminating dirt streets filled with immortals. Fast-paced music thrummed in the background. Laughter rang out.

A slight hesitation from Roux. Then, "Would you agree to a truce until we return to Harpina?"

"Not even to spare my life." Truth. He asked for too much. Looked like her pride won this round, after all, escaping a brutal battering.

He heaved a sigh. "How about a temporary cease-fire that ends as soon as the wraith is dead?"

Oh. Well. A more palatable outcome. *Sorry, pride. You gotta take one for the team.*

Before she could respond, a series of raps sounded at the door. A feminine voice with a tone so perfect it could only belong to a siren called through the block, "Yoo-hoo. Mr. Sausage Man. It's go time!"

Blythe spun. She recognized that timbre. The one

she'd heard inside her head when she'd first awoken in Roux's arms.

Speaking of the Astra, he closed his eyes as his shoulders rolled in. A pose of dejection.

"Tonight's date is here," he muttered. "I had to pick the first contender while you slept. I went with the siren who sang to you."

Why did he look and sound so disgruntled about this? Did he have no desire to use the women of Ation as his own personal harem?

An admirable trait. Not that it mattered. "That's my cue to beat feet, I guess," Blythe said, stepping in the direction of what she hoped was a private bathroom with a tub and running water. She'd change into something less comfortable and head out.

Her gaze caught on the crown anchored to his backpack, and she missed her next step. The urge to race to that gorgeous array of crystals, to hold it, to try it on and see how it fit drifted through her.

Focus. She reached the door, turned the knob, and peeked inside—yep, a bathroom with a wooden tub and copper pipes.

"You will stay here." Roux's lids popped open and narrowed. "In fact, you will remain within my sight at all times."

I will, will I? "Aw, does little Rue and his Winky Boo Boo seek a chaperone?"

His lips compressed into a thin line. "Word of the tournament hasn't yet spread far or wide enough. One rule should hold particular interest to you—you aren't to be harmed. You are the sister of my Commander's *gravita*, and I will protect you unless you attempt to compromise my task. Force me to choose between you and my mission, however, and I will. I'll kill you myself, and I'll do it without hesitation."

That, she believed. Which meant she hadn't detected reluctance a bit ago. On the contrary. She'd sensed resignation. He planned to bed his babes in front of Blythe. But so what? Someone make her a bowl of popcorn. She'd offer commentary from beginning to end. From the size of his penis to his inability to find a G-spot with a miner's hat and a map.

Except, why should he be allowed to experience a single moment of pleasure? And why should she let him call the shots? It was bad enough that the females of this world already believed Blythe required a male to fight her battles for her. A humiliating truth she would rectify as soon as possible all by her lonesome.

Yeah, she'd made a mistake earlier, thinking to use him to slay Penelope on her behalf. Eight years out of practice had screwed with Blythe's brain, that was all. If she couldn't defend the honor of her family and harpies in general, no matter the odds stacked against her, all in the name of vengeance, she didn't deserve the nine stars decorating her wrist.

Another series of raps came, followed by another and another. No way was Blythe sticking around, bowing to his dictates, and making things easy for him. Let him spend his date searching for "the sister of his Commander's *gravita.*"

"Ready or not, I'm entering," the siren called, her patience gone. She kicked at the door. Hinges pulled, and wood split. "I'm Monna, by the way."

"Enjoy your night. Or not." Knowing she wouldn't survive her next actions if she reactivated the link to Penelope, Blythe buried every ounce of her hatred. A bandage to a hemorrhaging wound that wouldn't hold for long.

"Harpy," he rasped. "What are you planning?"

She grinned, earning a double blink. And okay, yes, without the hatred coloring her perception, she couldn't deny the reaction appealed to her. Or that his powerful body stole her breath. Of course, she liked looking at lightning, too. That didn't mean she should reach out and grab it.

Splinters rained from the door frame. Any second the siren would breach the perimeter.

"Catch me if you can, Rue." Blythe blew him a kiss, spun on her heel, and sprinted toward the windows. With the dress clutched close, she dived through an opening, soaring into the night.

9

THE CHASE

"No!" Roux teleported to the window and leaned out, reaching— "No," he repeated as he swiped air.

His gaze cut through the darkness, Blythe's descent as clear as if halogens spotlighted her. In a split second, he calculated her trajectory. Then he materialized in the exact spot she was to land, intending to catch her— A curse exploded from him. He hadn't moved an inch. Thanks to his oath to stick near his dates, the ability to teleport deserted him.

All he could do was watch as the harphantom hurled toward the ground.

Foolish woman! Why would she do this? Did she *want* to hurt? She had wings, yes, but they were tiny and not meant for flight.

A patter of footsteps let him know his date had entered the room. He cared not, keeping his attention fixed on the harpy. Despite the ruby and its weakening effects, Blythe managed to land with great ease and grace, rolling to her feet. Relief engulfed him.

She paused and craned her neck. Meeting his gaze, she bestowed another diabolical smile upon him and extended her middle finger in the air.

Like a bullet, she shot off, disappearing in the masses. Many more immortals than he'd counted upon his arrival to the royal lands. They celebrated around a bonfire, playing music, laughing, and fighting viciously.

"Don't mind me," his date cooed. "I'm just admiring the view."

He pivoted on his booted heel. She stood merely two feet away, wearing something akin to a mortal bikini. The lovely black siren with curves for days had helped save Blythe; he'd thought to honor her by choosing her first, not encourage her advances.

Although, if he responded to her touch the same way he'd responded to Blythe's, the date might go differently than he'd anticipated. After he caught the harpy. Which he would do.

He swiped out his arm and grabbed the siren's biceps. "Come."

"Sir, yes, sir." She wiggled her brows at him. "I assure you, that's why I'm here."

He pressed his tongue to the roof of his mouth as he transported her to Blythe's landing spot. He could flash only within the realm itself, and only to places he'd seen. "For this date, we'll be traveling at lightning-fast speeds and hunting a harphantom."

"Ohhh. An adventure. I'm impressed. I'm also all in." She melted against him and traced her hands up his chest. "By the way, you can be all in, too, if you know what I mean."

The contact aggravated his sensitized skin, and he stiffened. Why respond as usual with this stunning female when, only minutes before, he'd luxuriated in blissful contact with Blythe? A woman who despised him. Except when she lost her memory and ate him up with her eyes.

With the memory, his muscles bulged, burned, and hardened. His leathers pulled tight.

Roux scowled. Why did he crave her touch, and hers alone, as if he would die without it?

Had the torture master turned his talents on himself?

Chuckling, the siren rubbed against him. "You are loaded for bear, and I'm living for it. Rowr!"

He set her away and snapped, "If you'd like to keep your hands, do not touch me without permission." And, all right, okay. Perhaps he understood Blythe's violent reaction to his manhandling. Next time, he wanted her willing.

A bitter laugh lodged in his throat. As if she would *ever* be willing again.

"Sure, sure. Permission. Got it." The siren winked, all innocence, not the least bit abashed or discouraged. "Hey, for no reason in particular, do you happen to have a safe word?"

A muscle jumped beneath his eye. How was he supposed to deal with the females of this land? "Just…try to keep up with me."

He stalked off, not waiting for her response, tracking Blythe's scent. He approached a crowd congregated around a bonfire.

To the siren's credit, she followed without complaint.

"He's here!" someone shouted.

The music stopped. Every female in the vicinity scrambled over, forming a circle around him. That circle tightened as the immortals drew closer. A chorus of "Dibs" accompanied dreamy sighs.

"I hear he's a villain, not a hero," someone said, and many of the sighs turned to purrs.

Then the women got serious, preparing to rush at him. Roux readied his claws.

"Don't you dare touch! He's mine tonight," Monna screeched, the tenor of her voice different than before. "If you screw this up for me, I swear I'll sing all of you into the flames."

Sirens had an aptitude for compelling other species with their melodies, and hers struck him as far stronger than most.

Everyone scattered. A path opened up, and Roux increased his pace. There. A banshee was changing into the leather dress Blythe had carted from the room. Without thought, Roux flashed over, gripped the banshee by the throat and lifted her off her feet, constricting her airway before she was able to issue an ear-destroying death scream.

"What did you do to the harphantom?" he demanded. "Tell me!"

Her eyes bulged, and her face turned purple. Mouth floundering open and closed, she pointed a trembling finger in the direction he'd been headed.

He tightened his hold. "Did you harm her?"

"She didn't," a gorgon next to the banshee assured him. Despite her calm tone, the snakes growing from her head slithered and hissed with aggression. "All she did was snag the dress as your charge raced past us."

Truth? "If you have lied, I *will* find you. Both of you. I'll kill you and everyone you love." He released his hostage, and she collapsed on the ground.

"So fierce!" someone squealed behind him.

Females! He kicked into gear. Things only grew worse from there as he and the siren journeyed across a hilly expanse. Monna used the opportunity to explain all the reasons he should sleep with her. Everything from scratching an itch to giving her the baby she'd dreamed of having for so long to proving "once you go siren, no others are worth admirin'."

"Hey! Are you listening to me?" she whined. "I said this Monna knows how to make you moan. There's no better time to demand I prove it. Hint, hint."

Tracking, tracking. Dirt gave way to pink sand and mile after mile of abandoned desert. Though Blythe's scent continued to provide a path, he never caught sight of her. Somehow, she remained at bay.

"What is located in this direction?" he asked, interrupting his date's newest diatribe.

Monna gave a slight shudder. "Wraith Island."

Ah. Blythe sought the individual who'd hobbled her. "How far is it? How many wraiths reside there?"

"Five hours or so on foot. And one wraith? Ten? A hundred? Who knows? Anyone foolish enough to venture onto the island is never seen or heard from again. Not even our queen attempts to rule the species. The wraiths govern themselves, led by Penelope the Husk Maker. She's responsible for tagging your phantom, which means your phantom is now hers, and you'll never get her back. You might as well forget her and focus on a different bedmate. Hey, here's a totally random thought I'm offering for no particular reason. I'm very bendy."

Husk Maker. Because she drained her victims dry?

Roux picked up the pace, jogging. Running. The citizens were right to avoid the wraiths; they were extremely dangerous. Oh, the damage this Penelope could do to Blythe...

The next hour passed in silence, wind kicking sand in every direction. The grains ruffled his hair, filled his nose, and pelted his skin, stinging like needles. Nothing he hadn't borne before. The siren, on the other hand, began to lag, despite using his body as a shield. Was she deterred from flirting? Not even slightly.

Another hour passed, seeming to take an eternity and a blip at the same time as the landscape changed again. From sunny pink sands to dark and gloomy skies overlooking rock bundles.

"Do you have a mate at home?" Monna asked. "Is that how you're able to resist all this?" She motioned to her admittedly lovely body.

He held his tongue, supplying only a grunt.

With twenty-two minutes remaining on the six-hour date clock, a large body of choppy water came into view. Even as a thin white vapor blew over the surface, he caught sight of a bobbing dark head at last. Blythe! She didn't appear to be drowning but swimming strong and fast toward a large island with a heavily wooded mountain rising from the center, its top shrouded with a much thicker mist.

"Stay here," he ordered. But, when he tried to flash, he failed. Roux swallowed a curse. His oath. He couldn't leave the siren behind.

"Sorry, lover," she said, understanding, "but abandoning me for any amount of time isn't how this date of ours works. If you want to flash, flash, but you gotta take me with you. Them's the rules you agreed to."

"Very well. We do this together." He slung an arm around her. "Prepare yourself. This might be jarring."

Just as before, she melted against him and ran her palms over his chest. "I'll be sure to hang on real tight."

Flash. They materialized directly in front of Blythe, chin-deep in the icy water. He treaded his feet, holding the siren with one hand and snagging the harphantom with the other as a wave rolled past.

Monna screeched. Blythe fought him, but it was too late. He held fast and flashed to the beach.

Upon landing on solid ground, the siren curled against him, muttering, "So c-c-cold, k-k-keep me warm."

Blythe wrenched free from his clasp. He expected an immediate attack, but she stayed where she was, drenched and glaring, her eyes a haunting mix of black and blue. The gown clung to her water-dotted skin. And he'd considered the garment transparent before. Every curve defined…

Roux licked his lips. His flesh might be the temperature of ice, but his blood burned white-hot. The sight of her body, a perfect hourglass…

He thought he heard Monna exclaim, "So big! And still growing! By the way, you touched me first, and I consider that my permission. Stay silent if you agree."

Focus on what matters. Right. Anger overlaid his attraction. Blythe had endangered herself as well as his mission. She must be stopped from ever doing so again.

"Don't look at me like that." Blythe's teeth chattered. "You're making it difficult to contain my hatred for you."

"Go ahead. Unleash it." He stepped toward her in challenge. "Let the wraith drain more of your strength."

She jumped to avoid contact. A mistake. Her knees buckled. She careened to her backside and stayed put, panting and glowering up at him. The hem of the dress—nightgown—whatever bunched above her knees, revealing more of her legs.

Roux scrubbed a hand over his drying mouth. Too beautiful, and too stubborn. That's what she was. Why not keep the ruby on her until the end of the tournament? Forcing her to dial down her abhorrence for him could only aid his task. There would be fewer attempts to take Roux out or reach Wraith Island. The weaker his charge, the less damage she could do.

As long as he kept her by his side, she would be perfectly safe. Yes. He liked this plan. Once he'd successfully crowned the new queen of Ation, he would work to free Blythe. Until then...

Best to hobble her in other ways, too. He reached behind his back and summoned the chains from his pack. The metal links with accompanying shackles appeared in his waiting grip. If—when—he did this, Blythe's loathing for him was sure to double. Triple. Harpies were notorious for their aversion to fetters. But so what? Wasn't as though he had a chance with her, anyway. Or that he even desired a chance.

The burn to touch her and be touched *by* her would go away sooner or later.

"Know you brought this on yourself," he grated, revealing the contraption to Blythe.

"Ohhhh. Is that for you or me or me and her?" Monna squealed with happiness. "Never mind. I say yes! I'm into it."

The harphantom clambered to her feet. "Don't you dare come near me with that thing."

"I dare anything when it comes to the well-being of the Astra and the safety of my task." Perhaps her safety factored into the equation as well. He kept his gaze locked with hers as he prepared the cuffs for her wrists. "I gave you a chance to behave. Now I'll force the issue."

"I won't go down easily," she snapped.

"I know. But you will go down." He wasted no time, flashing closer and caging her in his arms.

She fought hard, injuring herself to injure him. He absorbed any abuse. Twice he lost his grip on her. *Such soft, slippery skin.* A thousand times, he lost his mind. *Such lush, feminine curves.* Fire consumed his veins, a distraction he couldn't afford. In the end, he had to drop the shackles, pin her atop a mossy rock with her arms over her head, and straddle her waist to subdue her. Unexpectedly winded, he summoned the chains.

"Is it my turn yet?" Monna asked.

"Go ahead," Blythe spit up at him. He missed her playful smile. "You're the Astra's torture master, after all." Her eyes flashed black. "Do to me what you did to the boy."

Boy? He clamped the first manacle in place. "What boy?"

"The one in your memory. I've seen how much you enjoyed chaining him. He lay upon that table, helpless, pleading for mercy, as you peeled and seared his flesh, piece by piece."

She'd seen his memories, without the aid of *alevala*? The blood rushed from Roux's head, a piercing ringing filling his ears. Before he had time to think, the truth spilled from his tongue. "My father did the peeling and the searing. I did the pleading."

10

THE BARGAIN

Blythe reeled. She had no words to give as Roux transported her and the siren back to the bedroom at the palace. He released the other woman immediately, then secured Blythe's chain to the bed's canopy rail, securing her arms above her head.

He muttered, "The so-called adventure date is officially over," while escorting the other woman to the door. A slab of wood now in major need of repair. "My obligation to you has ended."

The siren gaped at him. "But we haven't... I didn't get to... Give me a chance——"

The Astra slammed the block in her face. He didn't acknowledge Blythe as he stalked to his backpack, gathered a set of tools, and worked far longer than necessary to repair the damaged entrance.

For an eternity, she stood where he'd left her, trying to make sense of the words he'd spoken with such a flat, almost dead cadence.

My father did the peeling and the searing. I did the pleading.

Had he told the truth? Maybe. Or spun a lie to garner undeserved sympathy? Maybe not. *Think this through.*

She'd known the visions in her head had come from his memories. But she'd been so focused on the older male who resembled Roux in every way but one, she hadn't studied the child. Now she considered nothing else. The child did resemble Roux—greatly. Same pale, wavy hair. Same bronze skin. Same yellow eyes with those spinning striations.

The two were indeed related. They were probably even father and son, just as he'd claimed.

Bile burned Blythe's throat. How could a man hurt his own child in such a way? Parents were supposed to be protectors. The thought of purposely maiming her own daughter sickened her. That sickness worsened when she considered any young one, even the Astra, enduring such repeated anguish and agony.

The savagery she'd witnessed. The tormentor's delight. Roux's hopeless desperation.

Blythe tensed as a question struck. What did this realization mean for her vengeance? Something? Nothing? A traumatic past didn't excuse what Roux had done to her family or her people. Nothing did. Nothing *could.* Deep down, she still despised him, her determination to mete punishment unwavering. And yet, the sense of urgency had faded.

Stop allowing your hatred to be your coffin. Live your life. Find happiness.

Laban's advice echoed inside her mind. Well, the hallucination's advice.

Maybe Roux's death could wait until the completion of his task? She could even turn the delay into a belated wedding gift to Taliyah. The newlyweds wouldn't be condemned to five hundred years of defeat, forcing all of harpykind to go into hiding with the General and her Commander, simply to survive. A win-win for everyone but Erebus.

But what of the other consort-less harpies Roc and his army were responsible for? Was their vengeance to be delayed as well?

Although, they might be consort-less, but they were still harpies. What if they preferred to deliver their own brand of justice?

Okay. Wow. What a difference a small piece of information made in a person's mindset. This wasn't good. This wasn't good *at all*. If Blythe didn't strike at the first opportunity, she was nothing but a fool. Right?

The shackles rattled as she plopped onto the foot of the bed. She sat statue still amidst a beam of silvery moonlight as Roux finished the door, returned to his chair, and dug items from his backpack. Weapons. A notebook and pen. More weapons. A pillow. Even more weapons. A can of soda. More weapons.

Who was he, Mary Freaking Poppins? What else was in that bag, and how soon could she steal it?

The crystal crown caught her eye. The circlet dangled from the side, as usual. *Even more beautiful.*

The urge to hold it and wear it resurged stronger. If she hadn't been chained, she might have marched across the room to claim it. Who didn't want to be queen? But, just as before, the urge tapered, allowing her to refocus on Roux. Mistake!

Candle after candle sparked to life on its own. More and more soft, golden light caressed the Astra, creating a glittering force field around his powerful body. Her heart rate quickened.

Head bowed, he wrote in the notebook and sipped his drink. Must be writing down observations about the realm and the women within; he concentrated with all his might.

He. The male who'd survived horrors of unimaginable proportions.

It wasn't long before the sun rose, pouring morning light through the windows. A delicate wind snuffed out every candle. Smoke curled from the wicks, soon creating a hazy, dreamlike effect. Still Roux wrote.

A dozen times, Blythe opened her mouth to initiate a conversation. His task. His past. Their current predicament. A few questions about Isla. Had he seen the girl before coming here? How had she looked? Acted? But Blythe choked and stayed quiet. Maybe it was better not to know. And why make nice with Laban's killer? Even if a hallucination had maybe kind of offered permission.

A firm rap at the door preceded the clicking of a lock. The gorgon she'd seen at the Oath Stones strolled inside the room, carrying a tray piled high with food. The snakes protruding from her scalp currently slept and hung well past her shoulders.

"Hello, gorgeous," the other woman said. "I thought I might bring you a little me with a side of pancakes."

The vampire, a harpy, a siren other than Miss First Date, and an Amazon elbowed each other in the hallway, fighting to be the first through the door on the gorgon's heels. Each held a tray of her own and raved about the dishes.

"Grandma's secret sexy recipe!"

"Guaranteed to stimulate your fiercest appetites."

"Once you taste mine, you'll forever pine. It's a guarantee."

The females jockeyed for the best spot to leave their offerings, utterly ignoring Blythe. Thank goodness. Oh, the utter humiliation of being bound to a bed in front of witnesses.

"By the way. Who gets to date you next?" Trayless now, the vampire anchored her hands on her hips. "We gotta have an answer so the lucky lady has time to prepare her nether regions for pound town."

"Nether regions?" The Amazon elbowed her in the stomach. "We talked about this."

"What? I didn't want to sound crass while being crass."

"We are picking up the pace," Roux said without glancing up from his writing. "There will be multiple dates today. I'll start with the first female to leave this room. She may return in one hour."

The jockeying started up again, with the harpy making it into the hall first, the gorgon second, and the Amazon third. The harpy celebrated her victory with a smug little dance while the others pouted and threw fists. And daggers. Amid the brutal battle, someone accidentally shut the door—with someone else's head. Suddenly Blythe and Roux were alone once again.

The scent of bacon, syrup, and fresh fruit made her mouth water and her stomach rumble. Unlike other harpies, she didn't have to steal her food in order to prevent sickness. A perk of being a royal phantom.

"Well? Unchain me already. Let's feast," she commanded, so snotty she annoyed even herself. "Apparently, we only have an hour."

He didn't glance her way, either, but he did stop writing. "The she-beast is hungry, is she?"

She rolled her eyes. "You do realize she-beast isn't an insult to me, yes? It's a compliment. But yeah, I'm hungry."

That snared his attention. He set the notebook aside, asking, "Do you want food or the Phoenix I mentioned? Or both?"

"Food." And maybe soul, just not the Phoenix's.

"Very well." Roux stood and breathed deep, as if steeling himself for a coming blow. He popped the bones in his neck and rolled back his shoulders. Muscles and *alevala* rippled before her eyes.

Mmm, mmm, mmm. Look at those washboard abs.

Dang. Ogling him now? Trying to ignore her fluttering belly, she quickly averted her gaze. So he had a physique sculpted from fantasies and power? So what? She had no interest in bedding him. Nope. None. Like any harpy who'd lost her beloved consort, Blythe was dead from the neck down.

Well, mostly dead. On the verge, anyway. Perhaps a libido took time to wither completely? Yes, yes. That must be it. Her foe's incredible strength had nothing to do with anything. This was simply her body's last-ditch effort to revive.

From the corner of her eye, she watched as Roux swiped up the tray closest to him and dragged the stool at the desk to the foot of the bed. He eased atop the stool's rounded top and balanced their breakfast on his lap.

Did he think to feed her by hand? "No way," she spat,

facing him. Too intimate! Too reminiscent of the time she'd had no memory of their past. She'd sat on him, in total lust with his ferocity, feeling as if she'd stumbled upon a treasure of untold riches, delighting in his reaction to her teasing.

"If you wish to eat this food, yes way," he said. His pupils immediately pulsed, momentarily covering his irises. Two *alevala* jumped, switching places.

Ohhhh. What was this? Was he fighting a battle within himself again?

Was *she*? Blythe realized she was panting ever so slightly. Panting. With desire. For him. So close she had only to reach out to touch him…

No! No, no, no. The desire wasn't for him but sex. There was a difference.

Desperate to eradicate the tension in the air and prove herself right, she rushed out, "Why don't we bargain?" She would do almost anything to avoid having his fingers near her mouth.

His gaze dropped to her lips, and his lids turned heavy, sinking to half-mast. A good look for him. "There's no need. Without an Oath Stone, I cannot trust you to keep your end of an agreement."

The tension thickened. Irritated, she snapped, "That sounds like a *you* prob—"

He shoved a strawberry onto her tongue, silencing her. A heated protest dissolved as the sweet juice awoke her taste buds.

After she swallowed, she tried again. "Look. I decided not to—" The tanginess of pineapple hit her awareness, and she moaned. His scent in her nose deepened the richness of the flavors.

"See. No need."

Okay. At this rate, they'd get nowhere. Blythe did the only thing she could. She kicked the tray from his lap before he could feed her anything else. Instant outburster's remorse! Bye-bye pineapple. Bye-bye strawberry.

Roux looked at the food splattered over the floor, then her, then the food, then her. He blanked his expression. "Very well. You may go hungry. Act like a she-beast, and you'll be treated like one."

When he made to rise, she slammed her foot atop his shoulder to hold him down. "Unchain me, and I'll act like a mildly mature human adult. I'll stay put. I promise. Consider this a test run for my level of honesty. While we eat, each feeding *ourselves*, we can exchange questions." Win-win for her. There were mysteries she longed to decipher. Also, freedom!

He arched a brow. "You think there's something about you I wish to know?"

"Yes." A confident statement. "I'm the daughter of your worst enemy, and I've had more dealings with Erebus than anyone you've ever met. You must be curious to learn his greatest weaknesses. Or perhaps you'd like to learn the plans I'm privy to."

Roux snorted. "And you'll tell me all without lying, yes? Me, the male you despise."

"Well, yeah. Why not? Daddy Dearest arranged for my passage here, only to betray me. I'm looking forward to returning the favor. Also—see! You have questions. In a show of good faith, I'll answer this one for free. Erebus is the reason I'm wearing a wraith's jewel with my see-through jammies."

When she angled her metal-bound wrists to trail a blunt-tipped claw down the center of the ruby, he fol-

lowed the action with his gaze and gulped. *Got him!*
"What do you say?"

Roux gave a clipped nod. "I agree to your terms. We
may ask up to three questions each about any topic. The
other person cannot refuse to answer. If you lie, even
once, I'll know, and I'll keep you chained even after
my task is completed."

"Please," she retorted. "You'll be dead long before
then."

His eyelids slitted. But he rose, unhooked the chain
from the bed—without freeing her hands—and strode
off to sit at the desk, where the bulk of the food trays
rested. With his back to her, he waved her over.

Testing her at the starting line? Blythe stood and
stomped over, plopping in the chair across from him and
digging in. He watched her. Intently. She tried not to notice or care that flutters had re-erupted in her stomach.

"So. Why did your father torture you?" Better to
start with a bang, letting him know she wouldn't be
pulling her punches.

He blinked. "You wish to know about my childhood,
when you have only three questions? An answer that
has no bearing on our situation?" Confusion flittered
over his expression. "Very well. I'll tell you. My twin,
Rowan, and I were not conceived in the typical way.
Mars—"

"Whoa! There are two of you?" The second question
exploded from her before she had a chance to filter it
with common sense.

He smirked, the striations in his eyes spinning at
warp speed. "There are, yes. And now you have a final
question remaining."

Hey! "That last one doesn't count." Might as well give a protest a shot. "It could have been a statement."

"But it wasn't."

"No," she grumbled, honest. "It wasn't."

His next smirk was even more irritating than the original. "As I was saying, Mars—our father—was bored and wondered how he might have turned out if he'd lived different lives as a child. So he cloned himself, creating the two of us. Rowan, he kept in luxury and pampered. Me, he kept in the dungeon and tormented."

Oh, wow. A thousand other questions whirled inside her head. Roux the Astra. A clone. A freaking clone of the Roman god Mars. An exact copy. All because the (clearly) egomaniacal warrior had wished to know the difference a childhood filled with torment wreaked on a boy?

The unbridled pride required to do such a thing. The total lack of compassion. Roux's childhood was far worse than she'd suspected, wasn't it?

Rather than partake of the meal, he crossed his arms over his chest. "My turn. Death is involved in becoming a phantom, even for the daughters of Erebus. Tell me about yours."

She frowned. Why would he wish to know such a thing? Unless he thought he would discover her greatest weaknesses? Yeah, that had to be it.

Well, too bad, so sad. The story revealed nothing. "I was nine years old. A year away from leaving home to attend harpy camp, where I was expected to learn to control my temper in order to better kill my enemies. My mother and aunt summoned me, explained the circumstances of my birth, asked if I wanted to be stronger, then stabbed me in the heart. First with fireiron, then demonglass, and finally cursedwood." The three substances that made up trinite. "When I revived, boom, I was a phantom. And yes, I was stronger."

He thought for a moment. "The actual conception of a phantom isn't Erebus's preferred method of creation."

"Nope." Usually, the Dark One killed an immortal of another species first, injected them with his death venom and seared his brand into their spirit—among other things—binding their will to his. "Don't worry. I'll turn my sights to Erebus soon and end the phantom-making problem at the source. Like I said, I owe him as much as I owe you." Mood instantly soured, she sank her teeth into a bacon sandwich and ripped. The flavors burst on her tongue. Man, the ladies of Ation had no modern equipment that she'd seen, but they'd found a way to excel in every way possible, anyway.

Roux continued to watch her, the intensity of his gaze making her squirm.

"What?" she demanded.

"You harpies and your need for vengeance. It never ends."

She replied between bites. "As if you Astra operate another way. I admit, though, I'm surprised you didn't ask me how Erebus betrayed me."

"Betrayal is betrayal." A pause. Then, "Do you wish to become General, now that the rules for leadership have changed?"

Again, another question that revolved around her. "No. I'm on a different career path now." Only a few months ago, a harpy had to be a virgin to rule over the species. Since the Astra's arrival and Taliyah's ascension to the throne as replacement for the slain Nissa, that requirement had gotten the boot.

With nine stars earned, only one challenge stood in the way of Blythe's reign. Defeating her sister on the battlefield.

First, she had no desire to cut another beloved family member from Isla's life. Second, Blythe didn't want to harm her sister, and that's what it would take to win a true battle between them. And third, she had her vengeance to oversee.

"Ah, yes," he said, a little too silkily for her liking. Uh-oh. Had they switched to flirt mode again? "Your new career path. Let me guess. Destroyer of Astra."

"Exactly. DOA for short. An acronym with a second, equally applicable meaning."

He arched a brow, Astra-speak for *do tell*.

Her pulse fluttered. *"Dead on arrival."* Meal forgotten, she reached up and grazed the ruby with the pad of a finger. "That's my company motto."

His gaze followed the action and heated. "Funny. This Astra has never felt more alive."

Yes. They had definitely switched. "What do you want from me, Rue? No, don't answer that." She had a solo query left, and she had to make it count. What should she demand to know?

Thinking...

Oh! Here was something sure to ruin the mood and educate her about his physiology at the same time. "Why did your *alevala* kill the shifter?"

He shrugged. "My memories are tainted. In fact, you are never to peer at my *alevala*."

Big tell. Huge! What part of his past didn't he want her to see? Unless...

She gulped. Was he concerned about her well-being? "I feel cheated. You're gonna have to elaborate and tell me why your memories are tainted."

"Because I am tainted." A flat statement. He clearly believed what he'd said with every fiber of his being.

Why would he think that? "Are you tainted because of all the fated mates you've killed during your battles to obtain a blessing?" Petty of her, yes, but a girl had to use the weapons at her disposal.

A tinge of color dotted his cheeks. "Couldn't the same be asked of you? How many mated ones have you slain?"

The food she'd consumed settled like lead in her stomach. He wasn't wrong. But as soon as she affirmed the truth, that yes, she had killed many fated mates on the battlefield, Roux would want to know how she could turn around and blame him for his actions. And he would have a point. But grief was an insatiable beast that fed on pain, and it didn't care about points.

"Ask your final question," she told him, swiping a sugar cookie from a tray. Though she was no longer hungry, the sweet treat helped sooth her nerves.

Roux's study of her intensified. "Why are you able to function after the death of your consort, when other harpies cannot?" The fact that he used the softest, gentlest tone—a tone she should never, ever hear from someone like him—made the impact of his words a thousand times worse.

Then. That moment. The easy exchange was utterly obliterated. She bolted to her feet, her chair skidding behind her. The cookie splattered on the floor.

"What are you implying?" she demanded, wings buzzing.

"Oh, yes. I'm curious, too." A feminine voice filled the room, startling and unwelcome.

Blythe found the culprit with her gaze and scowled. Penelope splayed on the bed, her head propped onto an upraised palm. She'd selected the same redheaded bombshell guise as before, with a much sexier outfit. No firstone dagger in sight.

"Well, this is awkward," the wraith said. "Not the jubilant reception I expected. But please, do continue. I'm enjoying myself immensely."

11

THE MENACE

And the threats keep coming.

"Take a seat and be quiet, girl," the intruder commanded. "Your superiors need to have a grown-up conversation."

Shock held Roux immobile for two heartbeats as Blythe paled and obeyed, stumbling back and plopping into her chair, no longer as graceful as a ballerina. Black flooded her eyes, and croaked sounds left her. Attempting to hurl curses at the invader? Though she fought her position, she remained seated.

He catalogued several thoughts at once. The sight of the harphantom's weakness did something to him. Roused a hidden protective instinct he'd never known he possessed. A wraith had entered his private bedroom without his knowledge. She wielded some kind of control over his harphantom, making her the one who'd applied the ruby. A certain enemy who'd accomplished the impossible by sneaking up on him without alerting his defenses. How?

He'd sensed no hint of aggression from her. Or perhaps he *had* sensed something but his desire for Blythe masked it. So much desire. White-hot. Blistering. How did she continue to touch him without inciting pain or irritation?

He'd been seconds away from yanking her into his lap and pressing his lips to hers.

He would have kissed her. Tasted her.

He still wanted to.

The wraith might have saved him from making an unforgivable mistake, but he planned to kill her regardless.

"Nothing to say, Astra?" she inquired.

He didn't jump up or accuse or reveal a single beat of concern. Didn't display any indication of his thoughts. He knew better. As soon as an opponent realized their effect on you, they owned you.

"I have plenty to say," he offered pleasantly. "But I don't think you'll like any of it." At last he deigned to stand, putting himself between Blythe and the visitor.

The wraith looked him over. "My, my, aren't you a delicious treat? More so than I expected. I'm thrilled to say rumors are true for once."

He studied the buxom redhead who reclined on the bed, perfectly at ease in the midst of a brutal warrior and his chained prisoner. She must know what many did not. Though the Astra Planeta could create worlds, they couldn't handle spirit beings at will. One of the reasons Erebus had utilized his armies of phantoms to such a degree throughout the eons of their war.

But, even if Roux could handle this wraith, he couldn't kill her yet. The ruby linked her to Blythe, and that link was currently open. If the wraith died right now, Blythe died as well. She might not revive.

Frustration pricked his nape. "If you came for the harphantom—"

"Let me stop you there. I came for *you*, darling. But let's not get ahead of ourselves. Introductions must first be made. I'm Penelope the Available. *Very* available. And you are…?"

"Already tired of this conversation. Why are you here?"

She smiled, unbothered by his harshness. "I'll call you Sir Hugsalot. Hugsie for short. Since I'm a business-woman by nature, I'll cut to the heart of the matter. For starters, I'm here to welcome you to our humble world. For enders, I'm owed one hundred meals in heels." Her pitch hardened. So did the glint in her golden eyes. "I've taken the liberty of creating a list of names. You will fetch each female, or I *will* reclaim my sweet Blythe. You did notice my mark on her, yes?"

"Try to take her from me. I dare you." He offered no more. While he couldn't handle a wraith, he *could* hurt her. There were ways.

Behind him, Blythe grunted, no doubt fighting her weakness with every fiber of her being and spewing silent curses his way.

Penelope eased into an upright position, her smile growing wider. "I see you haven't yet realized your pre-dicament. Let me explain it in a way you'll understand. I can aid your mission…or ruin it."

He raised his chin a notch. "I promise you, wraith. My predicament is far better than yours."

"I do hope you won't make me teach you otherwise." All teasing seduction, she glided to her feet, revealing a short pink dress with a deep vee up top and a ruffled skirt that did little to hide her panties. Tracing a sharp red nail between her breasts then plucking a piece of folded parchment from beneath the gown's fabric, she said, "Last chance to agree to fetch my meals."

He arched a brow. "If you'd done your research, you'd know I never reverse my decisions."

She patted her mouth as she yawned. "I guess I hoped you'd make an exception since you cannot save yourself from battle by altering the atmosphere and putting anyone to sleep. Yes, I know about that."

"I can manipulate the air in other ways." Maybe. Probably. Creating airborne pain toxins required a whole different skillset. "You will remove the ruby or—there is no or. You have no other options."

"Don't be silly. I have *all* the options." Penelope waved the parchment in his direction. "Are you sure denying me is the correct course? Even though I'll rain more torment upon you than you've ever known?"

As if such a thing were possible. With a father like Mars, a mentor like Chaos, and a head full of mental prisoners who reviled him, Roux had already experienced the worst torments imaginable. His memories offered a fresh filleting every morning, and nothing anyone else did to him could ever compare.

In an attempt to prove it, the escaped prisoner screamed. Rage echoed through the chambers of his mind. So annoying. Who was this persistent male?

Where did he hide, and why did he make himself known only at times like this?

"I'll take your silence for a yes, you wish to deny me." Penelope shrugged, resigned, and returned the parchment to its proper place. "Very well. I'll allow you to enjoy the rest of your morning. But we'll be seeing each other again real soon. That, I promise you." With a wink, she glided to the wall of windows and whisked outside.

He waited several beats, lest she return, before concentrating on Blythe, who sagged in the chair, limp. Should he offer to feed her his blood? His soul? Other phantoms had smashed their lips all over his body. Why not her? Yes, it was a process he'd always detested. While souls regenerated and the pulling sensations were temporary, the memories lingered, festering with all his others. But. He had to admit he was curious to learn how he affected his charge.

If her mouth felt half as pleasant as her hand…

The fire reignited in his veins. Soon, he burned. Before he could make the offer, Blythe vaulted to her feet, her strength oh, so clearly returning. Well. Time to chain her to the bed, then.

Her eyes narrowed. Extending her shackled arms in front of her to ward him off, she snarled, "We both know Miss Murder just proved enemies can sneak up on you. Meaning, yes, you're a terrible guard dog, and I've gotta be able to defend myself if I have any chance of surviving. Don't you even *think* about—"

He flashed mere inches from her and clasped her by the biceps. Anger, irritation, and embarrassment collided within him. "I never make the same mistake twice. The wraith won't succeed again." He lifted the harphantom off the floor and hauled her to the bed, where he rehooked her to the metal links. "If you hadn't guessed, she-beast, the breakfast and our bargain are over."

Blythe fumed for the next four days while Roux lived his best life, going out with one beautiful immortal after another, completing his nine remaining dates as vowed. But, yeah, okay, sure. Those rendezvous had sucked for everyone involved. The guy had zero game. Like, none. Basically, he pretended he was alone while the women fawned or sexually harassed him. He never spoke a word. Not even when he spent quality time sharpening too-sharp weapons while sneaking searing glances at a certain prisoner who remained chained to his bed, making said prisoner wonder what thoughts wove webs inside his head.

But back to the dates. The hopeful females always arrived with winks and smiles, and they always left with grumbles of disappointment. No matter their species, lack of dress, or suggestion of activities, Roux remained gruff and utterly uninterested. Touching wasn't allowed. Ever.

So why did he welcome mine?

Oh, she knew he liked the sight of her. But no ordinary attraction explained such an extraordinary exception. Not that he'd made another play for her.

The only time he truly interacted with her? When he unhooked her from the bed, and they shared a meal at the desk. They had exchanged no more questions, but they hadn't traded other insults, either. It was just...he was so different than she'd imagined. Rough around the edges, yet also smooth. Withdrawn, but open. Cunning, but courteous.

Did she catch herself enjoying his companionship? Occasionally. But oh, how she abhorred those moments. They marked a true betrayal to the life she'd once shared with Laban.

Had Isla begun to heal at least, or did she worsen now that she was without a mother? Had anyone guessed Blythe's whereabouts and told the little girl? Did the darling cry herself to sleep?

Tears stung Blythe's eyes. Tears. Big, fat drops of sadness and regret.

What are you doing? Focus! She'd come to Ation for a reason. Not just for herself, but for Isla, too. A new morning was dawning, sunlight streaming through the bedroom windows. The sixth day since Roux's arrival.

As usual, the Astra sat in his chair, sharpening a blade and staring at her again. The sadness evaporated. Heart thumping, she looked away fast. She shouldn't like being the object of his unwavering concentration. No, she should not.

In a bid to distract herself, she dropped her gaze to the weapons scattered around his feet. She would run scenarios in her mind, figure out all the ways she could maim him with each, and…oh, wow. A beam of light spotlighted the crystal crown. *Stunning.*

Foolish Roux. How could he leave such a magnificent piece lying on the floor? Anyone could come in at any time and steal it.

How dare they! Mine! Well, not hers. Not yet. Blythe should at least try it on. What would it hurt? Guaranteed the crystals made her superiority pop.

She eased upright, her chains rattling. The familiar clink snapped her back to reality. Ugh. What had she been thinking? If she crowned herself, she would become queen of Ation. Would she then need to fight the winner of the tournament while wearing the ruby?

Not a bad plan, as long as she retrieved the firstone dagger and kept her hatred under wraps. As queen, she would force the final battle between her and Roux. A confrontation Taliyah couldn't halt. There'd be no allowing the Astra to win his task before Blythe killed him either, as she'd previously considered. Their course would be set.

On the other hand, if she waited until after the task, she could launch a sneak attack at the perfect time. But again, she must retrieve the firstone dagger. Which she could do with a simple bargain.

The wraith desired a hundred "meals." No big thing. Send the women of this realm to certain death? No problem. Go without Blythe's loyalty, go without her mercy.

For the return of the dagger, she would happily provide Miss Murder with the hundred—plus interest. That dagger was more than a murder weapon. With it, she had a work-around for the ruby. She wouldn't need to be strong to defeat Roux, only sly.

So her stomach churned at the thought of attacking him from the shadows? So what? The best way to achieve a goal? One step at a time. This plan got her from A to Z in only three moves. Meals, crown, Roux.

"I know that look." His harsh tone filled the room. Sharpening, sharpening. "Do not cause me trouble today, harpy."

Oh, he thought he knew her, did he? He probably expected her to fire back with a venomous barb. She returned her gaze to his and smiled sweetly instead, cooing, "But what if I really, really want to cause you trouble today, Astra?" She put the queen and dagger ideas on a mental shelf for further thought later. Four full days remained until the tournament's start. She had time to weigh the pros and cons for such a permanent decision.

Roux dropped his chin but not his gaze, one hundred percent pure alpha male. "Proceed at your own risk."

Warm shivers danced over her skin. Dang him! He'd upped his sexy.

Looking away had worked the first time, so she did it again. Only, her focus locked on the pulse thumping at the base of his throat. A pang of hunger cut through her.

Hunger. For the Astra. For his blood. His soul.

His powerful body.

Her heart raced. The chains. The chains must be weakening her defenses. *Get the metal off, whatever the cost, now, now, now!*

"Take me to the Oath Stone," she beseeched, dangling her bare feet off the edge of the bed. Having refused to don the flimsy excuse for a nightgown he'd offered her last night, she wore a leather vest and pleated skirt. Wartime attire, exactly what she needed right now. "I'll vow not to kill you and not to run until the start of the tournament. I'll stick to palace grounds. I'll even agree to attend the first day of the tournament with you, so that you'll have ample opportunity to recapture and rechain me."

He ceased sharpening the blade. The muscles in his shoulders tensed. "If I leave you chained, you won't attempt to kill me or run, either. With Penelope determined to mete punishment for my refusal, I prefer to keep you dependent on me."

At least he didn't lie about it. "Aw, is the Astra afraid of the wicked wraith?"

Pursing his lips, he shook his head. A single jerk of negation. "You cannot manipulate me into doing as you wish."

Oh, really? "Please, Rue," she pouted, batting her lashes at him.

Minutes passed in silence, the air between them thickening— Roux stood, a slow unfolding, and prowled closer, bringing the scent of cedarwood and spiced oranges with him.

Her breath hitched. He stopped before her, a tower of might and menace. His inhalations came a little heavily.

The moisture in her mouth dried. She went still. His irises. They all but crackled with flames. In that moment, she craved so many things. Bad things. His hand, gripping her nape. His breath, fanning her bare skin. His body, pressing against hers.

"What do I get out of this deal?" he demanded.

Oh, no he didn't. Up went her hackles. "What do you mean, what do you get? You get to live a few more days."

His pupils expanded and retracted like a pulse before the striations executed a slow spin. "Every day you are free of chains, you will place your palms on my chest of your own volition. For five minutes."

She...was confused. Of all the things he could have asked for, why this? A brief touch. Why not a kiss? Or sex? "I don't understand."

"Your understanding isn't part of our bargain."

He was beyond irritating, but he wasn't wrong. "Fine," she said with a nod. Because why not? She would've ceded much more to get her way. "You've got yourself a deal."

He hesitated only a moment before unhooking the

chain and removing the shackles with a flick of his wrist. Clasping her hand in his, he hauled her to her feet, then flashed her to the Oath Stone.

Today, thick gray clouds obscured the sun, bathing the land in shadows. Wind raged, whipping tendrils of her hair across her cheeks. A coming rain scented the air and charged the atmosphere, zapping her veins.

"We've spoken our promises." Roux's stare never wavered from hers as he burned a symbol into the stone with the tip of his finger.

This is actually happening? She had won this round?

He arched a brow, all *your turn.* "When you verify your agreement, the deal is sealed."

"Great. Wonderful. But I have no symbol of my own." She'd never needed one. Among harpies, a symbol was reserved for Generals.

"Only requires your blood," he said.

Hey! Was he a little *too* eager for this? Was she about to walk straight into a trap? "Imma need you to restate our terms first, bud. Let's make sure we truly agree."

He worked his jaw. "Why don't you *tell* me the terms?"

Even better. But how to word this, ensuring she earned herself some wiggle room? "I, Blythe the Undoing, vow to stay within eyesight of Roux the Crazed One for the next four days. During that time, I vow to put my hands on him for five minutes a day. I will not kill him until the tournament begins. In return, Roux won't shackle, chain, or bind me in any way." Now she arched a brow at *him.* "Satisfied?"

His attention dropped to her lips. "Not even close. But I agree to your terms, anyway."

"Then let's seal the deal." She swiped the tip of her

index finger across one of her fangs. Then, with a grunt, she did it. She pressed the welling red droplet into the symbol.

A current of energy jolted her from the inside, and deep down, she knew. The deal was indeed sealed. For better or worse.

"This is good," Roux said, almost smiling. Fifty years of tension melted from him, rousing her suspicions all over again. What did he think he'd won with this? "Let us return to the palace."

"The palace?" Where they must cloister themselves in a bedroom, alone? Blythe lurched back. "You've cooped up this freedom-loving harpy long enough. From now on, we're gonna *Pretty Woman* this sitch, Warden. You bought me, so you pay my bills. Congratulations. We're going shopping."

12

THE CHALLENGE

Bargain: Day 1

Roux cloaked himself in sheets of the realm's atmosphere and trailed behind Blythe as she explored the overcrowded markets of Ation City. Booths abounded, vendors selling everything from fruit pies to clothing to well-crafted swords.

As graceful as always, the harpy pilfered a dagger as she walked past a table, and no one noticed. She stole a kabob next, moving faster than a blink, and dined on the meat as she continued. Again, no one noticed her expert level sleight of hand.

"I have gold," he informed her, slightly bemused. The coins filled a pocket of his pack.

"What does that have to do with anything?" she called without glancing back at him, finishing off her meal and moving on.

He happily followed, unseen by the masses. For days he'd debated the wisdom of keeping a rabid harpy in chains while fighting the fervency of his growing desire for her. Little had he known she would present him with the perfect solution, granting him everything he'd craved.

Blythe flittered around other shoppers, pausing to listen to different conversations. The entire population seemed to have gathered here, everyone buzzing about the upcoming tournament. An event that would require an arena of some sort. So why hadn't one been built? Did the women already have a spot in mind?

Tonight, he would traverse the palace in secret. Something he should have done long before now, but couldn't for three reasons. One, he could not leave Blythe alone and helpless. In her weakened condition, she needed a protector. Two, he'd enjoyed watching her, even as she tossed and turned on the bed, unable to sleep. And three, he'd spent a good amount of time scouring the corridors of his mind for his screamer or plunging the depths of his subconscious for any helpful information he'd tucked away over the centuries. So far, he'd made no real progress with either matter.

"Why'd you kill Minerva? She wanted nothing to do with that cursed crown."

The statement caught his notice. Did the speaker use the word "cursed" literally or figuratively? And did it matter to his cause? He slowed to listen to the rest of the conversation.

"She was ahead of me in line, so, she had to go."

"Line? What line?"

"Dibs on the Astra. Should I add you to the list?"

"Nah. I'll take your spot." The woman swung a

sword, removing her friend's head. "Think I'll remove the rest of my competition, too," she said, focusing on Blythe with narrowed eyes.

Roux balled his hands into fists. The harphantom noticed the killer's attention, he knew she did, but she displayed total nonchalance, blowing a kiss in his direction before branching off. Despite her many abilities, she couldn't see his shielded form. Not fully.

He continued to follow, snared by her confident swagger. The longer he watched, the tighter his leathers became. Wasn't long before his muscles tensed, as if he geared for battle. Maybe he did—another bloody war with himself.

What madness had he entertained, to demand the lethal beauty touch her palm to his chest for five minutes each day? He could barely tolerate her presence nowadays. The sight of her, with her sleek black hair, pale blue eyes, and curvy figure kept him on edge. The scent of all that honeysuckle and rose constantly invaded his nostrils, making him totter on that edge. And the hunger she incited. He was starved, always.

If he didn't know better, he might think she was his *gravita*. The one female in existence made for him. As Taliyah was to Roc. As Ophelia was to Halo. But that couldn't be right. Roux wasn't like the other Astra. Unless he was, and he just hadn't known it until now?

But what were the odds? Millennia upon millennia without any kind of physical desire and then, boom, the old dog suddenly learned new tricks? No. On the other hand, he'd only just met Blythe. How like Fate to give a clone—a being never meant to exist—the female who would forever despise him, living only to end his life.

He gave his lips a nervous swipe of his tongue. No,

he thought again. She wasn't his *gravita*. So far he had produced no stardust for her. The only sure sign. There must be some other explanation for his...tolerance of the harphantom. When she touched him later this evening, he would unearth the truth.

Well, well. He now had a logical reason for accepting her bargain. One based on strategy rather than romance.

His every instinct went on sudden, high alert. There. A vampire in a sun hat snuck toward a preoccupied Blythe, her fangs bared and her claws flared. The widow had yet to notice the forthcoming attack.

Roux prepared to *handle things*. Blythe beat him to it. Moving at warp speed, she took the vampire to the ground with the grace of a gazelle and the ferocity of a lioness. Stab, stab. She blinded the vampire with the kabob, then swooped down to fit her lips over her opponent's throat. A glowing light seeped from the other woman's pores.

Disappointment sucker punched him. *She's feeding.*

He should be overjoyed. Now he had no need to offer any part of himself.

As the vampire attempted to break free, Blythe ripped off the sunhat, allowing the bright light to sear the other woman's sensitive skin. Some vampires in Ation could withstand the rays, others could not, just like in other worlds. Good to know.

The vampire screamed and writhed in pain. All around, conversations ceased.

Still acting as if she hadn't a care, Blythe straightened, wiped her mouth with the back of her hand, and sauntered on.

"Hey!" someone shouted. "Someone needs to teach you a lesson about messing with vamps, and I'm just the one for the job."

A gorgon swooped out of nowhere, beheading both the first and second vampire with a swift swing of her sword. No, not just "a" gorgon but a member of the welcome party. "You know the rules," she shouted. "No harm comes to the phantom. We keep our vows and twist them, but we don't forget them."

Grumbles erupted, resentment spreading like wildfire. Multiple glares landed on Blythe.

She stopped at a booth filled with shoes. Crimson wet her hands as she pointed to a pair of leather boots and casually asked the vendor, "How much for those?" There wasn't a hint of black in her irises.

"Too much for you." The banshee looked ready to unleash her most potent death scream. Such an act killed some immortals and gravely injured others.

The harphantom hiked her thumb at him, telling the shoe saleswoman, "I'll let you squeeze the Astra's biceps if you give me the boots."

"Blythe," he snarled, dismissing the clouds and marching closer. "You cannot—"

"Yes! Deal!" the banshee rushed out. "By the way, I have a strict no refund policy."

Blythe stuffed her bare feet into the shoes, then had the audacity to wince in his direction. "Sorry, bud, but a deal's a deal. I believe we discussed the fact that my debts are your debts, so you better pay up. I don't mean to underhype the issue, but your very honor is at stake."

He could not allow her to get away with this. He would—

The banshee shot out her hand and, yes, she squeezed his biceps. As his skin prickled with irritation, the touch affecting him like every other throughout the centuries, a dreamy moan slipped from her lips.

"Totally worth it," she sighed.

With a huff, Roux grabbed both of *Blythe*'s biceps and flashed her to their bedroom. Near the foot of the bed, to be precise. She'd made him endure the touch of another. Now she must offer her touch in return. Wait until she finished shopping? No longer.

"You owe me," he said, whipping off his shirt. Excitement replaced his anger. The motionless *alevala* were ultrasensitive, but nowhere near the cusp of action. Here, now, he warred no longer. He knew what he wanted. "Pay up."

She glared at him. "Now isn't a good time."

"I don't care."

For a long while, she said nothing else. Didn't move. Soon, though, she was panting her breaths. The scent of honeysuckle and roses strengthened, filling his head with all kinds of ideas...

"The five minutes do not begin until at least one of your palms rests on my skin." He inhaled deep, puffing up his chest. *Touch me.*

"There isn't a clock in this realm, and I refuse to touch you a second longer than promised. So how will we know when my five minutes are up?"

"I have an internal clock. I'll tell you when to stop. If you don't trust me to be up-front and honest, count down in your head. I don't care," he repeated. He inhaled deep again...

"Whatever," she said, flippant. Finally, blessedly, she did it. She slapped her hand against his pectoral. The vampire's blood still covered her flesh but it bothered him not a bit. In that moment, *nothing* bothered him.

Ten seconds passed. Twenty. The softness of her. The delicious heat. The *connection.*

Forty. Zero irritation occurred. At the one-minute mark, the barest tendrils of pleasure uncoiled, and he stifled a groan. Only iron determination prevented him from clasping her wrist and guiding her fingers elsewhere. Or crowding her onto the mattress.

The thoughts in his head. The things he imagined doing to her, if ever he did get her into bed. So many things. His control wavered. His fingers twitched at his sides. Soon, he wasn't just panting, he was pant-growling. Muscles hardened. *All* his muscles. Hunger clawed at his insides. He wanted this female. Needed her. Badly. More than he'd ever needed anything. Roux would commit terrible deeds to strip her.

Reason through this madness? Impossible. He could only peer down at her as she looked anywhere but at him, maintaining a bored expression. And yet, the pulse at the base of her throat hammered rapidly.

A wild thought invaded his head. Did she like the contact, too, despite her feelings for him? That thought spurred another. Something wilder. Did a part of her, possibly, desire him in return?

The clock ran out before he could deduce the answers. Part of him longed to beg for one more minute. Even a second. But she must have kept track of the time, as suggested, because she severed contact before he could make an announcement.

He nearly roared at the loss of the connection.

"All done," she said, flipping her hair over one shoulder. But she couldn't hide the trembling in her fingers. "Obviously, you got the better end of our deal. I'll be in the bathroom, washing off Astra funk. Enter at your own peril."

* * *

Silvery moonlight filled the bedroom. Blythe lay unnaturally still atop the mattress, too uncomfortable to move. Hours had passed since her hands-on interaction with Roux, but her skin felt far too tight. Her insides ached.

The Astra occupied his chair, per usual, polishing his weapons, watching her with a greater awareness than before. To better guard her, now that she was unchained, yes. But he wanted her, too. There was no mistaking the ferocity and passion he radiated. Not any longer. Not while she felt it, too.

Every so often—like now—she snuck a glance in his direction, unable to help herself. Perfect nocturnal vision displayed every detail of his rough features. The wide brow. The prominent cheekbones. The patrician nose. The strong jaw covered in golden scruff.

Once again, she caught herself panting with desire. The same consuming fire that had threatened to engulf her ever since she'd rested her palm on his muscular chest and wonder had lit up his incredible eyes. A thousand times, she'd almost demanded he take her to bed and give her pleasure for her pain. He *owed* her, after all.

Except, no enemy should be allowed to affect her physically. And Roux wouldn't be able to do so, if he didn't resemble Laban in some way. Yes, that *must* be the reason. Both were strong, blond, and, well, male.

Wait. What was this? Though Roux remained seated in the chair, he also stood. But the standing Roux was too bright to be a spirit yet not solid enough to be a body. Sitting Roux looked as if he'd been powered down.

That brightness... He'd projected his soul out of his

body, hadn't he, making himself an open smorgasbord to any phantoms nearby. And oh, how tasty he appeared. A feast of power.

No one would be able to see him, except a phantom like Blythe.

As he ghosted through the door, a warrior on a mission, she jolted into an upright position. To follow him or stay here and search his stuff, maybe even rig his weapons to fail? Oh, oh. Since he'd left her, she might be able to bypass her oath and leave him, whisking to Wraith Island to wheel and deal with Penelope. Worth the risk?

While options two, three, and four appealed greatly, curiosity got the best of her. Blythe shoved her hatred into that hidden corner in her mind. Strength returned faster than before. More strength than before, too. She should have no problem slipping into a spirit plane.

A grin bloomed. Roux might sense her, as he had before, but he wouldn't see her. Therefore, he couldn't prove she'd acted inappropriately. If anything, she was doing something right, keeping her oath by remaining within his sight. Kind of.

Blythe gave chase, passing his notebook. Backtracking. Okay, so, maybe she could spend a minute or two spying for the good of her cause.

She flipped through the pages of the book. Uh… A flush heated her skin, and she fanned her cheeks. He'd written the same word over and over. *Feast.*

Her lungs emptied. Was the thought directed at her?

She needed to get out of here before she talked herself into becoming his next meal.

On the way out, her gaze got caught on the crown. Once again, she backtracked. *Must touch…*

Trembling, she reached out... If she wore this magnificent circlet, Roux might— Roux! Gah! Blythe stilled and huffed an angry breath, hit by another realization. The crown clearly had some sort of mystical draw. It must. From now on, she'd have to be careful around it.

Right now, nothing mattered more than finding Roux. She rushed from the bedroom. An unfamiliar vampire and siren stood sentry in the hall. There to ensure the honored guests remained within? Rolling her eyes at such a feeble block, she hurried on, unnoticed. Following the Astra's scent—there was no missing it, even in this form—she glided down a narrow staircase.

There! He entered and exited rooms. Anytime he encountered one resident in conversation with another, he stopped to listen. Discussions about the "sperm donor" caused his features to twist before he marched on. Debates about who might win the tournament elicited interest. So. He sought info about the coming battle and its probable victor. The woman—queen—he must kill to complete his task.

Blythe listened while taking in palace details she'd missed on her way in. Elaborate buffets. Comfy sofas. Flameless torches. Murals depicting a bloody battle of some sort between warrior women of every species. True to the realm's history?

On the fourth floor, they entered a room filled with women who were throwing what looked to be popcorn at a white sheet that hung on the wall. That sheet showcased an old episode of *New Girl*.

On the third floor, a group of ten immortals congregated with Roux's dates at a long, rectangular table. They passed pieces of parchment around.

Following the Astra's lead, Blythe leaned over someone's shoulder to study the parchments herself. Hmm. One was a blueprint for what looked to be an underground fight club. The other had nothing but text. A vow? Oh, yeah. Definitely a vow—Roux's. Considering there was a promise in there to date ten women, this must be the pledge he'd made to save Blythe.

Back to the underground fight club. Was the *tournament* to take place there? How intriguing.

"Okay," an Amazon said. "I call this Get You Some meeting to order. And, guys? We're down to the wire here. Did you hear me? The wire. We gotta figure out how to murder a phantom and trap ourselves a torture master once and for all."

13

THE TEMPTATION

Bargain: Day 2

"Wake up, Warden." Blythe reached for Roux, only to draw back. Touch him free of charge? No!

Still and quiet, he sat in his chair by the hearth, his eyes closed. He should have looked at peace. He didn't. Tension roiled from him.

"There's something I want to do, which means you gotta come with me so I can keep my promise," she said. "Also, you need to… Nothing. Never mind." She'd meant to tell him to hide the crown, too, but the words dissolved in her throat.

Now that she understood the crystals possessed power, she knew better than to approach. But, really, was there a valid reason to forever shield the headpiece from her view? No, of course not. Look how pretty it was, bathed in morning light. This masterpiece deserved to be examined daily.

Blythe stepped forward, reaching— Argh! Snared again. Scowling, she drew back. *Focus.* In a matter of minutes, multiple someones would knock on the bedroom door to offer the Astra breakfast and a blow job.

"Wake. Up," she commanded, clapping her hands.

Slowly he parted his lids, revealing stormy irises. Bothered by the council's plot to betray him? Or something else? Yeah, must be something else. The male considered himself too powerful to harm. And it was as irritating as it was sexy.

He scanned her once, twice, and gulped. Tension pulled the corners of his lips down as he gripped the arms of the chair.

Did he approve of her new look?

When his leathers pulled tight, she almost grinned. Oh, yeah. He approved.

While he'd slept the approaching dawn away, she'd cleaned up in the bathroom and dressed with care, selecting a sheer white dress with bright red cotton undergarments. All of which she'd had to adjust for her wings. *Worth it.*

He scrubbed a hand over his face and rasped, "What does the she-beast desire, exactly?"

Time to take advantage of his appreciation. "I want to swim in the lake." Get her peepers on Wraith Island again. There'd been no sign of Penelope in the market. Maybe the wraith would appreciate a curbside visit. Maybe not. Perhaps Blythe would encounter a different wraith and pass along a message. The day was ripe with promise.

"The water is ice-cold," he reminded her.

"So? I don't recall asking his most delicate royal highness to get in. If you prefer, you can watch me from the shore and stay all hot and bothered. Yeah. That's right. I noticed your hard-on." The best way to cover her desire? Exploit his. "And yes, I'm very aware it's pointed in my direction. And *only* mine."

A muscle jumped in his jaw. "No swimming."

Okay, so, taunting him hadn't been the smartest course of action. Noted.

"Why do you wish to venture into the territory of the female who controls you, anyway?" he demanded.

She kicked into a swift pace in front of his chair. "Look, I'm used to activity. Exercise. I've been cooped up for far too long, and I've gotta expend some energy before I combust." Truth.

"Energy?" Something akin to hope flickered in his eyes next. "Is the wraith no longer able to drain you?"

In other words, had Blythe ceased hating him. "Or," she added, with a roll of her eyes, "we can return to the market, and you can use your muscles to purchase more supplies."

A scowl twisted his features. "Fine. I will take you swimming. In exchange, you will answer a question for me."

The old one or a new one, such as how she planned to inconvenience him today? Either way, triumph lit her up inside. Already a step closer to her goal! "Deal," she said. "Ask."

"Did you get all hot and bothered as well?"

Her breath caught. His tone. Like melted honey poured over ice. He had sensed her desire. Or at least suspected she harbored it. "Yes," she grated. "But I thought of Laban." Because she always sometimes thought of Laban. Just not often enough anymore.

Roux's scowl returned, and shame slapped her. Un-

able to meet his gaze, she dropped her attention, landing on the thumping pulse at the base of his throat.
The perfect place to tap his soul. Mmm. Even his vein
looked good. How sweet would he taste? How much
power would flood her system before she vomited him?

"Do you need to feed, Blythe?" A softly uttered question.

Maybe? "I—"

A knock sounded at the door, bringing her back to
her senses, saving her from making a huge mistake.

Demonstrating pure frustration, Roux grabbed his
backpack and stood. "We leave now." With two long
strides, he reached her side and yanked her body against
his.

Blink. Suddenly, they stood on the rocky, mossy beach,
enveloped by a cold, boisterous wind that whipped tendrils of Blythe's hair across the Astra's face.

She peered up at him, struggling to rein in an unexpected sense of comfort. Being in a man's arms shouldn't
feel this good. Especially this man's arms. But it did feel
good. So, so good.

He reached up and smoothed those errant locks of
hair behind her ears. A gentle caress. Defenses crumbled, and she leaned into him. The urge to rest her head
on his shoulder was nearly irresistible. To drink in his
strength and his heat. To forget the past and their trou-
bles and just be, if only for a moment. But she couldn't
ignore their history. She *shouldn't*.

"Blythe," he said, looking as though he had a thousand things to say. "If I could go back—"

"But you can't." She stepped free, earning her freedom. Anything else he had to say, she didn't need to

know. An apology wouldn't make things better. "I'm swimming, you're watching."

She turned away and yanked the dress over her head. For the first time, he got an unimpeded view of her undergarments. As she folded the outer garment and set it aside, being sure to exaggerate her movements, Roux's hitch of breath made her belly quiver. Ignoring the tremors in her limbs, she strode into the tempestuous waves. The iciness wasn't pleasant, but a girl had to do what a girl had to do.

"Don't venture too far," he commanded. "Stay within my sight."

"No worries, Warden. I haven't forgotten our deal." Or the fact that she must touch him again sometime today.

Groaning, she dove underwater and didn't come up until she needed air. Blythe swam laps for ten…thirty… sixty minutes. Then another hour. By the end of the third hour, some of her excess energy burned off, and she treaded water near Roux, who did indeed sit upon the shore, watching her every move. He'd donned her least favorite expression: the blank mask.

"What are we doing when we leave the lake?" she asked.

"Returning to our room."

Ugh. "We should explore the land together. You know, listen to gossip. Find a way home. Stuff like that."

He snorted. "Trust you to aid my cause? No. Expect you to sabotage me at every turn, then use whatever we learn against me? Yes. For now, the best path to my victory is spending as much time as possible indoors."

"Okay, we'll circle back to our next activity." She floated to her back, peering up at a gray sky. "What's it like being a clone? Are there differences between yourself and others?"

"There was one difference in particular," he grumbled, "until recently."

What did that mean? The touch thing?

There's no irritation with you. Words he'd spoken as he'd guided her palm across his chest, broadcasting shock and wonder.

She chewed on her lower lip. Did every other touch bother him? But what made hers different?

For the first time, she went digging for his memories, rather than fighting them as they attempted to resurface. She bypassed delightful glimpses of a smiling, laughing Isla. Blips of Laban, crooking his finger at her. Her mother. There. The tortures inflicted upon Roux by his father. Mars, the original Roux. The peeling of his skin. The whippings. Stabbings. Torchings. And those were just the things she'd seen! No telling what other horrors he'd suffered as a child. But, um, yeah. That explained why he disdained contact with others. Get hurt enough, and you came to expect it. But it didn't explain what made her touch different.

"Care to elaborate?" she asked, tiptoeing around the issue as she bobbed through a wave.

"No."

Figured. "Mars is dead, right? Why haven't you claimed his throne as your own?"

He couldn't hide his disgust. "I want nothing that belonged to him."

Daddy issues. Something they had in common. She swam a little closer to the shore. "You mentioned a pampered twin brother. What happened to him?"

"He died," Roux said, his eyes flickering with red.

A warning to change the subject. She didn't. "Were you close to him?"

He pursed his lips. "I was, and I wasn't. He visited me upon occasion and sometimes snuck me treats. Most times he oversaw my next fileting."

Her chest tightened big-time. Did this guy have any *good* childhood memories?

"How could you leave your daughter behind?" he asked, making her stomach roil. "She is a sweet child. I met with her and—"

"You what?" Rage pierced Blythe, all sympathy gone in an instant. The next thing she knew, she was flying onto the shore, her wings fluttering wildly. She shoved the Astra to his back and sank her claws deep in his throat, preparing to rip. "Why did you seek her out? What did you do to her?"

He lay in the sand, broadcasting more of that awful, tantalizing wonder. In a blink, she became aware of his hands on her hips, holding her steady.

"Answer me!"

"I didn't seek her." He tore his focus from his fingers and met her gaze. "She sought *me*. Invited me to a tea party."

A tea party. Of course. A harpy tradition. Invite an enemy to drinks and laugh as they downed their own death. "Well? What did you do after she poisoned you?" His answer would determine Blythe's next moves.

"She didn't poison me. She told me I have a prisoner in my mind who I've hidden from myself, and he will punish me for my actions. Though she was wrong."

Prisoner? In his mind?

"Isla needs you," the fool continued. "Yet you came here."

"I came here *for* Isla." She spit the words at him. "You murdered her father. What kind of mother allows such a wrong to go unpunished? And who are you to question me about her well-being? You would have killed her too if I hadn't intervened."

His fingers flexed, his grip tightening. "You think you stopped me from doing anything that day? No, she-beast. You might be a warrior, but you did nothing. I'd already stopped myself. I spotted her. Was in the process of drawing back. Then you appeared. I would never harm a child. *Never.*"

Maybe true, maybe false. But it changed nothing, the damage already done. "You know what? I'll go ahead and answer your original query." She ignored the heat of his hands. The only source of warmth as cold wind whipped her water-dotted flesh. Rejected the decadence of his scent. Overlooked the delicious awakening of his body beneath hers. "I left her because you gave me no other choice. To allow you to live is a far greater insult to her."

A firm shake of his head. "You lie to yourself. Your choice is always your choice."

The response only fueled the fires of her rage.

Rage? No hatred this time? She jolted, surprised. Must be a mistake. But...nope. No mistake. The link to Penelope was closed. But, but...why wasn't Blythe's hatred engaged?

"All right, Warden. I've had my hand on you long enough." One by one, she plucked her claws loose, desperate to be free of this male. "Consider today's obligation met."

Disgusted with herself, she stood and swiped up her dress. Working the material over her head, she scanned the area for any hint of a wraith. Another citizen of Ation. Someone! But no. A wasted trip then.

"Blythe," Roux rasped, sounding even more forlorn than when they'd first arrived.

"No. Take me back to the palace. We're done for the day."

Bargain: Day 3

Roux castigated himself for ever mentioning Isla to Blythe. He'd ruined a peaceful, informative, and sensually charged interlude. A mistake he wouldn't make again.

He arranged dinner on the desk and claimed his usual seat. "Come here and eat." His tone registered, and he cringed. Perhaps he should be nicer?

The harphantom kept her back to him. Currently, she crouched in a window, her feet resting on the bottom ledge. Despite the windstorm whipping locks of that sleek black hair in every direction, she remained perfectly balanced. At ease but not.

She'd perched there most of the day, peering out at the surrounding village. Ignoring him. Searching for a way to escape him?

Only two nights remained until the tournament kicked off and their bargain reached its completion. There would be no more touches. No more brief moments of comradery. No other charged Q and A's.

Could he bring himself to shackle the grieving widow again?

"Come here and eat," he repeated softly.

"Not hungry," she muttered.

He sighed, a common occurrence lately. She hadn't

eaten breakfast or lunch, either. Should he force the issue?

In the end, he merely picked at the food and watched her. Always he watched her, his desire for her only ever worsening. And now that he'd clasped her tiny waist in his hands, he thought of little else.

His fingers constantly jerked in remembrance. His skin rarely ceased tingling, and his blood always burned white-hot. The ensuing steam caused his muscles to bulge and the *alevala* to jump. He relished and resented every sensation.

If only he could travel back in time and spare her consort. The harphantom would hate him no longer. But even in this impossible fantasy, Roux had no chance with her.

He scrubbed a hand down his face as a familiar scream echoed inside his head. Last night, he'd searched his mind for the escapee. A failed expedition: he'd found no one out of place. No hint of an illicit—or secret—presence. But whoever it was only seemed to make himself known when Roux dealt with his feelings for Blythe. Which made him wonder…

What if he *had* absorbed the consort? Or, if not the consort himself, perhaps a part of Blythe's grief over the male's loss. No telling what was left behind when her spirit tore free of Roux's. It was only fair, he supposed, since she'd taken some of his memories.

Outside, the sun began its swift descent, the light in the room dimming. Soon candles, torches, and the hearth blazed to life. The same thing had happened each evening, compliments of some sorceress's enchantment. He'd noticed the citizens of Ation used both magic and technology to see to their needs.

In a sudden burst of movement, Blythe hopped backward, landing on her feet inside the room. She pivoted on her heels and tripped his way, crying, "What's happening? My feet won't stop moving."

He jerked with realization. He should have expected this. "Fighting will do you no good. The vow compels you."

Her eyes widened. His heart thudded. As she neared, he ripped off his shirt and swiped the food from the desk. Perfect timing. She climbed over the surface on all fours and slapped her hands on his pectorals. The softness! The connection!

Animalistic noises brewed on the back of his tongue, vibrating in his chest. The pleasure he'd experienced before? Nothing compared to this. His sensitized nerve endings hummed with relief for the first time since she'd last touched him.

Roux grabbed her waist and hauled her onto his lap. Of her own free will, she straddled him, settling against him more comfortably.

"I hate you," she hissed. All the while she kneaded his muscles.

"Do you?" He rocked her against him. Once. Twice. A gentle caress. "Why aren't you weakening?" Because she thought of *him*? Roux rocked her with force.

She gasped before flashing her fangs at him. "Why are you so annoying?"

He blinked. An evasion. So telling. "You aren't. You're thinking of *me*. You don't want to, but you are."

"You don't know what you're talking about." Softness in her eyes, blades in her tone. "No matter what occurs in this realm, I'm going to kill you, as premeditated. That's a promise."

"Lyla," he intoned, uttering the nickname without thought, "if you sit on me like this tomorrow, I might willingly go to my death."

14

THE NEED

Bargain: Day 3½-4

Hours after the emotionally and sexually charged interlude ended, Blythe still wasn't calm. She tossed and turned in bed, undeniable hunger gnawing at her, stronger and more intense by the second.

Hunger.

For Roux.

Every part of her ached for his touch. Even her wings reacted to him. Maybe it was the way his heart had raced beneath her palm. Or the heat of his skin searing hers. Or the sheer, unadulterated strength he'd presented. Perhaps the roughness of his voice when he'd called her Lyla.

Mmm. Shivers cascaded through her. Would he use the ridiculous nickname tomorrow? Why did she want him to? What was wrong with her? And what was wrong with *him*? He'd put on a clean shirt, then returned to the chair near the hearth, where he'd remained. He'd kept his chin down and stared for hours— Whoa! He was staring even now. Staring *hard*, his eyes wild.

New shivers plagued her. Firelight bathed him, setting him aglow. He wasn't sharpening or polishing a weapon but white-knuckling the arms of the chair, as if holding himself back from a battle. Ferocity seemed to seethe beneath his skin.

A familiar electric charge crackled between them. Her lips parted. Breathing with any kind of finesse grew difficult.

Look away. But she didn't. She couldn't. She'd been utterly snared.

Aching worse, she shifted atop the mattress. Had he woven an ancient lust spell over her? Nothing else explained such ferocious desire.

When morning sunlight filled the bedchamber, she jolted with excitement. A new day—a new touching. The final one. Why not get it over with? Yes. Get it over with so she could finally, blessedly ponder more important matters.

Blythe climbed from the bed. Roux watched her, the arms of the chair cracking. A woman on a mission, she glided across the bedroom.

"This is not the time to toy with me, she-beast." The harshness of his voice nearly melted her bones.

"Now that's a lie, Warden," she purred, jumping onto his lap. "I've discovered *always* is the time to toy with you."

He swooped his hands to her waist and jerked her closer. "If you truly wish to wreak havoc, double our contact today. That should do the trick."

"Don't think I won't." She ripped his shirt down the middle with a simple tug, settled her hands on his pecs—and petted him of her own free will. *Silken heat poured over hard stones.* "I might even go for a triple, and there's nothing you can do to stop me."

He squeezed his lids shut for a moment, hiding his fiery irises. "Prepare yourself," he grated, rocking her against him. "You're about to witness the next erection of my famous pants tent."

She chuckled, genuinely amused by him. "I'll try not to be too scandalized." Mmm. Oh, yes, there it was. Big. *Very* big. Enormous. Annnd she was already panting for it, for him, wanting to both leap off him and burrow closer. But she stayed put, letting him continue to rock her against him as she struggled not to moan. Or notice the soul-glow in his throat. Or the rushing vein ready to be tapped.

When two *alevala* jumped in his skin, changing places, she recalled what had happened to the shifter and hastened to avert her gaze. Although…perhaps Blythe would be spared from such a gruesome fate? After all, she *carried* some of his "tainted" memories. Seeing more shouldn't liquefy her face.

His grip constricted on her, strong enough to bruise. "Look at me, Lyla."

Not the nickname! "No." Not until she calmed her inhalations, doused all the fluttering in her stomach, and cooled down. How she burned.

Hoping to distract them both, she uttered the first question to pop inside her brain. "Are you a virgin, Roux?"

He stopped rocking her, and there was no stopping her next moan. "What does it matter?" he asked flatly.

"It doesn't." Right? She couldn't think. "But are you? A simple yes or no will suffice." As much as he reviled being touched…maybe. But wow. Just wow. "I mean,

to my knowledge, you've never made use of your concubine."

"If I say yes, you'll want to know why I seek any kind
of intimacy with a woman who despises me."

"Uh, to be fair, I want to hear the explanation even if
you say no." She faced him. A mistake. He snared her
all over again.

A calculating gleam lit his narrowing eyes, and oh,
did she like it. "Take off your shirt," he said, "and I'll
tell you."

Well. The Astra certainly wasn't above using circumstance to his advantage. Of course, he probably figured
a refusal was imminent, considering she currently wore
a top and a pair of panties. The jammies she'd donned
before bed. But sometimes sacrifices must be made for
the greater good. Keeping him off guard was definitely
for the greater good.

"You can look," she said, whipping off her shirt and
bearing her upper half, "but you can't touch."

His lips parted. "Exquisite," he breathed, and her
stomach hollowed out.

Staring at her breasts, he ran his hands up her sides.
Would he break her rule?

To her astonishment, he stopped just before he
reached the no-go zone. "So soft," he praised, sounding drunk.

She held her breath, waiting for his next move. What
would he do?

He reached back, grazing his fingertips over her
wings. The gentlest of touches yet ripples of heat sped
through her entire body. "So perfect," he said as her
nipples puckered.

A whimper escaped her, his admiration a potent brew

of power and confidence. Unable to remain still, she toyed with the ends of his hair. "The price has been paid, Warden. Give me what I desire."

His Adam's apple bobbed—and still he stared at her breasts. "I am a virgin, yes. The touch of others has always been...unpleasant to me. If the sensitivity didn't stop me, the screams did."

Wow, wow, wow. Even though she'd expected such an answer, she hadn't expected such an answer. First, he'd just admitted it. Second, she kind of wished he'd refused to respond. To know he had spent countless centuries devoid of affection *after* he'd endured countless centuries of torture and pain...

The urge to hug him bloomed. An urge she couldn't allow to grow. *Focus on the conversation.* "I remember the screams very well. I've heard them. Do they spring from your childhood?"

He licked his lips. "They aren't memories. I'm able to absorb immortals if I choose, trapping them inside my head." With barely a pause, he exploded into motion, gripping her hips and yanking. Hardness met softness, and pleasure whipped her. Then he thrust just as she arched her spine. They rubbed against each other.

A dam broke. Neither of them stopped. They slowly ground together. Panting. Moaning louder and louder. She couldn't think...needed to think. The goal was to ruin his concentration, not her own. Maybe?

She gripped his shoulders, holding on for the ride. Every lash of pleasure robbed her of more sense, sending her thoughts spinning into an endless ether. So so so so so good! Her gaze dropped to his mouth. "Have you ever been kissed?"

"Never," he rasped.

"Do you want to?"

He snapped his teeth at her. "More than anything."

Her heart galloped. "Do you hope to lose your virginity? With me?"

A muscle jumped in his jaw. "Yes, Lyla. With you. Only ever with you."

Whimpering, she leaned into him. With her lips hovering over his, she said, "Tell me why you waited, and I might take off my panties."

He double blinked. One of his hands shot into her hair, fisting the strands. With the other hand, he cupped her backside and took control of her motions. "Because," he all but hissed. "There's your answer. Now take off your panties."

With great effort, she managed to focus and brush the tip of her nose against his. "Because why?"

"Because," he repeated, tightening his grip. "I don't know, can only guess."

Did he maybe, possibly consider Blythe—widow, mother, enemy—his *gravita*?

For some reason, the very idea pushed her toward the edge of climax.

Teeth clenched, he said, "You spent so much time in my spirit…my body must not consider yours…a foreign invader."

Oh. Yes. Okay. That made more sense. And she wasn't disappointed about it. She wasn't! She slowed her gyrations, easing from the ledge. Being his fated mate would have made it easier to subdue and kill him, but so what? Easier wasn't always better.

And what was she even doing, fraternizing with the enemy like this?

"How much time is left on my clock?" she demanded, going still.

He bared his teeth. "You zeroed out two minutes and thirteen seconds ago. I didn't want to stop you. You looked like you were having such a good time."

No he did *not* say that.

A knock sounded at the door. "You're needed on the third floor," a woman called. The siren. Blythe recognized the voice. "You're the guest of honor at a mandatory council meeting."

She shot to her feet as if she'd been caught cheating on her consort. In a way, she had. Voice like ice, she said, "We'd better dress and go."

"Not until we finish our conversation." Scowling, radiating sexual frustration and iron-hard determination, he gripped the damaged arms of his chair.

"There's nothing else to say."

They glared at each other, both struggling to inhale, exhale. Something!

Tremors overtook her. Afraid of what her expression revealed, she turned and strode to the closet to dress for battle.

"Perhaps Penelope has made trouble for you at last," she said, strapping on a leather uniform and tying combat boots to her feet. A girl could hope, anyway.

"Perhaps," he intoned, standing and donning a fresh T-shirt. "Stay here. I'll return shortly."

Let him leave without her? Not happening. "I'm going with you. I'll act as your bodyguard." To prove she meant business, Blythe strutted over, smiled, and clawed out his throat with a swift swipe. "Two. See? Your reflexes are off. You require protecting."

His scowl might have softened the tiniest degree.

Amusement might have glittered in his eyes. *She* might have softened. A surprising outcome.

"Very well," he said.

Spirits restored, she smirked and tossed the organ into the hearth, then wiped off her hands on his shirt. With a spring in her step, she strode to the door, opening up to the siren. "We're ready to dazzle at the council meeting. Lead the way."

Roux did his best to remain alert, but he struggled to maintain his composure. He followed his harphantom down the empty, winding hallway.

As she trailed the siren, the graceful sway of her hips beckoned his gaze as if it belonged there. Maybe it did. There was an old adage among the Astra. If you touched it, you owned it. He'd had his hands right there and there and there.

With a little more time, Roux might have brought Blythe to a climax. She'd been close; he'd sensed it. What he wouldn't give to see her delicate features soften with the satisfaction he had bestowed.

He rubbed his throbbing fly. What other delights had he missed, thanks to the siren's interruption? Holding Blythe's soft, pliant body afterward? Sharing more about his life, encouraging her to share more about hers? Comradery? Belonging?

Now wasn't the time for regrets. No doubt he was headed to some kind of setup.

Roux sighed. He should have spied on the citizens of Ation more than once. Should've explored the amphitheater beneath the palace more than once, too. Hadn't the Commander told him to beware of some kind of monster? Not that Roux had spotted any sign of vicious beasts down there.

Instead of furthering his cause, he'd spent the bulk of his time considering Blythe. Just like he was doing now. But how could he not? She seemed to be fashioned for him alone. No one had ever fit him so perfectly. And at times, she wanted him, too.

He'd begun to think she might be the missing puzzle piece of his life. Or the prize of prizes he deserved after surviving centuries of horror and pain. Problem was, he didn't deserve *her*.

But he craved her, anyway. He *needed* to learn the taste of her lips. Soon. He dreamed of tossing her onto her back and *doing things*. Soft things. Rough things. *All* things. He planned to start at her mouth, dabble at those plump breasts with their irresistible amber crests, and work his way down. Then back up. Then down again. He wouldn't stop until she shattered. Or he did.

Inside him, pressure mounted, nearly unbearable, and a growl rumbled in his chest. If he failed to find relief soon, he might end up tearing this palace to shreds.

How could he win her? How? She might want him, but she didn't like him. He liked her far too much. Liked her unwavering determination to avenge those she loved. Her unshakable fortitude to oversee a goal. The way she teased him. Played with him.

A shrill scream echoed inside his head, the loose prisoner making himself known.

Enough! Determined to stop the intrusion at last, Roux drew to a halt and retreated into his mind...there! An unauthorized shadow, slinking away. He gave chase, resolute. He would learn the being's identity and lock him up or die—

"Warden? Yo! Rue. Your presence is requested."

Blythe! Was something wrong? Yanked from the chase, Roux blinked into awareness. Frowned. The harpy stood directly in front of him, and she was patting his cheek.

Pale blue eyes offered...was that concern? "What happened? Where'd you go?"

He'd stopped in the middle of the hall, he realized, without allowing his instincts to take over. Anyone could have attacked him with any weapon, and he would've been unable to stop them.

Why would he allow such a travesty? Because deep down he wanted Blythe to touch him? Or was some part of him beginning to trust her? If his instincts no longer considered her a threat...

This wasn't good. This wasn't good at all. In Ation, Blythe the Undoing was his *only* threat.

"Perhaps the sway of your hips hypnotized me," he croaked. As close to the truth as anything. Let her know the wealth of power she wielded over him? No.

"How wonderful for me. An unexpected weapon for my arsenal." She winked at him. Actually winked. And her irises remained blue. Then she scowled, as if regretting her show of playfulness. "Well? What are you waiting for? Let's go," she snapped at the siren, who stood off to the side, eyeing them thoughtfully.

With a shrug, the other female kicked into motion. "No questions about the trouble you're in?" she asked, as he and the harpy followed.

The irritation in her voice scraped against his eardrums. A common occurrence with her ilk. When a siren's emotions infused her words, anyone within hearing distance usually experienced a bodily reaction.

"None." He tore his gaze from Blythe and focused on their companion. His first date, Monna. A true beauty, with short dark hair, round brown eyes, and darker skin. Thick black slashes tattooed into her arms.

Why couldn't he crave *her* touch? Life would be so much easier.

Monna huffed with greater irritation. "You should care. Things are about to go nuclear."

Would *Roux* go nuclear if ever he got Blythe into bed?

Could he get her into bed? Should he? How much more would she hate him afterward? Did it matter? Hate was hate.

The siren cast a scowl over her shoulder. "Still no questions about what's going on?"

"Nope," Blythe said.

"None," he repeated.

"You know what? I'm glad we didn't work out." Monna put her nose in the air. "You're the absolute worst." She opened a door to the very conference room he'd explored during his search of the palace. "In here."

He flashed in front of Blythe, entering first. The remaining members of the welcome party sat at the table, each glaring at him. A refreshing change from the usual leers and catcalls. No sign of the wraith.

Spine ramrod straight, the siren sat. The lone open chair waited at the end of the table. Had they purposely removed the other chairs? Last time, there'd been twenty females seated in here.

"Pop a squat," one of the Amazons commanded.

"Thanks. Don't mind if I do." Head high, Blythe sauntered around him to claim his chair. She acted like a queen before peasants, aware of her superiority and unafraid to show it.

To his bafflement, he almost smiled as he took a post behind her. With harpies, sass was never far from the fore, and Blythe the Undoing wielded more than most.

Saying nothing, he crossed his arms over his chest and scanned their disapproving audience. One minute passed. Two. Three. The first one to break the silence would prove themselves to be the weakest in the room. Patience required strength.

The vampire flashed sharp, white fangs at him. "It's been brought to our attention that you somehow broke your vow to us."

"I broke nothing," he replied easily. Had Penelope witnessed his time with Blythe and informed the others? Was this her big play?

"Is that so?" The dark-haired Amazon banged her fist on the tabletop. "How about the fact that you left the palace grounds without being on an official date?"

"I'm able to flash. I was no more than a split second away the entire time I was gone." Something he'd carefully considered before whisking Blythe to the lake. "Again, I broke nothing. Also, the rules stipulated I had to date each member of my welcome party. Technically, Blythe Skyhawk is part of my welcome party. She stood among your midst."

"Therefore, in light of your egregious transgression," the Amazon continued, "we've decided you owe each of us— Oh. I see." Frowning, she scanned the others, as if unsure how to respond. "Is he pardoned? He's pardoned, isn't he?"

Murmurs of disappointment arose, but one by one, reluctant nods came.

"Tricky, tricky Astra," someone muttered.

As if these females were any better. They intended to betray him at the first opportunity.

"Now that that's settled, I'm guessing the meeting is over," Blythe said, reclining and kicking up her legs. "The big guy is starved. Someone make him a sammich. Extra pickles."

The women ignored her, no one even sparing her a glance.

The taller of the Amazons offered him a tight smile. "Minus the wraiths, roughly ninety-five percent of the realm has signed on to participate in the tournament."

Exactly as hoped. Even those who had no interest in sex or sperm sought a way home.

"This assembly is concluded." The tall Amazon banged a gavel.

The council members stood, their customary leers returning. Some winked at him. Others blew him a kiss. The manticore made a crude hand gesture.

He showcased no reaction. But Blythe...might have. Had she stiffened, as if she were upset by the attention he received from the others? Surely not. Wishful thinking on his part, nothing more.

"What about that sandwich?" he asked on her behalf.

"Food-wise, you're on your own today," a gorgon said as everyone else filed out the door. "We're busy preparing for the festivities. Unless you're hungry for gorgon? Because I'm already hot and ready to be served. No?"

He didn't deign to respond.

"Tomorrow," the Amazon piped up, pausing in the doorway to glance at him, "someone will collect you at sunrise and escort you to the opening ceremony."

Opening ceremony. The moment his truce with Blythe ended.

He nodded. "I'll be ready."

15

THE SURPRISE

"Come." Roux extended his hand to Blythe as soon as they were alone in the conference room. "I will feed you."

She reciprocated, linking their fingers without thought. Thought came after. Dang him! His new-found charm had to stop. Roux, with his tragic past, sexy-rough features, and desperate passions was nothing to her. Less than nothing. That hadn't changed and wouldn't. Ever. But she didn't let him go. Not yet.

"Where are we going?" she grumbled.

"A village we passed when I carried you to the palace."

He transported her to a clearing with ancient fae-type beings scattered about. Eleven of them, to be exact. They ranged from the palest white to the most flawless black, with hair in every shade imaginable. All wore dresses made of leaves and flower petals. They flittered about, either gardening or cooking.

The scent of roasting vegetables coated a cool breeze, and her mouth watered.

"Not the sandwich you requested, but food," Roux said, sounding proud of himself.

Ugh. Why was even *that* charming?

Noticing the enormous male in their midst, a fae shrieked. "He's back!"

The others shrieked as well, practically stampeding each other to race off. Dude. "They are not your biggest fans."

"No. They are the first of the fae-nymphs," Roux explained, resignation replacing his pride. "Mars filled his harem with them. By force. To escape him for good, they came here."

Her chest clenched. Roux had been a victim of the god too, yet he garnered the same reaction as his perpetrator. Perhaps another reason he'd always despised being touched. *He'd never known if someone reacted to him or his father.*

The clenching worsened as the Astra led her forward. They'd never let go of the other's hand, she realized with a start.

He stopped near a pot of simmering soup, clasped her by the waist, and hefted her onto a waist-high tree stump, putting them face-to-face. Their gazes caught for a moment. His attention dropped to her mouth before he got busy filling two clay bowls with the rich, creamy potage. One for her, one for him.

"Thank you," she said softly. Trying to tune him out and gain control of her emotions, she dug in with a small wooden spoon. Mmm. Tasty. "Four and a half stars. Will eat here again."

"If nothing else, I can satisfy *this* hunger," he muttered.

Seriously! Did he have to be so charming? "You know, I can so snag an organ from you right this second, yes? Probably two. Or more. Let me enjoy my meal in peace." And maybe sneak a conversation with one of the fae-nymphs and get a message to Penelope. *The enemy of my enemy is my friend.*

"Lyla, you may take any organ at any time." The heat in his eyes said what he didn't. *I've never forgotten. It's foreplay.*

She squirmed atop her stump. They finished the soup in charged silence.

"More?" he asked. "Dessert?"

"No thanks." Now probably wasn't the best time to indulge in a vice.

He placed their dishes in a basket partially filled with dirty utensils, then turned to help her down. As if she wasn't a harpy in her prime, well able to hop off a perch, she waited to accept his assistance.

He clasped her waist, lifted her, and slid her down his body. Slowly. Tendrils of pleasure uncoiled. Her feet reached the ground, but she didn't remove her hands from his shoulders. For balance. She breathed in the intoxicating aroma of cedarwood and spiced oranges, her head fogging.

Maybe she could indulge this vice instead?

"Is there something you'd like to do to me, Lyla?"

The low, rough quality of his voice caressed her ears, and she shivered. "I've already touched you today," she stated, panting a little.

"I believe I've mentioned I'm good with doubling up." His gaze dropped to her mouth again. "I have no limits with you."

No limits. Because she was special. She melted into him, even as she chided him. "This has to stop."

"This? What is *this*?" He cupped her backside, massaging sore muscles. "I'm merely standing here. Breathing."

No, he was tempting and smoldering and seducing. How could he affect her so strongly? How had her consort's hold on her body lessened to such a degree, allowing it to happen? Had the father of her child been nothing more than a passing fancy? Why hadn't she had any more hallucinations of him? That manticore had been the love of her life. Her addiction. Now he was relegated to be little more than a memory she took out of a box and played with occasionally...when she wasn't playing with the Astra.

Shame and guilt stabbed her. How could she want Roux at all? If she were being honest, he didn't look anything like Laban, so she couldn't trick herself into blaming a resemblance between the two. Not anymore.

"You know exactly what *this* is."

"Tell me." A heated demand as he deepened his massage. "Let's make sure we understand each other."

Oh, they understood each other all right. More than she liked. "I mean it. D-don't do this," she said, ashamed of her desperation. A weakness only he inspired. If he kissed her, she would kiss him back.

Could she live with herself?

"I will not *do this*, as you call it." He released her and eased back. Promise glittered in his eyes. "Yet."

* * *

The first rays of sunlight streamed through the bedroom windows. Blythe lay on the bed, where she'd tossed and turned all night, as usual. Roux wasn't in his chair by the hearth, staring at her, at least. He'd shut himself inside the bathroom ages ago, leaving her alone with his parting word.

Yet. The worst of all the words! Now anticipation crackled in her cells.

What was he doing in that bathroom, anyway? Going on a date with Palmela Handerson? Yeah. That had to be it. Blythe had turned him on, and now he hoped to turn himself off.

Good! Maybe he would emerge with his smolder dialed down, and she'd be able to think clearly again.

Right on cue, he stepped from the enclosure wearing a black T-shirt, leather pants, and eight layers of tension. Well. The date must not have gone well. The smolder endured at full capacity.

Why she wanted to smile, she didn't know.

He strode her way, a brave prisoner on his way to execution. "Get up." He stopped out of range. "The tournament is soon to begin."

Right. The tournament. The urge to smile faded. Their truce was over. From now on, there'd be no more forced physical contact. No more straddling her enemy or sharing an almost kiss. And that was good. The time had come to choose a warpath. Become queen, putting their battle on a forced timeline? Or let him win his task, and take care of business afterward? In other words, strike now or later?

Which one, which one? Both came with pros, and both came with cons.

No wonder she hadn't pulled a decision trigger yet. Get this right, and she would win big. Get it wrong, and she would lose everything. Nerves already frayed, Blythe climbed from bed. "Guess we're back to being enemies."

"We were always enemies, harpy."

True. "You acted like a besotted suitor yesterday," she quipped, stretching.

"Yesterday, I didn't have to chain you. Today I do."

And...what? He resented the need? She strutted to the wardrobe, almost glancing his way. But bad things happened when their eyes met. Or when they stood next to each other. Or when they touched. Terrible, wonderful, awful, amazing things.

Now or later?

Blythe cast a glance to the crown. To wear or not to wear? The crystals glistened in the sunlight, summoning her closer for a better look. The next thing she knew, she was kneeling in front of it, holding it. Heavier than she'd expected. Colder, too. Not that she minded.

Pinpricks of light didn't just glisten within the crystals; they swirled. So lovely. She *must* try the piece on. There was no reason not to. Become queen...yes! This was her destiny. Meant to be.

Blythe lifted the gorgeous coronet—

"What are you doing?" Roux swiped the headdress from her clasp.

"Hey!" She shot to her feet, reaching, but the crystals vanished into thin air. "Give that back!"

He clamped onto her wrist, snarling, "I will not."

Will murder him right here, right now! Her nails elongated, the tips sharpening. She tensed to strike.

"Final chance to heed my warning, before I make a new crown from your entrails."

"Go ahead." He lifted his chin. "Try."

She wouldn't try, she'd do! Except, just as soon as she met Roux's gaze, the spinning, jewel-toned striations in his irises wiped her mind of all thought. That blip of blankness cleared the way for a mortifying realization. She'd fallen victim to the crown's spell. *Again.*

The Astra had just prevented her from choosing a war path before actually choosing a war path. Although, the answer struck her as obvious now. Avoid the crown and postpone her vengeance.

Yes, that felt right. It bought her more time. Time to win the firstone dagger from Penelope. To plot and scheme at home, away from the Astra and his sense-highjacking intensity.

"Sorry," she muttered, deflating. Deep breath in. Out. Uh…had she just *apologized* to the Astra? Roux should infuriate her, not calm her. That was a consort's job.

Hello, guilt. Hello, shame. *Hate myself.*

Weakness washed over her limbs. *Hate the wraith.*

Her knees wobbled. "I meant, you're welcome." She put her emotions on lockdown and shimmied free of his grip. "Now we know the crown gets more powerful with every punch."

"There have been other punches?" He scowled, his eyes flittering with red. "Why didn't you tell me?"

Was he serious? "Like there aren't a million obvious reasons, Rue. Though, really, only one of those reasons matters." She selected today's attire, another uniform. A well-made leather vest and pleated skirt

with her combat boots. Perfect. "I didn't tell you because I didn't want to."

He opened and closed his mouth. "Do not push me,
Blythe." With a huff of frustration, he stabbed his fingers through his hair. Muscles flexed. In his arms, *alevala* switched places. He froze. "Unless you *want* to
push me further and see what happens."

Roux stepped forward, putting his body less than an
inch from hers. Challenging her. And yes, highjacking
her good sense.

"Do you, Lyla? Are you ready for *this*?"

Yes. No. Maybe? Her heart skipped a beat. "I think
you've forgotten the threat of chains. But I haven't. As
soon as you come at me with those shackles, the fight
is on." A fight the ruby guaranteed she'd lose.

"I expect no less."

Would he truly keep her bound in front of so many
foes?

Daring him to complain, she very obviously pilfered
two of his daggers from the desk and stomped toward
the bathroom.

"What if we agree to a second truce?" he asked, his
tone flat.

Hmm. Blythe halted in the doorway and executed
a slow turn. He wore his blank mask, but oh, his body
language told a different story. He feared her response.

"Go on. I'm listening." What price would she pay
to maintain her freedom? But more importantly, what
price would *he* pay?

"I won't put shackles on you today, and you won't
attempt to kill me or escape. We'll use the reprieve to
catalogue our surroundings and learn what we can about
the threats against us."

It wasn't a bad idea, actually. But like she'd really make this easy on him. Not after their last negotiation.

She hit him with a smug grin. "I'm waiting to hear what *I* get from this bargain."

His lids slitted. "I think you know what you get."

"Tell me, anyway." How much power would he cede to her?

"You get...whatever you want."

Her eyes widened. Tremors swept through her limbs. Whatever she wanted? As in *anything*? For the Astra to make such an open-ended offer, it could mean only one thing. He would cede *much* power.

Did Roux have...feelings for her?

"Deal," she said, an embarrassing wobble in her voice. "I'll let you know when I decide."

"I'm Tonka, by the way."

Blythe eyed the day's escort. A fellow harpy who hadn't sided with her on the day of Roux's arrival. The female led the way with Blythe behind her, and Roux trailing Blythe. She had no doubt the Astra tracked her every move. The heat of his gaze bored into her back, keeping her blood white-hot.

"Oh, so you're deigning to talk to the *it* now?" she asked the harpy with forced breeziness.

"What can I say?" The blonde was as happy and chirpy as could be, as if her dreams were coming true right before her eyes. Grinning, she spread her arms wide. "This is an amazing day."

"Is it? Do tell."

"Kerry—you might know her as the manticore—has decided to fight on behalf of the entire royal council," the harpy said. "We are united, making us one, after all. She is our representative."

They thought they were doing something big with this move? That they'd cover all their bases in the effort to "trap" Roux, letting one woman risk her life while the others plotted from the sidelines? No need to ask why they'd chosen Kerry over everyone else. If her abilities were anything like Laban's, she could rip out throats with her teeth and paralyze her opponents with a toxin that leaked from her claws.

"Not gonna protest?" Tonka asked. "I don't know if you noticed, but she's not like other females of her kind. She mean."

"Why bother protesting?" Every member of the welcome party was a dead woman walking whether they entered the tournament or not.

On the second story of the palace, they descended another flight of steps.

"What'd you do to be banished to this realm, anyway?" Blythe asked, changing the subject.

Bitterness contorted Tonka's features. "The year of General Nissa's coronation, I discovered her in bed with a lover. Rather than murder me to keep her secret, she sent me here."

Ouch. In those days, the virgin rule had been strictly enforced. Had anyone learned General Nissa liked to entertain gentleman callers *regularly*, she would have lost her seat of authority.

Finally, their threesome hit the first level of the silo. In the center of the rounded foyer was a stone wishing well. Or what looked to be a wishing well. It seemed to grow from the floor itself.

Tonka climbed onto the ledge and saluted Blythe and

Roux. "See ya down below." That said, she stepped off and whooshed through the opening, disappearing into the darkness.

Roux grabbed Blythe's arm before she could follow suit. "We go together, she-beast."

She should protest. But she didn't. She nodded, letting him wind his strong arms around her and gather her close. His heat and scent enveloped her, a dangerous combination, and she sort of sagged against him. Not intentionally. It happened without thought. Beneath her cheek, his heart raced.

"Hurry," she rasped. She needed this to end, like, now, before she did something worse than burrow closer.

He slid his hands to her backside and squeezed, reminding her of the last time they'd stood like this. How close they'd come to crossing a line they'd never be able to uncross. "I could hold you here until release becomes your price for our bargain."

Ahhh. Diabolical Astra. This had been his plan all along. "A game of sexual chicken?" she asked, sliding her palms up his chest. "While the fight rages to become the center of your blessing task, no less."

He petted her hair. A simple action, but her eyes shut, a feeling of homecoming washing over her. Almost better than— No. No, no, no. Her eyelids popped open. Game over. Roux won.

"I'll pay your toll," she stated, dropping her arms to her sides. Cold invaded her veins. "Consider us even."

He frowned, evincing confusion, but gave a little nod. "Very well." He took her hand, flashed her to the ledge of the well, and stepped into the black hole in the center. Down they fell, whisking through shadows like bricks tossed into water.

Her heart jumped into her throat.

The second they passed a layer of blue light, they slowed, floating to a stop on a foundation of compacted dirt and smooth rocks.

Blythe immediately extracted her fingers from the Astra's. From his strength and heat. His scent. The unexpected comfort of him.

A gaggle of voices offered a distraction, drawing her gaze. Oh, wow. Okay. Underground fight club indeed. She stood in a massive torch-lit cave that was both tall and wide. Taller and wider than many mortal buildings. The dazzling crystal ceiling—the same crystals as the crown—couldn't be reached if a dozen ladders were stacked on top of each other.

Up ahead was what looked to be a Roman coliseum of old, ringed by stone bleachers. A canopied dais topped the north section—a dais she, Roux, and Tonka climbed countless steps to reach. The other councilmembers were already there and seated. Minus the manticore, of course. And surprise, surprise, there were only two open seats. One meant for Tonka the harpy, the other meant for Roux. Message received. Blythe was unwanted.

Only a handful of spectators sat in the bleachers but countless others waited on the sand below, armed and clearly eager for the first battle to commence.

"Amazing, isn't it?" Tonka asked, motioning to the cavern. "The original captives of Ation still talk about the dragons who torched the realm's surface, causing widespread destruction. While the fire-breathers hibernated within the walls of this underground labyrinth, our strongest soldiers dug down to hunt them. Once the creatures were eradicated, the settlers turned the area into the fight zone."

Forget the chairs. Blythe moved to the edge of the dais. There was no rail to perch upon, only a long drop to splat.

Roux sidled up to her side, and she halfway expected him to wind an arm around her waist to ensure she stayed put. When he didn't…yeah, disappointment set in. Which disappointed her! Her hatred might have gotten buried, but it hadn't faded. The seeds still grew in the rich soil of her heart.

Get it together, girl.

Tonka joined them at the ledge and shouted down at the masses, "Who's ready to make her dreams come true?"

Deafening cheers rang out. As they died down, the harpy proclaimed, "Imma count down to ten. Anyone in the ring when I finish is officially entered in the tournament. There will be no backtracking afterward. The only way out is death or victory. Now is the time to change your mind and hustle into the stands."

More cheers. Then, the countdown began. "Ten. Nine. Eight. Seven. Six."

Between the "seven" and "six," a swift click-clack of footsteps caught Blythe's attention. In unison, she and Roux stiffened and spun. Too late. A large beast—Penelope's beast, Amal—was already airborne and mere inches away.

It slammed into Blythe, ramming her belly with its snout. As she hurled over the ledge, pinpricks of warmth registered at the collision site. The warmth quickly mutated into streams of fire that poured through her veins.

Down she tumbled, unable to flail. Unable to move, period. Her muscles had petrified. Courtesy of Amal's toxin?

"Five. Four."

Roux must have calculated the trajectory of her fall, as well as her landing, because he flashed to the bleachers, extending his reach to catch her. If not for a horde of wraiths who materialized above him, each projecting Blythe's image, causing him to shift his stance.

"Three. Two."

Blythe landed in the sand. Impact bruised her brain, stole her breath, and broke several of her bones. She twitched for a millisecond, shedding the toxin, then lumbered to her feet.

"One."

New cheers sounded all around her. She lifted her gaze to Roux's.

Eyes of bloodred narrowed to slits. Because he knew what she did: the wraith had proven more diabolical than expected.

"No one can harm the harphantom!" At his sides, his hands fisted again and again. "That was our deal, and our deal still stands."

"He's right," Tonka announced to one and all, so smug it grated on Blythe's every nerve. "Our deal still stands. His female is a combatant, plain and simple. As he agreed, he cannot interfere with the outcome of the tournament in any way, shape, or form. In the ring, you may do whatever you wish to the phantom."

Yeah. Exactly what Blythe had figured.

She rolled back her shoulders, denying the urge to rub the ruby entrenched so firmly at the base of her throat. No doubt the wraith planned to drain her the second the battle began.

"Today is a free-for-all," the harpy continued, again speaking to the masses. "When the horn blows, you'll have ten minutes to take out as many of your competitors as possible."

Every other combatant focused on Blythe, target number one.

Determination stiffened her spine and aggression filled her wings. "Bring it," she snapped. Somehow, some way, she would survive this. Then oversee her vengeance as planned.

No other option was acceptable.

16

THE PROBLEM

The horn blasted, echoing from the cavern's rocky walls. Roux reeled. Blythe had been drafted into the battle. She must fight to the death to become Ation's queen. As soon as she wore that cursed crown, Roux must kill her.

Horror deluged him.

The battle whipped into a swift frenzy, and there was no way to stop it. A ten-minute countdown had commenced.

As hundreds of immortals converged on each other, a good percentage of them aimed their menace at a stalwart Blythe. He returned to the dais. At the edge of the dais, he drove his claws into a stone pillar. *Will not flash down there. But I want to. But I won't.*

The harphantom disappeared in the masses. Dead

bodies piled around her. Strain coiled through Roux. The escaped prisoner screamed in his head. Easy to ignore. He didn't care who the escapee was or why the being reacted to Blythe and only Blythe. Roux cared only about the harpy's survival and well-being. *Will not flash.*

"I told you this would happen, Astra, and I never, ever lie." The recognizable feminine voice sent a tide of fury crashing down his spine. Penelope the wraith appeared at his side. "Well, except for the times I do, in fact, lie. But only then, I promise."

"You did this to her," he snarled, never turning from the fray.

"Oh, I did indeed. Quite well, actually." How smug the wraith sounded. "Thank you for noticing."

Nine minutes, five seconds remained. Swords swung. Whips lashed. Spears flew—along with body parts. Streams of scarlet sprayed and flowed. Grunts, groans, and curses filled the death-scented air. The injured and the dead toppled in every direction.

Roux leaned forward, attempting to get a closer look. *Come on, come on.* How was Blythe? If she were harmed...

The screaming grew louder.

"Why so glum?" Penelope simmered, as if she felt sorry for him. "I did warn you that I would strike, and you all but demanded I do my worst."

Where was Blythe?

The wraith floated in front of him, blocking his view. "If you haven't guessed, I'm draining your female this very second. Who knows how long she'll last out there? Oh, that's right. I do. I know. The answer is not much longer."

How he wished to choke the life from this spectral being. How he wished to think! But the screams. Images of Blythe being bombarded with injuries assailed him. In these flashes, he saw open wounds. Missing limbs. Hemorrhaging organs.

Not knowing what else to do, he focused on Penelope and gritted out, "You want your meals. Very well. I'll provide them. Now cease draining her."

With a satisfied grin, she returned to his side. "Question. How can you provide me with two hundred meals when nearly everyone in this realm is scheduled to die within the next ten days?"

Eight minutes. "Before, you expected only one hundred meals." Was that a head of sleek black hair he spied, rising from beneath two of the fallen? Yes! Though unsteady, Blythe made it to her feet with someone else's daggers in hand.

"The price is double for my trouble, darling. You know how it goes. Inflation, and all that."

Roux winced as a gorgon plowed into Blythe. The gorgon's hair-snakes sank their fangs into the harphantom's face. Despite her weakness, she managed to work a dagger between their bodies and gut her opponent. But her wobbling worsened when she climbed to her feet. Compliments of an opponent's venom?

Blood dripped from the punctures in her brow, blinding her. She swung her weapons at everything and nothing. A vampire sensed easy prey and swooped in with fangs bared. Roux opened his mouth without thought, intending to shout a warning. His oath erased his voice, keeping him quiet. There would be no interfering with the tournament.

His claws sank deeper into the pillar. Just before

the bloodsucker reached her target, a banshee cut her down with a sword. Relief crested—and crashed. At least eighteen others switched their focus to the pale, trembling harphantom.

How much longer *could* Blythe succeed in this condition?

With no other recourse, Roux bit out, "I will feed you in Blythe's place." A thought that left him shuddering. Without the use of jewels, wraiths fed like phantoms. Lips to skin. A method he usually avoided by fair means or foul. But Roux wanted Blythe healthy, whole, and able to steal as many of his organs as she wished. Faced with the possibility of losing her, he could do nothing but trade his pride for the truth. Feeding this wraith was the only way to keep the harpy safe.

"I'm intrigued by the offer, but I'm not yet sold." Penelope fluffed her mass of red hair. "I seek the meals to feed my subjects, you see. And I know what you're thinking. I'm such a benevolent queen."

A manticore—the original manticore—plowed into Blythe. The two hit the ground and rolled over the sand. Behind him, the royal court clapped and cheered. Razor sharp claws raked across the harphantom's throat, and she jerked, blood pouring from the wounds. When she froze, Roux tensed. Was the manticore's venom working through her system?

Seven minutes remained in the heat, but less than a second remained in her current battle. She must revive in time. She must!

As the manticore tensed, preparing to render another strike—this one delivered by her lengthening teeth— time seemed to slow. He rushed out, "I'll consider feeding your wraiths as well, but you must allow Blythe to regain her strength while I'm contemplating it."

"I'll give you both one minute. No more. But probably less."

"Do it!" he commanded, time returning to normal.

The manticore was in the process of whooshing down, intending to bite—the harphantom jolted with new life. With one hand, she reached up and caught her opponent by the throat. With the other hand, she punched. Her attacker staggered, her jaw broken.

Look at the Undoing go.

A warrior without equal, Blythe glided to her feet. Color returned to her cheeks. All grace and brutality, she repeatedly kicked her rival in the face. Savage stomps meant to cause as much damage as possible. Before the manticore could recover, the harphantom stepped inside her, vanishing. Seconds later, the manticore was using her own claws to rip out her own throat. Blythe had taken control of the body.

Only then did he breathe a sigh of renewed relief. Pride squared his shoulders. *That's my female.*

No, no. Not mine. Not outside of their private quarters, where they seemed to be the only two people alive.

Unless she *was* his?

He hadn't produced stardust for her but…maybe. If she belonged to him, he might belong to her, too. Though he'd never heard of a harpy receiving two consorts, stranger things had happened. Surely.

If he belonged to her, she would have to forgive him. They would talk more. Tease and play. Touch. Kiss. So badly he yearned to kiss her. To do all the things he contemplated every night while she tossed about in bed.

I will make her scream my name.

"Thirty-nine. Thirty-eight. Thirty-seven," Penelope counted, reminding him of their ongoing negotiation.

Concentrate! "How many wraiths serve you?" he asked as another combatant swooped in to finish off the manticore.

The royal court twittered with disappointment.

"Oh, only twenty-two."

Only.

"Like me," she continued with the most annoying calm, "they dine exclusively on hatred. That's why we were sent here. Too many immortals hold grudges. We weakened them, so they found a way to dispose of us. But I digress. I sense you hold enough hatred to feed my lot of wraiths for *years* to come."

She sensed correctly. "During the tournament, I will feed you and your wraiths. But only once a day. And I will not wear a jewel." As much as he would detest having their mouths on his skin, he preferred temporary contact to a permanent connection. "In return, you cannot drain Blythe during heats. Or at all."

"I'm considering thinking about it… No deal. I can't help it if she opens the link herself. There are moments I *will* feed on her, despite the timing."

He nodded stiffly. "I agree. Do you?"

"No, not yet. I want to know why you're doing this. The harpy still hates you. Otherwise, I couldn't drain her at all. Besides that, you're required to kill her if she wins the tournament."

Yes. The very reasons he required time to think this through. "I owe you no explanation for my actions."

"Fair enough. But what happens if your female dies without my interference?"

Feeling like an injured animal backed into a corner, he grated, "Our bargain will stand. Do. You. Agree?"

"Yes. I accept the terms, Astra. For the next ten days, you'll flash to the island at sundown. No exceptions. If you fail to appear, even once, I'll drain Blythe the Undoing to death before the next battle commences."

Fresh energy poured through Blythe, her wings flapping with new life. Not as much energy and life as when she was fully charged on souls, but enough to get her through the death match.

Why had Penelope ceased feeding? Because her point had been made? *Figure it out later.* Blythe popped the bones in her neck and her shoulders, then cracked her knuckles. *Let's finish this.*

She raced into the worst of the fray. Dodging blows, clawing when appropriate, claiming a plethora of fallen weapons as necessary. At some point, the internal tempest she'd experienced since her consort's death faded. Old battle instincts overtook her, and oh, it felt good. Fighting as she was born to do. Taking down one enemy after another.

Sand flung from her boots, grains sticking to damp skin. Warm blood coated her hands. Tissue collected under her nails. Did a certain Astra watch her with his customary smolder? Or did he worry, as Laban would have done?

Anger accompanied her next strike, sending a witch to the ground, minus her intestines. Comparing Roux to her consort needed to stop. So did relaxing in his presence and seeking his embrace.

Two more combatants fell by her powerful strikes. Approaching her next target, she scanned the arena.

Wow. The masses had thinned by almost half. Only six hundred or so remained. How much time was left on the clock? She'd lost track.

Eager to take out more competition, she picked up the pace and two short swords. One. Three. Five. Eight others went down. Man, she kind of adored the swords. Lightweight, with scalelike blades over the metal. Organs shredded at record-breaking speed. Maybe she'd keep the pair after the hostility ended.

She didn't mean to do it, but she shot a glance up—and nearly ground to a halt as shock stole her breath. Roux didn't watch her with worry. Not even a trace of it. Rather, it was pride that radiated from his muscular frame.

But that couldn't be right. She—Blythe wheeled to the side as an Amazon caught her unaware, slicing the tip of a sword through her biceps. *Deserved.* Allow yourself to become distracted during a scuffle, and you welcomed injury and loss.

She rallied quickly, misting as the Amazon swung a dagger. Blythe solidified behind her attacker and used her short swords like scissors. Chop. Headless Amazon.

Sensing an approach from the rear, she misted again. The siren who'd come for her tripped over the falling Amazon. While the two went down, Blythe hacked off the newcomer's head.

Each new victory put a spring in her step. With her next set of victims, she spared a second or two to take a bite of their souls before rendering the final blow. Those small nibbles added up, charging her up. Blythe began to cut through her opponents as effortlessly as butter.

Just as she raised her swords to take out a harpy—no mercy, even for her kinswomen—the horn echoed from the cavern walls. The combatants went still. Silence reigned. Well, as much silence as possible when so many people huffed and puffed from exertion.

Blythe scanned the competition, on the hunt for true threats. Her, her, and her. Respectively, a harpy she recognized as a legend of old, the Phoenix Roux had mentioned, and a former Amazon queen, judging by the marks branded into her flesh. All three glared her way.

"Congratulations," Tonka called from the dais. Funny, but she didn't exude as much joy as before. "If you're still alive, you made it to round two. Which starts bright and early tomorrow morning. Tonight, you're invited to a celebration party. Attend at your own risk. In the next round, things aren't gonna be so easy."

17

THE WRENCH

Roux paced inside the bedroom, waiting for Blythe to emerge from the bathroom. He did not wish to attend the celebration. He would rather spend the rest of the day locked away with her. They had much to discuss. His appointment with the wraiths. His duty. Tomorrow's battle. What had happened at the well during their game of "sexual chicken."

He bit his tongue to silence a grunt. When would she exit?

Lively music started up outside the window and cheers followed. The party was to take place right outside the palace?

Irritated, he flashed over to look out. Despite a dark, stormy sky, hundreds of females congregated below.

Throughout the circle of silos, blazing bonfires popped and snapped, roasting meats and vegetables.

Cries of "Bring out Mr. Sausage Man!" rose over the music.

He worked his jaw. When the bathroom door swung open behind him, he forgot everything but Blythe. Roux's gaze whipped to her. An automatic reaction. If ever she stood nearby, she held his attention captive. And no wonder. The sight of this woman.

His heart punched his ribs. Without the wraith draining her, she exhibited pure vitality. Long black hair hung loose, gleaming. Her baby blues sparkled, and her cheeks glowed. The ruby glittered. She wore a clean vest that pushed her breasts together with a single button and a short skirt. Multiple daggers were strapped to her thighs—visible through slits each time she took a step.

"I guess we need to have a conversation now," she said, looking anywhere but at Roux.

"I'm not ready to talk." The words slipped from him unbidden, barely more than a growl and far different from what he'd meant to say. He wanted his mouth on hers. Consequences be damned.

"Well, what you are ready to do, you don't get to do. Not with me, anyway." Chin up, she sauntered over to shoulder him aside and peer outside. "Pick someone from your wannabe harem."

Her inner armor was strapped on tight tonight. Perhaps he could strip her of it. How he loved when she softened. In those moments, she couldn't hide her desire from him.

A desire she once claimed stemmed from thoughts of Laban. But what if it didn't?

Roux positioned himself behind her and leaned forward, flattening his hands on the window's frame. His body all but caged her in, and he loved it. "You sound jealous." Was she?

She humphed and slowly pivoted to face him. "Warden, I've never been jealous a day in my life. But if it ever happens, you'll be the first to know. Because my dagger will be buried hilt deep in your ball sack."

He inserted his knee between her legs. They stared at each other, searching, searching. Soon panting. His cells became kindling, sparks erupting inside him. "Are you saying you wouldn't care if I spent the night with someone else?" he asked with a silky tone. "Perhaps even multiple someones?"

"Care?" She snorted. "I welcome such an occurrence. In fact, I'm happy to pick another for you. Yeah, I'm liking this idea. We're going to attend the party, you and I, and find ourselves a couple of bang buddies. You choose mine, I choose yours, and the madness between us will end."

Sharp possessiveness sliced him, nearly unleashing a roar of denial that struggled against a fraying tether. He snapped his teeth at her, then nodded. "Very well." If she wished to go this route, they would go this route. How far would she push it? "Pick a companion for me. Perhaps I'll make proper use of this one."

As she sputtered for a response, Roux wrapped his arms around her and flashed to the land below. The crowd had already doubled in size, clusters of women as far as the eye could see. Many were already drunk and dancing around a bonfire.

A storm continued to brew overhead, the wind growing noticeably colder. A thousand different scents clashed. Roux burrowed his nose in Blythe's hair, breathing in the delectable fragrance of honeysuckle and rose. Mmm. Nothing better.

"We should get started," she rasped, clutching his biceps.

"Yes." Let her go? He didn't think he could. "We should."

She didn't back away. His ribs squeezed tight. Whatever happened between them in the coming days, she must win the tournament. He could then escort her to Harpina and lock her up while he researched ways to cut out a phantom's heart with trinite without cutting out a phantom's heart with trinite. Maybe he would visit Nova, his home world. There, he could traverse the Hall of Secrets. A terrible, wonderful place where secrets had collected over the ages, each whispering from the walls. Surely someone somewhere had faced a similar dilemma and found the perfect solution.

There was a way to do this and ensure Blythe lived. There must be a way. What if he could claim her metaphorical heart instead of the literal one?

Of course, hadn't he already cut out her figurative heart when he'd murdered her consort?

"Couple of ground rules," she said, as he wrestled to remember their current topic of conversation. Even the crowd faded to the background. "When you're selecting my evening lady caller, try to remember I prefer those who haven't invaded Harpina."

Roux flinched at the harsh admonition, but he still couldn't bring himself to let her go. Despite the barb, she hadn't stiffened in his arms. She seemed almost… absorbed by him.

"Noted." His gaze dipped to her lips. Lush, soft, and cherry red. He swallowed. "What else?"

"I like the usual things, I guess." She batted her lashes at him. "Sexy and strong with a sense of humor and a total obsession with me."

Was this how she was when happy? Vibrant and full of life? Eager to tease and flirt? To tempt and lure?

"Lyla," he rasped, and there was no stopping the movement of his hands. He dragged his fingers up and down her sides. Anytime he grazed a patch of bare skin, new goose bumps erupted across her limbs.

"Yes, Rue?" She grinned, then frowned. The grin reappeared a second later...only to fall again. Then it snapped back and lingered.

Warring inside herself, unsure what to welcome or fight with him? He knew the feeling! "I like sexy and strong as well. If she doesn't rip out my organs, even better. Just in case you were wondering."

Her frown reappeared and stayed put. She said, "Good to know. But do you think you can keep the sausage factory closed to the public for an hour? I'd like to reacquaint myself with the ladies free of your interference. To better select your perfect match, of course."

In other words, she planned to check out the competition, plot against Roux, or trash-talk. Or any combination of the three. He heaved a heavy sigh. Forcing her to remain at his side wasn't something he wanted to do. With this harphantom, free will mattered.

"Go," he said, sliding his hands down to enjoy a final squeeze of her backside. "The sausage factory closed for maintenance as soon as you issued your threat."

The smile returned, and he almost regretted his sudden bout of morals. "The Warden has jokes. How unexpected."

"The Warden does not have jokes." Not usually.

214   GENA SHOWALTER

"Dang you. How is even your denial cute?"

Cute? "Do us both a favor and pick yourself for me, she-beast." There was no stopping the words. "I will do bad things to get your hands on me again." *Or my hands on you.*

"I—you—oh!" Frowning again, she pulled from his embrace one step at a time. A slow retreat, yet a retreat all the same. But even as she walked backward, putting more and more distance between them, she held his gaze. "I'd probably be doing the other women a favor if I did. You're terrible at first, second, and third impressions."

"The worst," he agreed.

She ran her bottom lip between her teeth. "But I have a sinking suspicion you're going to be amazing in bed."

"The best." He would not stop until she collapsed, utterly satisfied.

Black flickered in her eyes, there and gone, leaving soft baby blues. "I think I'll hate you more if I pick myself for you. But I still might do it." With that, she spun and bounded off.

A shout welled in the back of his throat. Muscles hardened, his leathers threatening to burst. He opened and closed his fists, considering flashing directly behind her, gathering her close, and returning her to their room.

The ease with which this female elicited a physical reaction frightened him. "Don't drink anything," he called. "People are already intoxicated. The brew is potent."

"Ahhh. Is Grandpappy Rue worried about me?" she called back. "Don't be. This isn't my first rodeo, cowboy."

The grace of her movements, even as she pushed and elbowed her way through the crowds, drew a moan from deep in his chest. But all too soon, he lost sight of her.

Roux curbed the urge to give chase, planting his feet in the grass and remaining at the edge of the congestion. If anyone attempted to harm her, she would take them out without problem. In that regard, he had no worries. The way she'd fought today had more than proven her capabilities. She wielded the kind of bravery and cunning too many forsook. Any warrior worth his wage would be overjoyed to fight at her side.

A group of leering, giggling shifters approached him, their drinks sloshing over the rims of their clay mugs. Roux set an internal countdown in his mind, concealed himself with shadows, and strode off. He would not miss his visit to Wraith Island.

He skirted the party's perimeter, listening to gossip, searching, scanning. Catching sight of Blythe again, he automatically altered his path to draw closer. She stood with a harpy. A beauty with light hair—a skilled warrior he'd noticed on the battlefield. A true competitor who'd cut through her opponents as if they were nothing but sheets of paper.

The pair engaged in a serious conversation. Serious, but not heated. Meaning, no trash talk. Did they know each other? What did they discuss?

Blythe reached up to hook a lock of silken hair behind her ear, the motion pure elegance. He would never tire of watching her.

The two females shook hands. Agreeing to some kind of deal?

Why not secretly listen to the rest of the discussion?

Guilt sparked, but he ignored it. For the success of

his blessing task, there was no line he wouldn't cross. He'd never lied about that.

A slight tendril of aggression brought him to an abrupt halt. Instincts buzzed. Someone approached, intending to inflict harm. The Phoenix, judging by the level of heat wafting from her. Roux rolled his shoulders. Let her try something.

"Hi," she said when she reached his side, striving for a pleasant tone but failing. "My name is Carrigan."

"So?"

"So, you had better watch yourself, Astra. That's my best friend you're eye-stalking."

He cast the Phoenix the briefest glance. Tall and toned, with red hair, fair skin, and amber eyes. On the battlefield, power had sizzled over her skin, flames barely banked.

"Your best friend is the pale-haired harpy? Someone you willingly agreed to pit yourself against in a battle to the death?" He shook his head. Roux would rather die himself than harm a fellow Astra. "I highly doubt that."

"I'm not surprised by that. You aren't nearly as smart as I am. Like any true friend, I'm going to help that pale-haired harpy, as you call her, get to the end and kill me. I'll revive, protect her from you, then force you to escort both of us home." Unshakable confidence laced her every word. "What do you think of my plan?"

"I like it." Few flaws. Phoenixes almost always came back from the dead, and when they did, they were always stronger. "I would have liked it better if you'd kept me in the dark and executed a successful ambush."

She smiled at him, a sensual curve of her mouth that would have hardened him in an instant if he'd been another male. As usual, a lone female affected his body, and it wasn't this one. "Do you think I'm destined to fail because you're an Astra? Some kind of superman, right? Well guess what, Mr. Kent? Every superhero has a weakness, and you are no different."

"Do tell."

"Your ego will be your defeat. What your beefed-up brain cannot comprehend is that I will win any battle against you by superior intellect alone. I had the foresight to consult an oracle before purposely coming to this realm, you see. I wanted to make sure I had a way out. And I do. I happen to know something you don't."

"Is *your* ego a weakness?" he asked conversationally.

She acted as if he hadn't spoken. "I was told I would be one of two finalists left in a tournament to the death," she said, smirking at him. "That I and my friend would escape, and a phantom would die or not, depending on *my* decisions."

Blythe struggled to keep her attention on Lucca, the famed harpy she'd cornered not too long ago. At first, they'd exchanged half-hearted insults. Then they'd bargained, becoming allies who swapped information tonight and returned to being foes tomorrow. Finally, she had a chance to get her burning questions answered. Though, granted, she and the other combatant had only issued softball queries so far, feeling each other out.

But dang it, Roux had been involved in a deep conversation with the Phoenix for the past ten minutes. What were the two chatting about?

Focus. Only an idiot wasted a golden opportunity like this. "Tell me about the Ation crown," she said. "I've felt its come-hither vibe and heard it's cursed. Is it?"

"Yes and no," Lucca replied, the braids in her hair slapping together as she wobbled her head back and forth. "To see it is to want it. But once someone is crowned, they cannot shed it until their death. So, they end up dying quickly because others want it. And not just because of the crown's intense draw. Legend claims only the queen will be freed from this realm. Your Astra's offer fed the tale, growing it into a beast. Why else would so many survivalists be willing to die for the chance to win a night with a surly warrior and his chopping block?"

"He isn't mine," she muttered, casting her gaze his way. He was fully engaged with the Phoenix. He kept his body angled toward hers and his eyes on her face. Hers. Not Blythe's. And he even clasped the other woman's wrist, locking her in place, as if he couldn't bear to part with her.

Hey! He was touching her. Willingly.

Was he enjoying it?

Blythe curled her hands into fists. Prickles ran the length of her spine, and she couldn't understand why. Or what they stemmed from. Because it wasn't jealousy. Nope. Not even the tiniest bit.

"Whatever floats your boat," Lucca said, palms up and out in a gesture of innocence. "No judgment over your appallingly terrible taste, I swear. Anyway. My turn for info. Tell me everything you've gleaned about the Astra's blessing task."

To say anything might well be a betrayal to Roux. But to say nothing was to end a fruitful Q and A.

Shouldn't she *want* to betray the Warden? Yes. She should. So she would. "He's gotta cut out the queen's heart."

"Yeah. With a trinite blade. That's public knowledge around here. What else you got?"

Hold up. He had to use trinite? Blythe pressed the tip of her tongue against an incisor. Erebus had conveniently left that part out.

"What happens when he fails?" Lucca added.

Ugh. Forget the guilt. "If he fails, he and his buddies get cursed," Blythe forced herself to admit. But she didn't elaborate. "Your turn. What can you tell me about Penelope, queen of the wraiths? You might call her Miss Murder. After she tagged me with her jewel, she stole my favorite dagger, and I want it back."

"Well, I know she guards a treasure room underneath her palace, and the only entrance is in her bedchamber. At least I think she does. No one had ever returned to verify the rumor."

Okay. Good to know. Now they were getting somewhere. *Gotta get to that treasure room.* And she needed to do it before the tournament ended. Now, her course was set. She must win the crown and kill Roux before he killed her.

Before she could stop herself, she glanced his way again. This time, their eyes met, and her breath caught. He was glaring at her, a muscle jumping in his jaw. Uh, was he angry with her? Had he guessed her thoughts?

The background music changed, the pounding beat becoming a siren's soft melody. Her questions ceased to matter. Mmm. She liked this music. Slow and haunting. Electric. Her limbs trembled. In her veins, blood raced and heated.

Suddenly every desire *Blythe* had ever harbored for the Astra surged to the fore. She needed to get her hands on him. Now.

Maybe he felt the same way. His features softened, his eyelids hooding and his lips parting. He looked... hungry.

"Does your favorite weapon happen to be a—" Lucca moaned, then giggled and fanned her cheeks. "Uh, did everyone in the world get sexy all of a sudden? Because wowzer. Even the Astra is starting to look good to me."

"He does look good, doesn't he?" she replied with a moan of her own. Her insides were fluttering, heating. Demanding. Pull her gaze from the warrior? Impossible. "Very good."

Lightning flashed as Roux stalked across the distance, closing in on her. He stopped directly in front of her, his scent making her head swim. "Dance with me," he rasped, extending his arm.

Dance? With him? Not what she'd expected him to say. Wings rippling, she placed her fingers in his. "Yes." No other reply was acceptable.

18

THE FEASTING

Something about the melody…

Roux had never danced with anyone. Never even swayed to music when he was alone. He wasn't sure he knew what to do, but stop this? No. Uncaring about his audience, he tugged his gorgeous harphantom close and wrapped his arms around her.

Oh, the softness of this female. Lush curves pressed against him. Pleased him.

He ignored the muted warning in the back of his mind. Forgot the Phoenix. Lost track of everything but Blythe's smooth palms skating up his chest, locking at his nape. They swayed together.

Those pale blue eyes mesmerized him. Undid him. He craved everything she had to give, all at once. Lived only to touch this woman and be touched by her. To possess her, body and soul. And be possessed?

Words spilled from him, unfiltered. "Give yourself to me, Lyla." He wasn't sure anything mattered more. "Every inch. Hold nothing back."

"Mmm. Every inch, huh?" she echoed with a sexy chuckle. "That's my line to you. And I'm betting there are a *lot* of inches." She toyed with the ends of his hair, and he leaned into the contact. "If I do, what will you do with me?"

"Whatever I want. Everything. Only what you desire. Whichever answer you prefer."

"That's an impressive list." Dazed, she rasped, "I say yes to each. Yes, yes, a thousand times yes. So kiss me, Astra, and make it count."

Kiss! Yes! Heart hammering, Roux swooped down. To his delight, Blythe rose to her tiptoes, eagerly meeting him halfway. Their lips pressed together, and she opened for him, allowing his tongue to thrust against hers. No, there was no allowing, no passively accepting his ministrations. The breathtaking woman greeted him with a thrust of her own and clutched him closer.

The pleasure of his first kiss! The sensations. The connection, deeper than ever before. Hands wandered. Bodies ground together. Heat left him fevered, wafting from an inferno that sparked in the marrow of his bones. Had anything ever tasted sweeter? Or more intoxicating? She was a potent wine enchanted with desire itself, and he only wanted more.

He kissed and kissed and kissed her, savoring at first. Growing more and more frenzied—and more and more mad.

How could he ever live without this now?

A new burst of lightning flashed overhead, quickly followed by another. And another. Thunder boomed, shaking even the ground. Through it all, the siren's song filled his ears.

The rest of the world vanished from his awareness, the desperate tasting speeding into a wild devouring. Never, in the whole of his life, had he drowned in anything other than physical pain or mental screams. Until now. Until her. Roux drowned in Blythe, and he had no urge to recover.

Icy raindrops fell, sizzling against his blistering skin. Blythe gasped, and the kiss paused. They fought for air, but they didn't spring apart. Separate him from this female? No. Not even when the heavens split and hammered the land with hail. He pressed his brow against hers, and she let him.

The most sublime sigh escaped her. "What are we doing?"

"Everything I've dreamed."

"Are you ready to stop?" she asked, soft against him.

"Not until you scream my name."

"Do it. I dare you. Make me scream and scream and scream and—"

He swooped in, silencing her with another kiss. They ate at each other. Clutched and kneaded. Rubbed. But all too soon, wandering hands and grinding bodies weren't enough. He required her surrender. Total and complete. In bed. Naked. She would be eager for him and him alone.

Roux lifted his head, ending the kiss, only to lick the seam of her lips. Between harsh breaths, he bit out, "I want more than your body. I want your thoughts. Give them to me."

"Can't think…" She stabbed her fingers through his hair, and nipped his chin. "Want to scream. You said

I'd scream." Diving in for another kiss, she jumped up and wrapped her legs around his waist. Hardness met softness, and his madness sharpened. "Give me what you promised."

A harsh groan barreled from him. The new alignment amplified every sensation rampaging through him—and added others!

Drunken catcalls and lewd suggestions hit his ears. He wrenched up his head and snarled at the offenders. Only then did he remember the celebration taking place around them. Despite the storm, the fizzling out of the bonfires, and the inundation of rain puddles, immortals loomed in every direction, watching him and the harphantom. Some grinned while teetering on unsteady legs, spilling their drinks. Some glared while doing the same. Those who remained stone-cold sober—the welcome party—exhibited smug satisfaction.

That smug satisfaction should bother him. And it would. Tomorrow. As for tonight…

Roux flashed Blythe to their private chamber, appearing beside the bed. The siren's song drifted through the windows, growing more and more muted as the rainfall intensified.

He gripped the object of his fascination by the waist and tossed her to the mattress, exactly as he'd imagined doing a thousand times. Before she ceased bouncing, he lunged over her, putting his mouth just over hers. Hovering. With one hand, he braced his weight. With the other, he plucked at the button holding her vest together. She watched him, her pupils expanding.

The sides of the garment parted, revealing the plush mounds he'd beheld in his every waking fantasy. "Let me touch."

"Yes." She arched her back, presenting herself to him. "Do it."

Trembling, he reached out slowly, so slowly, and tentatively cupped one of her breasts. He groaned. Gently kneaded. The utter softness. *Nothing better than this.*

Gasping, she flattened her hand over his. The sight of her. The sight of her in his grip. The feel of her. This. This was better.

Aching to see more, all, he jackknifed to his feet and yanked off her boots. His trembling worsened as he reached under her soaked skirt, hooked his fingers around the crotch of her panties, and pulled. The material slipped down her legs, past her feet. Feet he placed exactly where he wanted—far apart at the edge of the mattress.

She watched him with glittering eyes. "Deep down, I knew you'd be like this."

"Like this?" He lifted his shirt overhead and dropped the material to the floor.

"Mmm-hmm." Passion painted her flesh with a rosy flush. "Irresistibly demanding."

"Oh, you knew it, did you?" He undid the button on his leathers. "How often did you ponder this phenomenon?"

"Too often," she grumbled.

He gave a rusty chuckle filled with more strain than amusement. "That's good. Because I have never stopped thinking of you. And Lyla? I will demand *many* things from you."

Here, now, only one question remained. Where should he start? Instincts shouted *rush* while begging for *slow*.

Roux dragged his gaze down her curves, setting off a chain reaction of sensations. His blood burned hot, nothing but fuel. Energy pumped into muscles. Sweat glazed him, and ferocity whipped at his back.

"My Lyla is a prize among prizes." Strands of inky hair clung to her rain-dotted skin. A pulse raced at the base of her throat. The rise and fall of her bare chest left his insides clenching.

Where the skirt parted...

The moisture in his mouth dried, and he wiped a palm over his face. "No one compares to you," he croaked, throbbing for her.

"How do you know?" Remaining reclined on one elbow, she stroked a tiny claw around her navel. "I'm your first."

"Yes, but I'm thousands of years old." And then some. "I've seen much. Trust me when I say you are my favorite sight in all the worlds." His favorite *everything*.

She entranced him with a sensual smile. "I want to see you, too." Her gaze dropped to his zipper, and she licked her lips.

A hoarse sound brewed at the edge of his tongue. As the storm intensified outside, reaching a new pinnacle, obscuring the siren's song, he slowly opened the metal teeth. "Is there something specific you'd like to see, harpy?" To bare himself to her...to remove all barriers between them...

"Very much so. I— Wait. Hold up." A frown pulled at the corners of her mouth. She shook her head. "This isn't right. Something about this is wrong."

A denial threatened to detonate. But she wasn't wrong. Fighting for air, he dropped his arms to his sides. The most difficult action he'd ever completed. In that moment, however, he comprehended the problem—the siren's song.

He growled with more force. Without the tantalizing melody filling his ears and clouding his judgment, reason bombarded his mind in a rush. With reason came recognition. Fury pitched and swelled, fast and hard.

Now he understood the smug satisfaction every member of the welcome party had exhibited. The treacherous group had decided to bring Roux and Blythe together. Why? To introduce him to the pleasure he'd been missing all his life? Because mission accomplished. Now he knew what the harphantom tasted like. He'd glimpsed the rapture awaiting him in her arms. He could never be satisfied without her.

"The siren dies today," he hissed.

"She dies *badly*." Eyes as black as night, Blythe jolted upright, refashioned her vest as best she could, then smoothed her skirt, blocking his gaze from the lushest, sexiest, most exquisite view he'd ever come across. Another reason to rage.

How was he supposed to keep his hands off her now?

"Allow me to do the honors." She jumped from the bed and darted around him, lacking her usual grace. Her motions were clipped, her legs trembly.

A small mercy, he supposed. He hadn't left her unaffected.

After swiping up his bow and fishing two arrows from the quiver, she stomped to the window, aimed, and released a double shot. Roux flashed behind her as the missiles sliced through the siren. One dead center in her mouth, the other dead center in her throat. Both silenced her for good.

"There. Problem solved." To the others, Blythe shouted, "Anyone else want to join the choir?"

The rain lightened as the welcome party rushed over

to circle the fallen immortal. Comprehending what had happened, they glared up at Blythe and Roux. It was only then, as the countdown clock in the back of his mind ran out, that he pieced together the crux of their plan.

They knew about his bargain with Penelope. They'd hoped to make him miss today's feeding, giving the wraith a reason to drain the harpy. *Craftier than I realized.*

Other females stopped partying to frown at their mugs, as if they weren't sure why they held a mug filled with a mix of brew and rain in the first place. Other victims of the siren's song, meant to drink themselves into a stupor before tomorrow's battle?

Roux turned on his heel. "I must go," he told Blythe. He flashed to his discarded shirt, donned the material, and amended his pants.

"Go? Now?" Whirling around, she gaped at him, incredulous. The black faded from her eyes. "Where?"

"That isn't your concern." Admit the truth? Surely he wasn't so foolish. She would only insist on tagging along, and he needed a break from her. The tension inside him...something was soon to shatter.

"Not my concern?" she grated. "Are you meeting someone? A certain Phoenix, perhaps, now that I've primed the pump?"

Speaking of Carrigan the Phoenix, he would go somewhere quiet to recharge after he dealt with the wraiths, and carefully consider what to do about her and her threat.

"Well?" Blythe prompted.

"Does it matter? You planned to find me a—what

did you call it?—a bang buddy. Stay here. If you leave, I'll consider it a breach of our agreement."

"Breach? What breach? How? You can't just change the rules and—"

"I can. I did. I'll return shortly." He flashed to Wraith Island before she could issue another half comment. Only able to transport himself to places he'd seen, he landed on the shore.

To the left and right were mountains made of stone. Between them, a valley filled with dead trees. He followed a single, open path, flashing forward as far as his eyes could see. Before long, he came to a gated drawbridge, which led to a sharp-edged palace built from glistening ebony. The top disappeared in a wealth of gray clouds.

Penelope waited at the front door, grinning. Ribbons of red hair blew in a breeze a spectral like her couldn't feel. She'd changed clothes. Or rather, changed the image she projected. A long black gown now cinched at her waist and flared to feet several inches off the ground.

"I'm surprised you made it, Astra, considering the trap the council laid for you."

A trap that would have succeeded if Blythe hadn't stopped him when she had. Roux doubted he would have possessed the strength to end the encounter for any other reason. "Did you want me to fail, wraith?"

"Yes and no. I was undecided, honestly. On one hand, my followers could've drained you in retribution, taking you out of commission until you failed your blessing task, allowing me to keep the phantom forever. On the other, she couldn't possibly taste as delicious as you. Or as delicious without you around to inspire her hatred."

Yes, Blythe's hatred. How could he forget, even for a moment?

He fisted his hands. "Let's get this done."

Penelope's grin widened. "My, my, my. In such a hurry. You'd think the gaggle of females weren't about to offer you a jolly good time." She turned and glided inside, clearly expecting him to follow.

He did, the thump of his boots echoing off barren walls. No furniture filled the foyer. Or the hallway. Or the rooms they passed. The palace was empty. But then, wraiths had no need of such things. They rarely slept, and when they did, they simply floated around.

"Do you want a tour of the place, or shall we get straight to business?" she asked.

A grunt was his only response.

"My apologies, Astra, but I don't speak Surly." She tossed him a glance over her shoulder and sniffed. "Care to try again?"

"I want this done," he snapped.

"Fine. Just know you're missing out. The vacant bedrooms are really something special."

Up a flight of steps they went. Wait. He thought he sensed...firstone. Roux stiffened. If the wraith had firstone in her possession, she owned the means to slay him. Not just slay him but trap him. In the presence of firstone, he couldn't flash or utilize other abilities.

Not by word or deed did he reveal his concern, however. Instead, he memorized every detail about the castle, logging inconsistencies in the dimensions to examine at a later point. Now that he'd explored within these walls, he could return without anyone's notice. And he would. Remaining on another plane rendered the firstone useless. Mostly.

He would come tonight, in fact. No more spending his nights with Blythe under the pretense of guarding her. She was well able to care for herself. No more watching her. Wanting her. Imagining she straddled his lap and stroking himself.

Penelope soared past double doors, entering a ballroom with a royal dais and a throne made of—Roux did a double take. The throne was made of a dozen immortals frozen in time after being drained of life, their bodies contorted in different positions to fabricate a chair.

"Ladies," Penelope announced, "I'm both sad and happy to report tonight's delivery service is a go."

He pursed his lips as he surveyed the "ladies." Twenty-two wraiths waited in a line. Bones and hair in sackcloth; that's what they were. None had chosen a palatable form like their queen.

Hate wraiths. Before he left this realm, he would find a way to slay each and every spectral here. Had these creatures not appeared above him, bearing Blythe's image, his harphantom would not be forced to compete in the tournament.

Behind them, twenty-three prehistoric beasts like the one-horned monstrosity who'd pushed Blythe into the arena were chained to a wall. Each animal surveyed him with ravenous, beady eyes.

They'll get theirs, too.

"He's in a hurry," Penelope told her followers, "so there's no reason to make introductions or politely await your turn." She clapped, all haughty disdain. "Well? Didn't you hear me? Go, go, go. Feast!"

There was no time to brace. In seconds, the beings surrounded him, adhering their mouths to some part of his body. Not physically, but spiritually, and that was so much worse. They sucked on him from the inside. The pulling sensation never ended. Cold infiltrated his limbs and torso.

Phantoms did this, too. Which made sense, considering Erebus based the creation of his phantoms off wraiths.

Wraiths had come into being because of a curse. Knowing this, the Dark One used some kind of evil force to similarly curse those he killed, binding their life to his for the rest of eternity, forcing them to obey his every command.

Suction sounds filled Roux's ears, and pulling sensations worsened. The cold spread, going deeper. He cringed, the urge to fight nearly irresistible. From Blythe's exquisite kiss to this. From sizzling heat to frigid chill.

Weakness soon invaded. More than he'd expected.

The defenses in his mental prison crumbled. Prisoners rushed free.

"Oh, Astra. I forgot to mention." All calculation and delight, Penelope floated in front of him. "In your haste to save the harphantom, you neglected to set a limit to how much of you my people can drink during each setting. Therefore, I took the liberty of deciding for you. In case you're wondering, it's however much they want. Try not to die."

He attempted to respond, but he discovered he had no voice. Screams erupted. Thousands upon thousands of screams.

Do not black out. Do not...

19

THE LIGHT

Blythe paced before the crackling hearth, her wings flapping through the slits in her T-shirt, and her mind a mess. The storm had finally let up, but an icy wind continued to bluster inside the bedroom. Candles flickered all around, helping to warm the chamber without the presence of Roux the furnace.

If she'd been home, she might've taken Isla shopping or settled in an engaging book about torture techniques. But she wasn't home and she wasn't in the mood to read anything but the room—with the Astra in it. Where had he gone? Who was he with? The Phoenix, as Blythe suspected? What was he doing? Thinking? Feeling?

As she strode back and forth, stomping her feet, she scraped her claws over the hearth's stone frame. A romantic association between the Astra and the Phoenix shouldn't bother her. Roux's comings and goings didn't matter. Dead enemy walking, remember? But it bothered her. It mattered. She'd let him kiss her. They'd almost had sex.

To be perfectly candid, they absolutely, positively *would've* had sex if she hadn't come to her senses. He'd nearly lowered his zipper, and oh, how she'd hungered for him to do it. No male had ever tempted her more. She'd been consumed by his scent, his heat, his strength. Even his expressions. The usually stoic warrior had displayed everything from shocked wonder to fierce possession. His touch had been eager and firm. Confident despite his lack of experience. Which was another turn-on, dang it!

He reacted to Blythe alone. Yearned for her alone. Or he used to. And now? Had she opened the floodgates of passion for others?

On her next pass, she scraped the stone *harder*, surprised when the thing didn't crumble into dust. Part of her resented the return of her good sense. And she shouldn't! Wrong turns put you in the wrong location at the wrong time, doing your best to put out fires you were never supposed to ignite.

Lifetime consequences for a momentary pleasure? Not a fair bargain on any level. And yet, still she desired the intense blond giant. And this time, she couldn't blame the siren's song.

What's the matter with me? To a certain degree, Blythe had once acted this way with Laban, too, before she'd realized—or rather, accepted—that he was her consort. But Roux wasn't her consort. He couldn't be. To her knowledge, no harpy had ever gotten a new fated male. And, if such a thing were possible, which it wasn't, there was no way the second would be the one who'd murdered the original.

Unless Laban belonged to the harpy and Roux belonged to the phantom?

No. No! All other harpies possessed a dual nature, too, reflecting whatever their father happened to be. Again, they only ever received a single consort. Even if said consort had only appeared in a solo hallucination and had done the unthinkable, telling them to move on and live their best life.

What kind of spouse did that?

Blythe paced faster. Why couldn't she get herself together? If not for herself, for her child.

Sweet Isla. A whimper slipped free. Blythe stopped, just stopped, as a fresh tide of homesickness rose. What was the little girl doing right this moment? Did she need help with homework? Was she sleeping at night?

Regret joined the toxic assortment of emotions fermenting inside Blythe. Forget teaching the beloved child how to properly handle a foe. Why hadn't she shown her daughter how to properly love her family?

How could a mother leave her own child without even saying goodbye?

With a shriek, she pounded her fist into the wall. Stone finally cracked, and dust coated the air. Tears seared her eyes. Tears? Ugh! What kind of a harpy cried?

First a bad wife and mother, now a bad harpy. Her chin trembled. Was overseeing a vendetta always this complicated? So far, Blythe had done little to aid her own cause. She gotten herself stuck in an unfamiliar realm, a participant in a death tournament. Oh, yes, and she was kind of owned by a wraith.

She swiped at her eyes with the back of her hand, clearing her vision, then rubbed the ruby still embedded at the base of her throat. As firmly attached as ever. Not even the slightest wobble.

Why had Penelope ceased feeding from her during today's battle, then? And why hadn't the queen fed since its end?

An unexpected motion caught Blythe's attention. Wings fluttering, she spun, ready to defend herself against—Roux! He tottered on his feet only a few feet away.

"What's wrong?" she demanded, staggered by his deplorable condition. Not just pale but ashen. Shaky. "What happened?"

Clutching his head, he collapsed to his knees.

Stomach churning, she rushed over to crouch beside him. Was the Phoenix responsible? *She dies first!* "Talk to me, Roux." She checked his pulse. Thready. "Tell me what I'm dealing with here."

"Wraiths fed...screams started...won't stop." He would have toppled the rest of the way if she hadn't caught him and eased him to the floor. "Can't make them stop, can't make them stop," he chanted, thrashing.

The wraiths had fed on him? No, no way Penelope's crew had managed to overpower an Astra in his prime. A male who'd battled countless armies of phantoms for eons. Plus, there were no jewels adhered to his body. Not that Blythe could see, anyway.

Ignoring her own shakiness, she ripped his shirt down the middle. The material fell away, revealing moving *alevala*. Images jumping from one place to another, again and again, faster than a blink.

Her heart jumped in unison. She scanned him as

quickly as possible to avoid getting trapped. Nope. No jewels. Meaning, he hadn't been overpowered. There were no open wounds, either. The wraiths must have... what? Gotten his permission?

No way. He must have...but he wouldn't...unless he would. She gasped again. He had given them permission, hadn't he? He'd let them feed on him. He must have bargained with Miss Murder to save Blythe's life. No wonder Penelope had stopped feeding during the battle.

A gesture Roux might have made for his Commander. But maybe, possibly, he'd done it for Blythe as well?

She gulped, something akin to tenderness flowing through her. A river newly released from a dam, eroding shores made of pain and grief. Her tremors worsened as she cupped his jawline to lift his head and study his face. His eyes remained closed.

"Flash to the bed, Astra." The hard floor wasn't comfortable. Especially for a man of his size, who hadn't stopped flailing about. "I'll follow you there, I promise."

"The screams. Make them stop," he repeated, as if he didn't hear her. Maybe he didn't. He gripped and yanked at hanks of his hair.

Did he speak of the same screams she'd heard when she'd ghosted inside his spirit? If so... She shuddered, remembering the horrifying chorus, and how it had driven her mad in only a matter of seconds.

Not knowing what else to do, she smoothed her fingertips over his brow. His cheeks. "I'm here. I'll keep you safe."

Um. She would? There would be no better time to visit Wraith Island, reclaim her firstone dagger, then come back here to hack off his head. Or just hack off his head with a regular blade and discover whether his ability to recover from such a devastating wound was as developed as hers.

No. Absolutely not. He'd taken Laban out in battle. How could Blythe do any less with Roux? Sparing him now had nothing to do with his offer to fuel the wraiths and preserve her strength.

To her surprise, the Astra calmed somewhat as she caressed him. Heart thudding, she continued cooing and stroking, doing her best to disregard the soft, smooth texture of his skin.

"Yes," she rasped. "I'll keep you safe. For now."

When he leaned into her touch, instinctively deepening the contact, a barbed lump grew in her throat. How could this male who'd known nothing but cruelty for the bulk of his life seek more of her? The ruthless harphantom who'd been nothing but, yep, cruel to him.

Whoa. Hold up. Was she vacillating between regret and sympathy for Laban's killer right now?

Okay. Time to remind herself of Roux's callous side. So. Screw it. There was no better opportunity to do what was needed than to experience one—or two or twenty—of his past blessing tasks. If she experienced pain while witnessing it, so what? If she died like the shifter, she died. Again, so what? She would come back. This way, at least, she'd know her own reaction to the tattoos.

What had he been forced to do in the past, anyway? To Blythe's knowledge, none of the other Astra had ever spoken of his former deeds. And Roux himself had been super adamant that she never, ever look at his *alevala*...

What didn't he want her to see? And when had she started taking orders from her enemy? Or a maybe enemy.

Maybe?

She huffed out a breath. He *was*.

Curiosity riding high, Blythe did it. She slid her gaze to his chest. Inhale. Exhale. The pictures continued to jump, shifting too swiftly to lock onto. Hmm. Each of the marks seemed to be a different version of Roux. Even pieces of him. There. His eyes, flickering with sparks of red. There. His lips, opening wide to unleash a bellow. There. His hand, clenching tight.

Rather than chase a single image, she stared hard at the spot just over his heart. Finally! A connection snapped into place when those inked eyes appeared, meeting her gaze. Impact jolted her, air gushing from parted lips.

Her mind blanked, only to recalibrate in seconds, a scene taking shape…

Suddenly, she was lying on a familiar stone altar, her mind nothing but noise. No, no. Not her. Anything she experienced now, she experienced as Roux. But the altar. Wow. It reminded her of the one Roc had built for Taliyah, when he'd intended to sacrifice her.

Roux wasn't bound, but he wasn't free, either. He remained motionless.

He wore a loose white shirt and matching pants. Not to mention his customary blank expression. Above him, lavender sunlight shone from an azure sky. Around him, a crowd of—what *were* those? Shadow people? Or something else entirely? Dark outlines matched the shapes of many of the Astra, even those of Chaos and his attendants.

Eerie, yes, but tainted? No. So how had a memory like this killed an immortal in a matter of seconds, simply because she'd viewed it?

One of the almost-people approached the altar. This one had the shape of Commander Roc. Wait. Was Roux about to suffer the same fate as his leader's previous brides?

Yep. Sure enough. The silhouette of Roc tore into Roux, shredding his body. Tissue and blood flew in every direction. Through it all, Roux made not a peep. He lost limbs. Organs. Even his head.

So. He *could* recover from a beheading.

Abruptly, the scene spun into another. As the new one crystalized, she realized she was—no, *Roux* was standing before a shaded outline of the Astra named Halo…who pinned and shredded him just as Roc had done.

The scene spun again. Again, Roux died at the hands of a shadowy Astra. Then again. And again. It happened over and over, one murder revolving into another. Once the lineup finished, each one repeated, only faster. Same order. Same outcome. Then came another repeat, faster still. It came again and again and again. A never-ending spinning wheel of blood, pain, and death, leaving Blythe dizzy.

Sickness churned in her stomach. Hers, not Roux's. Or maybe theirs? She felt the burn of it through the haze of memories. Then the screams started. One after another, soon blending into a familiar cacophony of horror. She struggled to keep her thoughts together. A colossal chore, yet somehow she managed it. Kind of. Intelligence came in bursts. The Astra's blessing task. Had he been forced to relive the tasks completed by his friends? Only, he took the place of their victims?

Did it happen in real life? Or was this some type of mental torture?

Mental torture, she'd bet. Meant to be reminders of his childhood, when he'd been physically tortured by someone else who was supposed to love and care for him.

Poor Roux. How many times had he relived his friends' blessing tasks? Once? Or an endless cycle until a clock ran out? Either way...

How was this male still able to function? As she'd suspected, he'd known nothing but torment and betrayal throughout his life. How did he not hate the males he considered compatriots and friends? Or did he? Did a part of him resent them for what happened, whether it was real or not?

Blythe attempted to extract herself from the memory, but the spinning wheel held her captive. Roux died again. And again.

No escape? Stuck here?

Panic gripped her, but she fought it, focusing on her goal rather than the failure. *Disengage! Abort!*

She clawed and kicked, attempting to evade Roux's stream of chaotic consciousness, but an invisible tether held her in place. With no other options, she wrapped herself in that tether, letting it choke the life out of her...

Blythe came to with a gasp. Her eyelids popped apart, and she sagged to the floor beside her Astra. Or rather, sagged on top of him, resting her head in the crook of his arm. Though she tried to shift positions, she was too weak.

Sweat soaked her. Probably blood, too. Breath sawed in and out of her mouth as if she'd just sprinted across three different galaxies, chased by a posse of her worst fears. Roux had calmed, at least. He wasn't flailing anymore.

As she lay there, her mind ravaged into oblivion and her body absorbing his heat, her eyelids grew heavy and slowly slid shut. Darkness teased the edges of her mind.

Panic sparked. *About to fall asleep. With the Astra.* Her greatest foe. Her sworn eternal enemy. The object of her death vow. Yes, circumstances between them had somehow changed irrevocably, for better or worse. But this... No!

Blythe fought with everything in her, prying open her eyes and refusing to blink. But it wasn't long before her irises burned and new tears welled. Her lids got heavier.

She didn't care. There would be no sleeping with Roux. Adult harpies only drifted off with their consorts. No exception other than death. Unlike his carry to the palace, tonight's nap couldn't be explained away.

There was no way Roux was... He couldn't possibly be... She refused to believe...

Boulder-heavy eyelids sank low...lower...

What are you doing? Stop this!

Gathering what little remained of her strength, she attempted to rise. Her body betrayed her, refusing to obey her mind's commands—and she snuggled more comfortably against him.

Lower...

No, no, no. This wasn't happening. She refused to let it. She would do something, anything, and then...

The darkness came, and Blythe drifted into the oblivion.

20

THE CONFUSION

Roux woke as if someone had just punched him in the gut repeatedly. His eyelids popped open. Every muscle in his body went taut and hard as stone, as if he prepared to attack and defend. Instinct kicked on only a split second later, and he remained still, absorbing different details.

He lay on his back. On a floor. No wraiths loomed nearby. The screams had ceased, his prisoners secured in their cages, and he had no idea how it happened. Muted rays of morning sunlight seeped into a familiar bedroom, illuminating a cascade of dancing dust motes.

An unfamiliar weight pressed into his side. He frowned. Could it be… No, no, surely not. And yet, the harpy's tempting scent enveloped him.

Dare he hope… When he felt the caress of her warm

breath against his bare skin, a sensation he'd memorized as they'd kissed, his muscles hardened for an entirely different reason. She had draped herself over him? Willingly?

Slowly he craned his head. Another punch in the gut! She *was* draped over him. Willingly. In fact, she lay on her side, curled into him, looking as contented as could be. Her cheek rested on his shoulder, her face aimed up at his. They exchanged breaths. But she wasn't awake. She slept. She actually slept. As if she trusted him to oversee her protection while she was at her most vulnerable. But… That couldn't be correct.

Blink-blink. The image never shifted. Her eyes remained closed, her long lashes casting shadows he longed to trace over her cheeks. Her exhalations were steady, her expression soft. Lengthy locks of her silken hair spilled over his chest. Rosy color tinged the cheekbone he could see. Her lush lips were slightly parted.

She was so beautiful it almost hurt to gaze upon her. So delicate he feared her image might shatter at any second. So elegant, even in slumber, he felt as if he held the world's greatest treasure.

But.

What?

Why?

How?

What?

He scoured his mind, only bits and pieces coming back to him. By the time the wraiths finished feeding on him, he'd barely had the strength to stand. Or the wits to puzzle out a plan of action. Somehow, he must have focused enough to flash to Blythe. His sometimes

partner and always enemy. A foolish move on his part—
or the most brilliant.

Though she'd been presented with the perfect opportunity to attack him, achieving a measure of vengeance
at last, she had opted to cuddle him instead. How was
Roux supposed to process such an unexpected development?

Did this mean she considered him a consort? *Him?*
Roux? The male she still despised. His eyes widened.
Surely not. Harpies didn't get two consorts. But also…
maybe. He didn't know how. Or why. Or even why him.
Unless she were, in fact, his *gravita*.

Careful, so careful, moving more slowly than before, he wrapped his arms around her and flashed them
both to the bed. The soft mattress replaced the hard
wood floor, contouring to their shapes. Much better.
A breathy sigh left her, and she settled deeper into the
crook of his embrace.

A gratification he'd never known washed over him.
As if he was finally doing what he'd been born to do.
Beneath the sensation, however, hunger stirred. The
same hunger he'd experienced while they'd kissed.
Only stronger. Hotter. More insistent. But somehow
also softer. Sweeter. Calmer.

The conflicting impressions warred. Sweat beaded
on his brow. If he woke her with another kiss, would
she receive him? Castigate him for taking what didn't
belong to him?

He wouldn't risk it. No way he could start this miracle day with a misstep. For their next embrace, he
wanted—needed—her to be aware from the onset. Pride
demanded it. Not to mention a sense of honor he'd never
known he possessed. But then, from the very begin-

ning, Blythe the Undoing had excelled at bringing hidden things to the surface, exposing long buried truths. Besides, did he even have time to do half the deeds he imagined? He checked his internal clock. Forty-three minutes and thirty-seven seconds until round two of the tournament. A rough groan left him. No, not nearly enough time. Once he began, he didn't plan to halt until she begged for mercy. A process that could take days.

Focus on anything else. He peered up at the vaulted ceiling and tried to reason out what horrors awaited Blythe during today's battle. Too many possibilities. At least he didn't have to worry Blythe would be drained during battle.

Angling to his side, he traced a fingertip over the ruby above her sternum. The action, though gentle, woke her at last. She rapid-blinked. Spotting him, she didn't jump up or stiffen. No, she offered him a dreamy, dizzying smile she might grant to only those she admired.

"Good morning, Astra."

A trick? Maybe. But wait to touch her? No, not now. Not after that smile. *Invitation enough.*

Perhaps he could do *one* deed he imagined.

"Let's make it an even better morning." Desperate, Roux clasped her nape and swooped in to claim her lips with his own. She opened for him without hesitation, welcoming his tongue. He gave it. Aggressively. The kiss proved harder than he'd intended, but she met each thrust with the very moans of surrender he craved.

Fire raged through his veins. *More!*

As if she heard his thoughts, she panted, "Yes. More."

He thrilled. She might hate him, but she no longer wished to kill him. If she did, she wouldn't kiss him this way. Or sleep in his arms. With a bit of time and patience on his part, he might be able to convince her to become his new concubine.

She hooked a leg over his hips to force him closer, practically fusing their bodies. She petted his cheek. Kneaded his shoulder. His pecs. His abdomen. She stroked lower...

Every point of contact wrenched a new huff from him. *Careful.* Never had he barreled toward a cliff so fast, with such an uncertain outcome. Would she end this before he experienced his first climax?

He wrenched his mouth from hers to demand, "I want everything, she-beast." Conquer a world? No problem. Destroy it? No big deal. Relinquish this prize of prizes? No. "What do you want from me?" He let his mouth hover just over hers. "Tell me, and I'll give it to you. Whatever it is."

"I want... I need... I crave..." The words left her between panting breaths. Specks of black dotted her irises, glittering bright and brighter, as if her phantom and harpy warred for rights to answer him.

Unable to wait a nanosecond more, he stole her next words with a kiss and rolled on top of her, pinning her with his weight. Pinning her wings, too, which wasn't something harpies usually allowed. But she didn't protest. Instead, she moaned and spread her legs, creating a cradle for him. Yes! Need drowned out everything else inside his head, consuming him in an instant.

Her lush breasts drew his palms like magnets. He kneaded her through her shirt, nearly losing his mind as she arched her spine, seeking greater contact. His inhalations roughened. Thoughts fragmented. *More, more, more.* He tracked a hand down her belly and did something essential to his sanity: he tunneled his fingers under her panties and plunged one inside her.

His eyes flared wide. *She hungers for me. Greatly.* He'd heard talk of such a tantalizing reaction from one's female, but he'd never cared. Until now. He very much cared. *Will experience this every day for the rest of eternity.*

As he teased her, and himself, working the digit in and out, learning what she liked best, they both released a series of ragged cries.

"Lyla. My Lyla."

"Roux," she gasped.

They locked gazes like so many times before. This time, something was different. There was a deeper connection. An undeniable awareness—they knew exactly what they were doing, and they weren't ready for it to end.

"Never take this from me," he commanded.

All sultry indulgence, she slithered against him. "Does the Warden like his new toy?"

"The Warden *loves* his new toy."

"Does he love—" She went still. Her air of sensuality evaporated. A second later, she pulled her gaze from his, razing his fantasies of the impending pleasure. Dread infiltrated his excitement. He braced for a torrent of staggering disappointment. He knew what was coming—and it wasn't him.

"My consort loved me," she told him softly. Flatly. "You do not."

Anger scraped the center of his chest. "You mean your *first* consort, yes?"

Absolutely the wrong thing to say. Again.

"Okay, I'm done," she snapped. "I don't have two

consorts. I can't. And you should know I wasn't sleeping earlier. I was resting my eyelids. There's a difference."

"You were sleeping, Lyla, and *you* know it," he snapped back. Though he throbbed, his every frayed instinct insisting he continue, Roux eased his finger free of her body. There was no preventing his next action. As she watched, he licked her desire from his skin.

His eyes closed as he rolled to his back. The sweetness! His new reason for breathing.

A choking sound left her. "You cannot be this sexy. I forbid it." With a huff, she hammered her fist into the mattress. "Also, dial down the smolder. And stop enticing me!"

"As if I can stop. Apparently, I do it simply through existing." And what a stunning revelation. How was he supposed to function, knowing such a life-altering bit of information? "But then, I am your consort."

"You aren't. There's got to be another explanation." She pinched the bridge of her nose. "No, not another word from you. I'm not discussing this while I'm so obviously mentally compromised."

"For the record," he said, focusing on calming his rough breaths. Maybe she was right and there was another explanation. But maybe she was wrong. *There's a good chance I'm hers.* "I prefer you when you are out of your mind with passion for me."

To his surprise, she snorted. "I bet you do."

Amusement from her? Now? After all she'd admitted? With a jolt, he shifted to his side, facing her fully. Sparkling eyes of baby blue greeted him. Soft lips. Oh, yes. Amusement.

Think! He must be smart about this. Must do nothing to dampen her good humor. "Shall we discuss the fact that I can still taste you? Or would you prefer to focus on my plan to go straight to the tap next time."

"Uh." She blinked rapidly, as if wavering. In the end, she shook her head. "Neither, thanks."

Determination narrowed his eyes, and he pinned her gaze with his own to let her know the seriousness of his words. "But there *will* be a next time." A statement rather than a question. The female was a fever in his blood, contact with her both his cure and his sickness. He wouldn't be deterred from this for long.

"Maybe there will," she grumbled.

"Today," he insisted. "After the battle."

"What? No. Not then." Before he could protest, she added, "It's too soon. I need a couple days to think this through, or I'll just keep stopping you before we reach the best part. And no tempting me while I'm pondering, either. Lust for you clouds my judgment. Obviously." More grumbling.

He opened his mouth but went silent with another jolt, as if hit by lightning. The things she kept admitting! "Come again?"

"Only if you're good," she retorted. "Look. I'm as baffled by this as you are, but here it is. The truth, the full truth, and nothing but the truth. I can't have two consorts, but something is definitely happening between us. And despite everything, a part of me is genuinely rooting for you on this one, Astra, it really is." She threw her legs over the side of the bed and rose to pad to the closet. "I might not like you, but dang, I do want you."

No more hinting. She'd just issued a bold statement. Roux sat up in a rush. "How badly?" He must know!

"Dude. Keep it down before we're ambushed by the

horndogs. Geez." She riffled through the clothing selection, choosing the standard leather top and pleated skirt. "I think we can both admit we're attracted to each other, but there are obstacles in our path. Namely, if I allow myself to rock your world, I'm not sure I can ever overcome my guilt and shame."

A terse silence stretched before he softly asked, "You think I feel no guilt for what I took from you and your child—what I took from him?"

Peering at the floor, she chewed on her bottom lip. For a moment, she radiated nothing but tender vulnerability, and it shocked a growl from him. That growl acted as a cattle prod. She leaped back into pure harpy mode and anchored her hands on her hips.

"You know what? I just realized the gal who calls you Mr. Sausage Man has shown you more romance than I ever have," she said. "That isn't fair to you, now, is it?"

He eagerly shook his head. "It isn't. Will you give me some?"

"I think I just might. My Astra deserves a preview of what I have to offer."

Her Astra? He gulped. His heart raced. Was she about to make him suffer in the most amazing way…?

With the world's most seductive smile, she reached for the straps of her top. Oh, yes. She was. She stripped for him. Slowly.

His jaw slackened. He blinked. Scrubbed a palm over his face. Refocused. Licked his lips. Fisted the bedsheet with one hand and stroked himself with the other before realizing his actions. Seeing her fully unclothed…

Descriptions rushed through his mind, one after the other. *Perfect. Flawless. Incomparable. Breasts. Nip-*

ples. Stunning. Gorgeous. Exquisite. Navel. Beautiful. Breathtaking. Tantalizing. Mine.

"Do you approve of my version of romance, Rue?" she simpered at him. *Flirted* with him. This wasn't a punishment but a game.

He couldn't look away. Could only croak, "Yes."

"Good." To his consternation, she began to dress. "Don't worry, babe." She anchored her boots in place, then strapped on multiple blades. Each weapon belonged to him, and oh, did he enjoy seeing her don his things. "If I decide to give you a go, I promise I'll make your first time beyond story-worthy so you can brag to all your Astra buddies."

He heard the teasing note in her voice, but he knew. This wasn't a game, either. She'd called him *babe*. Babe. As if she bore a slither of affection for him.

This was a full-on seduction, and he never wanted it to end. "You will give me a go." No other outcome was acceptable.

She flashed a smile, causing his heart to stutter. "Are you worried about the outcome of today's battle?"

"Lyla." He couldn't keep the chide from his tone. "Nine stars decorate your wrist. You are one task away from ruling the entire population of harpies. Yesterday, you shot a siren in the mouth and the throat simultaneously after dispatching every opponent who challenged you with a viciousness not even the Astra have displayed. Entertaining worries concerning your ability to protect yourself would be a waste of my time and energy."

All hint of teasing faded from her, and for a long while, she simply stared at him with wide, vulnerable blue eyes, as if trying to figure him out. "I...thank you. That means a lot."

She reveled in his confidence? *Will remind her every day!*

"Well." She cleared her throat. "You should probably change into something that hides your newest tent. I've got immortals to slay and some thinking to do."

Not grabbing her and throwing her back on the bed proved difficult. The most difficult task of his life. Somehow he managed it, merely standing and adjusting his hard-on through his leathers.

"Anything I can do to help you think faster?" he asked, stuffing an array of armaments into his backpack and handing the pack to her. Ensuring her safety had never been so important.

"Just sit in the stands and look pretty without distracting me with your smolder. Imma bring home the big V." She hooked the bag over her shoulder and winked at him. "Maybe in more ways than one."

Blythe carted her borrowed backpack to the arena. She flashed into the crowded stands to take a seat alongside the other combatants. All six hundred and twenty-eight others, to be exact. Everyone else had beaten her here, including Lucca and the Phoenix. Why? What did they know that she didn't?

No one but Blythe looked confused as Tonka kept shouting, "You're number six hundred and twenty-nine, phantom. You go in order of arrival."

Well, well, well. The others must have known to come ultra-early to snag a smaller number. *Thanks for the heads-up, Lucca.*

On the other side of the stadium, Roux appeared at

the edge of the royal dais. He was a tower of strength and arousal, peering at her with unwavering lust. And yes, smoldering. Behind him, the usual suspects perched in lounge chairs and ate popcorn. But she refused to think about them. Or the Astra. Or her actions this morning. Or her actions last night.

Okay, so, maybe she would entertain one thought about the Astra. Did she hate him still?

She thought…maybe? But also maybe not. Did she still hate what he'd done to Laban? Yes. Therefore, the jewel remained in place.

Okay, perhaps two more thoughts. Or three. Whatever! This was such a screwed-up situation, a bona fide mystery, yet here she sat, consumed by her desire for Roux. Her maybe, maybe not consort. The way he looked at her…

"Who's ready to die?" Tonka, the harpy MC, called. She appeared at Roux's side at the edge of the dais, though she maintained as much distance as possible. Did she fear getting too close to a caged Astra? *I know the feeling.* "Who's ready to win?"

Cheers erupted all around but died soon after as the harpy waved her hands for quiet.

"Here's what is going down. Twenty-three groups of twenty-five and two groups of twenty-seven will enter the ring with ten unibeasts. One at a time, for fifty minutes each. Anyone who survives goes on to round three. You must remain seated until it's your turn. Leave and you are disqualified. By the way, disqualification equals death."

Unibeasts? Oh…dang. Blythe clued in, puzzling together today's festivities fast. More beasts like Amal to chase and maul combatants. Would any of the weapons in Roux's backpack work against such creatures?

"You'll go in the order you are numbered," Tonka added, and Blythe moaned.

She must sit here for the bulk of an entire day, watching immortals get mangled at best and eaten at worst. An inner groan filled her head. Yeah, she'd get to study the animals and learn their weaknesses, but the pro did not negate the con: going from one battle to the next. Which she'd have to do, no doubt. Guaranteed round three took place immediately following Blythe's heat.

There'd be no having sex with Roux. No conversation about expectations and feelings. Just more violence. And okay, yeah, she was kind of talking herself into liking this plan.

With a rattle, the gates that held the restless beasts in their cell rose. One by one, they charged out into the arena, snarling and hungry for a kill.

Below her, the twenty-five warriors formed a line in what must have been a hastily decided battle plan.

A trumpet blasted, and the first beast sprang forward, its teeth sinking into the neck of a shifter and ripping. The female beside Blythe gasped, her own hand fluttering to her uninjured throat. The creature spat out flesh and bone, and the shifter fell to the ground. A metallic bite filled the air.

After that, the line broke apart, every combatant for herself. Roars from the animals and the pained cries of the dying filled the air.

Finally, the dooming call of the trumpet rang out as the first heat ended with zero survivors, showcasing no discernible weaknesses for the beasts. Yikes! Blythe had guessed correctly about the means of suffering, however. Mauling and eating. The crowd cringed, hissed, cheered, booed, and shouted obscenities at the beasts. The aggression only seemed to make the creatures stronger.

During the ensuing heats, she took notes. The unibeasts poisoned with their ultrasharp, stony hide. Gouged and sliced with their horn. Kicked and left gaping holes in immortal bodies. They were faster than vampires, stronger than berserkers, and intelligent enough to learn and predict most of a foe's moves.

Survivors crawled away from the sand, bleeding and broken and invariably missing a body part. Lucca and the Phoenix fought in the same heat and worked together, both emerging successfully, though battered.

As the crowd dwindled, Blythe realized the women who'd be battling at her side had been hand selected to make things more difficult for her. Sirens, the lot of them. They eyed her with varying degrees of glee.

Were they able to command the beasts with their song or something, protecting themselves? Whatever. Her mojo returned with force, and she'd get through this. Somehow.

At the approach of evening, Roux vanished from the dais. She tensed. Where had he gone? *Why* had he gone? Did he plan to return?

She tried to tell herself it didn't matter but…it mattered.

21

THE BEATING

Roux endured his second wraith feeding with gritted teeth, clenched fists, and locked knees. He despised every moment of this, which made the spectrals love it more. They were dragging out this feeding as long as possible. Hours had passed, sheer determination the only thing keeping him on his feet.

Whatever he had to do, he would return to Blythe and witness her battle with the unibeasts.

"Would our resident rooster like a cock-a-doodle handy before today's session ends?" Penelope asked, eyeing the bulge in his pants as she reclined on her throne of immortals. Or rather, acting as if she reclined while hovering over the seat. "Yes? No?"

"I'm going to enjoy killing you," he told her. The wraiths sucked and sucked and sucked some more.

Every inner pull added fuel to the fire of his fury, while also dulling the fire Blythe had stoked in him.

"I'll take that as a soft no. Do let me know if you change your mind." The wraith heaved a sigh. "Although, I must say, you shouldn't come to our home loaded for bear if you don't want us to offer sexual favors. It's downright rude."

"I will kill you slowly," he grated. He couldn't be blamed for his condition. A sense of possession clawed at him. His harphantom was considering having sex with him. He couldn't not stay hard.

"She won't survive, you know," Penelope said, as if sensing the direction of his thoughts. "Our pets can move between the natural and spirit realm with ease. She'll have no means of escape."

"She will find a way to win." She must! He needed her well. Not for Roc. Not for Taliyah. For himself. Because she might be…his. The knowledge cemented in Roux's mind. She was. She was his. His female. His *gravita*. Stardust wasn't needed to prove it. He knew it beyond a shadow of a doubt.

From the very beginning, he had reacted to Blythe the Undoing in ways he'd never reacted to another. First, her beauty and grace captivated him. Then her touch entranced him. Now, having tasted of her teasing sense of humor…her unexpected gentleness… How could he resist her?

What had begun as physical attraction had ripened into a bone-deep awareness. And really, they weren't as terrible a match as he'd once assumed. Their jagged edges just…fit. He struggled with his emotions, but she felt everything in spades. Confidence was never an issue with Blythe. She knew herself, and she reacted to situations accordingly.

This morning, when she'd promised to rock his world, she'd even helped him figure out what *he* felt. Eagerness. Excitement. Anticipation. The stardust would come. It was only a matter of time.

I have a female. Me. The clone.

Joy burst through him. A ray of light in the darkest recesses of his mind.

"Are you *smiling* now?" Penelope made a disgusted noise.

"Will you demand your turn tonight?" he asked, ignoring her question.

"While you look like that? How can I do so now? The first bite a diner consumes is with the eyes, and I'm not currently digging your flavor." She scowled at him. "Don't take this the wrong way, Astra, but you and your brethren are weird."

"You've known more than one of us?" Some of the wraiths wrenched away from him, as if the tang of his happiness repelled them. The rest followed.

"I might have. Then again, I might not have."

Roux checked his mental clock. Blythe's heat shouldn't begin for another thirteen minutes, eighteen seconds. Enough time to ferret out a bit more information for his task.

"Who *might have* you met?"

The queen of wraiths shrugged. "Perhaps I followed Silver for a time, without his notice. It would have happened before I was sent here, of course. He's a hot piece, that's for sure. Has even more hatred than you. Perhaps I've also conferred with Erebus a time or twenty."

"Did the Dark One send you here?" Roux rolled his

head over his shoulders, straightened his spine, and flexed his hands, checking the extent of today's damage. His internal defenses were compromised but holding steady. His limbs weren't a hundred percent, but they weren't going to give out on him, either. "He usually only deals with those who will affect his war with the Astra."

"Oh, I'll affect his war with the Astra, all right, but he's not to blame for dragging me to this land, kicking and screaming. My mother is to blame for that." A note of bitterness crept into her voice. "The Dark One appears to me upon occasion, that's all. He's quite inventive, isn't he? And kind of delicious, if you're into evil villains who can only be counted on to betray you. A particular favorite of mine. I mean, who else would think to use a— Oh, oh, oh. Sorry, Astra, but I won't be spilling my secrets that easily."

Erebus, able to speak to those in Ation. Upon occasion. Without visiting. How? For that matter, how had the god gotten Blythe here? She'd mentioned her father's betrayal. At the time, Roux hadn't questioned her further because he'd known he couldn't trust her. Now he wasn't so sure. Would she tell him the truth?

After their first round of sex, or perhaps the third or fourth, they'd probably cuddle, and he'd have an opportunity to find out. Maybe, after a dozen climaxes, she'd be more inclined to help him rather than harm him.

"There you go, smiling again," Penelope muttered. "Can't you wait to unveil it after you leave? Honestly, Astra, it makes my stomach turn."

Twelve minutes, twenty-seven seconds until Blythe's battle. "Shall we bargain for information, wraith?"

"We shan't. You have nothing I want." She ran her gaze over his body. "Well, almost nothing."

He waggled his jaw. "What of your freedom from this world?"

Her eyes brightened, as if she suddenly glowed from the inside, but the light dulled in a snap. "You believe you'll escape. You're wrong. Why do you think Erebus stays on the other side of his doors when he—" She pressed her lips together in a thin line. "Well, well. Look who tricked me into saying more than I planned."

The god comprehended how to open doors into Ation. A tidbit. Roux had only to figure out how Erebus did it, then reverse the process. Maybe. His task for tomorrow. After he devoured Blythe.

"Smiling again." The wraith tsked. "Don't you dare rush off," she ordered when he tensed to leave. "Maybe we *can* bargain. After all, I know other things concerning your enemy. Many, many other things." She purred now. "In return, you can give me the same show the harpy gave you this morning."

She'd spied on them? Of course she had. Eyes and ears lurked everywhere in the palace.

Despite his rising irritation, he was tempted to stay and question the wraith further. But acting too eager might place him in a lesser position in her estimation. Better to return on his terms.

Eleven minutes, nine seconds left in the battle. Eight. Seven. Six.

"I'll consider it," he said. As she sputtered with indignation, he flashed to the underground arena, landing in the same spot he'd abandoned earlier. The edge of the dais. Without glancing over his shoulder, he knew every member of the welcome party still occupied the dais as well. They sat in their chairs, laughing and drinking champagne.

The harpy named Tonka popped to her feet, bubbly

liquid splashing over the rim of her glass. "Uh, don't
you have somewhere else to be, Astra?" she asked with
a worried tone.

He scanned the area below and stiffened. If he'd been
smiling before, he wasn't now. His harpy stood in the
ring, lined up with everyone else in her heat. They were
all sirens, the weakest of the participating immortals...
save for their voices. The group faced off with ten unibeasts on the other side of the circle, each animal paw-
ing at the sand, eager to begin.

Smears of blood wet the walls and drenched the sand.
Evidence of previous battles.

Having watched many of the preceding heats, he
knew the beasts had eaten the losers. A strong metallic twang scented the air.

"The last group isn't supposed to go for another ten
minutes, thirteen seconds." Other facts hit him. The
odds of only sirens ending up in Blythe's group, rather
than an eclectic mix of species, were not high. This had
been planned, and not in the harpy's favor.

"Not our fault. The combatants before this one can-
celed," the pale-haired Tonka explained, setting aside
her glass and approaching his side. She faced the arena,
not daring to meet his gaze. "They preferred to lose
their heads by sword rather than to feed a horde of unibeasts their vital organs. To each their own, amirite?"

He flicked his tongue over an incisor. This had been
a planned act, and, considering Penelope's change of
heart at the end of their conversation, the wraith participated. Was she supposed to keep him on her island
until Blythe's heat ended? A heat meant to conclude
with the death of his chosen female, he was sure. If not
by fair means, then definitely foul. Without him acting

as an eyewitness, the perpetrators could claim total innocence afterward.

The fury he'd experienced when he'd learned what was to occur today—nothing compared to what he experienced now. It burned through him, torching any semblance of calm.

"When I kill you," he told the councilmembers, using the softest of tones, "I will make sure you hurt in ways you never dreamed possible."

A mix of trepidation and aggression wafted from them.

"You can't blame a girl for taking a shot." The pale-haired harpy reached for a large ram's horn that rested against a pillar. "Besides, we've heard your threats before. So far you've been all talk and no action. How do we know you're even half as evil as you've been boasting?"

Did she hope to goad him into launching an attack? Would he then be accused of breaking a rule? He leaned down, getting in her face, forcing her to peer into his eyes. "You'll be the first to suffer."

She stumbled back, only to lift her chin in defiance. "Promises, promises. Now enough chatter. It's time for the final round."

She couldn't mask her trembling as she brought the horn to her lips. Her gaze returned to him before she inhaled deeply...and blew.

At the sharp blast of noise, combatants and beasts launched into motion. Roux watched, his jaw clenched, as the sirens rushed together to join hands, leaving Blythe on her own. A soft melody rose from them. As the song increased in volume, each of the unibeasts shifted its full focus to the harphantom.

Every note of the song ramped up their level of aggression, until they were foaming at the mouth.

Roux braced. No matter what occurred, she would pull out a win and kill each predator. Roux hadn't lied earlier. He had complete confidence in this female's abilities. But, despite her arsenal and skill, she would not emerge unscathed. The thought of her pain...

A growl vibrated in his throat, and Tonka backed away from him.

On the field of battle, Blythe charged toward her foes, clutching two short swords. A shout of warning died on his tongue. She needed different weapons. Swords served no purpose against a unibeast's thick, stony hide. A soft underbelly might be susceptible, but she'd have to get underneath a beast without getting torn to shreds. An impossibility. Then, at the last second, she vanished, reappearing in the circle of sirens.

Slash, slash, slash, slash. With her customary grace and elegance, she cut down the other immortals, her motions as fluid as water. Bodies toppled, one after the other. When the final competitor fell, the song died and the unibeasts ceased foaming. Their steps slowed as they shook their heads, coming out of a haze.

"So she can flash," said an Amazon behind him. "She didn't reveal the skill in round one."

No, she hadn't, he realized. She'd kept her talents to herself. As she should have.

The unibeasts reacted to the kills, rushing over to feast on the remains before any survivors could heal. Their hunger never abated, their stomachs bottomless pits. As screams flowed and ebbed, Blythe was momentarily ignored. She dropped the swords and unhooked a whip from her side. With a crack of her wrist, the end of the whip coiled around one of the beasts' necks. Yank.

It flipped over and she flashed, materializing

crouched on its belly and already ramming a blade into his heart.

Yes! "That's my female," he whispered, unwilling to distract her.

At the death of their comrade, the other beasts lost interest in their meals. They focused the full bulk of their attention on Blythe. Snarling, with thick droplets of drool leaking from fangs any vampire would envy, they formed a circle around *her*.

"All right," she called. "Who's ready?"

They surged at her in unison. And, when next she flashed, the animals dove to greet her where she reappeared, clearly expecting the action. But she had expected their counterattack and met the creature closest to her with a sword through its open mouth.

Unlike immortals, these beasts did not heal swiftly, and a second one died.

Eight to go, with roughly nine minutes on the countdown clock.

Roux barely contained a cheer.

Blythe took out three others in quick succession, leaving five opponents and a little less than five minutes. But she didn't do it without injury. Gashes littered her torso. Horn gouges had left holes in both of her shoulders and one of her thighs. Her right arm had no biceps, only teeth marks in the bone.

Heart in his throat, Roux reached up to grip a pillar, uncaring when cracks spread around his fingers. A scream tore through his mind, animalistic. Primal. There was something odd about it. At any other time, it would have bothered him. Right now, he couldn't think.

Blood loss had slowed Blythe's ability to heal. Not to mention her motions. No longer did she have the strength to flash. Though she tried, flickering in and out of view but getting nowhere. She seemed to operate solely on combat skill and sheer determination.

The creatures proved relentless. They gave no quarter, scraping her with their toxic flesh, slicing her with their horns and stomping on any part of her they could reach. Yet, she refused to give up, and took out another and another and another.

Only two monsters and two minutes to go. She just needed to outlast them.

Toward the end of the one-minute mark, she killed another but lost a hand, stumbled, and fell. As she rolled to escape a series of bites, she hemorrhaged blood in every direction.

Breath hitched in Roux's lungs. The remaining beast prowled around her, herding her into a corner.

She had nowhere to go.

Claws grew from its nail beds.

Her prey lunged in her direction—and slammed into the wall. As its stony flesh cracked, she reappeared behind it. In a single fluid motion, she rammed a sword hilt into the widest crack, breaking through and reaching its heart with her hand. The ability to flash hadn't abandoned her, after all. She'd faked it.

A howl of pain echoed as she yanked the heart out. Her specialty. The creature toppled, seized, then sagged into the sand.

Blythe dropped the organ and stumbled, collapsing. Blood poured from her wounds. Her eyes drifted closed.

"She outlasted the unibeasts, making round two officially over," Roux bellowed. He flashed and gathered her near lifeless body. At last the screams in his head quieted. "Stay with me, Lyla."

She panted shallow breaths. Alive! But she didn't open her eyes.

He straightened, clutching her against his chest. Where to take her? Staying in the palace, being surrounded by all those prying eyes and ears right now held no appeal. Nor did camping near Wraith Island.

An idea rose. He flashed into the circle of Oath Stones and scanned the area. Abandoned. Excellent. Silvery moonlight glinted off the rocks. Far too soon, the sun would rise, starting another day. Another battle.

While cold winds had plagued the royal grounds for days, warmth enveloped the private haven. After gently stretching out on the soft grass and arranging Blythe against his chest, facing away from him, he sliced his wrist and held the wound over her mouth.

Crimson dripped past her parted teeth. She needed the blood of her consort to heal. Would she tolerate Roux's or not? What if he was wrong and he didn't actually belong to her?

They would find out.

"Take everything you need, Lyla. Heal."

At first, she didn't act as if she'd heard him. Or react at all. But as more and more of his blood dripped down her throat, her eyelids popped open and narrowed. She grabbed his arm with her working hand, bit into his flesh, and gulped him down.

"That's my precious," he cooed. Careful to hold his arm steady for her, he stretched out at her side. "Not just blood. Soul, too, she-beast."

A soft light glowed around her lips. Usually, when phantoms fed on his soul, cold flowed into his limbs and an itch he couldn't shake tormented him inside and out. Here, now, satisfaction inundated him. Color was returning to her cheeks. Gashes were closing, and her missing hand was reforming.

She continued to drink with greedy abandon. Even as a new tide of weakness washed in, his satisfaction remained high.

He petted her hair, telling her, "No one fought harder or better than my Lyla."

When the suction ceased, he almost protested. Curiosity kept him quiet. Maybe a dash of uncertainty, too. He wrapped his arms around her and rubbed her belly. *Do not vomit me up, Lyla. Please.*

Tension roiled inside him as one minute bled into a second. Then a third. Another five minutes passed. She merely turned and settled more comfortably against him. With her head crooked on his shoulder, she molded her body to his.

He exhaled a sigh of relief. She'd kept him down. He was her consort. Her male. Pride infiltrated every inch of him, and he locked his arms around her once again. Possessiveness sparked and spread. *Mine. My female. Always. Never giving her up.*

Would she ever fully accept his claim, though?

Sighing, he stared up at the night sky. Perhaps not. The jewel remained embedded in her throat. A sight he suddenly resented. It represented the biggest obstacle between them.

"Thank you," she muttered with an almost drunk tone. "In case you were wondering, Astra tastes *good*. You are pure power."

The corners of his mouth twitched. "You will want more of me?"

"Babe, I'll demand it."

A full-blown smile bloomed. Since she hadn't brought

up the consort thing, he wouldn't, either. Yet. "I look forward to this," he replied.

"Good." She got more comfortable. "So, um, where'd you go earlier? During the battle, I mean. Not that I was obsessing over it or anything."

He kissed her temple. "I went back to the wraiths. As long as I feed them once a day, Penelope isn't allowed to drain you."

"That's...wow." Her voice wobbled. "That's some kind of a romantic gesture, Astra."

For the first time in his life, he felt the urge to tease another living being. "Oh? Does my harphantom approve of romance now?"

"To her absolute shock, she does indeed," was the prim reply. A yawn cracked her jaw. "Round three begins in an hour."

"Forty-nine minutes, twenty-two seconds, actually."

She pouted. "So, not nearly enough time to provide my own romantic gesture."

"There's time to *describe* it," he intoned. "Begin with the removal of your clothing and end with your shouts of pleasure."

A soft laugh left her, the warmth of her breath fanning his shoulder. "Talking about getting naked and drowning in sexual bliss will only drive us both to the brink of insanity. So, yes, you've convinced me to do it." She lifted enough to prop up her elbow and rest her cheek on her palm—and give him the sexiest grin he'd ever had the privilege to see, setting his blood on fire. "Why don't we pretend I've already verbally stripped us both so I can tell you everywhere I plan to put my mouth..."

"Yes! Start there and spare no detail."

22

THE COMEBACK

Blythe took her place in the underground arena with the rest of the combatants. Only a hundred or so had survived the unibeasts and very few hid their shock upon discovering her among their numbers.

She offered everyone a mocking smile and a middle finger salute. As predicted, frenzied horniness had left her cranky.

Teasing Roux before today's competition might have been a wee bit foolish. But she couldn't regret it. The guy was feeding wraiths on the daily to keep her strong. He tended to her. Charmed her. Beneath that tough, rough exterior might be—gasp—a candy-coated center.

He was just so different than she'd initially believed. Teasing him had become an enjoyable pastime. She had only to think of him to ache.

This wasn't supposed to happen. She wasn't supposed to like him. Or crave him. And sleep in his arms? Never.

Lifting her gaze to the royal dais, she caught his eye. And lost her breath. Oh, did she love the way his gorgeous irises lit up anytime he spied her. How his body all but vibrated with the need she had stoked.

Somehow, this male was her consort. The second. An impossibility somehow made possible. The evidence couldn't be denied. She had napped in his arms. His blood hadn't sickened her, yet drinking from others did. Even drinking from bloodfruit had bothered her. And his soul… Mmm. There was nothing better.

So what was she going to do about this?

"Congratulations, everyone," Tonka's voice echoed from the cavern walls. "You survived your worst nightmare. Are you ready for today's challenge?"

Silence met her query.

"Wow. Save the enthusiasm for later, okay?" the harpy griped. "We've decided to take it easy on you this go-round."

That did it. Cheers rang out.

Head in the game, girl.

When the celebration quieted, Tonka added, "When you hear the horn, all you must do is venture topside, find a queen of hearts flower, and bring it back here. Oh. And you gotta do it in fifteen minutes or less."

Groans of distress rose from the masses. Uh-oh. What was a queen of hearts flower?

Blythe searched for Lucca, intending to ask her. Of course, the horn sounded and combatants scrambled out of the arena.

A plan formed. Blythe flashed topside, waiting at the

well. A group of competitors shot from its shadowed depths, landed in the palace foyer, and sprinted outside. She stayed put, searching for Lucca... Yes! Payday, baby! The harpy and the Phoenix emerged from the well together.

Blythe jetted after them, blazing over grass, soon passing the circle of silos. Jockeying for a better position, she elbowed and shoulder checked anyone in her path. The combatants behind her ganged up to knock her feet together. Down she tumbled, the immortals trampling over her. She didn't stay down, though. Nope, she ignored the bumps and bruises, and surged to her feet, giving chase once more. No sign of Lucca now. Dang it!

As Blythe pumped her arms to increase her pace, she followed the females ahead of her. They aimed for Wraith Island.

She mentally shifted through the sights she'd encountered the last time she'd traveled this direction. A wooded terrain. A field of wheat. A small village. A cemetery. A stretch of gravel. Another wooded terrain, two other villages, then the beach. Unless... Were the queen of heart flowers found *on* Wraith Island?

If so, Blythe could flash and arrive before everyone else. If not, she would waste precious time. She also ran the risk of losing the crowd, her current GPS.

Considering she had no idea what she was looking for, she opted to remain near the other combatants.

Through the woods they went. Trees blurred at her sides. Suddenly, prickles on her nape alerted her to a possible threat. She scanned...and sucked in a breath. Erebus! Up ahead, he stood in the frame of a red door, wearing his customary black robe, with an expanse of a star-studded sky behind him. He held a length of chain, and he offered the smile she reviled most. Smug.

"I have a surprise for you, daughter," he called. "A good one."

Fury scorched her. How she longed to punch that grin off his face and rip out his guts with her claws. No doubt he'd popped in to distract her at a critical juncture. She hadn't forgotten the truth: she was nothing but Astra bait to Daddy Dearest.

Maybe Erebus even knew she'd come to kind of, sort of…like Roux. Or maybe the Dark One hoped to taunt her about her doomed situation, and the role she played in it. How she'd been granted a miracle, a second consort, but surviving the tournament meant cursing Roux. Did she really want to do that now?

Could she do anything less?

She garnered the strength to ignore the god, sprinting on. But again and again he reappeared, always standing in the frame of that red door. No one else seemed to notice him. In fact, several combatants misted through him. He occupied a spiritual plane.

"Last chance," he told her. As she approached the end of the woods, he tugged on the chain—yanking someone from behind his back.

Blythe nearly tripped over her own feet as she came to an abrupt halt. Her heart punched her ribs. This… this couldn't be. Wasn't possible. But the sight before her never altered. Laban. Her consort. Alive and well.

No, no. Must be a wraith in disguise. Or another hallucination. Finally. Her second sighting. He looked so different, yet the same. A spiked metal collar circled his throat. Like her father, he wore a black robe. His once golden skin was paler than before, the thick mane of dirty blond hair she'd loved to finger comb a tangled mess. His head hung low, but his dark eyes were lifted and glued on her.

He unveiled a small smile. "Hello, sweetness."

His voice! This was no wraith in disguise.

With a screech of shock, Blythe launched forward, slipping into the spiritual plane. At the doorway, she hit an invisible block and bounced back. Impact rattled her brain and momentarily blurred her vision. "You prick," she shouted at her father. "Let me touch him." Would her fingers ghost through him?

Erebus ignored her. "Don't be rude, Laban," he said with the tone of a teacher speaking to a misbehaving child. "Tell your mate how beautiful you find her, even when she's snapping at the hand trying to feed her."

"You are the most beautiful sight in the world to me, Blythe," the manticore croaked.

She came to her feet and pressed her hands over her churning stomach. "Let me touch him," she repeated.

"Deal with your friend first."

Friend? She heard the footsteps then, closing in fast. She turned just in time to spot an Amazon's fist flying toward her face. Blythe ducked and kicked, sending her attacker stumbling into the dirt.

The other female didn't seek revenge, but jumped up and hurried on, muttering, "You'll get yours soon enough," before disappearing past the line of trees.

"Well?" Erebus prompted. "I'll hear your thanks now, daughter. I put your male back together. He's not a hallucination. Aren't you so happy?"

She skidded her gaze to her father and…and…her attention snapped back to Laban. Alive and well? No, this couldn't be. No way, no how. She'd observed Erebus as he'd made some of his phantoms. A grotesque, awful process that involved the living, not the dead. "This isn't my Laban. It can't be."

"Oh. I assure you. It is indeed your Laban." The god's tone hardened. "And if you want him back, you'll kill Roux as planned. Soon. If not, I'll kill Laban for good. After I've told him all about your escapades with the Astra. He'll be riveted, I'm sure."

She…he… This was another trick. She knew better than to trust a known liar to keep his word. And yet, despite her growing hunger for Roux, she felt a draw toward the male at the end of that chain. A need to get nearer to him.

Just another trick? For all she knew, he was nothing more than an illusion crafted with potent black magic.

If he wasn't?

No! Erebus sought to distract her and circumvent her success.

Had the Blade of Destiny shown him a path to his own defeat? Loss was the only thing Erebus feared.

Determination came in like a freight train off the rails. Survive this round and plan. The Dark One had screwed her over for the final time. She would help Roux win his task and somehow save herself in the process. Then she and the Astra could face off about the past.

"Enjoy your defeat." She smiled and zoomed off. As she exited the forest, she came upon Lucca and the Phoenix, who were headed back toward the palace. Both were sliced and diced in multiple places and soaked in blood. Carrigan was missing a hand but in the process of growing a new one.

"You'll never get a flower and make it to the palace in time, even if you flash," an earnest Lucca said, trying to propel Blythe in the same direction. "The bees are good and mad. A third of the competitors have already lost their heads."

Bees? "Don't bet against me," she responded, preparing to blaze on. "You'll always lose big."

"You misunderstand." The Phoenix jumped into her path. "We picked a queen of hearts for you."

Blythe prepared to throw an elbow when the words registered. Uh... "Come again?" They'd gotten her, the Undoing, a flower?

"Here." Lucca withdrew an ugly orange bloom missing petals.

Another trick? Surely.

And if not?

With great reluctance, Blythe accepted the offering. "Why would you do this?"

"For the moment, you'll just have to trust that we have a reason. Right now, let's qualify for round four. Come on."

The pair dashed off, leaving her behind. Blythe hung back, immobilized by indecision. To follow or not?

What possible motive could they have for aiding her in a zero-sum game? Nothing struck her as good enough. And yet... She couldn't shake a lingering doubt. What did they know that she didn't?

Other combatants with shredded throats and missing appendages headed her way, many clutching the same orange bloom.

Not a trick, after all? Unless they were all in on it?

Deciding to risk it, Blythe flashed to the underground arena and presented her flower to Tonka.

"Son of a beast," the harpy muttered. "You move on to round four. Yay."

* * *

Roux thrust an arm into the air. Yes! Blythe had done it. She had obtained a queen of hearts flower and returned first. Others arrived soon after, and the horn blasted.

The harphantom immediately lifted her gaze, meeting his. A current of electricity arced between them, wild and sharp. Why did she appear so...desperate? Had something happened out there?

"Looks like your female survived," Monna said. She stood with him at the edge of the dais.

He ignored her, appearing at Blythe's side.

"Take me to our spot," she pleaded.

Something *had* happened. Roux gathered her close in a hurry and returned her to the Oath Stones, where sunlight bathed the land, casting a vivid sheen over the sea of soft grass and glistening rock.

"Tell me."

She slipped free and backed away. Opened her mouth. Closed it. Opened, closed. Then her shoulders rolled in, gutting him.

"Tell me." A command.

Pale baby blues wide and wounded, she wrapped her arms around her waist, saying, "The harpy and the Phoenix helped me. Gave me the flower. I don't know why. But before that..." Her eyelids narrowed. "You know what? No. Nothing else of importance happened out there. I'm not going to waste another moment of my life wishing for something I can't have. I'm going to take what I want while I can."

Motions jerky, she ripped off her top. "Strip, Astra. Let's do this." Her skirt hit the ground. She kicked off her boots and shed her weapons. Gloriously naked, she demanded, "Why aren't you stripping?"

Because he didn't understand her mood. Because her beauty had erased his wits. Because…he didn't know why. "I never thought I'd say this, but we will talk before we *do this*."

"I don't want to talk." She kicked his feet out from under him, and he let her do it. Let her dive on top of him and claim his lips in a mad kiss.

He kissed back because he couldn't not kiss back. While his body hummed with frothing delight, his mind wasn't satisfied. He wanted to be more to her than an outlet.

And he would be. Roux had learned enough about her to know she must be eased from whatever mood this was. He gentled his response and cupped her jawline. Applying the slightest pressure, he took control of the kiss. Reverence marked every brush of his lips and stroke of his tongue.

Her fervor tapered until she matched him stroke for stroke, brush for brush. Reverence for reverence.

With a groan, she lifted her head and pressed her brow to his. Clinging to him, she asked, "Why aren't you out of your mind with passion?"

Roux rolled her over, pinning her to the grass with his weight. "Your Astra requires more romance. And he's going to get it."

Wrapping her arms around him, she molded her body to his and dragged a knee up and down his side. "My Astra. Roux."

Those whispered words annihilated his defenses.

"That's right. I'm yours, and you are mine." With

his hands free, he gripped the neckline of his shirt and yanked. "I should inspect what's mine."

"You should. Twice."

He lowered his lips to hers and stole her breath. As she writhed beneath him, he kissed her jawline. The length of her throat. Lower. He tasted the sweetest peaks and most sumptuous hollows. Savored her cries of bliss and pleas for more. Relished the way she moved against him. Her sweet cries filled his ears, creating the most tantalizing music.

This. This was what he'd been created to do. Not to hurt or to inflict hurt, but to please this female. Through her pleasure, he found his own.

But the more he tasted, the more he wanted. Ever-sharpening desire lashed at his fraying control while frenzied desire burned at the fringes of his every thought. Sweat sheened his skin. Muscles pulled taut. Veins throbbed.

His palms, they tingled and heated. And heated. He expected to produce flames at any moment. Blythe didn't seem to mind.

"Roux, I'm going to… I'm so close…" Her body jerked, and she screamed a sound of complete satisfaction.

He lifted his head from between her legs and licked his wet lips. His chest puffed up. His control frayed further. Climax looked good on her.

He should give her another one.

With a drunken smile, she rasped, "Get inside me, Roux."

Yes. No. He fought the clawing need to obey. "No sex." Not until she asked for it before they even started. For now, they could do something he'd imagined.

He jerked to his knees and lowered his zipper.

Her jaw dropped. What did she think of him?

One thudding heartbeat, two.

She smiled with feline-like approval. "I am going to love being with you."

He gripped his shaft and stroked. She watched, as though riveted. As a ray of sunlight broke through the night's gloom, stroking her, he did it again. And again. She wiggled, her skin glittering. Brightly.

His jaw nearly unhinged as he swept his gaze over her sprawled form. He had covered her with stardust. Had claimed her as his own. His possessiveness tore off its leash. *My* gravita. Something he'd never thought to have. Or want. But he had one now—and he would keep her. Forever.

He would die before he gave her up. The task couldn't have her heart. Though she was soon to become Ation's queen, Roux refused to kill her. So decision made. No need for further pondering. He would succeed another way, saving both his friends and his female.

"If you're worried about getting me pregnant," she said, placing her legs outside his hips, "don't. It's not my season."

Pregnant? He gulped. The thought of creating a child...someone he could—and would—protect in all the ways he had not been. Becoming a family. *Want this!*

"Lyla, I'm not worried about anything right now. I think I might be happy for the first time in my life." He climbed up her body, kissed her, and rolled, putting her on top of him.

Magnificent female. All mine. "Though it pains me to say this," he began, urging her to her knees, "you won't be claiming my virginity today. But you will be giving me that story you promised me."

"Is that so?" With her mussed black hair, luminous eyes, and passion-flushed skin, she was all goddess. She wrapped her fingers around his shaft, saying, "When the pleasure is too much for you, just say my name... and I'll keep going."

23

THE PARTNERSHIP

Blythe meant to torment Roux until he gave her what she wanted. In a good way! But the guy who liked to sit in chairs and stare at her in silence was an animal in bed, and she kept losing her mind over it, forgetting her purpose.

As she licked and sucked him, he stayed rough and growly. Commanding. He displayed zero hesitation, threading his fingers through her hair and guiding her the way he wanted her. He loved what they were doing, and it showed. And even now, he watched her. Oh, did he watch, gauging every change of her expression.

Only want more. What had started as a screw you to her father and his tricks had morphed into a sensual indulgence she never wanted to end.

"You make me feel so good," Roux rasped. "Can't live without this. Never letting you go."

And he wasn't done. As she sucked him faster, he made observations about her. "You're desperate for me, too.

"You enjoy this very much.

"You'll need more every day."

He asked questions. "You've been starved for me, haven't you, Lyla?

"You'll give me whatever I want, won't you?"

Blythe couldn't think past her growing need. She sucked faster.

Hoarse groans left him as he fisted a handful of her hair.

Between panting breaths, he told her, "I never understood...why males waged wars...for their females... but this...you... I understand now." Strain radiated from him. "Need to see you."

The next thing she knew, she lay on her back, Roux looming over her, a fantasy made flesh. His pale hair was tousled. His pupils pulsed over his golden irises, reminding her of a heartbeat. Never had there been a more sensual sight. Or sensation. His erection pressed against her core, without penetration, perfect, and wonderful and terrible because she craved more.

Fierce, wild eyes locked with hers. He stared at her in that all-consumed, all-consuming way, and any remaining defenses she possessed crumbled, leaving her shockingly vulnerable. All she could do? Rock against him as emotion after emotion swamped her. Hope. Tenderness. Anticipation. Nothing she'd thought she would crave again...but everything she needed?

He dipped his head to kiss the corner of her mouth, rocking, rocking, and whispered, "I understand, Lyla."

Blythe opened her mouth to ask what he thought he understood, when she herself understood nothing, but the pleasure. "Roux. Forget your principles and get inside me."

"Don't tempt me." He kissed her hard and fast, preventing a debate. Always rocking against her, driving her toward the brink. "I meant what I said. You'll ask me before we start. You'll say, Roux, will you please give me what I need?"

"Asking doesn't sound like something I'd do." Pleasure spiked. "But I might just issue a demand."

"Even better." He thrust against her with more force, his shaft slipping over her sex, rubbing against all the right places. Again. And again. Sweat trickled from his temples. "Lyla. Not sure how much longer I can hold out. The feel of you…"

As she screamed, coming apart at the seams, he threw back his head, and came apart, too.

He collapsed atop her but quickly collapsed to his side. They both lay there for a moment.

"I am undone," he rasped.

"You aren't the only one."

Still laboring for breath, he swiped up a discarded T-shirt and cleaned her. When he finished, he tugged her against his furnace of a body.

She could do nothing but mold against him and marvel. With Laban, she'd always experienced the pangs of addiction at this point, as if she could never get enough. As if—she cringed with merely the thought—something had been missing, and she'd constantly sought to fill a void. Here and now, she wanted only to luxuriate in this seemingly endless sea of contentment.

But how could that be? What did it mean? Why wasn't the guilt attacking her with renewed force? Where was the tide of regret?

Roux must have sensed the source of her unease; he ran his fingertip along the jewel, frowning when it remained firmly attached. "Is there anything I can do to earn your forgiveness?"

No. Yes. Maybe? "I don't hate you. Not anymore," she admitted, the act disgracefully easy. "But I'll always hate what you did." How could she not? Her daughter had to live without her father.

"I *am* sorry I hurt you and your family, Lyla."

"I know." And she did. Looking back without her malice-colored glasses firmly in place, she could see that he'd accepted her vengeance as his due.

"Shall we discuss the tournament?" he asked, tracing his fingertips along the ridges of her spine. "You mentioned the harpy and Phoenix aided you today."

Not wanting to ruin the mood, she took the bait: the changing of the subject. "Yep. It was quite a shock, too. Since we were in the middle of a round, they claimed they had no time to explain. I should hunt them down and get answers."

"Or stay here with me. Carrigan, the Phoenix. She's dangerous. Be leery of her."

"Oh?" Remembered jealousy flared. Blythe traced the tip of a claw around one of his nipples. "Do tell."

"She says she received instruction from an oracle before voluntarily coming to this realm. That she has always known she will escape with me, and she alone will decide your fate."

"In case you're curious, she's wrong. *I* decide my fate." And she'd decided to win the tournament, find a way to save Roux's blessing task without dying, and defeat Erebus.

Should Blythe tell Roux about her most recent dealings with the god or not? And what of the Laban sighting?

No. Better to wait until she had processed everything. Roux would insist on deep diving into the encounter, and currently she had no answers. Honestly, she didn't know what to think about anything anymore.

Could she truly work with Laban's executioner? Could she willingly help save the Astra army who'd destroyed her daughter's life? Would Isla grow to despise her for such a deed?

Blythe, the first harpy in history to halfway forgive rather than fully retaliate? The madness!

"I think the oracle told Carrigan to align with Erebus," she said. "He expects me to kill you. An assignment he believes only I can carry out successfully." Something the Astra had already known. "It makes sense that he'd order Carrigan and Lucca to help me, and they'd actually obey. He probably promised them one-way tickets off realm. Which means they now grace the top of my hit list. Friends of my enemy are my enemy."

"According to Penelope," Roux said, kissing her temple, "not even Erebus is able to flash from this place. He visits her through doorways he fears to exit."

Yes, Blythe had firsthand experience with those doors. "Do you know of a way home?" Yeah. Decision made. Firm this time. Win the tournament, return to

Harpina with Roux, complete his task, stay alive, deal with Erebus. Then figure out all the rest.

"I have ideas. Namely, creating a doorway of my own. Something best done after the tournament, so no one else uses it."

Smart. "If that fails, maybe I can drag you into a spirit realm and Ation will lose its hold on us."

"Perhaps," he said, "but either way, we will leave this realm together. I will allow no other outcome." Determination hardened his voice, and she shivered. "Now, tell me what happened the other night, after I returned from feeding the wraiths."

When she'd stared at his *alevala*? "I saw an endless, spinning slideshow of your death and torture courtesy of the other Astra, who looked like shadow puppets."

He inhaled sharply, exhaled heavily. "My task usually involves entering an echo realm where memories of our tasks are recorded."

"Recorded? Why?"

"Someone always complains about a rule being broken. For a fair ruling, our deeds are rewatched, examined, and picked apart."

Okay. Yeah. That made sense. She'd bet her life Erebus demanded to view that replay every time he'd lost.

Roux continued, "I'm drawn into the echoes of the slain to experience their last moments alive. If I remain silent until the cycle is complete, I am successful. If I make a sound, any sound at all, I fail."

"And what is the purpose of such a task?"

"To break me, I suppose. And it's almost worked. The prisoners in my mind usually escape from the start, the noise as tormenting as everything else. Things get... jumbled for me."

Yawning, she snuggled closer. The trials of the day must have caught up with her. Fighting to stay awake, she smoothed a hand over his shoulder, petting him, offering comfort. "You've mentioned the prisoners before. Who or what are they, exactly?"

A moment passed. Then he said, "Tomorrow is a big day, and my harphantom needs her rest." He kissed her temple, more of his heat enveloping her. "Sleep, Lyla."

For some reason, she obeyed, letting herself drift off.

Hours later, a cozy, well-satisfied Blythe opened her eyes and stretched sore muscles, inadvertently rubbing against her deliciously ferocious Astra.

"There you are," he said, gliding his thumb over her jaw.

"What time is it?" she asked.

He kissed her brow. "Time for you to go back to the palace."

"I don't know about you, but I could go for a slice of chocolate cake first. Or the whole cake." Well, well. Her sweet tooth was officially back in business. "Probably best to acquire two, so I don't have to fork you for attempting to steal a bite of my dessert after I've stolen multiple the bites of yours."

"I will bring you all the cakes upon my return." He gently disentangled his limbs from hers and stood, leaving her lying on the ground, suddenly keenly aware of the cool breeze and setting sun.

The sky was a haze of dark blues and muted golds, a breathtaking scene as Roux gathered his clothing. "Return from where?"

"Wraith Island," he intoned with his back to her, sliding into his leathers.

"I'm going with you," she informed him. Fully awake now, she popped to her feet and tugged on her garments.

"Fine," he replied, surprising her with the ease of his agreement. "I believe there's a firstone weapon hidden within. You can search for it while the wraiths are otherwise occupied."

Uh... He was trusting her with firstone? "Look. I kind of know there's a firstone dagger hidden within Penelope's domain. Because I brought it, and she stole it."

The muscles in his shoulders bunched before he tugged his shirt overhead. "Will you strike at me while we're here?"

Okay. Fair question. Highly deserved. "I told myself I wouldn't, and I do plan to help you, but I don't know. Maybe, if you made me mad enough," she said, securing her own top in place. "Hey! Frowning, she examined her arm in the dwindling light. "Am I glittering?"

She was! And just as brightly as Taliyah did after Roc—Blythe jerked her gaze to Roux just as he pivoted to face her. His expression switched from chagrined to prideful.

"About that."

"You marked me as your *gravita* and didn't inform me the second it happened?" She jerked on her skirt, then her boots, reeling. He'd claimed her. Roux the Crazed One had officially, eternally claimed her as his fated mate. And now, everyone would know it.

"I considered telling you. And planned to. Later. Which is now," he told her, cautious as he finished strapping on his weapons. "I was kind of busy when it happened."

What was she supposed to even do with this information? Preen? Sob? What did this mean for her? For Isla?

Blythe was the sole being in all of history that Roux couldn't live without. The female he craved above all others. The one he *required*. An honor Laban had never given her. Not his fault, of course. Manticores didn't possess fated mates. They tended to jump from one companion to another. Something Blythe had feared in the beginning. But time and time again, Laban had proven his love for her. His utter devotion. And most days, she'd told herself the lack of a reciprocal meant-to-be connection hadn't bothered her. But deep down, she'd been troubled.

To share more with Roux...

She continued to examine her arm. The stardust was admittedly lovely.

"Don't try to wipe it off," Roux grated.

Her lungs compressed at his defensive tone. "I'm not," she assured him. "It matches my outfit." Then she shocked herself. She stepped into Roux's personal space and wound her arms around him, resting her head against his shoulder, seeking comfort.

After a minute of immobility, he shifted, returning her embrace. Tightly.

"I must admit, this isn't the reaction I expected," he said. "And I had no idea what to expect." After kissing her lips once, twice, then lingering and cursing, he asked, "Are you ready to go?"

"Ready," she said with a nod. More than ready, actually. There was no better way to end this day than screwing over Penelope and reclaiming the dagger.

"The second we arrive, I want you to mist." Roux

hooked a lock of hair behind her ear. "From there, follow me in silence. Upon entering the palace, I'll head to the throne room. You will launch your search."

"How long will I have?"

"The feedings vary in length but usually last at least an hour. For that reason, you will flash to the location where we first landed, and you will do so within sixty minutes of our arrival. No later. And no matter what happens to me, you are not to attack the wraiths."

"If a spirit-hag steals one of your organs, I make no promises. That's my shtick." But okay. His plan sounded simple enough. And once she got inside that palace, she'd have the ability to return anytime she desired. An ambush could be arranged...

Roux transported her to a rickety drawbridge shrouded by thick white fog. Blythe wasted no time with questions. She simply did as he'd requested and misted, taking a form not even other spirits could discern.

"This way," he told her softly. When he crossed the creaking wooden planks, she floated behind him. As soon as they exited, putting their feet on solid ground, the fog parted, revealing Penelope standing in a doorway, wearing a see-through pink nightgown.

Do not strike. Do not!

"How intriguing," the wraith said. "What's this you've brought me, darling?"

He stiffened, and Blythe would have lost her footing if she'd been walking. Had she seriously been spotted already?

"What did I bring you?" he asked.

Penelope waved to the Astra's groin. "Another erection. I'm beyond flattered. Truly."

Okay. All right. But also not okay. Not all right.

"That isn't for you," he snapped, and dang if it wasn't sexy.

"Sure it's not." The wraith winked at him. "Too bad for you the Astra aren't able to mist the way Erebus does. You would then be able to handle spirits."

"Enough chatter. Let's get this done."

"Tsk, tsk. So rude tonight. But I guess anything's better than your smile." Penelope spun and glided into an empty foyer. "Come on, then. The others are waiting."

Blythe could handle spirits, no problem. And she was sooo tempted to solidify just enough to lash out. How did Roux put up with this female night after night?

He stomped after Miss Murder. Unnoticed, Blythe branched off, heading in the opposite direction. Fifty-nine minutes on the countdown clock.

She'd never forgotten Lucca's claim that Penelope possessed a treasure room, and the only entrance was found in her bedroom. So, up the stairs Blythe blazed, on the hunt for the primary bedroom. No doubt a "queen" like ole Pen demanded the very best. Except the primary bedroom was as empty as the foyer. So were all the other bedrooms. She walked through every available doorway and got nowhere fast.

Could the entrance be hidden in the walls, maybe? Or the floor?

With the countdown clock ticking in her head, Blythe patted as many walls as possible. Searched the floors with an eagle eye. Hunted any well-portals that might lead below the palace. No luck. The most she managed to do? Uncover a vent.

"I thought about going first tonight." Penelope's sultry voice wafted through its slats. "In the end, I decided to go last and sample your deepest hatred. But you don't mind, do you, handsome?"

Roux's response was muffled, and Blythe pursed her lips.

"Mmm," the wraith moaned. "My suspicions were correct. You rival the phantom."

Frustration merged with annoyance when the sixtieth minute zeroed out, and Blythe had nothing to show for it. Though she was beyond tempted to make her way to the throne room, she set course for the front door, intending to head back to the drawbridge.

A pitter-patter of footsteps echoed. Seconds later, a unibeast clomped into the chamber.

Breath clogged in her throat. Uh-oh. She so did not want to deal with any of these creatures today.

It sensed something and stilled. As its beady eyes darted, she didn't dare flash. The use of power might trigger its most aggressive instincts. It had in the arena.

If it alerted the wraiths to her presence...

It prowled around the space, sniffing the air. Blythe held herself immobile...it walked right through her, and she breathed easier. But then it walked through her again. And again.

She moved. It moved, too, seeming to stalk her.

This went on for one minute. Two. Three. It never missed a beat and never failed to find her.

She chanced a step toward a door, gauging its reaction. It jumped in front of her, blocking the way, daring her to escape. Its ears flattened, and its eyes darted.

Her frustration and annoyance intensified. The unibeasts were intelligent beings; they learned and adapted.

Should she wait it out or risk flashing to the bridge?

Would Roux storm the palace, searching for her, if he beat her to the meeting spot?

In the end, she decided to take a chance. Blythe flashed to the edge of the bridge. She held her breath. No Roux. And no commotion at the palace. No stampede of unibeasts giving chase.

Relief cascaded over her—until the unibeast appeared right in front of her, with seven friends. Licking drool from their fangs, they circled her. She rolled back her shoulders and palmed a dagger. No choice. She had to fight.

"All right, fleabags. Who wants to die first?" she asked.

Tendrils of smoke curled from her skin, as if flames danced just beneath the surface. And mmm. The scent. Sweet and spicy, just like Roux.

Her eyes widened. The stardust was responsible?

The unibeasts snarled at her, gearing to attack. They leaped, and she braced. But at the moment of contact, they jolted and jerked, as if grazed by a cattle prod. They fell to the ground and shook.

Oh, yeah. Definitely caused by the stardust. What an amazing turn of events!

Just how powerful was her new armor? Grinning, Blythe kicked the creature closest to her. Nothing. No reaction. *Very* powerful.

Roux appeared at her side, waxen and clammy. Her grin vanished. Silent, he gathered her close and flashed to the Oath Stones, where he collapsed to his knees. He looked up at her with wounded, questioning eyes.

"The dagger?"

A lump grew in her throat. "I'm sorry," she croaked,

dropping down to pet him. Fury sparked as she smoothed damp hair from his brow. She would absolutely be killing the wraiths of Ation. "I didn't find it."

He squeezed his eyes shut and gave a clipped nod. "Then we try again tomorrow."

24

THE UNCERTAINTY

The next morning, the fourth day of the tournament, Roux cheered for Blythe from the royal dais. The combatants participated in some sort of endurance test known as "jazzercise." They jumped, kicked, and flailed for almost an entire day.

The fifth challenge started soon after and it, too, stretched on. It was then that Roux clued in. The councilmembers obviously strove to keep him separated from Blythe. And they were succeeding. After the sixth and seventh rounds, he and the harphantom had enough time to catch a swift nap, nothing more. There was no discussing what had happened between them. No touching.

He *needed* to touch her. To mark and claim her again. To know her desire for him hadn't waned.

As the eighth battle stretched on, his taut nerves frayed. Blythe raced a dangerous obstacle course alongside nineteen other immortals; tension mounted inside him. Didn't help that she had a chance to take out Carrigan and Lucca but spared them instead. The two were suspected accomplices of his greatest enemy, yet she showed them mercy? Why? And why did the wraith's jewel remain firmly entrenched in the hollow of Blythe's throat?

He didn't want to doubt her desire for him but... doubt crept in.

What if she had welcomed his touch and eagerly offered her own to trick him? What if she'd faked her pleasure? Was there a better plan? Lure the besotted Astra into a false sense of security, then take him out when he least expected it.

What if she worked behind the scenes to sabotage his task?

By trusting her in any capacity, he risked more than his life. He jeopardized the lives of his brothers. Men he loved. Men who relied on him to do his job. They'd always had his back. Had often put themselves in danger to save him. How could he endanger their futures for anyone, even a *gravita*?

But how could he not?

Tonka approached him at the edge of the dais and raised the horn to signal the end of the round. Not only did she act as the MC of the event, but she also acted as Roux's handler. The other members of the welcome party hadn't bothered to show up today. No doubt they planned an ambush of some kind.

"Your girl's sure to move on," the harpy grumbled. "Again."

"Yes." And he could not be prouder of her.

Covered in sweat and sand, Blythe swung a sword with expert precision, taking the head of a wolfshifter just before she crossed the obstacle course's finish line.

The horn's blare pierced the air. "And that's a wrap," Tonka called.

Roux planted his feet, remaining in place, ignoring the urgent urge to flash to his treacherous *gravita*, gather her close and bend her over their bed. The harphantom remained rooted, too, clutching the bloodsoaked sword. She was panting with exertion as she lifted her gaze, peering up at him.

Awareness arced in the space between them. Despite his jumbled mix of emotions, he wasn't sure he could function without her anymore. He'd tasted of pleasure and peace for the first time in his life, and there was no going backward for him. She was a lifeline, and he refused to let go.

He nodded his approval of her victory, and she blew him a kiss.

"By the way, tonight we're hosting a dinner to celebrate the combatants who reached the semifinals," Tonka said.

The tournament had done its job, thinning the herd. From hundreds of Ation citizens to ten semifinalists, including Blythe, plus the nine members of the welcome party, the thirty-nine women who'd chosen not to fight, and the twenty-three wraiths. And those from the villages who hadn't participated.

"You will come," Tonka added. A statement, not a question. "You don't even have to travel far. Food is being served in the conference room on the third floor."

Somehow, he found the strength to tear his attention from Blythe and face the other female. He arched a brow while tilting his head to the side. With an eerily quiet tone, he asked, "You have the means to force me?"

"Well, yeah." A flush stained the harpy's cheeks. "Your oath. Between courses, we'll be discussing round nine, which definitely, positively requires your input to ensure no rules are broken. And, because you can't interfere with the tournament, you can't refuse to listen to our questions."

He pressed his tongue to the roof of his mouth. Maybe his oath would force his involvement in this, maybe it wouldn't. Either way, he wished to hear more about this round nine.

"I'll be there. Make sure there's dessert." He hadn't forgotten Blythe's request for the cake. "Something chocolate, preferably."

A relieved sigh gusted from the harpy, and she grinned. "Okay, that was easier than I expected. Heck yeah, there will be dessert. If you're lucky, we'll serve the sweet treats on our bodies. Oh, and first course will be served in an hour. That way, we'll be sure to finish up before you're due at Wraith Island."

That, he highly doubted. Perhaps they intended to poison him and keep him from fulfilling his vow to Penelope? Too bad. His immunity to poisons, toxins, and venoms hadn't weakened. Or maybe they hoped to poison Blythe? Again, too bad. He would act as her taster. And probably feed her by hand.

The idea stuck, and there was no negating it. He *would* feed her by hand. And probably love-hate every second of it.

Blythe flashed to his side, startling Tonka, who backed up a step. "You ready to go, babe?" The harphantom leaned her head against his shoulder while gliding a palm up his chest.

Staking a claim? He almost grinned. And would have, if his doubts hadn't returned. Scowling, he slung an arm around her waist and transported her to their chamber.

He released her, stalked to his chair, and sat. "We're attending a dinner in an hour. Wash up and change," he said. "Then we talk."

She stood where he'd left her, her arms hanging at her sides, her expression lusty and yet almost vulnerable. "Why don't we take off our clothes and see what happens instead?"

He bit his tongue to stop a swift agreement. "Stay bloody, if you'd like, but we *will* talk. We approach the end of our time here, and I want things settled between us."

Moments passed in silence as she searched his face. Maintaining a blank expression required work, but he did it. "Guess I'll be washing up," she quipped, sauntering to the closet, where she withdrew multiple garments so sheer, he broke out in a sweat.

"We'll be flashing to Wraith Island straight from the dinner, so dress accordingly," he instructed, gripping the arms of the chair.

"Sir, yes, sir." A sassy tone, filled with determination. Blowing him a kiss, she strolled into the bathroom without exchanging the sheer garments for others and sealed herself inside.

He lurched to his feet and paced. Back and forth, back and forth. Did she plan to betray him or not? What would he do if she *did* betray him? A denial roared in his head.

Back and forth, back and forth.

With a growl, he plopped onto the bed; the mattress bounced with his weight, shifting something beneath him. He thought he sensed— Roux went still. The fir-stone dagger. *Here?*

Frowning, he scrambled to his feet and lifted the mattress. And there it was. The barest hint of a purple dagger, peeking out of a plain black sheath. Obviously a blocker designed to hide the dagger's nearness. If that tiny portion of the blade had not worked its way free, he might never have known the weapon waited within his reach.

Realization struck. Blythe planned to kill him. And what better time to strike an Astra than in bed, distracted beyond reason? No wonder she'd welcomed his touch.

Fury and pain tore through him, setting off a chorus of screams inside his head. The murder plan, he understood. Accepted, even. Tit for tat. But the faked pleasure...

He tasted blood as he stashed the dagger in a hidden pocket of his bag. With one act, Blythe had tainted his favorite memories. Rousing her passion and giving her pleasure had affected him. Undone and remade him, offering life rafts of bliss amid an endless sea of torture. To learn those recollections were nothing but lies...

Roux beat his fists into his chest once. Twice. Again. Then again. One of his ribs cracked. Perhaps others. Difficult to tell when his insides felt shredded. How far would she take this ruse? At what point might she strike?

Most important, what was he going to do about it?

* * *

"The she-beast is ready for dinner and dagger hunting, Warden," Blythe announced when she emerged from the bathroom exactly one hour later.

Roux reclined in his chair, firelight crackling behind him. With narrowed lids, he looked her over. A muscle jumped in his jaw.

Um, did he not like it? Because, for the first time, he was looking at her the way he looked at everyone else.

She'd chosen her outfit with care. A scanty, scarlet dress reminiscent of the "bait" Penelope had forced her to wear, with off-the-shoulder spaghetti straps, a deep vee to showcase plenty of cleavage, and slits that stretched from her hips to her ankles. A bejeweled belt cinched the scandalously sheer material at her waist.

Eerily silent, he eased to his feet. His hands balled and opened, then balled again. Whoa! His eyes. They flickered with sparks of crimson. She gulped. Before, he'd been a volcano soon to erupt, with molten lava seething beneath his skin. Blythe had blamed sexual frustration. Now she wasn't so sure. Never had he looked more capable of committing cold-blooded murder.

All this because she'd avoided having a chat about their expectations?

He flicked the tip of his tongue against an incisor. Finally, he spoke. "You look lovely, Blythe."

His tone. It was one she'd never heard him use before. Not with her. It sent icy shudders down her spine. And why hadn't he called her Lyla?

Disappointment set in. She'd expected heat from her Astra. Maybe a suggestive comment or twelve. A series of illicit touches, perhaps. Definitely a new application of stardust.

She tossed her arms up. "That's all I get from you?"

"Yes." He said no more but waved his fingers at her. "What more would you like me to say?"

So formal. She didn't appreciate it one bit. Had he somehow learned of Erebus's visit? Or discovered her father's evil plan to use a fake Laban against her? She still hadn't told him. Hadn't known how to broach the subject in the short minutes between heats. Should she do so now?

Maybe he resented her for leaving Carrigan and Lucca alive. He'd asked about the pair after every round of the tournament. Except today. Blythe just...well, she didn't want to murder the women who'd helped her until she knew beyond any doubt that they were working with her father.

Had Roux grown tired of her? In the space of an hour? Did she even want a consort so changeable?

Every day she'd felt herself soften toward the male. But what if the opposite were true for him and his feelings for her?

No. Surely not. The remnants of his stardust sparkled on her skin. He'd claimed her. For now, she'd claimed him. Whatever was going on, they would work it out.

Determined, Blythe strolled over, exaggerating the roll of her hips. His eyelids slitted further. Pressing against him, she glided her hands up his chest. She might not know how she felt about him, but she knew what she wanted—more pleasure. And she planned to get it.

"I crave you," she rasped. "That's what else I want to hear you say."

He narrowed his eyes. "I'd give you those words, but there's no time to talk. You made sure of that, didn't you, Lyla?" Suddenly *colder* than ice, he clasped her waist and flashed her to the third-floor conference room, the table piled high with a plethora of dishes. From a succulent bird stuffed with a mix of fruit and nuts to creamy potatoes and buttered vegetables.

Roux released her and stepped back at the first opportunity.

The savory scents made her mouth water, but her stomach only roiled in protest. All her life, she'd been confident in her feelings and her decisions. Become General. Give up everything for Laban. Lay the world at her daughter's feet. Kill the Astra. Now she knew nothing, and the uncertainty sucked.

Focus on the party. The welcome party as well as the other combatants were dressed to the nines, too, and already seated. All conversation ceased as the crowd noticed Roux and Blythe.

"Sit, sit, and we'll get started," Tonka said, motioning to the empty chair at the head of the table.

Thankfully—or not so thankfully?—they hadn't attempted to put Blythe at the other end. Nope, they'd saved her the spot next to Roux's. He escorted her over and even held out the seat for her.

She pasted a smile on her face. Brittle? Probably. But it was the best she could do.

Roux stared straight ahead...and anger began to overtake her uncertainty. She scanned the room's occupants, skipping over everyone but Carrigan and Lucca. They peered at her with expectation and maybe concern.

What? she mouthed.

Arena, Lucca mouthed back. *Midnight*.

Should she attend a meeting with possible foes? Yes, she decided only a moment later. She needed to know why they'd helped her. Or finally kill them. The real question was: Should she tell Roux about the meetup or keep quiet? In his weird, awful mood, he might protest. But could she sneak away without detection?

She chanced a glance at him. His eyes were now fully red.

Uh. No. There'd be no sneaking away. She'd just have to tell him and deal with the fallout.

She nodded at the harpy and the Phoenix.

"Now that our honored guest is here." An Amazon motioned to the food. "For our harpies, every dish is mine, so every bite you take is stolen. For our vampires, there's a nice blood pudding no one else will want. For Astras with a dessert fetish, our team of chefs made lemon blueberry cake since they didn't have the ingredients for chocolate. Seems our farmers are slower than usual since most of them are dead and all. I suggest everyone eat up. For many of you, this will be a last meal."

Roux had requested a chocolate dessert? For her? How…how sweet. So why treat her as an inconvenience? Had she angered him in some way? But how? She hadn't removed any of his organs in days. Not a single one.

"You mentioned round nine." He moved his gaze from one female to the other, avoiding only Blythe. "Explain."

Oh, yeah. Anger. Lots and lots of anger. Seriously, what had changed between the request for dessert— which must have happened after the round, when he'd spoken with Tonka—and the here and now?

"Yep, I sure did mention round nine, didn't I? One sec, though." Tonka mimicked the others, diving for the food, dumping spoonfuls of everything onto her plate. "A girl's gotta eat, amirite?"

Screw Roux. Blythe wasn't missing a meal because some guy had gotten his underwear in a twist about something he refused to share with her. Even if she deserved it! Half standing, she bent over the table and loaded up on chicken, greens, and honey-glazed carrots.

As she forked the first bite into her mouth, Roux latched onto her wrist and diverted her aim, claiming the bite for himself. He retained his hold on her until he swallowed. Then he stared at his empty hand as if trying to decide what to do with it.

"You may eat. There's no poison," he said, and nope, he didn't glance at her. Or prolong contact. He lowered his arm.

Okay, so maybe she could be nicer to him? "How kind of you to check for me, Astra," she said, and she meant it. Hoping to sooth him, she switched her fork to her other hand, then reached under the table to squeeze his knee. "Perhaps I'll offer you a reward."

As she slowly glided her nails up his thigh, a muscle jumped in his jaw again. Did he try to stop her? No. His breath hitched. Closer and closer she came to his zipper...

He stiffened and removed her hand at last.

"Or maybe I won't," she muttered, drawing back and spearing a carrot.

He scowled at the others. "Round nine. Tell me what I wish to know."

"Oh. Right," Tonka said, a pea falling out from the corner of her mouth. "Well, it's like this. Tomorrow, each of the combatants will be given a series of safe words. Oh, why wait? They are *stop, no, don't,* and *please.* After that, they'll be randomly called to the arena one at a time…where they will undergo the same torture for the same amount of time. Whoever utters a safe word is out. If not, and they survive, they go on to the finals. Since you are the Astra's torture master, you'll be overseeing each session. If you take it easy on someone, she'll be disqualified with this."

The harpy lifted a glistening black dagger.

Blythe's fork clattered to her plate. That dagger. Fashioned from trinite. The substance able to end her for good.

25

THE PAIN

Roux's nerves were well past frayed now. A second trinite dagger was in play. Where the citizens of Ation had gotten it, he could guess. Right or wrong, he would be taking it after he dealt with the wraiths.

He escorted Blythe to their room as soon as the dinner concluded. "Stay here. I'll return in the morning." He offered no other information. Wasn't sure he could speak much more without emptying the seething cauldron inside his head.

"Morning?" she demanded, spinning to face him. "You're staying out all night?"

As if she cared! "I have things to do."

"But…they have trinite."

"And you are well able to protect yourself." Truth.

"But—"

He flashed to Wraith Island, hating his task. Hating this realm. Himself. *Her.* As he'd vanished, hurt had flittered over her features.

His guts twisted. Just another lie. Anything to convince her greatest enemy of her affections. How better to lower his guard?

"You brought us a feast tonight," Penelope said with a grin as soon as he entered the palace. "Whatever happened to incite this, keep thinking about it!"

He hated her, too.

Roux did everything in his power to blank his mind and mute his hatred. The wraiths glommed onto him, anyway. Thankfully, he was only a little shaky when they finished.

Before his hostess could say anything else, he returned to the underground arena, where he intended to stay. During dinner, he'd observed Blythe's quick, stealthy exchange with the Phoenix and harpy. He knew the trio planned to meet.

Only two hours until midnight. Enough time to regain his strength and think about tomorrow's torture sessions.

As he drew the shadows around him, making his body blend in with the rocky walls of the cavern, he rolled through the facts. Ten females, Blythe included. What he did to one female, he must deliver to all. Though he was furious and, yes, okay, even destroyed by his *gravita*'s lies, he didn't know if he could harm her. The thought alone caused sweat to bead on his brow and acid to fill his stomach.

At the same time, he must do what he could to knock out as much of her competition as possible.

He considered and discarded one idea after another.

None of the combatants in the tournament would bow to mere threats. Mental torture rather than physical, perhaps? And if he broke Blythe's mind?

Sexual torment could solve the problem and teach the harpy a lesson at the same time. He could *force* her to desire him. *Fake it* then, *she-beast*. Let her see and hear the enjoyment others derived from his touch, too.

And if she didn't care?

He worked his jaw. He had to hurt her physically, didn't he?

Carrigan and Lucca arrived sixteen minutes early, beating the harphantom to the secret meeting. The pair rounded a corner across from the arena and stopped near the royal portal, located directly beneath the palace. Close enough to Roux that he didn't need to relocate. A blessing, considering he currently shook like, well, anyone who'd ever gone to war with the Astra.

Fitting, since he was at war with himself.

While the harpy evinced stress, pacing back and forth, the Phoenix remained still and calm. They'd washed the blood of today's battle from their skin and changed into the traditional leather dresses worn by the females of Ation, but they now sported a whole lot of dirt. What had they been up to before coming here?

"What if she doesn't believe us?" Lucca asked, pacing at a faster clip.

"Then she dies. It's that simple."

Roux tensed, the urge to strike now, now, now almost irresistible. *Threat!*

Wait. He sniffed the air. Did he detect the harphantom? The barest hint of honeysuckle and rose wafted to his nose. Oh, yes. She was nearby. Muscles hardened as he scanned the area. No other trace of her.

"If she dies," the harpy said, flinching, "we'll be stuck here."

Carrigan shrugged. "We're already stuck."

"Yeah, but with her, we've got hope."

"Okay, now I'm *really* curious why you wished to meet with me." Blythe stepped from thin air, appearing close to the other women, but just out of striking distance.

At the sight of her, Roux's central nervous system erupted in flames. His blood steamed in his veins, and his heart raced. She'd worn her hair free and loose, the sleek black mass framing her pale face, making her baby blues appear bigger and rounder than usual. The gown had been replaced by a short leather skirt and one of his shirts, tied at her waist, as if she'd ached to have something of his wrapped around her.

He almost reached for her. Then he remembered the firstone dagger. His hands curled into fists. Deep down, she wanted nothing to do with Laban's killer. She had only pretended to desire Roux in order to distract and kill him. The shirt was just another prop to sell her lie.

Lucca scowled at her. "We saved your ungrateful hide from a swarm of decapitation bees and determined royals. Was spying seriously necessary?"

"Yes," Blythe replied with a cold smile.

"She wasn't spying," Carrigan said with a smile of her own. "That's done in secret. I knew the moment she arrived."

The harphantom rolled her eyes. "Whatever you've got to tell yourself, hon."

Roux was inclined to believe the Phoenix, who merely gave another shrug.

"So?" Blythe spread her arms. "Why am I here?"

"To bargain," Lucca replied. "It may not seem like it now, what with the trinite dagger in play and all, but the former queen's advisors made a deal with Erebus to ensure your victory in the tournament. As soon as you don the crown, the Dark One has vowed to open a doorway out of Ation for them. Which is true, I'm betting. He can open one, all right, but that doesn't mean the group will be able to go through it."

Fury sparked in Roux. Not because of the deal offered by Erebus. That was expected. Roux even knew why the god wished for Blythe to survive. Who else stood a chance of defeating a male known as Torture Master? None. But the fact that Erebus had interfered to keep Blythe alive meant the Blade of Destiny had predicted her death before the tournament's end. So who was going to take her out? And how did Roux stop them?

Of course, there was another possibility. These females were lying, running a play of their own.

"Why are you telling me this?" Blythe demanded. "Why are you helping me again?"

She didn't know the answers? Hmm. Was she not already working with the pair to betray him? Interesting. So why hadn't she killed them yet? Simple curiosity? A sense of fair play for gifting her with the flower?

He pursed his lips. Did the reason really matter? She'd hidden the firstone dagger. That alone proved her guilt where Roux was concerned.

"I'm sure your Astra has mentioned my dealing with an oracle before I came to Ation," Carrigan said. "I believe we've found a path out of the realm. But. It requires Roux's aid, and he won't be in the mood to give it without you. And not because of his Commander's request. Don't think I don't see the stardust on your skin. Yeah, I know all about the warlords and their ways. After consulting with an oracle about my trip here, I made it my business to know. Though the stardust has faded, rather than brightened. Trouble in paradise?"

"Good to know I'm living in your brain rent-free," Blythe snapped. "What is it you'd like me to do for you in exchange for a ticket off realm, anyway? Spell it out for me."

"You will help Lucca survive alongside us. Then, and only then, will I show you the way out," Carrigan said.

"Are you kidding?" Radiating frustration, the harpy spread her arms once again. "What you're asking is impossible. The one survivor rule is etched in the Oath Stones. Trust me, I've experienced the compulsion that comes from making such a vow. There's no circumventing it."

"Maybe so, but if you want what we're offering badly enough, you'll figure something out." The Phoenix hiked her thumb in the other harpy's direction. "If she dies, I'll be happy to stay here for eternity just to spite you."

Lucca fluffed her hair. "I'm kind of important."

"Talk to the Astra," Carrigan suggested. She arched a dark brow. "Or not. If any Astra could be the first to ditch a fated mate, it's the Crazed One."

Blythe fumed and paced the bedroom all night, the Phoenix's words replaying in her head on repeat. *If any Astra could be the first to ditch a fated mate, it's the Crazed One.*

The Astra had marked her with stardust, then abandoned her as soon as trinite showed up? Okay, fine. His attitude had changed before the weapon's arrival. But either way—the nerve of the man! Had he decided to ditch her for good?

It was possible. After all, he hadn't drooled all over himself at the sight of her dinner party dress, as any smitten male would have done.

Had she lost her touch? One moment she'd been contemplating the pros and cons of making out with the too-sexy Astra, the next she'd wondered if he'd washed his hands of her for good. How she felt about the possibility? Besides awful. Big awful. Huge.

Which was foolish! Not getting physically involved right now—smart. Well, more physically involved. It saved Blythe from a boatload of guilt. Except, she still hungered for him. More than ever!

Why *couldn't* they be lovers, at least while they were stuck in Ation? Maybe they would bang the stupid out of each other. No lust meant clear thoughts. Clear thoughts meant better decisions.

Excuses, excuses. Justifications and rationalizations never got anyone anywhere but trouble. Her current predicament was living proof of that.

When the sun rose, Blythe bit her tongue and tasted blood. Still no sign of Roux. He was really gonna do it. He was gonna send her into battle without a pep talk or anything. Motions jerky, she changed into a fighter's uniform, loaded up with weapons and flashed to the underground arena.

"Sit, sit," Tonka called from the dais. "We'll be doing this one at a time in totally random order. Carrigan the Flesh Melter, you're first. On deck is Justice the Brain Smasher, followed by Umber the Lady Baller, Lucca the Blood Rainer, Helga the Slaughterhouse, Stefanie the Bone Collector, Blaise the Scourge of Fate, Daphne the Empress of Agonies, Vera the Living Terror, and finally Blythe the Man Hoarder."

Man Hoarder? Lips pursed, she climbed the steps of the amphitheater, joining the other competitors in the stands. Carrigan and Lucca nodded a greeting at her. No others glanced in her direction.

"I'm last again?" she asked. "Yeah. Sure. Totally random order." Once again, she'd get to listen to everyone else scream.

"Not our fault Fate hates you," the harpy quipped.

Her heart thudded as Roux appeared in the center of the arena. Two tables and a stool arrived next. Weapons adorned the smaller table. Chains hung from the other.

Pallid and a bit shaky, Carrigan headed down. Roux said something to her, his volume too low to pick up, and the Phoenix settled on the table and willingly chained herself down.

"Start the clock," Roux called.

"Clock started," Tonka called back.

For the next thirty minutes, the Astra sat on a stool— and Carrigan screamed. The same thing happened with the following eight warriors. Four and a half hours Blythe spent listening to bloodcurdling bellows and unheeded pleas for mercy while watching Roux, vacillating between fascination and horror.

He forced the women to chain themselves to a table he flipped upright. He then eased onto the stool before them, keeping his back to Blythe. Throughout each session, he remained relaxed, talking so softly she couldn't detect his words. He never touched his charges. Not with his hands or a weapon. Never displayed a sign of regret or remorse. Never hesitated to deliver the next round of anguish, however he was doing it.

Five women voiced their code word and died at the hands of the royal council, as promised. Thankfully, Carrigan and Lucca survived.

"Blythe the Man Hoarder," Tonka called, giddy, "you're up."

Blythe's stomach churned as she flashed to the sand. Walking would only delay the coming agony. Better to get it over with.

Perspiration dotted her palms. Oh, she didn't care about the coming pain. Nothing he did today could compare to the anguish of losing Laban. But. She did care about what this meant for their…relationship.

Ugh. The R word. But facts were facts. Whatever had transpired in the past, they were, kind of, a couple. She'd slept with him; he'd stardusted her. If she squinted hard enough, she caught glimpses of it in the light. Honestly? She really, really wanted more. He might be the storm in her life, but he was also, somehow, a calming harbor. She savored every moment in his arms.

With her head held high, she approached Roux. He stood before the table laden with weapons, his back to her. Behind him was the other table—crimson wet the chains. That blood had come as the women strained for relief.

What was he soon to do to her? She gulped. More importantly, what thoughts whirred in his mind?

The muscles in his shoulders bunched as soon as she reached the area. With a monotone voice, he instructed, "Lie on the table and shackle yourself."

Willingly shackle herself, exactly as the others had

done or resist like a normal person and appear fearful. Not off to a great start.

"Sir, yes, sir," she chirped a little too brightly. Limbs trembling a little, she cinched the cold metal around her ankles, then one of her wrists. Roux had to reach back to clamp the second shackle around the other, which he did without facing her. Suddenly, she had a direct view of the royal dais and the nine sets of eyes watching her with varying degrees of glee.

For their benefit, she pretended to get comfortable.

When Roux pivoted toward her at last, she forgot their audience. Forgot everything but him...her surprise second consort. The *alevala* rippled, as if preparing to jump from his skin. He'd blanked his features, but hadn't doused the red flickering in his irises. And oh, did those eyes project all kinds of torment.

He might have acted as if he didn't want her anymore, but he clearly despised the thought of harming her. Some of her anger dulled.

As he locked that crimson gaze on her, she only wished to hug him.

"It's okay, babe," she said for his ears alone. "I'll recover."

A muscle jumped beneath his eye. After sheathing a hooked dagger in his belt, he lifted his chin and approached her. He flattened his palms near her shoulders and leaned over to align his face with hers, forcing her to stare straight up at him. His scent enveloped her, fogging her thoughts as usual. Only a compromised judgment explained the delicious melting of her bones right before a torture session.

"I will ask you the same questions I asked everyone else, harpy." The coldness of his tone sent chills down her spine. "Whether you answer them or not, lie or tell the truth, I'm going to hurt you as much as I hurt the others. Know that every infusion of pain will be worse than the last. This won't get better until you speak one of four words. Do you remember those words?"

"I do." *Stop. No. Please. Don't.*

And he'd called her harpy? Here and now? Seriously? Why hadn't he used her nickname? Talk about a gut punch at the worst moment! Did he hope to put even more distance between them?

Would she do the same if—when—the situation reversed, and she oversaw his pain?

Could she? Should she?

"Prove you know them." His voice dipped. So did his head. He ghosted the tip of his nose against hers. "Tell me one."

The almost touch stole her breath. *Focus.* She opened her mouth to comply with his demand. Wait. "Ha! You won't trick me that easily."

He bared his teeth in a parody of a grin. "Very well. Pain it is."

"Do what you gotta do. There will be no tears tonight. Or ever. No accusations or blame, either. Just…be there for me afterward, okay?" Maybe they would have that talk about what had happened between them, after all. Hearing a pledge of devotion from him wouldn't be the worst thing.

He slitted his lids, as if she'd just shrieked obscenities. Um. Okay? Silent, he straightened, revealing two metal bands clutched in his grip. He fit each one around her throat and snapped them together. Then he lifted a table end, making her vertical.

Her chin caught on the suddenly too-tight neckband,

which restricted her airway. Not enough to choke her, but enough to keep her on edge.

He eased onto the stool, rested his elbows on his knees, and peered up at her. "Start the clock," he called without glancing at those on the dais. "We begin now."

"Clock started," Tonka returned.

"First question." Roux unsheathed the dagger, gripping it by the hooked blade rather than the hilt, and flicked his tongue over an incisor. "Do you hate me?"

"Uh...yes? No?" He'd seriously asked the others that question? "I don't know."

The next thing she knew, agony like she'd never known somehow entered through her nostrils, as if she'd sucked it down with her last inhalation and it infiltrated her every cell. Those cells seemed to explode in her veins. Her lungs flattened, breathing impossible, and her vision blurred. But just as soon as the pain began, it ceased, taking all the complications with it.

"That was the easy part?" she screeched. "How did you do that?" Better yet, what had he done?

"I'm able to manipulate the atmosphere surrounding me. I wasn't sure I'd be able to do it since I couldn't produce sleeping gas. But I can make the pain toxin. And harpy? The ability is supercharged here. With a simple thought, I will make you and only you inhale a poison unlike anything you've ever encountered." His blank expression never changed, but the red in his eyes never dulled, either. Even more telling, blood dripped from the hand holding the blade.

Her chest clenched. He hadn't cut himself with the other combatants. That, she knew. So why do it now?

Because he insisted on hurting when *Blythe* hurt? He must.

The knowledge affected her. Something softened in her chest even as her determination hardened into stone. There'd be no more screeching on her part. Whatever he dished, she would take. Happily.

"Next question," he said. "Do you plan to kill me?"

"I don't know," she repeated. "I'm still debating it."

Pain hit again, and yeah, it was even worse, exactly as advertised. He let it last longer, too.

"When did you find the firstone dagger?" he asked.

"Find it? I didn't. I—" The next wave of poison was pure agony, as if every inch of her insides had been scraped raw and bathed in acid. Sweat trickled here and there. Blood leaked from nearly every orifice; it even poured from the wounds the chains caused as her body involuntarily flailed. Multiple bones cracked.

"Fourth question," he said. "Did you ever truly desire me?"

Blythe struggled to concentrate. His question struck her as odd...maybe? She knew nothing but a creeping dread as she anticipated the fourth wave. *Need to respond. No, no, need to think!*

How much longer on the clock? What had happened to her determination?

"Respond to my final question," her tormentor insisted.

"F-final?" She had to endure the pain once more? Had a tear slipped down her cheek? What had he asked? She had a vague memory...oh! Desire. "I got wet, didn't I?"

More pain. More than she'd ever endured in her life. Her mind cracked, and so did another handful of bones. She might have bellowed. Or whimpered. She couldn't be sure. Knew nothing but agony.

"It's done," her tormentor shouted. This wasn't Roux, she decided. This couldn't be Roux. This was a stranger. The one who'd hurt her. "She has proven victorious."

Suddenly, the chains fell off and she fell forward. Powerful arms caught her before she hit the sand and cradled her against a firm body. Beneath her cheek, a strong heartbeat galloped.

"I've got you," the stranger said, his tone broken.

Only a moment later, softness pressed against her back and the steadying arms vanished.

"Drink," he commanded.

Blythe thrashed, shaking her head violently. Drink from the one who'd delivered such anguish? No. She needed Roux. The Astra. Her Astra. She wanted his stare and his intensity and his strength and his innocence and his ferocity and his rusty laugh and his unintentional jokes. Where was he?

"Drink." A harsher command with frayed edges. "Feed."

No!

Something warm and wet dripped upon her lips. The metallic scent drew out her tongue, and there was no stopping it. At the sweet taste of warm blood and crackling power, Blythe almost grabbed onto the source and bit down. But still she fought him. *Need Roux!*

"Calm for me, Lyla. Calm. Please. Breathe deep. Exhale. Inhale again. That's my good girl."

That nickname. She'd missed it more than she could ever admit. And the blood. She knew and loved the taste. Yes? She sniffed. Mmm. She did! It was Roux's. A tantalizing blend of cedarwood and spiced oranges. He was here, caring for her, the tormentor gone.

She sagged into a puddle of goo. As the droplets of

his blood turned into a river, she opened wide, guzzling greedily.

"Yes. Feed from me," he told her. "Take my soul, too, beauty."

Yes. Feed on Roux. She locked her mouth on his flesh and sucked a tendril of decadent, powerful soul. Most of her weakness fled in an instant, and yet her fatigue remained. Last night's lack of rest had caught up with her. But she wasn't worried. The Astra was here, and he was touching her. All would be well.

Blythe let herself drift into oblivion.

26

THE ARRIVAL

As the harphantom rested in bed, Roux stormed through the bedroom. Roaring inwardly with a rage like no other, he flipped over the desk and shredded the wood with his claws. Smashed the dresser. Punched holes in several walls. Dismantled his chair. Despite the noise, Blythe continued to rest.

His thoughts refused to settle. He'd hurt her. Hurt her so bad. How could he do such a terrible thing to his *gravita*? How?

The worst part and something she might not ever forgive once she awoke? Using the torture session to question her about her feelings for him. A cowardly, vindictive, foolish move. He *deserved* her hatred.

Knowing his requirement to ask the same questions of every female, as well as inflict the same amount of injury the same way, he'd started with Carrigan. She, of course, hadn't known what he'd even meant when he'd asked if she hated and desired him. But it was as she'd struggled to make sense of his words while combating pure agony that he'd begun to understand the crux of his mistake. He would rather not know the truth than torment his *gravita* like this. Yet he had been stuck, one hundred percent locked into his path, and there'd been no going back. With every combatant, his dread of Blythe's turn had magnified.

Roaring inwardly again, he punched new holes in the walls. Dust and debris coated the air. His knuckles shattered, skin splitting. Veins and an artery were severed in his wrist. Sprays of blood wet the floor before he healed.

"Roux?"

His heart stuttered in his chest. He flashed to the side of the bed. Her eyes remained closed, but any semblance of calm had left her. She tossed and turned; her features pinched.

"I'm here, Lyla. I'm here," he said, caressing her brow.

Though he'd done nothing to warrant the comfort of her nearness, he stretched out on the mattress and gathered his *gravita* into his arms. Just like that. She sighed with contentment and settled against him.

A tendril of hope unfurled. Maybe he wasn't doomed to lose her?

He clutched her close, afraid to let go. A sharp scream erupted inside his head, reminding him of his earlier roars and how the two possessed the same tone and tenor. As if Roux himself was somehow the escapee—or his twin was. But he knew better. His brother had never tasted freedom. Had he? Unlike the others,

Rowan preferred incarceration to freedom. No surer way to torment Roux for eternity.

Frowning, needing an escape from his current reality, he did something he despised. He turned his attention inward and ventured down, down, down to the darkest recesses of his mind. The closer he came to the prison, the louder the symphony of moans, groans, and grunts became. As his mental eyes adjusted to the gloom, a barred wall appeared, a pristine Rowan seated beyond it.

It was like seeing his childhood self in a mirror. Always a shock and horror.

"Hello, brother," Rowan crooned with a wicked grin. "I must admit, I expected you sooner."

He appeared exactly as he'd looked before he'd died: nine years old, dressed in a leather suit bestowed upon him by their father. At the moment, he leaned against the cell's back wall, a leg extended, with the other bent at the knee, acting as a resting place for an elbow.

The smug superiority he evinced scraped at Roux's nerves. "Have you left your cage?"

"No pleasantries, then? No warm-up before we dive into what it is you seek from me?" Rowan shrugged his shoulders. He might look nine, but he'd matured over the centuries. He stood and stretched. "Okay. I'll play. No, I haven't left my cage."

"Who has been running rampant in my head, reacting to my woman?"

"Ah. You mean the harpy. Our *gravita*."

Snarling, he gripped and shook the bars. "Mine! Not ours." He refused to share her with another, even his dead brother. "Mine alone."

Rowan unveiled another grin and strode closer.

"Who do you *think* has been running rampant? No, no. Let me guess. The female's consort, yes? No, no reason to verify. I see it on your face." He offered a sorry-for-you wince. "Unfortunately for you, you're as right as I am."

No. No! "I did not absorb him." But now he wondered... Isla claimed she'd spoken to a prisoner he'd hidden from himself. Could it be her own father?

"Are you sure?" Rowan asked. "Because I've seen his face. Have you?"

Laban...in his mind... No, Roux thought again, shaking his head. "Prove it." His twin had been a trickster in life, and he remained so in death.

"I don't have to prove anything. The suspicion alone will drive you mad. But sure. I'll keep playing this game. How about this? His cell door is open, allowing him to come and go as he pleases. He's there now. Just down that hall in cell block D." Rowan hiked his thumb to the right. "Visit him. If you dare."

Roux's gaze darted in that direction, where a wall of thick shadows hid what lay behind. He could navigate the twisting, winding corridors, but odds were good he'd lose track of time as well as the world around him. Here, now, he had only moments to spare. More than that, he wasn't sure he wanted verification.

How would Blythe react to knowing beyond any doubt that Laban lived in Roux's head, and that was the only reason she had desired him? *If* she hadn't faked her desire for him.

Would she resent him? How could she not?

Would she demand he find a way to free the male? Again, how could she not?

Would she leave him if he succeeded? Or hate him even more if he failed?

Would she think of Laban whenever Roux claimed her body?

Dread pricked his nape, and sickness filled his stomach. To risk his mission now... No. He couldn't. He wouldn't. And without verification, he shouldn't mention it to Blythe. Just in case Rowan lied. Yes, yes. All reasonable. Perfectly understandable. But how could he *not* tell her?

Roux had made so many mistakes with her already. Could he truly afford to make another?

Rowan leaned his shoulder against the bars. "You're going to lose her, you know? You are a clone, brother. Nothing but an experiment gone wrong. You were never meant to exist. The only purpose you served died when you murdered Father."

Words he'd heard before. Words he'd pondered throughout the whole of his life. Until Blythe. The woman he'd just tortured for information—the woman whose consort might be stuck in Roux's head. The very reason she might consider *him* a consort.

Might? Ha. The other male must be here, and she must perceive him. Nothing else made sense.

Roux did not wish to share her with anyone. "Why do you hate me so much?"

"Why do you hate *yourself* so much?"

He bared his teeth rather than offer an answer. "You lived a life of luxury while I suffered in agony. You had the adoration of Mars, and I had his disdain. You could have been a bright light to me, yet you chose to be more darkness. Why?"

The boy lifted his shoulders in another negligent shrug. "I accepted what you couldn't, I suppose."

"And what was that?"

"Only one of us was meant to survive. Father knew it, too. I think he hoped to prove himself the strongest of us. In that, however, he certainly bombed. Just as you will bomb with the female."

"I will not. I will fight for her, and I will win her." He jolted. Yes. Decision made. He would have her. Keep her. Find some semblance of joy in his life. He only wished he'd hidden it from his brother.

Roux backed away from the cell then. Looked like he'd be dealing with her whether he was ready to do so or not.

She'd said she wouldn't blame him for inflicting pain upon her. No tears. No accusations. Maybe she'd spoken true. But how would she react to the truth about Laban? Would Roux lose her for good?

"Where are you going?" Rowan asked with another grin. "*Why* are you going? Was it something I said?"

Roux blinked open his eyes, the hearth-lit bedroom coming into view. He was panting. Sweat bathed him. He still held the harpy, but his grip had tightened. *Can't lose her. Just...can't.*

Blythe awoke with a start, gasping. Took a moment for her mind to switch from off to on. Sunlight illuminated the ceiling of her bedroom in Ation. She lay in bed with Roux. The Astra rested on his side and peered at her; his expression contorted with strain. The most he'd ever demonstrated.

She rolled toward him, instantly concerned, and

cupped his strong jaw. "What's wrong, babe? Tell me, and I'll fix it."

He croaked, "I am so sorry."

He was sorry? But why? What— Her brow wrinkled. Wait. Memories returned in a snap. The tournament. The torture session. The something that had bothered her suddenly crystalized, and she sucked in a breath, jolting upright. Only then did she notice the destruction surrounding her.

Every piece of furniture except the bed and her wardrobe had been demolished. Holes littered the walls. Panels had been ripped out of the floor. Someone had thrown a nasty temper mantrum.

"Lyla," he croaked, sitting up and reaching for her. "Forgive me. Please. I loathed the thought of harming you, but I wished to knock out some of your competition. I chose the route that involved no contact."

She scrambled off the mattress, standing on a pile of debris, and whirled to face him, pointing an accusing finger. "I don't care about the pain. I told you I understood, and I meant it. But you didn't just torture me for the tournament. You did it for answers." The questions he'd asked… Do you still hate…the firstone… faked desire… "That is beyond reprehensible for anyone, but especially the Astra who marked me with stardust. I am so—"

"I'm sorry!" he interjected. Shame etched his expression as his shoulders rolled in. "It is reprehensible, and I hate *myself* for it. If I could go back…"

"—turned on right now. I thought I told you to stop being so sexy."

He opened his mouth. Closed it. Opened. Closed.

Blinked. "You meant those words. Your eyes remained blue. I don't understand."

What confused him? Seemed so obvious to her. "You could have asked me about anything, and you chose desire. You are so obsessed with me, Roux." She twirled a lock of hair around her finger. Finally he'd had a chance to learn about Erebus. The strengths and weaknesses of her competitors. Something, anything, to advance his task. Instead, he'd cared more about Blythe's feelings for him.

And oh, wow, she'd known it, but she hadn't *known it* known it until that moment. The truth gutted her. How much this male must need her.

"I mean it. You are absolutely wrecked," she whispered, awed.

He squeezed his lids shut for a moment. "I don't think I'll ever understand you." A pause. A heavy sigh. "I found the dagger, Lyla." Agony coated the words. "You hid it from me."

"What are you talking about?" She wracked her brain, but came up empty on offenses. "I didn't hide anything from you."

"Lyla." Another croak. He flashed to his backpack, dug inside, and withdrew the firstone dagger. Extending his arm to offer the weapon, he admitted, "I found it under the mattress."

Wait. It was the same dagger and sheath Erebus had given her. And okay, yeah, she did look pretty guilty. But come on! "Okay, now I'm kind of insulted. As if I would really be dumb enough to stash a critical piece of revenge in such an obvious location."

A frown pulled at the corners of his mouth.

"Penelope obviously framed me," she continued,

"because I most certainly did not find the blade when I toured the castle." Wait again. Different realizations clicked. A light dawned. "Okay, I get it now. You found it last night, just before the celebration dinner." The reason he'd treated her so poorly and left her alone all night.

The frown vanished, leaving remorse in its place. He bowed his head, and her stomach flipped. Roux, in a position of contrition...

"Explain your withdrawn behavior before that," she said, her voice a bit shaky.

Again, his shoulders rolled in. "The jewel. It remains firmly entrenched. I haven't known what to think. The female who purred for me so sweetly still hates me so fiercely."

The vulnerability he currently displayed, yeah, it got to her. An urge to soothe him sparked. "There's no denying the appearance of my guilt. I *did* promise to murder you when you least expected it."

His tension only heightened. "I also know of your meeting with Carrigan and Lucca." He covered his eyes. "I spied on you."

"Okay. So? That was a smart move on your part. That's what any warlord worth his salt is supposed to do with someone suspected of plotting against him." She would have done the same. "I'm only mad I didn't sense you. And maybe a little more turned on." No wonder she'd chosen this male as a second consort.

He was just so cunning and ruthless. Ferocious to the extreme. More so than she'd ever realized.

His hand dropped, but his head shot up. He stared at her as if she were some strange creature in a zoo.

"So you heard their offer," she pointed out, ready

to be done with the particulars so they could get to the good stuff. "They'll provide a way off Ation if I keep the harpy alive somehow."

"Yes. I heard. But what do you mean, turned on? I *betrayed* you, Lyla."

"No, you acted intelligently, Rue. I'd given you no reason to trust me. In fact, I would have been disappointed in you and questioned your mental capabilities if you'd trusted me. Then I would have had to question my own mental capabilities for finding you sexy."

His mouth opened and closed again. Hope lived, died, and was resurrected in his eyes. "You seek pleasure from me?"

"I'm demanding it, as requested." She dipped her gaze over his body and licked her lips. "I think we can both agree that after putting me through all that pain, you owe me pleasure. Soooo much."

Suddenly, he materialized directly in front of her. He cupped her cheeks and—cursed, then jumped backward, severing contact. His features contorted. "There's something else you should know." Hands fisted, he stared down at his booted feet.

Ugh. What else could there possibly be?

"There's a chance I…absorbed Laban. That he is one of the prisoners you heard screaming in my head."

"Oh."

His gaze lifted, meeting hers, projecting hope, fear, regret. "And that is the reason you have come to believe I am your consort."

The words hit her like a punch to the gut. Laban… trapped inside Roux… Her desire for the Astra an illusion born of a deception… No. Just no. "That can't be right." But…it kind of made sense and proved Erebus had lied that day in the forest.

What if Roux *was* right?

Widowhood had been different for Blythe compared to other harpies. The familiarity in the beginning. The desire to keep living after a consort's death. The lack of repeated hallucinations. Craving—claiming—another male.

Shock punched her again and again, leaving her cold, shaken, and yes, heartbroken. What did this mean for Blythe and the Astra? For Laban? For Isla?

"I haven't seen or spoken to him," Roux continued, braced for a blow. "I've hunted for him without success. Until we have a face-to-face, I won't know for sure."

"I'll go back in," she rushed out. "I'll find him." And if she got trapped inside the warrior, like before? A risk she must take. To think that she'd abandoned Isla, ventured to a prison realm, and repeatedly fought for a chance to kill the male who might be playing host to her daughter's father… Blythe nearly vomited. "We need to know the truth."

He offered no reaction at first. No emotion, his expression under strict control. Then he nodded. A clipped bob of his chin.

"Momma, Momma! I did it! I'm here!"

The familiar voice hit her ears, a riotous mix of joy and horror bombarding her. Please be a hallucination. A memory. Something! Heart thudding, she spun. No, no hallucination. She could do nothing but watch, eyes widening, horror amplifying, as little Isla flew across the room and jumped into her arms.

27

THE COMPLICATION

Roux could barely believe his eyes. Blythe's child. Here in Ation. The complications this presented... The danger.

More pallid by the second, the harphantom met his gaze, her baby blues vulnerable and wounded. Inside him, muscles clenched on bones. Only moments ago, she'd blown his mind. Not the least bit upset over his behavior during the torture session but charmed. And now that she knew his suspicions concerning Laban? How would she treat Roux? Deep down, he knew the revelation had changed everything—for them both.

He rubbed a fist into his too-tight chest. Most of his life, he'd felt as if he lived in the shadow of someone else. As if he were Mars, but not Mars. Blythe, Roux's *gravita*, was supposed to belong to him and only him, and he might have to share her with another male?

Whose name would she scream in bed?

"Whatever happens," he vowed, lifting his chin, "I will protect the girl with my life." As though she were his own. In a way, she was, yes? "No harm shall befall her." Roux would stop at nothing to keep his word. No matter how the harphantom felt about him. No matter what she decided to do regarding their situation.

The assurance helped alleviate some of her fears; bit by bit, her color returned. Inhaling deeply, she set the small girl on her feet, crouched, and cupped her cheeks. "How long have you been here, love?"

"I just got here." Isla cast her gaze to Roux and smirked. "Told you I'd see you soon."

He should have listened. Something he'd learned: when a harpy threatened you, believe her. "That you did. But how did you know where to find me?"

"Yes," Blythe said with an enthusiastic nod. "How did you know? For that matter, how did you get here? Did anyone hurt you when you arrived? If they gave you even the smallest scratch, Momma will do murder."

Isla rolled her eyes. "No one hurt me, 'cause I'm superpowerful. And Grandpa Bus is the one who told me 'bout seeing Roux. He visited me after we left the Astra's body, and he asked me a whole lotta questions 'bout him. But he didn't open the door for me until today."

"Grandpa Bus—" Blythe sucked air between her teeth.

"Erebus," she and Roux hissed in unison. Their gazes met. They nodded stiffly. Because they both understood. They were a team against the evil one right now.

"What questions did he ask you about Roux, honey?"

"Hang on, I gotta remember, 'cause there were tons." The little girl thought things over for a minute, then brightened. "Oh! He asked what I heard and saw while I was trapped inside the Astra. If I'd learned any of his secrets. What I think of him. If I'd like to kill him forever dead, and if so, how did I plan to do it." A hard glint entered her mismatched eyes. "If I wanted Roux to be my new daddy."

He went stiff all over. *Will rip out the Dark One's organs two at a time.*

"And what did you tell…Bus?" Blythe asked with a strangled tone.

"I didn't tell him nothing, promise." Isla spread her arms, all *Why don't you know this already?*, reminding him of her mother. "He was a stranger back then, and smart kids never talk to strangers. We rip out their intestines. Right, Momma?"

"That's right, sweetheart." The harpy offered her daughter a wobbly smile of approval. "Did you ever speak with—" she drew in a deep breath "—Grandpa Bus before the Astra invasion?"

"Nope. Only after." The little girl glanced between Roux and her mother, the first sign of concern falling over her features. "Am I in trouble for coming here? Are you and Roux friends now?"

"You are not in trouble. But I need you to help me understand everything that's happened while I've been gone, okay?" Blythe reassured. The girl relaxed, but Roux grew stiffer. His *gravita* had avoided the question about being friends. Something he realized he craved more desperately than her body. "What else has Bus said to you?"

Isla chewed on her bottom lip. "Well, a few days ago

he visited and told me how you were in so, so much danger but he could save you if he could get a message to you. I told him I'd deliver it, because I knew I could do a better job than anyone."

Dread curled in Roux's stomach as he awaited the response.

"I—I see." Blythe licked her lips. "What message did he have for me?"

"Well, he told me to tell you that the Phoenix and the harpy are big ole liars. That they have a 'genda of their own."

A lie meant to confuse Roux? Or the truth...to confuse him? Had the pair actually found a way off the realm?

Frowning, Isla scratched her temple. "What's a 'genda?"

"It's a personal plan." Blythe slid her fingers down her daughter's arms to clasp her small hands. "Did Bus say anything else?"

"Yep. He told me you guys are wrong 'bout some stuff, but that was okay, because he's gonna prove the truth as soon as you get home. He's real excited 'bout it, too."

So, either they were right or, yeah, they were wrong. Roux scrubbed a hand over his face. He hated Erebus Phantom with every fiber of his being. The only good thing the male had ever done was contribute to the conception of his daughters.

Once again, the color drained from the harphantom's cheeks. "Anything else?" she croaked.

"Nope. That's it, I think." The little girl scanned the destroyed room and gaped with amazement. "Can I break something, too, or do only adults get to do it?"

"Break whatever you want, love."

As Isla skipped off, laughing, picking up pieces of wood and glass to smash into walls, Blythe straightened and approached Roux. The urge to wrap his arms around her nearly overpowered him, but his thoughts stopped him. Would she derive comfort from Roux or Laban? And the little girl might not be ready to know her mother had chosen a new consort.

Isla might not ever be ready.

"I knew Erebus was pure evil," she whispered, "but I didn't realize the depths of his depravity until now. To send a child into Ation…to use her against us…" Rage simmered in her quiet tone.

Us, she'd said. "We will get her home." No matter what measures they must take. "Let's talk about what will happen tomorrow. When the tournament ends, you'll be crowned the winner."

"Obviously."

"You need to kill the Phoenix and the harpy. They are a hazard we cannot afford."

"Now hold up."

He didn't. "No doubt the royal council plans to attack you the moment you claim the royal title. I'll deal with them. In fact, I'm greatly looking forward to it. You must only ensure the girl's safety. When the last female is dead, I'll flash topside to cut a hole into the atmosphere."

"By hole do you mean door?" she asked. "Either way, I plan to stay by your side."

"It's a door, but it's also far more. I'll be cutting through planes and dimensions, and if you are nearby, you could be maimed. Once the process is completed, I'll walk through the opening, if I can, and explore where it leads. When I know it's secure, I'll return and—"

"Uh, that's silly," Isla interjected, rejoining them. "I'll just open a regular door, and we'll all go through together. I mean, it'll probably take me a second. Two tops."

Both he and Blythe gaped at her.

Mother crouched before daughter once again. "You know how to open a portal between two worlds, sweetheart?"

"Well, yeah." Isla spread her arms. "I watched Grandpa Bus do it. How hard can it be?"

"Ah. I see." Blythe offered a too-bright, encouraging smile. "While I adore your ambition, and I'm so very proud of your confidence, no one can leave this land through an ordinary portal. There's always an invisible block."

"My door won't be ordinary. Duh." The little girl hiked a thumb at her chest. "I'm superpowerful. A goddess! I can do anything. Grandpa Bus told me so."

Roux ground his teeth. Had the god filled her head with praise simply to convince her to venture here and save her mother? How disappointed would she be when she failed? And she would. He wasn't even sure *his* idea would work. But he had a second and third option to try. If he required a fourth, he'd come up with a fourth.

"I'm a goddess, too, sweetheart," Blythe responded, "and I can do a lot of things. But I can't open a doorway out of here."

"Don't worry. I can show you how." Isla smiled with pure innocence. "I promised I'd wait till you won the crown. Are you really gonna be a queen, Momma? Does that mean I'll be a princess? Because I really, really want to be a princess. So bad!"

The harpy cast Roux a *help me* look before peering past him and frowning. "Sunset comes. You should go. The wraiths are waiting."

He checked his internal clock and blinked with astonishment. She wasn't wrong. Yet, somehow, he himself had lost track of the seconds. "I'll return as quickly as I can."

To his surprise, she straightened and took his hand to give him a comforting squeeze. He squeezed back, wishing he could kiss her. *Needing* a kiss. Desperate for it. But under no circumstances did he want her using him to kiss *Laban*. He'd lived in another's shadow his entire life. Always second place. Never more than a clone.

Tensing, he flashed to the island. As always, Penelope awaited him at the door of the palace, wearing a new piece of lingerie. Only difference was, she offered no smile before leading him inside.

"I know how you like to get this done," she said, "so, let's get this done."

"Pouting because you're soon to lose your meal tickets?"

"You assume I don't already have a plan to ensure you and your female remain?" She humphed. "How you insult me, darling."

"I know you already have a plan. I also know that plan will go nowhere."

"We'll see."

In the ballroom, the army of wraiths stood in a line. No longer did they resemble haggard skeletons with hair. No, with their newfound energy, they'd chosen to don beautiful skins, like their queen. They ranged in color from the palest white to the darkest black.

After what Erebus had done... After *Penelope's* actions—planting the firstone dagger under the bed to incriminate Blythe—the cauldron of hatred inside of Roux refilled, already bubbling over. He knew the wraith was responsible for the blade. Should have guessed from the start, but lust had made him stupid.

"Ladies." Penelope clapped twice. "Chop, chop. Feed, feed. Our illustrious guest is impatient to leave us."

The females zoomed over, glomming onto him. He withstood the newest feeding with ease. Though each bottomless pit of spectrals took more than usual, he had plenty more hatred at the ready.

As they fell away from him one by one, overfull and moaning, Penelope glided a circle around him. She tilted her head this way and that. "There's something different about you."

Before he could respond, not that he'd had any intention of doing so, she swooped in and sniffed at his neck. Licked. Sucked down a mouthful of strength.

With a groan, she eased away from him and wiped at her mouth. "You're tastier than usual tonight, which means something happened with the phantom. But what?" Gliding around him again, she looked him up and down. "What, what, what?"

"If you are finished eating..." He yearned only to return to Blythe and Isla.

"Not quite yet." Circling, circling. "After this, you'll owe me one more fine dining experience. Unless I decide to break our deal and drain your female at her most crucial moment, of course. Or anytime afterward. Even if you manage to get her out of the realm, my link to her will remain."

Trying to provoke him?

Then she added, "Perhaps you should give me a new reason not to harm her."

Ah. She sought to herd him into a new deal, and he could guess the parameters. "You expect me to take you with us." A statement, not a question.

"Not me. All of us." Grinning at last, she swooped back in, feeding once again. This time, however, she stumbled away with a gasp, her eyes wide with astonishment. And perhaps envy? "You carry the scent of a child on your skin. A girl. Why? How? Tell me!"

"You are done," he stated flatly. As she sputtered, he flashed to the bedroom.

A quick scan revealed mother and child lay on the bed. Heart pounding, he padded over as quietly as possible. Their eyes were closed, with Isla curled into Blythe's side. The sight left his chest clenching worse than ever...and inspired his mystery prisoner to issue a high-pitched scream.

He bit his tongue, tasting blood, but he couldn't stop himself from reaching out and gently smoothing a lock of hair from Blythe's brow. Protective, possessive instincts clawed at him. *Will never give her up.*

Thinking to take a post in the center of the room and remain on guard all night long, Roux straightened and stepped away—Blythe shot out an arm and wrapped her fingers around his wrist, stopping him.

He craned his neck to meet her gaze and nearly lost his breath. With one gentle tug, she drew him toward the bed. Understanding, he crawled onto the mattress and molded his front to her back.

The protectiveness and possessiveness sharpened. And yet, at the same time contentment spread through him, the scream tapering off.

"What are we going to do?" she whispered.

We. He liked that.

Roux told her the truth. "Whatever it takes."

The day came. The final round of the tournament. Blythe opened her eyes to find Roux standing sentry in the center of the bedroom, framed in the golden outline of dawning sunlight. A sweet gesture, but she'd rather have him molded to her.

The Astra sensed her awareness and cast her a burning glance. Heart drumming, Blythe gently extracted herself from her sleeping daughter and padded to her consort. They had much to discuss, but now wasn't the time. Hungry for contact, she wound her arms around his neck and pressed her body against his.

Immediately he settled his hands on her waist and yanked her closer. Warm shivers rained over her spine. The desperation in his spinning eyes thrilled her...and it had nothing to do with Laban. It wasn't the manticore she considered when she breathed in his spicy, sweet scent.

"I think I should be gone when Isla wakes, to keep my mind on the coming battle," she whispered. A barbed lump grew in her throat. "Whatever happens to me, get her home."

His fingers flexed on her, a thousand emotions flashing over his face in a split second. The one she savored? Tenderness.

"Nothing will happen to you," he told her, low and fierce.

Deep breath in. Out. "Make sure nothing happens to you, either. I'll be very upset if my victory peach is bruised. I have plans for him."

"Do you, now?" He flashed her to the private bathroom, spun her around and molded his body to hers. His tantalizing heat engulfed her. "He has plans for you, too."

A soft cry parted her lips as he ran her earlobe between his teeth and ground against her backside. "By all means," she rasped, "proceed with yours."

"Very well. I'll do as I'm imagining and get you good and frustrated so you're extra mean on the battlefield." He dragged his fingertips up her thigh and tunneled his fingers under the large shirt she'd worn to bed. Under her panties.

"Yes," she mewled, arching into his touch. She lifted her arms and combed her curling claws through his hair.

Playing, playing. His warm breath fanned her cheek as he brought her to the brink of climax. "After you kill everyone, I'll finish you off." With that, he flashed off, leaving her throbbing with need.

Argh! Bad Astra. Bad. But good and frustrated? Check.

What was she going to do about that male?

Vibrating with aggression, Blythe cleaned up to wake up and strapped on an array of weapons. Then she flashed to the underground arena, at the edge of the battlefield.

Two hours till showtime.

The four other combatants had beaten her here. Of course. Each stood on one of five small round pedestals forming a circle in the center of the sand.

Blythe claimed the only free pedestal for herself.

The one that put her back to the royal dais. Spectators—the few who hadn't participated in the tournament—trickled in.

"Nice of you to join us," Lucca offered with a jaunty salute.

"It's to be a straight-up battle to the death, then?" Blythe asked. A clash between a gorgon, an Amazon, the Phoenix, and the harpy. Anticipation acted as boiling fuel.

"That's my guess," the Amazon said.

As the minutes ticked by in terse silence, Blythe's mind tumbled from thought to thought.

To save or not save Lucca. A question she must answer. Soon. What she knew? She'd be a fool to do as the Phoenix planned and let herself be taken out. Sure, she would survive the sting of fatality, if anything but trinite was used to end her life. But. For help home, Carrigan demanded Lucca's ultimate survival. Allowing the harpy to win the tournament and don the crown would only lead to her murder.

Speaking of the trinite, which of her opponents would wield it today? Surely the royal council had given it to someone.

Blythe sensed the moment Roux and Isla appeared. The air changed, thickening with shock. Murmurs arose from the stands as well as the other combatants.

"Look at her," Carrigan breathed with wonder. "So tiny. So adorable."

"I want one," Lucca said, making grabby hands. "Give her to me."

The Amazon shrugged. "I've seen cuter."

"Smart move, bringing a cute kid here to distract everyone," the gorgon spat at Blythe, "but it's not going to help you."

She ignored them all, mapping out a strategy in her head. No outcome had ever been so important. Nothing would dissuade her from the prize. Total victory.

"So, when you hear the horn, go for gold or whatever. I don't really care anymore. There are no rules. No time limit, either. Last one breathing wins." Tonka's preoccupied tone poured through the stadium. Then she began to baby talk with far more focus. "You are too adorable. Yes, yes, you are. Come here to me. Let me rock you to sleep."

"Stranger danger!" Isla cried. Then, sounding almost smug, she added, "My mom says I get to disembowel strangers anytime I want."

Tonka laughed, as though delighted. "Such a spicy little pepper. I'm still going to hold you—" Her pain-drenched scream registered next. "You cut off my hands!"

"You shouldn't have reached for the girl," Roux stated flatly, and Blythe might have fallen in love with him that very nanosecond.

Sexy Astra. Did he or did he not carry Laban inside his head? What did it mean for her either way? He *wasn't* Laban and...she didn't want him to be. She *liked* him. Somehow, he just fit her.

Focus! Head in the game.

Perfect timing. The horn pierced the air, and the fight was on. Blythe launched herself at the Amazon.

Carrigan and Lucca went for the gorgon. Clearly, the Phoenix and the harpy had the same plan as Blythe. Remove the two other competitors, then figure everything else out.

Didn't take long to deduce the reason the Amazon had made it all the way to the finals. The power of her punch and concrete-like fist shattered Blythe's jaw and knocked out several of her teeth. As she wheeled backward, spitting blood and enamel, the other woman followed the punishing blow with a vicious stab that would've slammed a blade through the underside of her chin if she hadn't misted. By the time she materialized, a split second later, her bones had healed, and her teeth had regrown.

The Amazon used her warp-speed momentum to throw another punch. Blythe expected the action, ducked, dove *through* the other woman. Upon landing, she flowed to her feet, solidified, and kicked backward.

As the other woman stumbled forward, Blythe spun and lifted her sword. Her opponent had already recovered and swung a sword of her own. Their blades met with a clang, metal to metal. No trinite.

"I'm not letting you win," the Amazon snapped.

"I'm glad to hear that," Blythe replied. Taking time to trash-talk allowed her to regain her bearings and do what needed doing. "I enjoy my victories so much more when there's resistance." That said, she misted *into* the Amazon. As she'd done to so many others in the past, she took control of the inhabited body and forced the woman to hack off her own head. Then, she slipped free just as Carrigan and Lucca finished off the gorgon.

Was the gorgon the one to wield the trinite?

She intended to check the fallen warrior's array of weapons. Instead, she was forced to concentrate on the scarlet-splattered Phoenix and harpy, who'd locked in, stalking a circle around her.

"Well?" Carrigan demanded. "Have you made a decision?"

Had she? What to do, what to do? Was the gorgon the one to wield the trinite? Or did Carrigan and Lucca have an agenda of their own, as Erebus suggested? Did the royal council intend to betray Blythe afterward, as Roux believed?

Guess she'd have to roll the dice and trust the only person who had safeguarded her since his arrival. "I have, yes," she said, lifting her sword. "No deal. I'm taking no chances. I'm going to kill you both."

28

THE WINNER

Roux sat next to Isla on the dais, white-knuckling his knees. Blythe blocked attacks from both of her competitors. But the partnered pair worked well together, driving her in different directions throughout the arena, and it wasn't long before the two landed a series of blows.

When one struck, the other prepared to do the same a split second later, leaving their foe little time to think, defend, or render a strike of her own. In a matter of minutes, she was stripped of all weapons. No. No. Maybe she'd shed them willingly for some brilliant reason he couldn't compute.

Most of her wounds healed in seconds but several remained, gushing crimson. He gripped the arms of his chair. Why? Still she fought, using her claws and teeth.

"She'll win," Isla announced with her usual pride and confidence. "She's the best."

"She is," he agreed. But watching her suffer pain, the day after he himself had inflicted more than she'd ever before braved...it wasn't easy or fun. He would rather endure a thousand more centuries of his former blessing task.

"Yes!" he and Isla shouted in unison when Blythe dodged Lucca's strike while swinging a sword she hadn't held a moment ago. Suddenly the harpy's head flew across the arena, minus her body.

His jaw dropped as realization dawned. Somehow, she'd misted the weapon without misting herself, hiding it from view. Not something he could do. Pride flooded him.

Carrigan bellowed her rage and anguish, wings bursting from her back as the headless body hit the sand, spurting blood. Flap, flap. Those wings produced a gale force that knocked the harphantom to the other side of the arena. As Blythe came to her feet, the Phoenix strolled forward, hips swaying.

"You will pay for what you did to Lucca. One life for another." Without a pause in her step, Carrigan held up a dagger. Flames spread over her hand. The hilt. The blade. Metal melted, dripping down her arm.

A curse exploded in Roux's head. The trinite blade, hidden beneath the metal now hardening over her flesh. Beware of the monster underground. *Hello, monster.*

The Phoenix had never found a way out, had she? Instead, she'd hoped to trick Blythe into trusting and sparing the harpy, allowing Carrigan to end the harphantom without much of a battle.

No wonder the worst of Blythe's wounds had yet to

heal. If the Phoenix sank that blade into the harpy's heart…

At his knees, his claws cut through his leathers. His skin. Muscle. The tips embedded in bone.

"Well, well," Blythe said without fear. "Aren't you the tricky one? I'm going to enjoy burying you in a grave of your own making."

"As final words," the Phoenix replied, "those are pretty terrible. Care to try again?"

"I'd rather *show* you my final words."

Both Blythe and Carrigan picked up speed, jogging…running…sprinting at each other. Slammed together. Exchanged blows and sprang to their feet. Ducked and dodged. Moved at speeds he struggled to track. He knew when Blythe attempted to ghost inside Carrigan because she bounced back.

The Phoenix possessed a block, similar to Roux's, though surely not as strong. Bet she'd paid a witch good money for hers. Too bad it wouldn't save her in the end.

"Do you think we can stop for donuts or something on the way home?" Isla asked him, her calm unshakable. "Momma loves sweets."

"Victory first, home second, sweets third." How he maintained a composed facade, he might never know. The combatants fought on with skill and cunning, and completely without mercy.

Isla wiggled in her seat. "Have you talked to your secret prisoner yet?"

He stiffened. Of all the topics to bring up… "I have not."

"You should."

He wouldn't ask if that secret prisoner happened to

be her father. He refused to get her hopes up, just in case he was wrong. *Please be wrong.*

"I knew you brought a child here!" Penelope's gasp hit his ears, and he growled. The wraith hovered off to the side, staring at Isla as if she'd finally found her holy grail.

Isla regarded the spectral without fear. "Who are you?"

"She is our Chosen One. Our key. Give her to me." The wraith jerked her attention to him. "Give her to me now, Astra, or I drain your *gravita*."

Chosen One? Key? He knew of no such lore among the wraiths. Especially considering a young phantom-goddess from Chaos's and Erebus's line.

A cry of distress rose from the battlefield, claiming his focus. He swallowed a roar. A pale Blythe stumbled, *without* taking a blow. She was being drained right this second. He leaped to his feet, grating, "The girl is mine. So is the mother. You will keep our bargain, wraith, or I will—"

"What?" Penelope demanded. "Time is running out, Astra. You can have mother or child, but not both."

"I don't like you," Isla remarked easily.

"Kill her, kill her, kill her," the councilmembers chanted.

"Last chance," the wraith spat at him. "I'll do it. I'll let your woman die."

Rage boiled in his chest as Blythe wobbled on her feet. "Mistake, wraith." He might not be able to touch her, but he could reclaim what was his. He flipped a switch in his mind, and the hatred she'd stolen in her nightly feedings—what she hadn't burned through—ripped free of her, slamming into him.

Suddenly *Penelope* was hit by weakness. Her mask of beauty slipped, revealing the skeletal creature beneath. Another underground monster unearthed.

Too late. Laughing, the Phoenix cut Blythe's throat with a brutal slash of trinite as she spun—the roar barreled from Roux as one of Carrigan's fiery wings sliced through the harpy's belly, cauterizing the edges of the wound at the same time, slowing the healing process.

As Blythe dropped, hitting her knees, the Phoenix executed another spin, clearly intending to use the other blazing appendage to remove her head. But Blythe misted in and out again, avoiding the blow.

Penelope bellowed, rallying. "You think this stops me? Say your goodbyes to your *gravita*, Astra."

Breath congealed in his throat as Blythe shot to her feet. She punched the Phoenix, nothing more, but Carrigan wheeled back as if she'd been gutted. A bright gleam of red glittered from her throat as she toppled. The ruby! It had come off the harpy, who had adhered it to the Phoenix. Now Penelope had no idea she drained Blythe's competition.

Picking up a sword, his woman smiled as Carrigan lumbered to her knees. Swing. Too weak to defend, the Phoenix lost her head. Literally.

Panting, hands fisted, Blythe stood fast as the body of her foe toppled a final time. Whether the Phoenix could heal from such a wound while being drained by a wraith or not was irrelevant. Blythe had done it; she had delivered a death blow, winning the tournament!

But how had the ruby fallen from her perfect skin? The only way would be for Blythe to have forgiven him. Acquitting him of all charges. Which meant...she had.

His eyes widened. Wonder bloomed through him.

"All hail the new queen of Ation," he shouted.

A collective denial rang out.

The councilmembers spoke over each other. "This isn't possible."

"Wasn't supposed to happen this way."

"The crown belongs to us!"

"No one will be leaving this realm!"

Blythe's gaze flipped up, finding Roux on the dais. The connection and chemistry between them arced, a lightning bolt to his systems.

He saluted her, and she winked.

Oh, how he longed to stalk over and yank his harpy into his arms. Maybe on Laban's behalf, maybe not. Either way, Roux could not let her go. He was keeping her, and that was that. What else mattered?

As if she'd read his thoughts, she nodded. *Soon*, she mouthed.

Yes. Soon. They would have their talk and plan their future. He could decide how to handle the blessing task. But harm her? Never again. He'd do everything in his power to make amends with Isla. Never could he take her father's place. Never would he try. But no matter her feelings, he intended to oversee her protection for the rest of his days.

Realizing she'd lost her leverage, Penelope screeched—the last sound she made. In a blink, Blythe was standing before her, little more than mist, and splitting open her torso. The wraith vanished as her guts spilled out.

"Told you," Isla told Roux as Blythe materialized at her side. "She always wins."

He smiled. "That she does."

Aggression rose from the royal council. He spun, facing them. "A single battle remains, and it's ours."

Sensing their end, the females attacked him in unison. As blows were exchanged, he and Blythe pressed together, forming a wall in front of the little girl. Block. Strike. Block, block. Slash.

But the child didn't stay put. Moving out from behind them, Isla stretched out her arms. As her brow furrowed and her nose wrinkled, the air at the opposite end of the dais rippled. The underground began to shake, dirt billowing, rocks falling. Then, a colorful door appeared, with a lock above the handle.

The girl grinned up at her mother. "See."

For a moment, the battle paused. An Amazon was the first to recover. She hurried over and twisted the knob. That knob held.

"Gotta use the key, dummy," Isla taunted, revealing the length of ornately carved silver in her palm.

Roux flashed over and tore the Amazon away from the door, allowing Blythe to transport her daughter there. Isla inserted the key, twisted, and removed the key. A click sounded, the knob turning on its own. Hinges creaked as the block opened, again on its own, welcoming the scent of honeysuckle and roses and revealing a bedroom Roux had seen in the Harpinian palace. A room he knew to be Blythe's. The king-size bed was unmade, the dresser scattered with weapons. Heaps of ash filled the hearth. A portrait of Roux graced the center of the mantel, a cluster of darts embedded into both of his eyes.

A giant rock fell, barely missing the dais. Mother and daughter stumbled to the side. The Amazon wrenched free and soared through the doorway without bouncing back. Roux almost couldn't process the feat.

The other councilmembers forgot all about their opponents and attempted to follow the Amazon through the opening. Before they could make it, he flashed inside the entrance, dragged the Amazon from the room, then herded the others backward.

"Go," he shouted to Blythe, fighting off the enemy as the shaking worsened. "Get Isla to safety. I'll follow you as soon as I keep the promise I made to these women."

She looked ready to protest until a bigger rock smacked into the stands. She scooped the girl into her arms and, as he turned to the side, she zoomed past him, shooting through the opening.

Relief bathed him. His girls were safe.

The councilmembers were undeterred. They sprang forward, attempting to claw their way past him. Without Blythe and Isla to worry about, he altered the air, ensuring his foes inhaled the same poison he'd fed the combatants.

One by one, his tormentors screamed and collapsed, writhing on the floor. Wounds appeared. Blood poured.

A delightful sight indeed. "For days you did your best to harm my female. Now you will learn the error of your ways." He unleashed his worst power, forcing their spirits to rise from their bodies. Drawing those spirits closer. Absorbing each one in his skin. What were a few more prisoners?

The other inmates recognized what was happening and screamed protests about overcrowding. He didn't care. As if fettered by an invisible chain, the radiant spirits whisked to him and absorbed through his pores. Inside his head, he was right there to greet them with another smile before tossing them into cells. Their screams joined the chorus of noise, and satisfaction filled him.

The cavern shook with far more force, rock after rock tumbling. A serenade of roars erupted in every direction. Distinct roars Roux recognized. Dragons. Not exterminated, after all, but hiding.

The monsters in the underground.

Roux pivoted on his heel, ready to return to Harpina and— The door had vanished.

He patted the air, but it was gone. Either it had faded…or Isla had closed it. Her version of payback? No matter. Working his jaw, he flashed topside, into the sunlight to await the dragons. As the ground beneath his feet quaked and cracked, he summoned his backpack and the array of weapons inside it.

Perfect timing. The first dragon burst from the earth, flinging large clumps of dirt. With a flap of its wings, the horned, scaled creature the size of a cottage launched into the air and spewed a stream of fire. Another dragon followed suit a few yards away.

Aggression and malice prickled Roux's skin. Focused on his goals, he withdrew a retractable spear. After he killed the fiends, he was getting off this realm. One way or another.

29

THE CULMINATION

Blythe's eyes widened as ferocious roars filled the bedroom. *What was* that?

She stood in front of Isla with her daggers steady. She would slay anyone who came through that mystical door. Not that she believed a councilmember would get past Roux. The giant Astra blocked the entrance, his back to her. Before him, the females dropped and screamed. The cavern shook with increasing force. Dust blustered into the bedroom, tickling her nose.

"Roux!" she shouted. "Finish them and come on!" Wait. "The door. It's fading." She gasped. Wrong. The door was just…gone. No more roars. No more cavern or dust. Panic overtook her. She dropped the daggers and slapped at the air, searching for some remnant. Nothing. A whimper escaped. "Where did the door go, sweetheart?"

"I think I ran out of power," Isla replied, her voice strained.

Stomach churning, heart thundering, Blythe crouched before her daughter. The darling had grown pale and trembly. "Are you all right? Were you hurt?"

"I'm okay." Despite the hint of weakness, the little girl flipped her fall of dark hair over her shoulder, as sassy as ever. "Told you I could do it."

"Yes, but *how* did you do it? And can you do it again after you power up?"

"'Course I can do it again." Isla puffed up her chest. "Creating the door was as easy as I expected. The key was the only hard part. I had to design it myself, since Grandpa Bus never crafted one. But I don't need to make another door and key, Momma. You're home."

"I'm not leaving the Astra behind." Today, Blythe had made some life-changing decisions. As she'd fought the Phoenix, she'd known Roux would protect her daughter until his last breath. Then. That moment. She'd had no more hate to give, the root of bitterness in her heart withered. And when she'd proven victorious and glanced up, catching the Astra's eye, desire for him—for a future with him—had overwhelmed her.

She wanted him, and so she would have him. If Laban truly did reside inside Roux's head, they could search for a way to free him and help his spirit move on to the afterlife. It was the right thing to do, yes? Unless Laban wished to stay there and have some sort of contact with his family?

Ugh. That part still required contemplation.

And what if Roux desired Blythe only because of her first consort's presence, somehow tapping into Laban's emotions and experiencing them himself? *Will I lose him, too?*

A worry for tomorrow. First up, getting her male home. No doubt he'd find a way on his own. The guy was an unstoppable force of nature. But why not help him for once? As harpies like to say, couples who slayed together stayed together. They could take care of vengeful wraiths, a (possibly) recovered Phoenix, and whatever had roared.

"Are you going back to kill him?" Isla asked, her brow wrinkled.

How to explain? Should she even try right now? "We'll discuss my plans for him later. Here's what we're gonna do now," she said, exploding to her feet and rushing about to grab what she needed. Isla's key. Bag. Her own clothes. Favorite toiletries. Weapons. "I'm flashing to Ation." Since she'd visited already, she didn't need another door to facilitate her arrival. Only her departure. "You'll stay here. Tell Aunt Taliyah what happened. She'll supply you with a phantom feast tonight." An assembly line of powerful immortals would strengthen the girl like never before. "In the morning, if I haven't returned, you'll open another door. Under no circumstances are you to speak with…Bus again. He's a very bad man who harmed Mommy."

"Oh." Isla narrowed her eyes. "He didn't tell me that part."

"He's crafty. He fooled me, too." Again, Blythe crouched before her daughter and hugged her close. "I love you with all my heart. You know that, yes?"

"I do. I love you, too."

"When I get back, we'll chat about everything that's

happened. I'll explain in detail. All right? Go on now. Do as you were told."

Isla hugged her a second time before rushing from the room. Tears burned Blythe's eyes. She stood, anchored the bag to her shoulder and breathed deep. *To Ation we go.* She flashed to the palace—a searing wind enveloped her. What the—*what*?

The palace was in rubble, and she balanced upon the remains. Cracks forked through the land, flames shooting forth. If Carrigan revived, she'd have to dig her way out. One threat eliminated at least. But for good or for a short time?

Blythe cast her gaze farther out. Smoke blackened the sky and tainted her inhalations. The only light came from multiple fires. Flames all around. Every silo a heap of stone and lumber.

A roar ripped through the darkness, and she detected as much pain and fury in the undertone. Battling Roux?

She flashed closer to the source, in the direction of Wraith Island. There! On the beach, in a haze of fire and smoke, Roux brutally murdered a dragon. The massive creature flopped to the ground, alongside four others.

Her heart beat with more force. Though she stood hundreds of yards away on moss-covered stones, the Astra heard the erratic drum. He must have. His head snapped up, his crimson eyes lasering to her. He was panting, splattered with blood, and so sexy she felt gobsmacked. His clothes were singed, his skin streaked with soot.

Onyx water stretched out behind him. On the island itself, the palace blazed like a bonfire. No sign of the wraiths.

Between one blink and the next, Roux appeared before her, a looming tower of menace. "You came back for me."

"I planned to tag team any threats with you, but I see you've finished the game on your own." She dropped the bag and threw her arms around him. "Let's celebrate your victory."

He dipped down to kiss the hollow of her neck where the ruby once resided. Voice throaty, he said, "You forgave me for our past." The menace got replaced by raw savagery.

"I have." She smiled at him. "We can't go back and change our beginning, but we can start fresh and change our ending."

"Yes." He slammed his mouth to hers and tangled their tongues together. A ruthless claiming. This man owned her mouth.

Driven by desire, she yanked at his clothes. He shredded hers and drove her to the carpeted stone. They devoured each other. Clutched and kneaded. As his white-hot palms covered her with stardust, preparing her body for his invasion, a frenzy quickly took hold of them both.

"More," she commanded. "Give me more. All. Everything."

"You are mine. Understand? Mine!" He gripped her chin and captured her gaze. "Want me," he demanded harshly. An order he clearly expected her to obey. "Only me."

Stripped of all artifice, she offered a hoarse, honest response. "With every fiber of my being."

"Never letting you go. Keeping you forever."

"Always."

He bared his teeth as though she'd dared to protest. "Woe to anyone who tries to take you away from me."

Too intense! Too good! All-consuming. He kissed her again and slowly worked his way inside her. Sweat dotted brutal features tight with strain. Their exhalations mingled until they inhaled the other's ragged breaths.

"This is…you are…" He didn't stop until he was fully seated, filling her. His eyes rolled back in his head. "Everything!"

The pleasure…aah! She was coming undone already. Coming, coming, coming, flooded by euphoria spiced with connection and possession. Her inner walls spasmed around him, no part of her unaffected. Roux owned her, period. Had marked her inside and out. Just as she had owned and marked him.

She'd promised to give him a story for his first time, but as he rocked inside her, harder and harder, driving her bliss higher, he became the author of the tale. Confident and assertive, an animal reduced to nothing but need. Body, mind, and being, he took her—branded her.

Blythe couldn't tear her gaze from the savagery of his expression. At this moment in time, he hid nothing from her. She saw it all, everything he felt for her. The consuming lust. The desperation and ferocity. An adoration she'd never noticed before. He looked at her as if she were his lifeline. The very reason he breathed.

"Say my name," he commanded with his next plunge. "Let me hear it on your lips."

"Roux. Roux." Tension built all over again, reaching for a new pinnacle and…almost there…yes, yes… She came all over again. "Roux!" she cried, shuddering beneath him. Muscles clenched and limbs quivered.

He followed her over, throwing back his head and bellowing, "Lyla!"

When they sagged to the ground, panting and shaking, she curled into his side, wholly content. Felt so natural, being with him this way. As if they were two puzzle pieces joined together.

She combed her fingers through his hair and nibbled on his earlobe. "I hope you're not worn-out, Warden. This she-beast is far from done."

Hours later, Roux clutched his female against him. Nonconstrictive but tight. There would be no slipping from his grip.

The contentment he felt right now...the sublime satisfaction... Nothing compared. He wanted this, wanted her, every day for the rest of eternity. He'd meant what he'd said. Anyone who tried to take her from him died screaming. But.

As they lay naked together, water crashing on the shore, smoke drifting over the blackened sky, worry infiltrated his thoughts. Had Blythe made love to Roux, or Laban?

"Do we need to stay on guard for angry wraiths?" she asked with a yawn.

"No. After the door closed, the dragons rose from hibernation beneath the cavern. Penelope healed and led her wraiths against them, but the dragon fire engulfed them, their ashes raining upon the land. If the wraiths recover, I'll be amazed."

"Are you kidding? How is that even possible? I was only gone a few minutes."

His arm encircled her neck. With a little rearranging, he pinched her chin and tilted her face up toward his. "You missed a lot. Someone from a village used magic to screw with the time here. Hours have passed. I would have cut a hole in the atmosphere, but I feared bringing the dragons with me. They were starved for fried Astra."

Her eyes widened. "Hours? Is time still screwed up?" If so, what would it mean for their return trip?

"Don't worry. I'll get us back." He pressed a soft kiss into her lips. "Just want to hold you awhile longer. *Without* thinking about the task." Or her status as the queen of Ation. That he must remove her heart with trinite, killing her, or doom his brothers-in-arms to defeat. Unless he found another way.

He'd told himself he could do so. But could he? Would he? If he failed… He could not fail.

Sweat broke out on his brow. "There's a more pressing matter to attend to, anyway. Laban."

"Uh, I won't talk about the task, and you won't bring up Laban." She squirmed and repositioned, draping her chest over his and resting her folded arms across his pectorals. Arousal surged anew, sharper and deeper despite this first true taste of rapture. "Instead, we'll discuss my rules. For starters, your concubine gets the boot *immediately*. I know you never slept with her, but I don't care. She goes or dies, one or the other."

The corners of his mouth twitched. "I like your jealousy. And I agree. She goes. In return for my capitulation in this matter, you will move into my bedroom at the palace."

"Capitulation, huh?" She snorted. "I'll bunk up with you, but not right away. Not until I've spoken to Isla."

"Though I wish for you to speak with her at the same time I speak with the concubine—immediately—

I know it will take time for the little girl to adjust to her mother moving in with the male who killed her beloved daddy." He wanted nothing to do with adding to the child's suffering. Wished only to protect her from further hurts.

"Thank you for understanding."

"But whether we are living together or not, we *are* together. From this moment forward. Say it."

Baby blues glittering, she smiled. "Stop bossing me around, Warden. Haven't you heard? It's easier to catch a harphantom with orgasms than orders?"

"I've already caught my harphantom, and I'm not letting her go for any reason." He slid a hand down her spine and squeezed her backside. "But I *am* willing to give her more of those orgasms."

Her eyelids grew heavy, and her smile softened, turning wanton. "Perfect segue for my second rule. You give me pleasure where and when I want it. And, Roux?" she said, wiggling against him. "I want it here, and I want it now."

30

THE RETURN

Mmm, mmm, mmm. Blythe did like watching Roux work. After a night of pleasure, whispers, and swimming, they'd napped as the sky cleared of smoke, then woke to bright, golden sunlight. That sunlight now bathed the decimated land and framed the Astra's powerful body.

He stood at the shore, shirtless, his *alevala* on display and moving. Sweat slicked back his hair. Glistening muscles bulged with every action. To create his door, he literally shredded one dimension after another with his claws.

"Try not to damage my new world too badly," she began, stretched out on the sand in a brakini, her arms lifted, her fingers intertwined under her head. "I'm planning to offer authentic escape-realm tours of Ation.

For a hefty price, immortals can stay here and solve a series of riddles that lead to your exit portal. If they fail to crack the riddles, they'll die here. Yes, yes. I'm liking this."

He frowned. "My portal is a bust. The layers repair themselves before I can get to the last."

"Use the dragon fire." Small flames lingered at the palace. "See if the heat cauterizes the layers. I mean, we know the flames can't burn through the layers themselves, but they might halt any regrowth for whatever's torn. And if that fails, I'll create a door like Isla did, and use her key. I mean, I watched her do it and everything, so how hard can it be? And if that fails, we just wait until *she* opens one."

Blink. He hovered over her, his hands near her temples as if completing push-ups. "I like the way your brain works." With a smile, he descended, kissed her quick, then vanished before she could get her arms around him.

With a laugh, she sat up. He appeared only seconds later, on the shore, a lit torch in hand. Dragon fire, the ends flicking a bright, neon red. He attempted to create another door. As he shredded and burned, burned and shredded, tension seeped from him. He looked over his shoulder and winked at her. "I like having your gaze upon me."

"You like having any part of me on you." And she more than enjoyed his reaction to her.

"You aren't wrong." He continued shredding, asking hesitantly, "The feeling is mutual, yes?"

"Oh, yes," she assured him, hiding a grin. She even enjoyed his vulnerability with her.

She hastened to dress in a T-shirt and jeans, knowing he'd give a victory shout any moment.

Perfect timing. He stopped. His smile faded. "Lyla! Come." He tossed the torch. "We go now."

Excitement warred with disappointment. The honeymoon had come to an end. Time to tackle life's problems.

After swiping up their packs, she teleported to where he stared and followed his gaze. The once blue sky looked burned in spots, with a curtain of air ripped down the center, revealing a dark, shadowed expanse beyond it. "Where does this lead?"

"The heavens outside of Ation's orbit." He took her hand and kissed her knuckles. "Remember what I told you. We are together now."

"Together," she agreed, and dang if she didn't beam him a schoolgirl-with-a-crush smile. "Trust me, babe. I have plans for you." For starters, she would teach him how to have fun. Give him the laughter he'd been missing most of his life. A new purpose for both of them!

He led her through the opening and suddenly they were weightless. An empty void offered no light or sound. Before she could adjust, the Astra flashed her to her bedroom in the harpy palace. As easy as that.

"Momma!" Isla called, scrambling from the bed where she drew a key in a sketchbook, rushing over to hug Blythe. "You came back without my door."

"We sure did."

Roux's blank mask descended, his tension returning. He squeezed her hand before releasing it, and said, "I'll give you two time." Then he was gone.

Blythe heaved a sigh and ruffled her daughter's hair.

"Hey, sweetheart. Let's sit down and have our talk, okay? Just like I promised."

"Mind if I join you?" Erebus's voice filled the room, and she gasped.

She darted her gaze to her most hated enemy. "You."

Isla merely waved, saying, "Hi, Grandpa."

The current bane of Blythe's existence stood on the other side of the room, leaning one shoulder against the wall. Dressed in a familiar black robe, pale hair in its usual disarray, while he displayed his customary smug grin. "Our little Issy defied the Blade of Destiny, adding a fork in the road of our lives. A true surprise, I must admit. Perhaps I'll allow her to live, after all. What a shame to waste so much power."

"Sweetheart," Blythe grated to her offspring, "go find your aunt Taliyah and let her know Grandpa Bus is here."

"Are you gonna kill him, Momma? Please, don't! Please!" Isla tugged on her arm. "He always talks like that. And I know he did something bad, but he's gonna apologize."

"I told you to find your aunt Taliyah." Blythe gave her daughter a nudge toward the door. "That's what you're going to do. Now go." The girl didn't need to witness what was about to go down.

"Yes, yes," Erebus cooed. "You should go, child. We wouldn't want you to learn of Roux's need to kill your mother to complete his task. Or hear how the Astra hopes to become your new daddy."

"Go!" Blythe's cold tone left no room for argument.

"Fine!" Isla stomped her foot as fat tears welled. "But I'll expect your apology later, too." With that, she flashed away, leaving Blythe flabbergasted. Teleportation was a skill she hadn't mastered until the age of sixteen.

"The real surprise," Blythe told her father, picking up the conversation as if there'd been no lag, "is you coming here to face me on your own rather than sneaking in one of your phantoms to deliver a message."

The taunt missed its mark. He merely grinned, unabashed. "The last phantoms I sent gave Roux a message meant for you as well. What fills your life and empties it at the same time? You, my dear, know the answer mentally. Today, you'll experience it firsthand." He extended his palm, a length of chain twined between his fingers. Of course, Laban stood at the other end of the links.

Laban stood with his shoulders back and his head high, but his gaze downcast.

"This trick is old," she snapped.

Her first consort finally lifted his gaze, and her chest squeezed. He projected something she'd never detected from him. Guilt and shame.

Unease skittered down her spine, dousing her rage. Without that rage, new realizations registered. Being in the same room differed from being on opposite sides of a doorway in two faraway realms. Here, now, a familiar scent wafted to her nose. *His* scent. Laban's. What if…

Roux appeared at her side, radiating concern. "I heard Erebus—" He spotted her guests and growled.

"Erebus was just attempting to convince me that my first consort is alive," she stated.

"Blythe," Laban croaked, and tears welled in *her* eyes. Such desperation. "I'm real. I'm here."

"No." She gave her head a violent shake. "No!"

"I assure you," Erebus purred, "he's telling the truth. Go ahead. Touch him. You know you want to…"

She halfway expected Roux to grab her arms to prevent her from making contact. He didn't. He glared at the manticore with blazing red eyes while huffing his breaths. His hands remained fisted. The blank mask he usually donned in front of others was gone. Torment etched his features, and all she wanted to do was fall into his arms.

"Laban." Erebus gave the chain a tug. "Go on. Give your mate proof of life."

Heart jumping, she whipped her attention back to the male she'd never thought to see again. Torment etched his features as well. Peering at her, he tripped forward, approaching.

"Touch me," he beseeched when he stood mere inches away.

Though shaking and hesitant, she reached out with a shaky hand. Contact. The pads of her fingers met the warmth of his cheek, and she gasped. He was solid. Real. Not a phantom or illusion.

But, but… "I don't understand." Her mouth floundered open and closed. Her vision blurred. Two consorts. Here. Together. She didn't…she couldn't…

She looked to Roux for help. What was she supposed to do? What was she supposed to feel?

Still he glared at the manticore.

"How can this be?" she asked Laban, the words broken. "I watched you die." Had thought his spirit lived on in Roux's head. But he didn't. Which meant both Laban and Roux were her consorts. And…and…and… she could make sense of nothing.

"I'll explain while I hold you." He reached for her,

only to dart his gaze to the Astra and lower his arms. His lips pressed into a tight line. But, as he returned his attention to Blythe, vulnerability overtook his expression. He opened his arms. "Please, love. Let me hold you."

Please, love. The same two words he'd spoken the day he'd died. Or she'd thought he'd died. A day that had changed the course of her life forever. But here he stood before her, alive and well.

A sob sprang from her aching throat as she fell into him. He enfolded her in his embrace, his warm breath fanning the top of her head. How she'd missed this male. How she'd loved him. How— Wait. Had she truly just thought of her feelings in the past tense? Surely her affection for him hadn't changed so quickly, along with everything else?

"Why don't we give these two fated mates time alone?" Erebus cocked a brow at Roux. "They have much to discuss. And you have a mystery to solve. If the prisoner in your head isn't Laban, who is it?" Laughing, he vanished. The chain, no longer in his grip, clattered to the floor.

"Roux," Blythe croaked, pulling from Laban. Whatever she did or did not feel for her original consort didn't change what she felt for Roux. Affection. Admiration. Love? She knew she liked him. Greatly. Knew she hungered for him wildly.

She reached for him, but he sidestepped, avoiding her touch for the first time. Her stomach sank.

"For once the Dark One is right. You require time. Together. Alone." He pivoted, presenting her with his back. Then he was gone. But, but...

Laban offered her his hand. For several agonized

heartbeats, she offered no response. The urge to hunt down Roux and force him to discuss this with her proved strong. Suddenly she reminded herself of a rope in a vicious tug-of-war.

In the end, she slipped her hand into Laban's and allowed him to lead her to the bed. The chain dragging behind them.

He sat at the edge and attempted to pull her onto his lap. Blythe resisted and eased beside him. Things were…complicated. No need to complicate them further by encouraging one male over the other.

"Explain what happened while I get you free of this," she said. She pulled and clawed at the metal collar locked around his neck. No hinges. No give. Tears burned her eyes. Give up? No! There had to be a way; she had only to find it.

"Don't worry about the collar, love." He clasped her wrists, forcing her to stop. "What I have to tell you…just know that I'm sorry. So very sorry." Guilt and shame filled his eyes once again.

"What is it?" Her stomach churned. "Tell me!"

He breathed deep, as if bracing for a blow. "More than a decade ago, Erebus came to me. He told me he could make me a phantom and remain unbound to him."

"He. Did. What?" Fury burned through her. "And you accepted?"

"No!" His irises blazed with menace. "But he did it, anyway."

Yes, that sounded like Erebus. She pressed her tongue to the roof of her mouth. *Grandpa Bus has much more to answer for than I realized.* "Why didn't you tell me before this?"

"Admit to my strength-loving female that I was too

weak to defend myself against her father?" He gave a clipped shake of his head. "No."

His words sank in, and she blinked. "You kept quiet about this, ensuring I grieved your loss? Do you know how selfish that is?" Her fury blazed hotter. And hotter. To become a true phantom, one must die first. Without knowing it, Roux had delivered the death blow that had turned the manticore into a phantom.

All the grief on Blythe's part had been for nothing. Isla's anguished tears—for nothing. Roux's guilt—for nothing. The once terrible chasm between them, born of her pain, could have been avoided.

Claws extended from her nail beds. Would she have done anything differently if she'd known the truth? Yes. But which things? Could she regret, even for a moment, the time spent with Roux? Witnessing his wonder as he experienced his first taste of pleasure. Teasing him from his stoic masks. Hearing him cheer as she battled on. But even still…

"If I could go back…" A ragged noise slipped from Laban. "But I can't."

"No, you can't. And neither can I." Laban's pride had caused this, plain and simple. Yes, Erebus carried blame. A lot of blame. But her former consort carried so much more. He'd been a partner. An ally. Yet he'd betrayed her trust in the worst way.

"We can move forward." Maintaining his hold on her, he said, "We can move forward stronger than ever, love. I know we can."

Could they? After a betrayal of this magnitude?

Did she want to? She could have spent the past two months helping him adjust to becoming a phantom. Searching for him. Focusing her rage on her true enemy—her father. Instead, she'd blamed an innocent man. A treasured consort.

She licked suddenly dry lips. "You don't understand, Laban. Some things have happened."

"I don't care. Nothing has to change what's between us." He adjusted his grip and squeezed her hand. "I'm different, yes. But my love for you hasn't dwindled in the slightest."

He still didn't understand. Heartache doused her anger. He'd hurt her with his actions, yes, but she had no desire to hurt him back. And she was soon to *destroy* him. Guilt flooded her, and she bowed her head.

"I want to be with you," he stated. "We can return to our life. Raise our daughter. Together. Think of her joy when she sees me."

Pressure joined Blythe's guilt, the two nearly flattening her lungs. He didn't know she'd slept with Roux. Or that the Astra was her consort, a fact that hadn't changed simply because of Laban's return. And the manticore definitely didn't know she might not want things to go back to the way they were pre-invasion.

During the final battle of the tournament, when Penelope had begun to drain her, Blythe had chanced a glance up at Roux, perched beside her daughter, on high alert for any perceived threat to the girl's life. She'd thought, *My family.* In that moment, she'd let go of the past in favor of grabbing hold of her future. Nothing had ever felt so right. Nothing.

"Laban. I must tell you something, and you must hear me. All right?"

He ran his tongue over his teeth. "If you intend to explain the Astra's blessing task, don't. There's no need. Erebus told me Roux is set to take your heart with trinite, ending your life. But I don't want you to worry over what's to come, love. I'll kill him before he has a chance to try. You'll be safe with me. I swear it."

The guilt delivered a series of punches, stealing her breath. Her first consort intended to protect her even though she'd betrayed him. But, at the same time, protective instincts surged. "You won't kill him. Or harm him. Or even go after him." She didn't mean to snap the words, but she definitely snapped. "He's a good male."

"Good?" Stiffening, he leaped to his feet and spun to face her. "You dare to defend the one who murdered me?"

"He's never lied to me!" she shouted as an avalanche of emotions tumbled through her. Anger. Frustration. Confusion. More guilt, now tinged with sorrow. More fury, too. They fed off each other, magnifying. Deep breath in, out. "A lot has happened since you died. What I'm trying to tell you is… Roux… He is… We…"

Laban's nostrils flared. "No. Don't say it. After everything I've been through."

"You're not the only one who suffered," she pointed out, her tone bleak, knowing she must hurt this man who loved her.

"I'm not sure I can bear to hear this from your lips as well as Erebus's," he whispered.

So her father had already taunted him with the information? *Yes, Grandpa Bus is gonna die bad.*

Laban scrubbed a hand over his face, his burst of temper fading. "Just don't say it," he repeated.

"I must. Because you *do* need to hear it from my lips." Without truth, what did they have? Deep breath in. Out. "Roux is… He is my consort. Something I still don't understand. It is impossible. Beyond impossible.

But it's also true." A harpy shouldn't be able to have two mates, and yet she did. "Even without answers, I... I'm with him now. I can't turn off what I feel for him just because you've come back."

"But you can, love." Eyes bright, Laban dropped to his knees between her legs. "You only *think* the Astra is your consort."

As gently as possible, she told him, "I know what I feel." And yet, despite the strength of her feelings for the Astra, Laban drew her still. Yet, it paled in comparison to what she felt for Roux.

How?

He gave his head an emphatic shake. "I've been with your father for weeks. Sometimes he forgets I'm there and mutters to himself. Again and again, he's cackled about the trick he's played on you. How Roux isn't your consort. How you are his downfall."

Heart in her throat, Blythe fought for air. Was he right? Erebus had proven the deceitfulness of his character again and again. She just, she didn't know anything anymore.

Springing away from the bed, away from Laban, she croaked, "I need time alone. Need to think." Before he could respond, she flashed to a place known as No Man's Land. A pocket garden realm created by the Astra, at her sister's insistence.

Several other harpies loitered around, laughing, chatting, and sniffing flowers. Screw being polite. "Out," she screeched. "Now."

They obeyed as if their lives depended on it, and she plopped onto a wooden bench. What was she going to do?

31

THE DEATH

Roux sat at the edge of his bed, his elbows resting on his knees, his head bowed. Screams reverberated through every inch of his being, a never-ending chorus. The prisoners had escaped. For the first time, he didn't care. And he wasn't bothered by them. They were no more than an irritating blip when compared to the travesty of his life.

He should have returned to the Commander and Taliyah to finish issuing his report of the happenings in Ation—and events soon to happen, now that Blythe was the realm's queen. Instead, he'd fired his concubine and come to his bedroom hoping to ease the turmoil in his mind.

Could it be eased? Laban was alive and not trapped

in Roux's head, as assumed. His *gravita* now possessed two consorts.

A humorless laugh escaped him. The harphantom wouldn't have two consorts for long, though, would she? No doubt she was already making plans to ditch the newest as quickly as possible. His hands curled into fists.

He couldn't blame her for it. In a matter of days, he was supposed to cut out her heart with trinite, bringing harm to her yet again, ending her once and for all. Either that, or he welcomed a curse upon the Astra.

Pain stabbed his chest. Of every torture he'd endured throughout his life, this was unquestionably the worst. Were Laban and Blythe already in bed? Touching? Groaning each other's names? Cuddling and whispering sweet everythings? Was she making him laugh? Lifting the never-ending gloom off his life with the simplest of smiles? Kissing?

"There you are."

The relieved statement penetrated his awareness. Huffing and puffing, he lifted his gaze to find Ian beside him. The Astra's incredible height and powerful build swallowed much of the space.

Roux almost offered the Commander's salute. Once, Ian had led the Astra. Had he not refused to sacrifice his bride during the original blessing task, he would still be at the helm. Now he held steady at ninth. He remained the strongest among them, however, and also the charmer. Able to seduce any female and befriend any male. What few failed to realize until too late? Beneath his affable exterior lurked a ferocious interior.

"Here I am," he said, not recognizing the animalistic quality to his own voice.

"Roc is eager for the rest of your report— Whoa! What's this look for?" The other male waved a finger in Roux's face. "Did you hear Taliyah is quote unquote going full harpy on you and roasting you on a spit? Because she is."

Movement drew his attention to the left. Silver materialized beside Ian, saying, "Did you find— Ah. There he is. Roc sent me to find out what's taking so long. Shall I transport us all together?" Mass teleportation was his specialty. Along with the ability to torch his foes with only a glance and read hundreds of minds at once.

He frowned as he looked Roux over. "What's wrong with you? Why is your face like that? Did Ian tell you Taliyah is determined to string you up by your intestines?"

"Enough about Taliyah. My face is fine." For once, Roux wasn't schooling his expression to hide his emotions, that was all.

With a growl, he sprang to his feet and paced before the pair. Why not tell them his problems? He wasn't a sharer by nature, but he'd never needed advice more.

"I am Blythe's consort, and she is my *gravita*," he announced. "She chose me, we slept together, and I—"

"Whoa, back up. This is you we're talking about. Do you mean you slept together or that you *slept together*?" Silver demanded. "There's a big difference. Huge. If you're confused, just check the measuring stick in your pants."

Even now, her sweet honeysuckle and roses scent enveloped him, making that stick…uncomfortable. "I meant it in every sense of the word. I marked her with my stardust." In essence, he wed her. For better or worse.

"Whoa," Ian echoed, pulling up a chair and getting comfortable. "Just so we can be sure you truly understand the meaning of the word, describe to us in great detail about this so-called sleeping."

Roux glared at the warrior. "We're moving on. Besides the sleeping, I also tortured her." Guilt cut through him. Followed by excitement. "Though she did find that part quite sexy." Had his chest just puffed with pride? Another growl escaped him. "I must discover how to win my task without harming her. Perhaps I can offer her first consort's heart? I am happy to kill him all over again. Unless she protests." He scrubbed a hand over his face. "By the way, Laban is alive, thanks to Erebus."

His companions said nothing, so he kept going. "Blythe is mine. Mine! I do not share what is mine. I *won't* share. If she tries to let me go, after promising to stay together, I *will* do murder. Except, I won't. Like a fool, I desire her happiness more than anything. And little Isla deserves a father." He scrubbed his chest next. "What should I do? Tell me. Someone. Anyone. Please!"

Silence greeted him. He glanced at the others. Both males watched him with slack jaws.

"Well?" he snapped. "Give me advice."

"I must admit I'm having trouble getting past the first part of our conversation," Ian finally piped up. "You're telling me our Roo Coo lost his manginity?" He looked to Silver, his brow wrinkled. "That *is* what the harpies call it, yes? Manginity?"

Silver scratched his jaw. "I think they prefer the term *popped his ejacucap.*"

"Ah, yes. You might be right." Ian returned his attention to Roux and grinned. "Congratulations on the loss of your ejacucap, my brother. This calls for a celebration." He held out his hand and a bottle of his favorite whiskey materialized. He removed the cork with his teeth, saluted Roux, and downed the contents.

"Did nothing else I said register?" Roux grated.

Another Astra arrived. "Did you find him?" Halo scanned the others before locking his amber gaze on Roux. "Did Ian and Silver not tell you Roc is ready to hear the rest of your report? If you're hiding from Taliyah—"

"Roux had sex with Blythe," Ian blurted out. "We're celebrating." He offered the empty bottle to the other male. "Would you like a drink of the whiskey I no longer have?"

"We're all hiding from Taliyah," Halo said, stroking his chin. "This is smart."

Roc himself suddenly appeared. Tall, bronze, and commanding. He scowled when he spotted Roux. "What's wrong with your face? No, never mind. There's no reason to hide in your room. Taliyah is now distracted with—"

"Roux had sex with Blythe." Once again, Ian interrupted a speaker. Something only he dared to do. But then, as Roc's biological brother, he had certain privileges the others did not. "Oh, and he mentioned stardusting her, torture, and the return of her first consort."

Surely the Commander would have brilliant words of advice for Roux. The male had dealt with his fair share of disasters while courting Taliyah, his twenty-first bride but the first to survive.

"What should I do?" he croaked. "I cannot live without her."

Roc patted his shoulder. "Kill the original consort, command Blythe to forgive you, and enjoy your newfound happiness. No mercy. Iron fist. That's how I handle Taliyah."

Ian, Silver, and Halo snickered. "Yes, brother," Ian said with a grin. "Your iron fist is the stuff of legends."

"All right. Where is he? Where's Roux?" The feminine shriek echoed from the walls. "I've got things to say!"

Roc winced. "Guess she's not distracted, after all. My best advice? Run, soldier."

Roux didn't run. He flashed outside the harpy's bedroom door. If the first consort received a private conversation, the second should, too. He deserved a chance to fight for what he wanted.

No sounds seeped from behind the entrance. What were the two doing? Were they even inside?

The blood rushed from his head. He lifted his fist and knocked a little too hard. Cracks spread through the wood. Booted footsteps thumped. Then the door swung open, revealing the manticore, who carried his own length of chain.

This male desired what belonged to him, and only one of them could have her.

Attack! Roux breathed in. Out. And remained still as a statue.

Laban narrowed his eyes, aggression suddenly pulsing from him. "She's not here. You should not have come." Despite his words, he stepped back and waved to encompass the room. He didn't do it gracefully, however. His movements were jerky, as if he kept changing his mind about what to do. "Enter. We will talk."

Halfway expecting to be stabbed in the back—hoping it happened, giving him a reason to strike—Roux strode inside. No ambush. Too bad.

The other man shut the door as Roux turned on his heel. They faced off like two foes on a battlefield.

Roux chose to break the silence. "She told you what I am to her." A statement, not a question.

"She did. You might be happy to know she was confused by her feelings for both of us." Laban grinned coldly. "Then I explained how she's been deceived. How Erebus tricked her into thinking you are her consort. It's only a matter of time before she cuts you loose."

He stiffened. Did the male speak truth?

No. No! Roux would not travel this road of thought. The very road he'd traveled the whole of his life, anytime he'd wondered about his purpose, believing he was destined to live and die alone. His time with Blythe had changed him, teaching him better. *She* was his purpose. His reason for being. He loved her, and love was never a mistake.

His eyes widened. He did; he loved her. She filled every corridor of his heart. Her grace. Her ferocity. Her playfulness. Her strength. Her bravery. Her everything. From the first moment he'd spied her, a part of him had known she meant something to him. That she could do what no one else had been able to: finally complete him.

To forgive him and shed her hatred as she'd done… she must love him, too. Nothing but love could conquer so pure and justified a hatred. Erebus could do many things, but he could not manipulate emotions.

Only one question remained. Would Blythe be able to cut *Laban* loose?

Roux fisted his hands, and the manticore braced, as if he expected a blow. A minute passed in tense silence; neither of them moved.

"I meant what I said, Astra." Laban grated the words. "You shouldn't have come. You are doing exactly what he wants and—" He slammed his lips together, silencing himself.

Why not finish the thought? Did it really matter? "I will leave." The urge to strike was only growing stronger. Though Roux could have flashed away, he walked toward the door. Taking his time, hoping against hope Blythe would return before he exited.

Laban moved to block his path, fury and regret glinting in his eyes.

Why regret?

"It's too late now, Astra. So. Let me tell you how the rest of our conversation is going to go. In a moment, I'll say something that horrifies and disgusts you. You'll attack me. In the process, you'll ruin your chance with Blythe, and Erebus will win your war."

A terrible suspicion flittered across Roux's mind. He almost flashed then and there. If he was proven correct...

The manticore might be right about what happens next.

In the end, he stayed. *Must know.*

He offered a stiff nod. "Let's hear what you have to say."

"Another mistake on your part." Radiating strain, Laban ran the length of chain between his fingers. "Ten years ago, Erebus came to me. He made me into a deathless phantom, something Blythe now knows. What she doesn't know? What I lied to her about? Erebus bound me to his will. He told me to fall in love with her, so I did. Maybe I was always meant to love her. Maybe his command was responsible. Perhaps the fact that he replaced my heart with a clone of the god Mars is responsible. We might never know."

Breath sawed in and out of Roux's mouth. Each new

sentence hit him with the force of a cannonball, proving his suspicion was, in fact, correct. "Tell me the rest."

"I was commanded to keep her safe until the Astra Planeta invaded her world. And I did. With every ounce of my strength, I did. But Erebus issued other commands once he had me in his possession. Do you wish to know what I was ordered to do if you came to my room today?"

No. "Tell me," he croaked.

"I am to kill Isla and ensure the blame points to you."

Bile seared his throat. That...that Roux had not expected. "Harm your own child?" He gave his head a violent shake. "No. You will not kill your daughter."

"You think I want to?" Laban shouted. He dropped the length of chain and reached up. With only a flick of his wrists, he removed the metal collar. It dropped, too. A loud clink pierced the airwaves. "This was merely for show. You realize that, yes? I was to wear it until our private confrontation, and I always do what I'm told. I have failed to stop myself from completing any of Erebus's previous orders. Remain quiet about my transformation. Let you kill me the day of your invasion. Try to convince Blythe to pick me over you. I won't be able to stop the next action, either. So, you have a choice, Astra. Let me murder my own child or kill me and lose Blythe, just as I told you. Exactly what Erebus hopes you'll do."

Roux reeled. He couldn't...he didn't...

"Kill me," Laban snapped, raising his chin. "That is what *I* hope you'll do. What Blythe and Isla *need* you to do. I know you love them because I know your heart better than my own." He pounded a fist into his chest. "I know you're a good male. So do this. Don't make me beg for my own end. Let me go with at least a shred of dignity, knowing I finally did the right thing."

As rage and protectiveness collided, Roux did it. He didn't think any more. Didn't give himself a chance to change his mind. He simply struck. In one fluid motion, he withdrew a trinite dagger and slammed the blade through the manticore's heart. A true death for any phantom.

Blood trickled from the corners of Laban's mouth as he offered a sad but relieved smile. "Thank you," he rasped. "I'm sorry you've lost Blythe. If I can't have her, you were a decent second choice. Tell her..." He went quiet then, his gaze sliding to the side. Soon, he stared at nothing and began to evaporate.

Roux both panicked and rejoiced. Isla was safe, but his relationship with Blythe was over. He'd just ended her first consort's life. Again. He'd made this so easy for Erebus. Because no matter how fervently Roux explained the situation, the harpy would not believe him. She would accuse him of being jealous, and she would be right. On the surface, he looked guilty as sin.

How much more would Blythe hate him now?

Blythe perched on the bench in No Man's Land, crouched and balancing on the back. Her mind had yet to settle. At least the scenery soothed. Golden sunshine bathed flowers of every color and winding stone pathways. A sweet fragrance saturated a cool breeze.

"I thought I might find you here."

She glanced up to see her half sister striding toward her, tall, pale, lithe, and scowling. A General filled with confidence—and dressed for war.

"Are we to do battle?" Blythe asked. "The harpy

General against the new Queen of Ation? Very well. I should probably warn you, though. I'm not really in the mood to go easy on you this time."

Taliyah joined her with a snort, stretching across the bench. "No battle, even though I'm furious with you for trying to sabotage the Astra and putting yourself in harm's way. But mostly for not bringing me a souvenir from Ation. Just came to chat. So, chat. Tell me you're okay."

"Not willing to lie to you." She heaved a sigh. "Where's Isla?" The little girl deserved to see her father the second he'd appeared, and Blythe was ashamed she hadn't gone to her first.

"I've got her polishing the royal weapons, so she'll be *very* preoccupied for a few weeks. By the way," T-bone added, "you are the only harpy in history to score two consorts. I didn't even think it was possible. No one did. Oh! You'll be pleased to know I've spoken with Neeka about your situation."

"She's here?" Blythe could get real answers—real help—with her situation?

"Nope. She's still with the Hell king and having a great time secretly ruining his life, but we've managed to sneak in a few conversations here and there. Well, after he and Roc fought. It was glorious. Anyway. Neeks asked me to tell you this: Your heart is your heart, whether it's this one or that one, so you can toss it *and* keep it."

"What does that even mean?" Blythe demanded.

Her sister shrugged.

This sucked. She rubbed the aching spot between her breasts. "What am I going to do?"

"That's easy. You do whatever you want. Either you

pick one and ditch the other or keep both. Yeah, that's probably the better plan. Keep both."

Hardly. "Juggling one possessive alpha male is tough enough, thanks."

"Okay, so which one do you prefer to juggle?"

That, she didn't need to ponder. The answer, as shocking as it was, remained clear as crystal.

She chewed on her bottom lip and craned her head to peer at Taliyah through lowered lids. "The one who's going to cause all kinds of problems."

"Wow. Him? Truly?" her sister asked, wide-eyed. "Gotta say, I totally didn't see that one coming."

Blythe, either. "He's difficult, complicated, harsh, vexing, frustrating, punishing, hard to read at times, and maddening always. But he's also gentle, wonderful, lusty, and supportive. He *lives* for me, T. Like, I'm his everything." Roux hadn't wanted to, but he'd given her time with Laban. Because he cared for Blythe. "I don't feel as if something's missing when we're together." Something she'd often forgotten after the manticore's death.

"But?"

"But. It's too fast. In the big scheme of things, I've basically only known him for a matter of minutes."

"You've only known the other one a matter of minutes, too, there are just more of them. But let me tell you a secret. With the Astra, it's easy to feel fast and fall hard. It's their intensity. It sucks you into their orbit and there's no chance of escape."

No *desire* to escape. "Also, Roux isn't the father of my daughter. Oh, yes, and he's supposed to kill me to save his people."

"And yet it sounds as though you've already made up your mind. So what are you here pondering?"

"How to break the news to Laban and Isla," she admitted, her shoulders slumping. She'd made so many mistakes lately. She couldn't afford to make another.

"Well, that one's easy, too. Do it swift and firm. But do it tomorrow. Tonight, we celebrate your return."

Leave Isla wondering what Momma would do? Leave Roux hurting longer than necessary? No. He'd endured enough heartache in his endless life. "Forget the party. I'm solidifying my future tonight."

"Fine. But you owe me big-time. I mean it."

She rolled her eyes.

"Come on." Taliyah jumped to her feet, took her hand, and tugged her from the bench. Arm in arm, they strolled through the door, exiting the garden. They entered the bustling market in the town square, near the street Blythe had occupied the day the Astra invaded.

Her gaze landed on a familiar sight, and her breath caught. Roux. He was waiting for her.

He stood outside Chop Chop, the at-home guillotine store, leaning one shoulder against a window display and radiating a wealth of ragged emotion. Regret. Guilt. Shame. Resignation. Fury. Several harpies eyed him as if he were a hot fudge sundae on a sultry summer night, but he didn't seem to notice them.

As soon as their gazes met, he straightened and stalked over. "Leave us," he commanded the citizens around him. His hands remained balled as the others scrambled away as fast as their feet could carry them.

"This is my cue, I guess, though this is the first and only time I'll take an order from a subordinate. You're welcome," Taliyah muttered and branched off in the other direction.

Blythe closed in on her consort, meeting him halfway. Her heart skipped several beats. "Hey."

"There is no easy way to tell you this." He lifted his chin. "I killed Laban. I used trinite. He won't be coming back."

Wait. What? Her stomach twisted into knots. "That isn't funny, Warden." Roux would never do such a thing for real, knowing the anguish she'd endured last time. He just wouldn't.

"This is no joke. He is dead by my hand. Before turning him into a phantom, Erebus gave him the heart of another clone. Laban was never your consort. He was always your father's puppet. He—"

"Wait!" What was happening right now? "I know Laban was a phantom," she cried, things cracking in her chest. Laban was truly dead now? Gone forever—again? Taken from Isla a second time? "Why? Why would you do this? He was my consort." Heart or not. "How could you hurt me like this? *How?* You saw what it did to me after the invasion."

If Roux had cared for her, even the slightest bit… Stinging tears welled, and there was no stopping them.

She'd chosen this male, and he'd dared to betray her trust in the worst way? Had broken her heart again, rending the organ in two.

Neeka's words chose that moment to drift through her mind. *Your heart is your heart, whether it's this one or that one, so you can toss it and keep it.*

"I did what I must to protect you and Isla—I did what the warrior asked me to do." His words were broken at the edges. "He was under Erebus's control, with orders to murder the girl. He couldn't fight the compulsion, and he knew it. I did what I must," Roux repeated, "exactly as I promised you in Ation, even if it means the end of us."

No. No! Stumbling back, she gave her head a vehement shake. Laban told her he *wasn't* under her father's command. And even if he were, he would *never*. He adored his daughter, just as Isla adored her daddy. And yet…

Deep breath in. Out. Roux wasn't a liar in any way, shape, or form. He'd always given her the truth, no matter the cost to himself. He'd confessed about the interrogation. He'd even told her about his fear of playing host to Laban. Today she'd learned the male she'd trusted for years had lied to her from the beginning, hiding what her father had done to him for the sake of his pride.

Her lungs emptied. What Roux claimed *did* make sense. Laban and Roux possessing the same heart explained why the Astra had seemed so familiar to her the day of his arrival. It also explained how she could have two consorts, when such an occurrence was impossible.

What if…Erebus *had* controlled Laban's will? What if the two *had* tricked her into believing the manticore was her consort? What if Laban *wasn't* strong enough to fight the god's control?

How easily he could harm Isla. And in ways no one would see coming. Not Blythe, and certainly not Isla. Which made it the perfect plan on her father's part. Thank goodness the child hadn't yet learned about Laban's survival.

A whimper caught in the back of Blythe's throat, the truth suddenly clear. Erebus *had* tricked her all right. But not using Roux.

With hot tears streaming down her cheeks, she rasped, "I believe you."

32

THE HEART

Roux blinked at his crying *gravita*, feeling as if he were both dying and reviving inside. "I don't understand." A hint of wonder invaded his jumble of emotions. "You believe me?"

"Yes," she croaked.

He scooped an about-to-crumble Blythe against his chest and flashed to his bedroom. He laid her upon the mattress and crawled in beside her, baffled.

She'd chosen to trust him, without proof. Did she—could she—love him? Even a little?

Could he make this easier on her, even in the smallest way? "I am so sorry, Lyla. So very sorry. I wish there'd been another way."

"Don't be sorry. You did the right thing. You protected Isla." She rolled on top of him, burying her face in the hollow of his throat. "Besides that, I'm the one who owes you an apology. I made your life miserable, but all along, you were my consort. The one I should have defended."

"Not me. Mars." A fact he both celebrated and despised.

"No. Not Mars. You. Mars was a tool. You, Warden, are a treasure."

He almost couldn't process the compliment. A treasure? Him?

Overcome, he enfolded her in his arms. "If you think I would change anything that has happened, you are wrong. You have Isla. Now I have you both."

She only sobbed harder. Never having comforted a crying female before, he wasn't sure how to proceed. But he loved this specific female, and he only wished to see her happy. Therefore, he gave it his best. As gently as possible, Roux wiped her tears away. He stroked her hair. Kissed her brow. Offered soft words of assurance.

"You are a warrior, Lyla. A goddess. Stronger than anyone I've ever encountered. I will do everything in my power to help you get through this. Isla, too. This I now truly comprehend—pain is no match for love."

After a while, she calmed. Exhaling a shuddering breath, she traced an X over his chest. "You are pretty wonderful, you know that, Roux?"

His eyes widened. First a treasure, now wonderful. "I'm unsure how to respond."

She took pity on him and changed the subject. "We probably need to talk about the blessing task before we exchange accolades."

Yes. "I won't be killing you. That is an unshakable certainty."

"Condemn yourself and the other Astra to five hundred years of defeat, allowing Erebus to ascend? No. That doesn't work for me. Not after what you've done for me, Isla, and yes, Laban. Besides, I like having you around."

As a strangled sound brewed in the back of his throat, he scrubbed a hand down his face. "I can't hurt you." Not ever again. "I won't."

"And that's exactly what my father is counting on. After everything he's done, we cannot allow him to win. Maybe, if I cut out my own heart with trinite, sacrificing myself, I'll revive as Taliyah did during Roc's task."

"No. I have to be the one to wield the blade." A cold sweat spread across his skin. "Maybe…maybe we can gift the Ation crown to another, and I can kill her? You haven't donned the circlet yet, so you aren't technically queen. There's time."

She shook her head with assurance. "I'm the only Ation female here, and I earned that headpiece. It's mine. But don't worry. I have another idea about how to handle our situation. Something an oracle said is rattling around in the back of my mind, and I think I'm beginning to understand what she meant. I just need to ponder it further."

"Tell me." Please. "Put me out of my misery."

"Nope. Sorry. Too many prying ears. I don't want anyone taking measures to stop me."

"Someone is *already* taking measures to stop you. Erebus and his Blade of Destiny."

"Not with this. Just…trust me. Okay? Let me make a grand gesture to win your affections. It's my turn."

"You *already* made a grand gesture and own all my

affections. There's nothing left for anyone else, I promise you." Trusting had never come easy for him. Took years for the Astra to demolish his defenses. But this was his Lyla. The *gravita* he loved. The female who'd chosen him. "But," he said. "Yes, I will trust you with my most valuable possession."

Her most sensual, calculated smile bloomed, and he drew in a deep breath. "Oh, I'm your possession, am I?" Her voice dropped to a throaty purr. "I guess I'm okay with that because you are mine."

How he loved when she staked her claim.

"I want you, Roux."

The soft statement nearly set his cells on fire. "After everything that's happened…everything that's going to happen…are you sure?" He refused to take advantage of her while she was at her most vulnerable.

"Babe, I've gone *hours* without your stardust," she said, kissing the hollow of his neck. Then she dragged a claw tip down the center of his shirt, slicing the garment in two. The sides gaped open, and she swooped down to lick his skin. "Do you want me, too?"

"More than I've ever wanted anything," he rasped, his palms burning. Already stardust was rising, ready to paint her soft flesh.

"Then take me. I'm yours. Now and forever."

"Now and forever." He wasted no more time. He clasped her nape and claimed her lips with his own.

Their tongues thrust together, already frenzied. He shredded her clothes, and rolled her to her back, pinning her to the mattress with his weight. But he didn't take her right away. Though he was half-mad with desire for her, he lifted his head and met her glittering gaze.

"I have a fantasy." He rubbed the tip of his nose against hers.

"Oh, yeah?" Grinning, she reached around to grip his backside. "Tell me. Maybe I'll do it…"

"You *are* the fantasy."

A delighted laugh bubbled from her. Then she folded her hands behind her head, getting more comfortable beneath him. "Well, then. Do this fantasy right. She's ready."

He snorted. This. This was the life he'd never known he wanted. Never known he'd needed. Playful and fun. Passionate and intense.

"I'll be right back," he said, and she lost her grin fast.

"What!" Out came the scowl. "You're leaving me right now? Is this how you plan to make me scream from a distance?"

With a grin of his own, he flashed away, then returned a few minutes later with a sack full of chocolate truffles. Treats he dumped all over her. "I'm told you have a sweet tooth."

"You're forgiven." As she gobbled up one, then another, he stripped.

Naked, he crawled over her and tasted the chocolate on her lips.

She chased his mouth for more, and he gave it.

"I will give you a good life, Lyla." He fed her the words between kisses. "Sometimes I will frustrate and anger you, but I will never not love you."

Gasping, she cupped his cheeks. Soft and vulnerable, she held his face inches above hers and searched his gaze. "You love me?"

The truth slipped out. "She-beast, I *live* for you." *My life raft. Never letting go.*

* * *

Over the next few days, Blythe spent time with both Roux and Isla. Sometimes one-on-one. Sometimes together. The little girl still knew nothing about her father, and she never would.

After Blythe explained to the child how many times the Astra had helped save her life, Isla had begun to soften toward him. A wonderful start to something special.

When the final morning of the blessing task dawned bright and early, Blythe slipped from bed, leaving a sleeping Roux behind. A difficult thing to do, to be sure. He looked so peaceful. So beautiful. *So mine*. Making him smile had become her new favorite activity.

Heart clenching, she flashed to No Man's Land. Only the General was present, all other harpies forbidden from entering today.

Taliyah had dressed for war but wrung her fingers and chewed on her bottom lip. "Are you sure you want to do this?"

"I am. And don't forget we have Neeka's blessing." Blythe had indeed deciphered the oracle's cryptic message, and the genius of it still left her breathless. So did the danger of it. But for Roux, she would do anything. With one act, she could prove how much he meant to her, save the Astra from the curse, and screw over her father. *If* her plan succeeded, of course. And it would. It must. "Did you bring what I asked for?"

Taliyah held up an ice chest. "I did. And you're sure Erebus hasn't foreseen this?"

"He didn't foresee you taking your own life to save Roc. He didn't foresee Ophelia eating him and spitting out his bones at Halo's ceremony. The Blade of Destiny must not show him the decisions of the *gravitas*."

Taliyah cracked her knuckles. "All right then. Let's get started."

Get started they did. When they finished, she remained in the pocket realm, away from Roux. If he or anyone else sensed what she'd done... No, better to keep her distance. She swam in the lake and changed into a clean uniform. No weapons needed today.

Finally, the countdown clock zeroed out, the ceremony set to begin. Blythe flashed to the harpy coliseum, at the far end of the center stands, and strode forward. Wow. Talk about déjà vu. The grains flung from her boots. Half the bleachers were filled with cheering harpies, the other half with phantoms chanting with monotone voices, "Ha ha ha. Ha ha ha."

Up top on the royal dais stood Roc and Taliyah, the other Astra, Chaos, and a grinning Erebus, who thought he'd won this round. Sunshine illuminated the grim expressions of the others. Apparently, they believed the Dark One had won this round, too. A gentle breeze carried hints of spring.

Roux waited in the center of the arena, shirtless, wearing a pair of leather pants with a single trinite blade sheathed at his side. The Ation crown dangled from his grip. Mmm. So pretty! The man *and* the headgear. *Gimme!*

Never had her Astra appeared so strained. Tension pulled his skin taut over sharp bone and bulging muscle. She wished she could offer comfort, but she knew there was nothing she could say to make this easier.

When she stopped in front of him, she curbed the urge to hug him. Contact could only add to the difficulty. "Hey, babe. I'll take what's mine, please and thank you." She plucked the crown from his fingers and settled the dark crystals atop her head.

Oh, yeah. Satisfaction flowed over her. So much better. Woe to anyone who attempted to take this circlet from her. She'd meant what she'd told him; she would be turning the realm of Ation into a wonderland of horrors and delights.

"Where have you been?" he demanded. He squeezed his eyes shut and pinched the bridge of his nose. His *alevala* jumped. "Sorry. I didn't mean to lash out. This day has been...not great." He groaned and opened his lids. With eyes like wounds, he asked, "What are we going to do, Lyla?"

Okay. Here goes. "I want you to cut out my heart with trinite," she said, lifting her chin.

Pupils pulsing with shock and horror, he reared back. "Kill you? No. Never."

"Don't make me beg, Warden. Oh, what the heck. Please kill me, Roux. Please." She pressed her hands together. "A Skyhawk always makes a supreme gesture to romance her male. Let me make mine with flavor and flare. I'd really like to put on a show for everyone."

He glared at her. Shook a finger of accusation. Opened and closed his mouth. "I can't believe you just said that!"

"Well, I love you. Today, I get the chance to prove it in front of everyone."

His mouth opened and closed faster. A strangling sound left him. "You love me? Me?"

"I do, and I'm never letting you go." Okay, she couldn't stay away a moment longer. Blythe pressed her body against his and slid her arms up his chest, around his neck. "That's why you're going to do this for me. You'll cut out my heart with your trinite blade, keeping yourself and your little friends curse-free and ensuring Isla isn't placed in unnecessary danger by allowing our enemy to win."

"I will not do anything of the sort." He slung his arms around her waist, a quick snap and lock. "We will go into hiding and hibernate for five hundred years. All of us."

"And let Erebus ascend, so that he's stronger than ever when we awaken? Nope. My plan gives us the victory. All you gotta do is kill me."

His nostrils flared. "Kill you to save your life?"

"Exactly." She rose to her tiptoes to press a kiss into his lips. "Aren't I brilliant?"

The striations in his irises spun with dizzying speed. "Do you think because my heart is the same as Laban's I can turn on you? I assure you, I cannot. He and I are not the same. Just as I am not the same as Mars."

"Laban and Mars have nothing to do with anything. I'm trusting you with my life, Roux. Obviously. Do me the courtesy of trusting your she-beast, as promised? I have a plan, remember? I'd tell you, but I'm not gonna risk your task."

"Yes. But—"

"No buts." She pulled back, unsheathing his trinite dagger. Then she grabbed his arm and slapped the hilt into his grip. "Do you know how jealous everyone is going to be when they see my consort is fierce enough to slay me? Let me have this. Please, Roux. Please. I've never asked you for anything. And everything will be all right, I swear. I have a plan, remem—"

Roaring, he slammed the blade into her chest and

carved out her heart, exactly as tasked. Sharp pain registered, and her knees collapsed. Roux caught her as she fell, cradling her against his chest as they sank into the sand together.

Tears streamed down his cheeks. "Heal, she-beast. Heal!" He cut his wrist and placed the wound over her lips.

Blood dripped into her mouth. From the dais, Erebus issued a roar of his own.

Didn't see that coming, did you, Dark One? Weakness invaded, despite his medicinal efforts. Her hands and feet chilled.

As darkness and death came for her, Blythe smiled up at the male she loved and whispered, "You forgot to shout *one*, babe. Now let Taliyah…"

His *gravita* went quiet. Even the phantoms in the stands went quiet. The watching harpies gasped with shock. Whispers arose. "No, he didn't!"

"Did an Astra just murder his freaking *gravita*?"

"So he's single now?"

Dead. Blythe was dead. Her shredded heart rested in the sand only a few feet away. Roux had done that. He'd killed her. As denials exploded inside his head, he thundered another roar at the sky. Why had he done this terrible thing? Why, why, why?

Suddenly Taliyah materialized before him and tried to wrench Blythe from his arms. He resisted.

"Do you want her to come back or not?" the General shrieked. "Then let me work!"

Blythe's final words drifted through his mind.

Now let Taliyah…

Though it went against his every instinct, he released

the love of his life. It was only then that he saw the blade in Taliyah's hand.

She spoke as she worked, ripping off Blythe's top, revealing her mutilated chest. "Erebus exchanged Laban's heart with a clone's, right? Well, Blythe decided to use his trick against him." The General opened a cooler to reveal a severed heart. "She borrowed her own ticker this morning. Had me cut it with a regular blade. Then she grew a new one. I saved the old one." She placed the precious organ in the hole Roux's fist had left behind. "This should work. A heart powers everything and this one is unaffected by trinite."

He...she... "Should?" Roux snarled, slashing his wrist again, then pressed the wound to her mouth, ensuring his blood continually poured down Blythe's throat.

Seconds passed. Nothing happened. He waited, unable to breathe.

Still nothing happened.

More seconds passed.

"Nothing is happening," he roared. "Why is nothing happening? Make her live—"

"Dude. Chill," Taliyah injected. "Look."

He looked and shouted with relief. The organ sprouted arteries, and those arteries grew, attaching to the dead ones. Light burst through her cells and spread. It was working!

Color returned to her cheeks. The wound in her chest was closing.

Taliyah wiped her hands for a job well done. "By the way, Rue the Day. It goes without saying that I'll make a new coin purse from your testicles if you harm my sister again."

"There will be no need. If I harm her again, I'll give you my testicles as a gift."

Blythe sucked in a breath and opened her eyes. "Ow!" She blinked, attempting to focus. "Wait. My plan worked?"

He yanked her upright and clutched her against him, hugging her with every ounce of his considerable strength. "I love you. I love you so much, and if you ever ask me to kill you again, I will put you over my knees and spank you!"

She hugged him back with all her might. "Sorry I couldn't tell you what I'd done. I was afraid the task might skew in Erebus's favor if you knew the truth."

"Tell me you are all right," he demanded, cupping her cheeks and searching her gaze.

"Are you kidding? I'm better than all right. We're legends now." She shifted her attention to Taliyah, who lingered, unabashed. "Admit it. You're jealous, sis."

The General sniffed. "Only the tiniest bit. Hardly at all, really. Oh, and Papaw Chaos says the task is complete, with Roux the winner."

The remaining Astra flashed to the field, gaping as they formed a circle around Roux and Blythe.

"I honestly didn't think he would do it," Silver said.

"Is Roux my new hero?" Ian asked, scratching his temple. "Did that just happen?"

Throwing back her head, Blythe laughed, and Roux had never felt so alive. But now he needed to be alone with his *gravita*. To inspect every square inch of her to make sure she was truly well and whole.

He flashed her to their bedroom, tossed her to the mattress, stripped her, and looked her over. She didn't stay still for long. No, she jolted upright to wrap her arms around him. Then she fell back to the mattress, bringing him with her.

"Your turn to make a grand gesture to me," she purred at him.

"I will, oh, I will," he vowed.

And he did.

EPILOGUE

"All right," Blythe said, taking Isla's hand. "You ready, sweetheart?"

The little girl nodded. "Ready."

Mother and child stood before Roux, who appeared a bit nervous.

"Do it," he agreed with a nod.

"On the count of three. One. Two—" Blythe urged Isla forward and together, they ghosted inside Roux. This time, they weren't trying to hide their presence, and he wasn't resisting. Even better, there were no screams. He'd told her the prisoners had begun to weaken, as if he were draining them of strength, using them as fuel for the *alevala*. All but one.

They entered a dark void reminiscent of a midnight sky beyond Ation. Roux waited for them there.

Isla took his hand without prompting. "It's time, Rouxbear. This way."

Rouxbear? What an adorable nickname.

"If you become frightened," he began, and Isla rolled her eyes.

"You're forgetting how powerful I am or whatever." As the darling urged them both forward, a soft glow seeped from her pores, turning her into a walking star.

Blythe gawked. First a door to another realm, now this? She'd never seen her daughter display such a power before.

They moved deeper into the Astra's consciousness, until they came upon a maze of cells. The young boy she'd spotted in those visions of torture stood at the bars of the first. The one Roux hadn't drained.

The boy smirked at them.

"Ignore anything he says," Roux instructed. "That's Rowan. My twin."

As they moved on, coming upon other cells, Isla's light chased away thick, cloying shadows, revealing other prisoners withering away. She detected species after species. Vampires. Shifters. Banshees. Amazons. Gorgons. Minotaurs and manticores. Centaurs. Sirens. Merfolk. Sorcerers. Gods and goddesses. Even ladies from Ation.

When they reached the center of the maze, where the thickest shadows congregated, Isla stopped. Her light pushed the gloom back bit by bit, revealing...hmm. Another clone of Mars? He sat before the wall, leaning back, his cell door wide open.

"I don't understand," Roux said with a frown. "Rowan is the only clone I remember absorbing."

Isla piped up, "Roux, meet Roux. He's you. Well, your conscience. That's how he explained it, anyway."

"Surprise." The lookalike spread his arms. "I knew you'd be shocked to learn you even had a conscience. You certainly kept me locked away long enough, didn't you? Thankfully, my cell opened soon after you met the harphantom." He hiked his thumb in Blythe's direction. "I explained to the little one that I'd make you more miserable than she ever could, and she agreed to let me give it my best."

"Mission accomplished. You nearly destroyed me." Roux scrubbed a hand over his face. "Rowan said Blythe's consort was the one running rampant..." He narrowed his eyes. "Because *I* am her consort, and you are me."

"The little prick does like to cause you trouble," Roux Number Two said with a grin. That grin quickly fell, however. "I'm so tired of screaming, aren't you? Time to let go of the misery of the past and look ahead to the future. For good."

Poor Astra. He still looked shocked beyond measure. "I agree with him," Blythe said. "You deserve joy, babe." She squeezed Isla's hand. "All right, sweetheart. Take us home."

Only minutes later, they were standing in the bedroom Blythe and Roux shared.

"Can I go now, Momma?" Isla jumped up and down. "My friend Kaitlyn wants me to help her steal a dagger."

She smiled. "Sure. Go on."

Isla hugged her. To Blythe's surprise, the little darling gave Roux a hug, too, before she raced out of the room. Once again, he appeared shell-shocked. Not too shell-shocked to yank her into his arms as soon as they were alone and kiss the breath from her lungs.

"I love you," he rasped when he lifted his head. "I'm so glad you were my undoing."

Her smile returned. "That's good. Because it turns out, you were my undoing, too, and I've never been happier." She was about to suggest they rip off each other's clothes when a prickle started at the base of her neck. Air hissed between her teeth. "Erebus. He's nearby. Probably walking the hallways of Destiny, planning his next move."

Roux stiffened but didn't release her. "Any idea who he'll choose to complete the next task?"

"No. But I can find out. If you don't mind me challenging him?"

"Go," he said, then kissed the tip of her nose. "Make him suffer."

She beamed at her consort. "I love you so much, I'm almost embarrassed."

"Yes, but I love you so much more."

"That's true." Blythe winked and flashed into the spirit realm. A narrow corridor inside the harpy palace that had been carved between past, present, and future. Only those with a key could venture here.

And there was Erebus, with his key—the Blade of Destiny—in hand. Unfortunately for him, Isla wasn't the only excellent thief in the Skyhawk family; Blythe had stolen a piece of his dagger during one of his visits.

He stood before a wall of mist that peered into the throne room. There, six Astra congregated. Silver, Ian, Vasili, Azar, Sparrow, and Bleu. They, too, discussed who they thought would be the next to fight for ascension and what must be done.

Blythe approached her father's side and offered him a cold smile. "You lost. Again. Overplayed your hand with Laban."

"Yes," he replied, with a shrug, not bothering to glance in her direction. "I can't be terribly disappointed, though. I've been looking forward to this next task more than any other."

He did appear particularly gleeful. Enough to make her stomach churn. "Do tell."

"I won't. But time will."

* * * * *